KU-435-996

ENGLISH HUMANIST BOOKS
Writers and Patrons, Manuscript and Print, 1475–1525

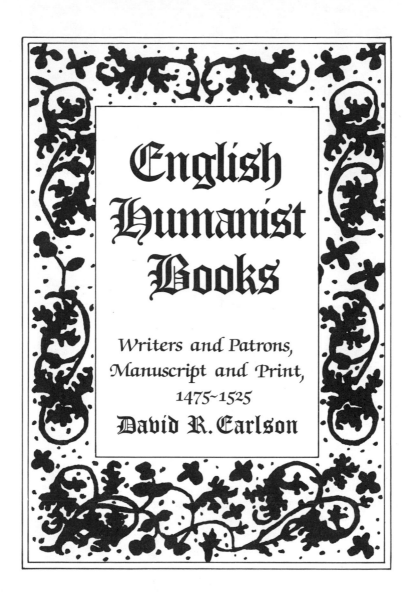

English Humanist Books

Writers and Patrons, Manuscript and Print, 1475~1525

David R. Carlson

UNIVERSITY OF TORONTO PRESS
Toronto Buffalo London

© University of Toronto Press Incorporated 1993
Toronto Buffalo London
Printed in Canada

ISBN 0-8020-2911-6

Printed on acid-free paper

Canadian Cataloguing in Publication Data

Carlson, David Richard, 1956–
  English humanist books : writers and patrons,
  manuscript and print, 1475–1525

  Includes bibliographical references and index.
  ISBN 0-8020-2911-6

  1. Humanism – England – History – 15th century.
  2. Humanism – England – History – 16th century.
  3. Books – England – History – 1400–1600.
  4. England – Intellectual life – 16th century.
  5. England – Intellectual life – Medieval period,
  1066–1485. I. Title.

  B778.C3 1993   942.05'1   C93-093049-5

This book has been published with the help of a grant from the
Canadian Federation for the Humanities, using funds provided by
the Social Sciences and Humanities Research Council of Canada

For my parents
and grandparents

 Contents

Acknowledgments

William Blake is exceptional. Otherwise, no one makes a book alone. In light of my subject matter, I should be especially conscious of the extent to which, although I acknowledge it mine, the present book too has been a cooperative venture. Most was contributed by William Barker, James Carley, and William Stoneman, the scholar-familiars to whom I owe my induction into the *arcana* of bibliographic study; between them, they taught me to look at books. I am lucky to know them, and I have benefited from their advice and help, general and specific, here and elsewhere, for years. Others contributed too. David Staines and David Shore criticized late versions of the whole typescript. C.J. McDonough tried again to improve my Latinity. David Galbraith offered good counsel and answered numerous specific requests for information. Lee Piepho provided crucial information at a crucial moment and later corrected a sizeable section. D.S. Chambers and Harry Vredeveld criticized sections in draft; Francesco Tateo and Erika Rummel advised on particulars, as did also C.G.C. Tite, FSA, whose hospitality during repeated visits improved my views of Thatcher's Britain. John Leyerle sent me to London in 1983, and Bonnie Wheeler made it possible for me to spend the summer in Oxford in 1984; it was during these trips that I began to collect material. Steve Daniels, Dennis Foster, Michael Holahan, Marlene Kadar, Seth Lerer, A.G. Rigg, Nina Schwartz, Willard Spiegelman, Fred Unwalla, and Annmarie Weyl Carr also contributed, even if they won't be able to recognize their contributions any longer. In North America and Europe, librarians and curators have shown me much patience and generosity, so it is misleading to single out only a few for thanks; nevertheless, I owe special debts to J. Conway, J. Samuel Hammond, T.D. Hobbs, and Erik Petersen. To Suzanne Rancourt, Judy Williams, and especially Prudence Tracy, all of the University of Toronto Press, I am likewise grateful. Funds for travel to collections, microfilms and photography, and release from teaching responsibilities were provided by the English Department and Research Council of Southern Methodist University, at various points during 1984–8, and the Social Sciences and Humanities Research Council of Canada and York University, where I held a Canada Research Fellowship 1988–91. The costs of the photography have been defrayed in part by a grant from the Faculty of Arts Research Fund of the University of Ottawa. To the numerous others who also contributed, thanks.

Ottawa
30 September 1992

ENGLISH HUMANIST BOOKS

Writers and Patrons, Manuscript and Print, 1475–1525

 Introduction

Humanists and Patrons, Manuscript and Print

This is a book about books: why they were made the way they were and how they were used, in England, during an important period in their history. In the late fifteenth and early sixteenth centuries, the technology for making books was changing, with the introduction of printing, and books were being put to new uses by an emergent group of professional humanists, who used them for their own advancement.

The question I have asked of the objects – the books whose stories are recounted herein – is one that a colleague of mine characterizes as the art historian's question: why is the thing this way, rather than some other? What conditions and what choices led to the books being the way they are? The only thesis I have is the methodological one implicit in such questions: writings exist not in the abstract, but only in the form of particular texts – real, material objects, products of the labours of various individuals, working together, within historically determined institutions and class structures. Writings always have material, social contexts that inform their meanings; the means by which pieces of writing are built and circulated are themselves meaningful, and impinge on the sense of the writings.[1]

These generalizations are as true for Victorian novels as for late medieval and early renaissance books.[2] In the late fifteenth and early sixteenth centuries, however, technological and historical developments cast such matters into prominence. Writings were fluid, mutable things at the time; and there was sensitivity among writers and readers to the nuances of a system of publication complicated in ways unparalleled before or since. The idea of textual fixity, or of 'final authorial intention,' seems to come up only after the advent of printing, which probably bears some measure of responsibility for it; revision – authorial, editorial, scribal, compositorial – was the rule. Writings enjoyed this greater fluidity at least in part because there was a wider range of means of publication available to writers – all of them equally methods of publication, all of them equally legitimate ways of delivering writings to interested publics.[3]

For the fifty or hundred years following the invention of printing around 1455, 'publication' was not yet synonymous with 'publication in print,' as it is now. At the time, all printing did was import an additional complexity into an already complicated system. To distinctions among various kinds of manuscripts – on vellum or on paper, large or small, unadorned or illustrated, rubricated, and so on, professionally written or not, in this script or that – the advent of printing added, not only a gross distinction between hand-finished and machine-finished things, but also distinctions among various kinds of printed products: again, on vellum or paper, in folio or a smaller format, plain or decorated, in this type or that, printed abroad or at home, by Froben, or Manutius, or Bade; and so on. Different kinds and quantities of labour were invested in manufacturing these different kinds of books; and so the differences among the several current means of publication were meaningful. Particular connotations attached to the vehicles chosen to put writings about. Consequently, writings changed as they moved from one medium to another – the 'same' writing meaning something different when occurring in a different bibliographical context.

Humanists – new to England as a professional group at about the same time as printing – were more attuned to the complexities of this system of publication than anyone, and were quicker to exploit them. Their livelihoods depended on it. 'Humanism' has been a difficult concept to define and to use, having seemed to many to involve such ultimately nebulous matters as the idea of individualism or kinds of religious belief. I have tried to cleave instead to a minimal definition, which seems nevertheless to be particularly efficient. Fundamentally, humanism was a committed interest in antiquity, in ancient literature, Latin or Greek, and in ancient culture more generally, committed in the sense that it was polemical, arguing in favour of a revival of ancient standards and canons of taste. Such an interest entailed, on the one hand, an effort to return *ad fontes*, in order to gain understanding of antiquity; it also entailed, on the other, an effort to put the understanding of antiquity so gained to work on and within contemporary society.[4]

Humanism in this sense was something that individuals might put on and put off, by turns, in such a way that some of their work can profitably be characterized as humanist, and some cannot. Particularly for the study of such transitional figures as John Skelton, I have found it more useful to think in terms of humanist gestures – manifestations, intermittent perhaps, of the characteristic humanist desire to return *ad fontes* – rather than to attempt to categorize such figures as humanists or not, *tout court*. Likewise, humanism in this sense matured. By the sixteenth century, it was easier to gain a good working knowledge of ancient literatures and cultures, particularly Greek, in England than it had been in the fifteenth. The co-operative accumulation of tools for studying and of information about antiquity, of the kind that could be passed from teacher to student and so did not require continually to be invented anew, had consequences for humanist practice; simply, it was possible to know much more about antiquity in the sixteenth century. But the fact that fifteenth-century humanists – and again, Skelton is an example – did not, could not, in fact, attain to sixteenth-century standards does not mean that they were not capable of humanist gestures. No matter their competence, it was still possible for persons like Skelton – formed intellectually in England before 1480 – to take a committed interest in matters of antiquity and to put such knowledge of antiquity as they could obtain to work in their own affairs.[5]

In turning to antiquity and returning from it to their own present, the humanists' most important discovery may have been the figure of Maecenas, the great patron of Augustan Rome,[6] whose name the humanists were to make a byword for munificence. Maecenas had been liberal and judicious, providing both material ease and relative independence to his literary clients, counting among them Vergil, Horace, and Propertius; in return for his patronage, he earned esteem. The invention of contemporaries willing to imitate Maecenas was crucial to the humanists' ability to imitate Maecenas' ancient clients; for without Maecenas-like patrons, humanists could not have survived and the movement could not have flourished.

When Giovanni Gigli, for example, late in the fifteenth century, took to calling Bishop Richard Fox 'Maecenas meus,'[7] he was accomplishing several objectives at once. He advanced a claim, in effect, that he had already played Vergil or Horace and was willing to continue doing so; in addition to thus flattering himself, Gigli's claim also offered Fox a chance to be flattered. Gigli implies that, since he had already played the writer's role, Fox had some obligation to play Maecenas in return – to keep the patron's part in a putative bargain that Fox may not in fact have deliberately entered into. Calling Fox Maecenas would have encouraged Fox to act like Maecenas, in order that he might be flattered by the exchange. Underlying Gigli's remark, furthermore, is the unspoken assumption – a tendentious assumption nevertheless – that Fox did desire to emulate Maecenas; that providing for the well-being of writers was something that the wealthy and powerful of contemporary England wanted to do. Taking so much for granted implies, argumentatively, that, if Fox had not as yet felt a desire to be Maecenas, he should.

The answer to the question arising from Gigli's remark – why would someone like Fox have wished to patronize humanist writers? – is not simple. Humanists could be, and were, useful to patrons for particular jobs. They served their patrons as tutors; as secretaries, responsible for keeping up their employers' correspondence; and as orators, representatives, in other words, especially ambassadorial, who spoke on behalf of their employers; in an extension of their oratorical function, humanists also acted as propagandists for those who paid them. But humanists' ability to do such jobs had nothing to do with humanism *per se*; the same work could be done, and had been, by others who were not at all interested in antiquity.

Humanists functioned as propagandists in two ways. On the one hand, they made cases for their patrons' points of view on particular issues. A good deal of the humanist poetry written and circulated in England in the reign of Henry VII was propaganda in this sense, that, in it, humanist poets broadcast or apologized for specific positions on contemporary affairs. Inevitably, the positions championed in this poetry tended not to subvert the authority of those who ruled England, who were also those who could pay humanists. On the other hand, humanists also functioned as propagandists less specifically, as advertisements for the general qualities of their patrons. Humanists' willingness and ability to be living signs of the goodness of those who paid them had political consequences as well, albeit less immediate and concrete ones. By decorating the households and lives of their patrons as they did, humanists decorated and so justified the social inequities that the emergent absolutist state in England took over from the late Middle Ages and managed in the interests of the patronizing class.[8] Without social inequity, there could have been no patronage – a point More makes implicitly in the *Utopia*;[9] by the same token, patronage also fostered inequity.

For patrons, patronizing humanists was one of a number of forms of conspicuous consumption, to use Veblen's term,[10] by means of which members of the noble class asserted their nobility; it was a way for them to make plain in public the fact that they commanded sufficient wealth to be able to expend resources, the more magnificently the better, on the decorative, inessential, non-industrial, unproductive, finally wasteful labours of others. Artistic and literary patronage was particularly beneficial from this perspective, not only because it could involve wasteful expenditure on a large scale, but also because it did involve the exercise of judgment. Lavish patronage advertised patrons' wealth; judicious patronage – what became connoisseurship – bespoke not only patrons' ability to spend but also the fact that they had sufficient time free from purposeful occupation – leisure time, in effect, for wasting on decorative, inessential, non-industrial, unproductive interests – to cultivate good taste. Literary and artistic patronage put the benign face of good, or at least comparatively innocent, works on those who benefited from the inequities of the social system that made bosses of them, at the expense of others. It also enabled members of a social aristocracy like early Tudor England's to show who was boss, locally and abroad, and to establish position, competitively, in relation to their peers within the patronal class.

Here again, however, patronizing humanists did not necessarily return better dividends than patronizing other sorts of writers or artists. Before the advent of humanism, members of England's social aristocracy had already been able to advertise their wealth and status by means of patronage; humanism's arrival did nothing to alter this foundation of class politics and individual self-promotion on which the system was erected. Nevertheless, I think it is possible to see that humanism should have been especially attractive to early Tudor patrons for two apparently opposed reasons: first, that it was in vogue, a newly breaking fashion; and second, that it was fundamentally conservative.

Denys Hay has pointed out that there was some measure of 'keeping up with the Joneses' involved in the advent of humanism to England.[11] Most tangibly, in diplomatic dealings, first with the papacy and Italian heads of state, and later with France and the Empire, the English risked embarrassment or worse if their secretaries and orators were incapable of dealing stylishly with their foreign counterparts. As the papal curia, for example, became increasingly humanist, the English were bound to try to keep up; otherwise, the country might have looked poor and backward. For a monarch like Henry VII, concerned as he was to secure his reign and dynasty, in part by augmenting England's prominence in continental affairs, such considerations carried weight. It was a matter of prestige. Credit accrued to patrons, among their peers in the patronal classes, for innovation and currency; these were signs of knowledge and good taste, and thus of the leisure that made the cultivation of taste possible. For Henry VII to appear magnificent among his peers – and to some degree his political success depended on his ability to foster such perceptions of himself, as a monarch of wealth and so of stable power, to be taken seriously – it was necessary that he invest in humanists; and his example should have had the effect locally of encouraging lesser English patrons to do likewise.

Why humanism should have attracted patrons in the first place, in England or elsewhere, probably has something to do with the fact that the humanist attitude towards the past complemented the fundamental beliefs about social relations that made patrons patrons. Antiquity offered both republicanism and imperialism as governmental models; for some, the choice was vital. Ultimately, however, humanists had to take the side of autocracy. Autocrats made better patrons, to the extent that they commanded greater disposable wealth, more independently, and were most in need of propaganda and compelling apologies. More to the point, as Antony Grafton and Lisa Jardine argue, humanists liked authority: characteristically, the authority of the ancient past, to which they deferred. From this perspective, what humanists inculcated, in themselves and in those who listened to them, and so what ultimately interested the patronal classes, was an attitude of deference to authority.[12]

A further reason patrons in England were persuaded to play Maecenas was that it was in the humanists' interest that they should do so, and the humanists could be persuasive. The fundamental job of a professional group, like the emergent group of professional humanists, is to see to the group's perpetuation and its members' individual survival. In the long term, education and educational reform provided for the reproduction of professional humanism; in the short term, only patronage could provide for humanists' well-being. Humanists knew the costs of pursuing patrons and taking what they could get from them. Patronage inevitably entailed subservience to patronal interest, to particular, immediate causes, as well as to patronal class interest in general; inevitably, to one degree or another, it cost clients their freedom. Maecenas' client Horace knew as much;[13] so did Richard Pace, an early Tudor client, who wrote in 1517: 'I am free, but by nature only, not in choice; for I have bound myself to serve my invincible king, as a servant of the wise cardinal of York. To serve one's country supersedes all freedom.'[14] For the most part, early Tudor England's humanists seem to have paid this price happily, though in fact there was no real alternative. Starve and wander; find another occupation; or learn to live by patronage. Ecclesiastical preferment, courtly and governmental office, university fellowships and readerships, masterships in the schools: all these avenues to material well-being, open to those not born into it, depended on patronage, and patronage had to be solicited.

Such conditions fostered a sometimes unattractive professional ruthlessness, contradicting in practice the ideals of disinterested wisdom that humanists espoused in theory, though again there was no alternative. 'Omnia tuo compendio metiare' and 'Ne quid des, nisi unde speres foenus' are not now among Erasmus' best known bywords; they were nevertheless a necessary part of the humanist creed. Erasmus could only wish he were joking when he advised Andrea Ammonio:

> To begin with, put a bold face on everything to avoid ever feeling shame. Next, intrude in all the affairs of everyone; elbow people out of the way whenever possible. Do not love or hate anyone sincerely, but measure everything by your own advantage; let your whole course of behaviour be directed to this one goal. Give nothing unless you look for a return, and agree with everyone about everything. But, you say, there is nothing special about all this. Come then, here is a piece of advice just made to order for you, since you wish it; but, mind you, I whisper it confidentially. You are familiar with British jealousy; use it for your own profit. Always sit on two stools at once; bribe different suitors to cultivate you. Threaten to go away, and actually get ready to go. Flourish letters in which you are tempted away by generous promises. Sometimes remove your presence deliberately in order that, when your society is denied them, they may feel the need of you all the more keenly.[15]

Books were used most effectively in England in the late fifteenth and early sixteenth centuries by these people who had no choice, who were trying to make livings for themselves by their skills as writers. Here again, the fact that they were humanists is more or less incidental. Inasmuch as it was a fashion, and had the special attractions it did for patrons, humanism should have appeared the more promising to those who were ambitious to live by learning and writing; more than any alternative, espousal of humanism should have seemed to promise success in attracting patronage. Humanism aside, then, the issue is how, specifically and concretely, certain people were able to extract livelihoods, essentially by writing, from a system unaccustomed to the attempt. In the cases of such earlier figures as Geoffrey Chaucer, Thomas Hoccleve, or even John Lydgate – a somewhat less clear case, in fact – the pattern had been for writing to be complementary, but in the final analysis still subordinate, to some other primary occupation. Chaucer and Hoccleve were bureaucrats first,

and John Lydgate was a monk first, even though they all published writing too. Unquestionably, their writings benefited their
careers, but they were not yet professional writers; such men
were bureaucrats, courtiers, and ecclesiasts who also wrote. For
English literary history, the possibility of making a living by writing was, if not invented in the first instance, then propagated
and generalized in practice by humanists, in the period running
roughly from 1475 to 1525.[16] Others earlier and elsewhere had
invented humanism and made a vogue of it; early Tudor humanists exploited it, appealing directly to patrons, and making
reputations for themselves among their learned peers, of a sort
that might later be traded for patrons' support.

The principal tool they used for accomplishing so much was
writing, which they published – in the original sense of 'made
public' – by a variety of means, appropriate to various short- and
long-term aims. From the perspective of the centrality of patronage to professional profit, it becomes possible to understand
the importance attaching to the deluxe manuscripts that were
presented to patrons.[17] Presentation copies and the literature of
presentation may appear inconsequential, in terms of the influence of one piece of writing on others. It must be true that at
least some of the writing now surviving solely in unique presentation copies was never read by anyone, that the writing in question had no other circulation besides the presentation, that its
recipient did not read it or pass it on to anyone else.

Cases of presentation literature sinking without trace in this
way were probably rare, however; the state of the surviving evidence no doubt distorts the picture. There is intermittent evidence that writings formally presented, in deluxe presentation
copies, were also circulated in other, humbler forms beforehand,
or were also republished later. Likewise, there is evidence that a
presentation copy given to a monarch might later be loaned out,
to be read and returned. Additional means for circulating presentation literature were also used: oral declamation, or ephemeral copies unlikely to be collected, put formally presented
writings before larger audiences, though without always leaving
unequivocal evidence that they had done so. Moreover, there is
evidence that early Tudor writers paid attention to one another's
professional doings. Whether or not the contents of a particular
piece of writing could be known in detail – the kind of knowledge

that could come only by acquiring and reading a copy of the piece in question – contemporary writers were able to learn that a piece of writing, on some topic or occasion, had been presented to a patron, with consequences; and they were influenced in their own work by such intelligence.

Even if the literature of presentation had little or no afterlife of literary influence, the custom of presentation and the presentation manuscripts themselves would be of great literary-historical importance. Presenting a piece of writing appears to have been crucial to the process of securing patronage, the hinge on which patron-client relations turned; for this reason, apparently, humanists took seriously the business of presenting their work to potential patrons. It was in their presentation manuscripts that they invested most heavily – both of their learning and literary talents, and of their own material resources, which had to be spent on vellum or professional illumination, in order that the presentation might bring them something back in return. This willingness to invest bespeaks the humanists' understanding of the workings of the contemporary literary economy. There were no copyrights or royalties yet, no publishers or mass audiences, ultimately paying writers' bills by buying copies of their books. To the extent that writers were dependent on individual patrons for their material well-being, it was inconsequential to them that the presentation copies on which they spent so much might reach audiences of only one; it was this audience of one, not the many, that mattered.

The importance of deluxe presentation manuscripts, like the cost of their manufacture, was disproportionate to the size of the audience reached by them, though they were by no means the only form in which humanist writing was published in early Tudor England. In addition to presentations, writers also used their reputations to attract patronal favours, and reputations were made by the many. Although individual patrons could pay writers directly, a writer's peers could pay too, albeit indirectly, by their praises, out of which a profitable reputation might be built. Humanists also needed audiences larger than the patronal one, in other words; and for reaching them, they used other, more cost-efficient means of publication. These were chiefly two: ephemeral manuscript copies, made at home and circulated informally; and printed copies, the manufacture and distribution of which the humanists themselves did not control. The advantages of ephemeral manuscripts were that they could be made cheaply, in relatively great quantities, for circulation hand to hand, or, in some cases, for posting in public; they proliferated quickly and inexpensively by comparision with deluxe copies, while still retaining something of the immediacy of personal publication.

In this and other ways, humanists tried putting multiple manuscript copies of the same piece of writing into the hands of the many, thereby indicating their perception of the potential value of reaching broad audiences; but printing – to leave aside for the moment what it could cost writers who tried to use it – was by far a more efficient means. Humanists sought to exploit the possibilities for reputation-making that printing offered them, to the extent that it was desirable and possible for them to do so. In fact, print was not always accessible to them, and they could not afford to maintain personal presses. The printers had their own interests to pursue, which sometimes coincided with those of humanist writers and sometimes did not. Nor was using printing always desirable to humanists, for whom reaching as large an audience as possible was not always the prime requisite, in a literary economy still centred on personal patronage and professional contacts. Nevertheless, printers discovered certain uses for humanist writers, just as professional humanists discovered that they could use printers from time to time; over the course of the early Tudor period, the two groups found opportunities to cooperate, without one dominating the other.

The relations among these three basic modes of publication that the early Tudor humanists used – deluxe presentation copies, for presentation to potential patrons; ephemeral manuscript copies, for circulation hand to hand, characteristically among peers rather than social superiors; and printed copies, again for a comparatively broad and socially humble audience – are complicated. They vary from case to case, though in ways that show an internal logic; and these relations, as they were worked out in particular cases, will be examined in detail in the chapters that follow. Briefly, the humanists appear to have been careful – though not invariably successful – about fitting modes of publication, and combinations of modes of publication, to the ends that they meant to serve by circulating their writings.

This point in the history of the advent of humanism to England, roughly 1475–1525, comprehending the reign of Henry VII, has by no means been neglected. At one end of it stands the 'More circle'; the activities of Thomas More, Desiderius Erasmus, and those associated with them have been objects of much study. Beginning with More's *Utopia* in 1516, England was for the first time an exporter of significant humanist learning, rather than strictly an importer of it, and with More's appointment to Henry VIII's council in 1519, the humanist movement can be seen to have borne English fruit. Humanism in England had become mature: all-pervasive in English intellectual life, self-perpetuating, reified. The names are the well-known ones, of More, Linacre, and Lily, Pace, Starkey, Elyot, and so on.

Likewise, the earliest phases of humanism's arrival in England, before the accession of Henry VII in 1485, have also been the object of a number of important studies, especially those of Walter Schirmer, William Nelson, Roberto Weiss, and Denys Hay.[18] The humanist activity in England was different in this period. The numbers involved were small: individual patrons were few, institutional support was all but wanting, and the humanists themselves, again few in number, were almost entirely foreign-born and foreign-trained. Among English travellers to Italy in the fifteenth century were some who brought humanist interests home with them; about ten or a dozen have been identified. Papal diplomacy played an important part, both in causing such natives of England as Andrew Holes, Adam Moleyns, Robert Flemming, and William Selling to travel to Italy, and in bringing to England Italians with humanist tastes, like Giuliano Cesarini or Gaspare da Verona, but here again the numbers were small. Poggio Bracciolini was the first such Italian to come so far north; and in the sixty years or so after his visit of 1418–23, a few others, and none so accomplished as he, likewise made their ways to England: Piero del Monte, Tito Livio Frulovisi, Antonio Beccaria, and Stefano Surigone. In this period, between 1415 and 1485, such persons were able to find patrons in England interested in the new learning, but again only a few: John Tiptoft and William Grey – both of whom had themselves studied in Italy, with Guarino da Verona – George Neville, and the egregious example, Duke Humphrey of Gloucester. Extra-official teaching at the English universities may have helped support some expatriate exponents of humanism before 1485, like Surigone, as well as Lorenzo Traversagni and Caio Auberino; while they were in England, however, such men remained dependent on the favours of a small number of highly placed individuals, like Duke Humphrey, whose provision of patronage depended on the state of their personal fortunes (often unstable in fifteenth-century England) and their personal tastes.

The focus herein falls on the middle period, between the early humanist activity in England of the fifteenth century, documented by Weiss (whose study leaves off in 1485) and the others, and English humanism's sixteenth-century maturity, when, by 1520 or so, the humanist activity had become 'the New Learning' – the predominant, most pervasive aspect of English intellectual culture. The state of affairs changed in this meanwhile, between about 1475 and 1525. What had been the 'modest and amateurish' activity of a few foreigners and wealthy English dilettantes in the fifteenth century became the bold and professional mature humanism of England's mid-sixteenth century.

It may be, as Weiss concluded, that, 'when reviewing the features of the New Learning of the early decades of the sixteenth century,' that is, the achievements of More and his circle of English and foreign-born contacts, 'it is impossible not to recognize them as the natural evolution of the modest and amateurish activities of the English humanists of the fifteenth century.'[19] My sense is that the change Weiss identifies was ultimately institutional – a matter of the creation of institutions designed to inculcate humanist interests; and also that the ultimate institutional change was the product not only of 'natural evolution' but of numerous particular decisions, taken incidentally, though always subject to various contemporary non-literary and non-intellectual pressures, by individual patrons and humanists. The most important individual may have been a seemingly most unlikely one, Henry VII.

The supply of and the demand for humanist talent in fifteenth-century England seem to have remained small until the period just after 1485, the first years of the reign of Henry VII. Estimates of his capacity for appreciating finer things have varied;[20] in any case, he was the first English king to patronize humanism regularly – to give exponents of it gifts of one sort and another, to provide them livings, and to employ them in his own affairs – and his example was of consequence. There was no Erasmus or More among those Henry VII patronized, nor any

Erasmian correspondence to throw flattering light on their accomplishments. Nevertheless, a number of men, of persistently humanist inclinations, were able to make livings in England during Henry VII's reign as men of letters, essentially, in large measure or exclusively by the king's benefaction: Bernard André, who from 1485 functioned as the quasi-official propagandist of the Tudor monarchy; Pietro Carmeliano, another poetic propagandist who became Henry VII's Latin secretary; Polydore Vergil, who came as a papal subcollector and stayed on, as archdeacon of Wells and the prebend of Oxgate in St Paul's, to write the *Anglia historia* at Henry VII's request; and the group of largely native tutors whom Henry employed in the education of his children, John Holt, William Hone, John Rede, John Skelton, and the exceptional Bernard André.

Throughout Henry VII's reign, papal business continued to employ learned Italians in England, including Polydore Vergil, Giovanni Gigli and his nephew Silvestro, both bishops of Worcester, the papal collector Adriano Castellesi, and Pietro Griffo, another subcollector; and again, natives of England with humanist interests in antiquity travelled to and returned from Italy: William Grocyn, William Lily, John Colet, Thomas Linacre, William Latimer, and Cuthbert Tunstall all visited Italy before 1500. In addition to the patronage of his own that Henry VII offered directly to humanists, he also promoted the careers of others who in their turn patronized humanists: John Morton, William Warham, Richard Fox, Christopher Urswick, Thomas Ruthall, and John Fisher among them. Their beneficiaries included virtually all of the members of the next generation of humanism in England, the circle associated with More that flourished in the reign of the next king Henry.[21]

By 1500, the formal, official emplacement of humanist studies in the English universities still remained largely in the future.[22] Magdalen College, Oxford, and the Magdalen College School were exceptions of sorts, as were also, to a lesser degree, Winchester College and New College, Oxford. The Magdalen College School numbered among its many important masters and alumni two in particular who, already in the fifteenth century, contributed decisively to the introduction of humanist pedagogy in Latin to England – John Anwykyll and John Stanbridge; other Magdalen masters and students before the end of the century included Grocyn, Holt, Lily, Hone, John Claymond, Robert Whittinton, and the future Cardinal Wolsey, who was the School's master in 1498–99. Thomas Chaundler, vice-chancellor and chancellor of Oxford University between 1457 and 1479, was also warden of New College in the same twenty-year period. During his wardenship, College fellows included William Warham and William Grocyn; and while there, Grocyn is believed to have taught Stanbridge, Rede, and William Horman, later master of Eton. But the kind of humanist activity that characterized the Magdalen College School or New College before 1500 was institutionalized only after 1500, with the foundation of new schools and colleges deliberately humanist in orientation.

England's distinguished early sixteenth-century educational foundations – like the St Paul's School, under its first headmaster, William Lily; and, at a more advanced level, Christ's College (1505) and St John's College (1516), Cambridge, for the design of which John Fisher was responsible, or Richard Fox's 1517 foundation, Corpus Christi College, Oxford, which provided for a public lecturer in Greek – suggest that by about 1500, as Denys Hay observes, humanism in England had reached 'the take-off point.'[23] The numbers had become, if not suddenly, then decisively larger. During the first fifteen years of the reign of Henry VII, a large and disproportionately influential English population had come to be convinced of the value of humanist training, to the extent that they demanded it for themselves or those whom they employed. The fortunes of the movement in England ceased to rest in the hands of a few egregious individuals, once the demand for humanist training became the common prerogative of England's dominant groups, the 'political class'[24] of persons engaged immediately in running the country or in a position to employ others to administer their affairs.

One consequence was that humanism became self-sustaining in England, among the English, to an unprecedented degree; another was that the country became the more attractive to humanists born and trained elsewhere, needing to make careers for themselves. The apparently large and stable demand in England for the labours of humanists, compounded by the perception that England was rich in such resources as well-endowed ecclesiastical benefices while remaining poor in talent,[25] and then by unfavourable conditions in Italy – an over-production of humanists there and, following the French invasion of the peninsula in 1494, political turmoil[26] – served to entice significant numbers of foreign-born humanists to come to England seeking their fortunes in the late fifteenth and early sixteenth centuries. By then, the situation in England was such that they could expect material success for humanists to be had there. And come they did, most often to the royal court, the best source of patronage in a country where power and influence were increasingly centralized.[27] A number of these foreign-born humanists who made careers in early Tudor England became important examples of what humanism in England could accomplish, for its exponents as well as for its patrons: among them, André, Carmeliano, Giovanni and Silvestro Gigli, Vergil, or Andrea Ammonio, who was in England by 1506.

Henry VII's death in 1509 had consequences for the development of the humanist movement in England, but not the same sort of consequences that the demise of another important early English patron of the movement, Humphrey of Gloucester, had had sixty years before. Instead of a setback for the profession, Henry VII's death, followed by the accession of his son Henry VIII, occasioned an impressive outburst of humanist activity, in some measure animated by intergenerational struggle within the professional group. Henry VII's death was taken to presage an improvement in opportunities for humanists, and not only because of the legendary financial leanness of his final years. Henry VIII had himself been educated by humanists, and he came to the throne amid rumours that he would be particularly well disposed towards *eruditi*.[28] Those who had enjoyed Henry VII's favour – the senior generation – felt their security threatened by this change of monarch, and so seem to have been particularly eager to impress the new king; the new generation, neglected under Henry VII, now saw a chance to improve its lot, even if impressing the new king entailed denigrating members of the senior generation. Eventually, the outcome was the ascendance of the new generation. Though André and Carmeliano lived on into the 1520s, they fell quiet; by the end of the first decade of Henry VIII's reign, his court could boast the employment of More, Linacre, Pace, Ammonio, and other new men.

The chapters that follow, however, are not a history of humanism in this middle period, 1475–1525, or of its development in the still briefer reign of Henry VII, 1485–1509, even though such a history would be useful. Instead, they are a series of case-studies, of particular English publications of the same period, in manuscript or in print or both, and in manuscripts of various different kinds and printed books of various kinds. As it happens, these case-studies shed light on important figures and important events in this history of humanism in England late in the fifteenth and early in the sixteenth centuries: Pietro Carmeliano, Bernard André, Desiderius Erasmus, William Lily, and Thomas More among them. But the focus is meant to be on a particular aspect only of this literary history. The case-studies document the practice of literary professionalism in the doings of a few writers working in England in the period 1475–1525, who were all humanists of one sort or another; how, specifically, by working with and on the literary institutions that then obtained – particularly the institutions of patronage and of publishing, in all their forms – these persons were able to make livings for themselves, principally by writing and then making their writing public in one way and another. The issue is what was made of books under these determining circumstances.

Chapter 1

Filippo Alberici, *Cebes' Tablet*, and Henry VII

Probably at New Year's 1507, a Servite friar of Mantua, naming himself 'Philippus Albericus,' presented Henry VII a manuscript book containing a number of his own verse and prose writings, illustrated with numerous full-page paintings.[1] The purposes that brought this Filippo Alberici to England are not known;[2] while in England, however, during 1506 and 1507, he sought local patronage. Letters he wrote Richard Fox, the bishop of Winchester, contain plain entreaties,[3] and the point of his presentation to Henry VII in 1507 seems clear. Any number of Italian writers and others seeking patronage had made the king similar gifts over the years, though not usually such attractive ones as Alberici's.

The book Alberici gave Henry VII in 1507 would have made almost anyone a most impressive present; Henry seems not to have taken great pleasure in it, however. Alberici's gift did not earn him much if anything by way of a return that could have kept him in England or interested in English affairs. After further travels in France, Alberici had returned to Italy by May 1509.[4] He seems to have given up on the sort of literary work he circulated in England – the only writing he published after his return to Italy was a history of his Servite order[5] – and to have pursued a career in church business, at which he had some success. He was elected Servite vicar-general in 1515; with other members of his order, he probably travelled abroad about 1521 to agitate against Lutheran reform; in 1526, he was serving as his order's *commissarius* in the papal curia of Clement VII; in 1530, he removed to Naples to found a Servite house on properties given the order by Jacopo Sannazaro, and there he died in 1531. There is nothing in any of this to hint that Alberici retained any interest in England after 1508 at the latest; in other words, from the perspective of its benefits to him, his English sojourn of 1506–7 had returned nothing. His presentation to Henry VII at New Year's 1507 appears to have been a magnificent failure.

In presenting his work to Henry VII, Alberici was making a gesture that by the beginning of the sixteenth century had become commonplace and obligatory for persons seeking to make livings in England as exponents of humanism. An impressive number of such persons sought Henry VII's patronage, among them well-known figures, including Bernard André, Pietro Carmeliano, Giovanni Gigli, Thomas Linacre, Polydore Vergil, and Andrea Ammonio; others less well known, like Alberici or Cornelio Vitelli; and still others – 'An Italian, a poete,' for example, whom Henry rewarded with a gift of twenty pounds in May 1496, or the Giovanni Opizio who presented poetry to the king in 1497[6] – who remain anonymous or all but anonymous.

The tool used by such persons to elicit patronage in the first instance, be it from the monarch himself or not, was the presentation manuscript. Prior personal introductions mattered, as did reputation, particularly for obtaining forms of ongoing support, such as ecclesiastical benefices or bureaucratic appointments. Introductions often were made, however, and the issue often was resolved, with the offering of a literary gift to a likely patron by the humanist patronage seeker. Besides making an introduction, the presentation manuscript compelled the prospective patron to answer the entreaty embodied in the presentation. The prospective patron might ignore the gift, an answer eloquent enough in its way; or he might reward it outright, with a recompensatory gift. Such immediate recompense alone could be valuable; in addition, its value served as an index of a patron's disposition and inclinations, encouraging or discouraging the patronage seeker. Small immediate recompense might hold almost as little promise of future benefits as none at all. Initial generosity, on the other hand, encouraged hopes that more permanent forms of support might be forthcoming; certainly, it tended to encourage additional presentations.

From this perspective, the presentation manuscript was the crucial instrument for persons seeking to take livings, by their learning and literary skills, from a literary economy centred on personal patronage, as early Tudor England's was. In large measure, their success or failure depended on the immediate impression they could make by their presentations. Alberici's exceeded the norm. In terms of its decoration, its contents, and the attractiveness of its portrayal of Alberici, it was outstanding. The manuscript – thirty-two leaves of vellum, 203 x 145 mm, with generous margins, carefully written in a humanist hand, and lavishly ornamented (fig 1) – comprises a collection of Alberici's writings, rather than a single item, and this feature shifts the focus of attention, subtly perhaps but still sensibly, from the occasion of the presentation to the idea of a literary career. The manuscript is not a production for the nonce, speaking only to the immediate occasion and its political circumstance, as do many contemporary literary presentations; rather, by virtue of its inclusion of a series of writings, it pretends to represent Alberici's capabilities beyond the particular moment, his accomplishment as a whole. It is more an advertisement for the presenter than an attempt to meet a particular need of the potential patron to whom it was addressed.

Some of the contents do the important work of establishing Alberici's credentials, asserting that he had friends. Near the end of the manuscript is a poem 'Ad Henricum regem de honore per eum allato studiosis Cantabriae,' celebrating Henry VII's visit to Cambridge in late April 1506, evidently in the company of his son Prince Henry.[7] It has the appearance of a poem read out in Henry's presence on the occasion: it addresses the king directly, for example, and calls on the university to attest to the veracity of Alberici's recitation of the king's virtues.[8] If it had been so 'presented' to the king earlier, orally, in some ceremonial context, its re-presentation in Alberici's gift-manuscript, after the fact, would serve to recall for Henry the earlier occasion and Alberici's role in it. Presumably, these were happy associations for the king, tending to capture his *benevolentia*, and, more concretely, causing him to connect Alberici with the world of official learning, specifically the University of Cambridge, then the particular re-

FIG 1 London, British Library, Arundel 317, fol 1r: the beginning of Filippo Alberici's presentation copy of the *Cebes' Tablet*, for Henry VII, dating from 1506–7, with full-page border. Vellum page, 203 x 145 mm; writing, 130 x 95 mm

FIG 2 London, British Library, Arundel 317, fol 25r: full-page painting at the head of Alberici's 'De mortis effectibus'

FIG 3 Pedro Berruguete or Justus of Ghent, double portrait of Federico
(d 1482) and Guidobaldo da Montefeltro. Urbino, Palazzo Ducale

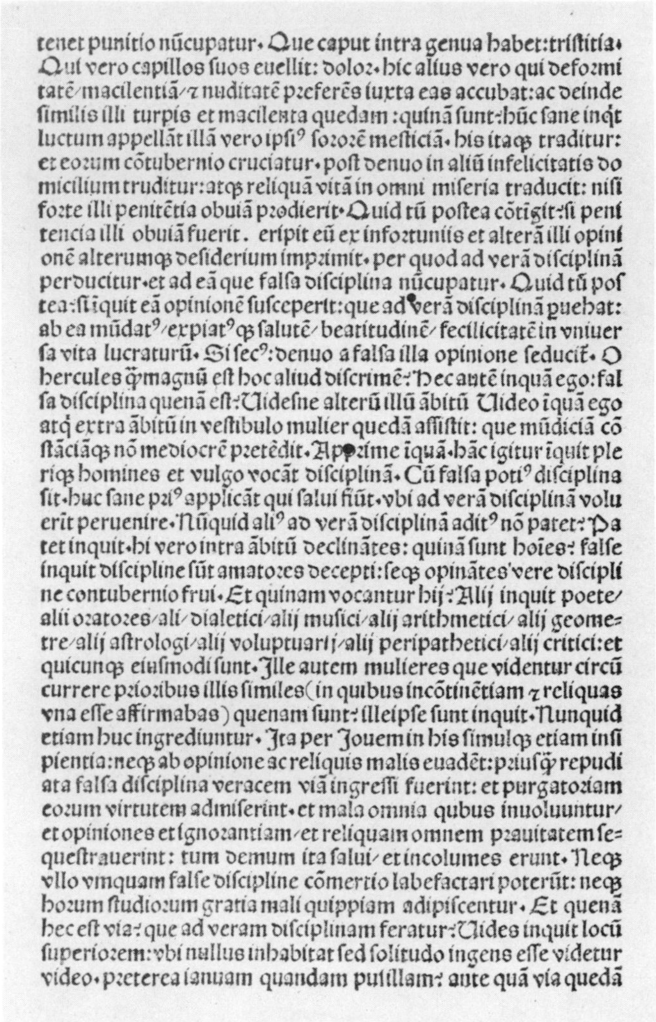

tenet punitio nucupatur· Que caput intra genua habet:tristitia·
Qui vero capillos suos euellit: dolo2·hic alius vero qui deformi
tate macilentia/7 nuditate preferes iurta eas accubat:ac deinde
similis illi turpis et macilenta quedam :quina sunt:huc sane inqt
luctum appellat illa vero ipsi9 foro2e mesticia· his itaq2 traditur:
et eo2um cotubernio cruciatur·post denuo in altu infelicitatis do
micilium truditur:atq2 reliqua vita in omni miseria traducit: nisi
forte illi penitetia obuia prodierit·Quid tu postea cotigit:si peni
tencia illi obuia fuerit. eripit eu ex infortuniis et altera illi opini
one alterumq2 desiderium impamit·per quod ad vera disciplina
perducitur·et ad ea que falsa disciplina nucupatur·Quid tu pos
tea:si quit ea opinione susceperit:que ad vera disciplina puebat:
ab ea mudat9/expiat9q2 salute/beatitudine/fecilicitate in vniuer
sa vita lucraturu·Si sec9:denuo a falsa illa opinione seducit· O
hercules qmagnu est hoc aliud discrime:Hec aute inqua ego:fal
sa disciplina quena est:Uidesne alteru illu abitu Uideo iqua ego
atq extra abitu in vestibulo mulier queda assistit: que mudicia co
staciaq2 no mediocre pretedit·App2ime iqua·hac igitur iquit ple
riq2 homines et vulgo vocat disciplina·Cu falsa poti9 disciplina
sit·huc sane p2i9 applicat qui salui fiut·vbi ad vera disciplina volu
erit peruenire·Nuquid ali9 ad vera disciplina adit9 no patet:Pa
tet inquit·hi vero intra abitu declinates: quina sunt hoies: false
inquit discipline sut amato2es decepti:seq2 opinates vere discipli
ne contubernio frui·Et quinam vocantur hij:Alij inquit poete/
alii o2ato2es/alii dialetici/alij musici/alij arithmetici/alij geome=
tre/alij astrologi/alij voluptuarij/alij peripathetici/alij critici:et
quicunq2 eiusmodi sunt·Ille autem mulieres que videntur circu
currere p2io2ibus illis similes(in quibus incotinetiam 7 reliquas
vna esse affirmabas)quenam sunt:illeipse sunt inquit·Nunquid
etiam huc ingrediuntur·Ita per Iouem in his simulq2 etiam insi
pientia:neq2 ab opinione ac reliquis malis euadet:p2iusq repudi
ata falsa disciplina veracem via ingressi fuerint: et purgato2iam
eo2um virtutem admiserint·et mala omnia qubus inuoluuntur/
et opiniones et igno2antiam/et reliquam omnem p2auitatem se=
questrauerint: tum demum ita salui·et incolumes erunt·Neq2
vllo vmquam false discipline comertio labefactari poterut: neq2
bo2um studio2um gratia mali quippiam adipiscentur· Et quena
hec est via2:que ad veram disciplinam feratur:Uides inquit locu
superio2em:vbi nullus inhabitat sed solitudo ingens esse videtur
video·preterea ianuam quandam pusillam: ante qua via queda

FIG 4 Lodovico Odasio, trans *Cebetis Thebani tabula* (Paris: Marchant 1498) sig B2v: the text is transcribed in appendix 2. Copy: Harvard University, Houghton Library, Inc 8008. Paper page, 186 × 128 mm; type, 150 × 90 mm

FIG 5 Hans Holbein, woodcut omnibus title-page border, depicting the tablet of Cebes, here occurring in a copy of Nicolò Perotti *Cornucopia* (Basel: Curio 1532). Dating from 1522, this is the fourth and final version of the tablet by Holbein, whose monogram appears near the lower left corner of the border. Copy: San Marino, California, Huntington Library, RB 137913

FIG 6 London, British Library, Arundel 317, fol 2v: full-page painting facing the beginning of Alberici's *Cebes' Tablet*

FIG 7 London, British Library, Arundel 317, fol 6v: the first *circus* of
the *Cebes' Tablet*

FIG 8 London, British Library, Arundel 317, fol 10v: the second *circus*
of the *Cebes' Tablet*

FIG 9 London, British Library, Arundel 317, fol 13v: the first part of the third *circus* of the *Cebes' Tablet*

FIG 10 **London, British Library, Arundel 317, fol 18v: the second part of the third *circus* of the *Cebes' Tablet***

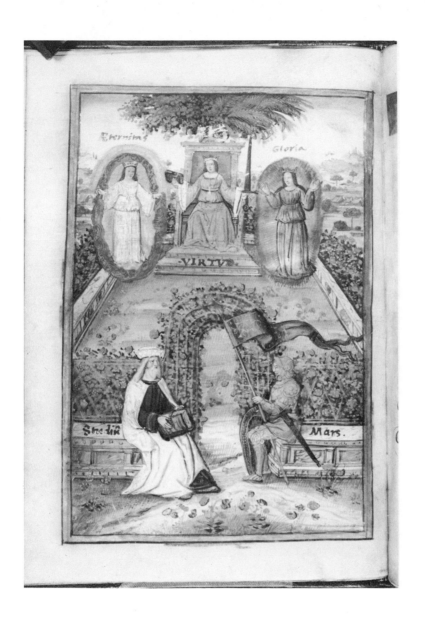

FIG 11 London, British Library, Arundel 317, fol 20v: the final part of
the third *circus* of the *Cebes' Tablet*

cipient of royal patronage. The poem would also serve to compel the king to acknowledge that he had met Alberici before, insinuating that the manuscript's presentation was not careerist effrontery but the continuation of a personal relationship into which the king had already entered.

The manuscript also contains a brief prose letter, ostensibly addressed by Alberici to Joachim Bretoner, *Anglus*. The letter in effect dedicates the final poem in the manuscript to Bretoner; it also provides Alberici an opportunity to state that he had not previously presented the manuscript's principal poem to some other patron. Bretoner was seneschal of King's Hall at the time of Henry's visit to Cambridge in 1506, and was presumably known to the king or to members of his family or court. By addressing the letter to Bretoner, invoking Bretoner's name, friendship, and esteem, Alberici further advertises his Cambridge connection; he also implicates Bretoner in his assertion of the originality of his presentation, calling on the Cambridge man to vouch for the fact that he had not previously dedicated the work elsewhere.[9]

The proper addressee of the letter, however, is the manuscript's recipient, Henry VII; from the perspective of the presentation, the letter to Bretoner functions as a warrant of Alberici's esteem for the king. The problem the letter raises was a genuine one: contemporary writers did succumb to a temptation to make the same piece of writing pay twice, or more often, by presenting the same piece of writing to more than one patron. The trick was easier to practise when works remained exclusively in manuscript circulation. Then, the only danger was that word of multiple presentation might travel; and as word did travel, potential patrons came to suffer anxiety over it. Whether or not Alberici had presented his work elsewhere before remains open to question. In any case, he was evidently sensitive to the threat to patronal self-esteem posed by the practice of multiple presentation. He at least wished to represent himself to Henry VII as sufficiently in awe of the English king to foreswear any potentially humiliating attempt to pass him used literary goods for new. The letter tends to confirm what such poetry was for, from the perspective of those who created it: whatever else it also did, the purpose of Alberici's writing – the purpose that is in the final analysis the writing's *raison d'être* – was to elicit patronage.

Alberici's presentation manuscript concludes with a

hundred-line *carmen* 'De mortis effectibus ex hyeme et nocte descriptis.'[10] It is a depressing little poem, and its inclusion in the manuscript seems unlikely to have done much to benefit Alberici, except that it is stylish, after the fashion of the other work in the collection; and thus it does the important work of establishing that Alberici was not a poet of only a single classicizing trick. Making much use of ancient myth, the 'De mortis effectibus' is strikingly pagan in outlook. The poem is a piece of morality and wisdom, on the inevitability of death, but it foregoes Christian consolation to maintain an ancient frame of reference. In it, a poet-narrator, gazing out on an early winter landscape at day's end, is struck by the fact of death. As night comes on and snow begins to fall, he imagines that he hears Earth – 'tristis Tellus' – lamenting winter's advent as if it were her own death and rebuking Phoebus for abandoning her. Earth's lament is cut short, when she suffers a deathlike agony; Earth's children – various 'nymphae' and 'dryades' – lament what they take to be her passing. Finally, the poet imagines seeing a stony altar, on a high, rocky wasteland, kept by the *Parcae*, where 'viventum genus omne' must come for sacrifice, 'nor is turning back allowed': 'Here, it is said, the fatal sisters do their spinners' work and keep the place with their unfailing observance'; 'in the end, reaching this final boundary stone is inevitable, and death leads on to the eternal shades.'[11] The poem concludes with a description of this altar, its furnishings, and the terrible inscription on it. Above it hangs a lamp that is put out, and the aversion of the face of the bird sitting on it denotes death; the horns of a goat's head, sculpted in marble, jut out from the altar, and from between them hangs a human likeness, shorn of hair; around this effigy circle fronds of monkshood, woven into a wreath; and from it depends a tablet inscribed with dark characters, reading 'By authority of Fate, with bloody hand, the cruel Parcae have here established their cruel threads and this their altar.' The scene is the subject of the manuscript's last full-page illustration (fig 2), which is specific to these details of the poetic description:

> Quid referam? Heu, vestram, mortales, noscite sortem:
>   Letantur nostro Fata cruore coli.
> Pensilis extincta est super haec altaria lampas,
>   Et volucris verso denotat ore necem;

Cornibus atque arae cadenti ex marmore capri
  Incisum mira prominet arte caput;
Inter utrumque pari pendet discrimine cornu
  Humana abscissis crinibus effigies;
Frondibus hanc circum serpunt aconita retextis,
  Qua pullis pendet scripta tabella typis:
CRUDELES PARCAE CRUDELIA STAMINA ET ARAS
SANGUINEA HAS FATO CONSTITUERE MANU.[12]

The burden of proof of Alberici's qualities as a humanist writer rests ultimately, however, on the manuscript's main item, placed at its head and occupying twenty-three of its twenty-eight inscribed leaves: a poem headed 'Tabula Cebetis qua sub picturis totus humanae vitae decursus declaratur, per F. Philippum Albericum Mantuanum carminibus intexta.'[13] The work is addressed to Henry VII by means of an introductory poem preceding it,[14] and it concludes with lines that again directly address Henry VII, along with his son.

Alberici's work here has literary-historical significance beyond the immediate context of its presentation to Henry VII, and the work's election for presentation should have seemed to Alberici particularly clever. In the first place, the piece translates into Latin hexameters, for an audience in England, a work of Greek literature: the *Cebes' Tablet*. No longer widely known, the work nevertheless remained a basic text for instruction in Greek into the eighteenth century and attracted the approbation of such a demanding reader as the revolutionary Milton in the 1640s.[15] Although the Greek original is now believed to date from the first or second century AD,[16] at the point of its recovery among Italian humanists late in the fifteenth century, it was believed to have been written by the Theban philosopher Cebes, a disciple of Socrates and contemporary of Plato, who figures as an interlocutor in the *Phaedo*.

Manuscript copies of the Greek work began to proliferate in Italy during the 1470s, and Greek texts were first printed in Florence around 1496 and by Aldus Manutius in Venice at about the same time. The first and most widely circulated Latin translation was made by Lodovico Odasio, tutor to the ducal family of Urbino, in the early to mid-1490s, and was first printed at Bologna in 1497. By the time the Odasio translation was seeing its fifth printing – in Strasbourg in 1508 – there were at least four other independent Latin translations and paraphrases in circulation, in manuscript and print, all of them Italian in origin; by then the work had been printed, in Greek or in a Latin translation, beyond the Alps as well, in Paris (1498) and Frankfurt (1507); and in 1501, Johannes Rhagius Aesticampianus – Ulrich von Hutten's teacher – lectured on the work in Basel.[17] Possibly, Alberici's translation was the first to reach England; in any case, the work puts Alberici in the avant-garde of European (not only English) humanism; in representing him to the king in these terms, the manuscript offered Henry VII an opportunity to own a piece of this avant-garde and to gain such esteem as could accrue to patronage of it.

From this perspective, a translation of *Cebes' Tablet* was modish; from another, Alberici's work could also have been seen as comfortingly traditional. *Cebes' Tablet* participates in a pair of literary traditions that flourished throughout the Middle Ages. It is wisdom literature – ostensibly a distillation of the sapience of the ancients – of a kind best known in the form of the *Disticha Catonis*; in addition, it is also a personification allegory, in which, in the guise of human beings, various abstractions take part. Alberici provided his work with summary *argumenta*, preceding each of his poem's major divisions, and these prose summaries are a guide to the work:

> A foreigner, Cebes, enters the temple of Saturn. He sees a painted tablet, now worn by withering age, the meaning of which he was not at all able to make out. An Old Man, who was a native of the place, saw that he and his companions were uncertain about the picture. When asked by Cebes, he uncovered the meanings veiled in the figures and, taking up a pointer, he explained the whole thing in order.

> The First Circle
> Here human life is shown. Those are infants, who are coming into life, and they display their heartfelt sadness by their various gestures, knowing in advance the sorrow to come. Genius, the god of nature, teaches each of them what he is to do. But Deception holds out the cup of error, for each of them to take up; some drink much, others little. From the

left, a crowd of Vices comes to meet them as they enter, while from the right come the Virtues; few follow the latter, most the former. There are those who would embrace the Virtues, but they are held back by Idleness; hence arises Luxury, thence arises Inconstancy. In addition, there is Fortune, who perches on a sphere, blindfolded; some she enriches, with her right hand, while she despoils others, with her left.

The Second Circle
Those whom Fortune has enriched beforehand lead a congenial life. Vainglory, Gluttony, and Pleasure embrace them. But when Fortune's gifts fail them, these people are immediately driven away; in order to recover their previous way of life, some take to murder, others to theft, and many to swearing falsely by the gods, for little reward. But some are shut up in a dark building, and these Sorrow, Lament, and Punishment afflict with sufferings. Whence they are lead to a glittering hall; when they have been purged of their crimes there, they are able to return to a better life. Penance batters the door with her rod and continually excites their hearts to honest deeds.

The First Part of the Third Circle
False Discipline comes to meet those who seek true knowledge; deceived by her appearance, the mortals follow her. With her are the False Poet, the Lying Astrologer, and the Trifling Sophist. Here the path forks, and the right fork leads to true Virtue; but it is wholly overgrown with thorns and infected with noxious vapours. And if any of those who undertook to travel the path to Virtue turn back, Night and Poverty punish him with their whips; and, when he has been hurt by their beatings, Circe turns him into a beast and finally drowns him in the Stygian lake, erasing him from men's memory.

The Second Part of the Third Circle
This path to Virtue is indeed altogether difficult and rough. But from all sides, divinities meet those who approach: here, Promise makes her offer to those wanting more; Hope en-

courages them to be able to attain all. There is also Delight, who raises up those who stumble on account of the hardships of the journey; and Skill is a man's companion half the way. There lies in the middle of the circle a huge rock; from its top, Constancy exhorts the weary with the fact that, once each has come so far, he finds the rest of the way most easy; and, with Truth as his guide, he goes on to Virtue's court.[18]

To this point,[19] Alberici's version and the Greek concur. Both describe an allegorical ascent, leading towards virtue, with the temptations and hardships that turn the many aside from the true path. Alberici's version is always more expansive – in such a way as to make it impossible to tell if he used the Greek original or one of the literal Latin translations that might have been available to him as the basis of his work[20] – but he keeps to the plot of the Greek original in all except its final section. In the Greek work, the description of the ascent ends with an account of *Eudaimonia* (Happiness), whose citadel is approached by way of *Paideia* (Education) and her daughters *Aletheia* (Truth) and *Peitho* (Persuasion), and by way of *Episteme* (Knowledge) and the *Aretai* (Virtues) who are her sisters; those individuals whom *Eudaimonia* crowns with wreaths of victory she then sends back to the world, which they are now able to understand properly. The Greek original concludes – in the apparently fragmentary condition in which it has survived – after the fashion of a Socratic dialogue, with discussion of certain points raised by the Old Man's description of the tablet, particularly the faithlessness of *Tyche* (Fortune) and the untrustworthy nature of her gifts.

To take the place of the Greek work's account of *Eudaimonia* and the virtues attendant on her at the end of its allegory, and its concluding dialogues *de casibus virorum*, Alberici fashioned a wholly original (and less frightening) ending for his work, which he summarizes:

The Third Part of the Third Circle
Queen Virtue sits on her golden throne, displaying the double strength of her power; for she signifies Learning by the book she holds in her right hand and Arms by the sword placed in her left. The path to her is pleasant. In her fore-

court sit Study and Mars, and they open the gates to those
who approach. Behind Virtue are the Laurel and the Palm;
with the one, she crowns victors and with the other, the
learned. At her right is Eternity, holding the rainbow in her
hands; on her left is radiant Glory.[21]

Alberici evidently meant this allegorical narrative – of Study
and Mars as the door-wardens of Virtue, on whom wait Eternity
and Glory, at the summit of the ascent depicted on the *tabula* –
to apply to Henry VII, to flatter his accomplishments as well as
to encourage him to persist in his putative devotions to 'Studium
et Mars.' Alberici had invoked the same qualities represented by
this pair of personifications in his encomium of Henry probably
occasioned by the king's visit to Cambridge in 1506. Calling him
'a mighty Caesar in intellect, likewise mighty in arms,' the poem
begins with the topic: 'You had praise enough, illustrious king,
and glory gotten of your own mighty valour, never to perish: why
– it is too much – why do you determine to wreath your brows
in garlands of the sacred branch of Minerva as well?' After re-
hearsing the king's accomplishments, it concludes on the same
note: 'Rightly, therefore, should be given you the insignia of a
double triumph: it befits you to be decorated with both the hel-
met and the laurel.'[22]

In using an allegory of this topic to conclude his *Cebes'
Tablet*, Alberici was acting without precedent; in applying it to
the Tudor king, however, he was not acting altogether unrea-
sonably. Henry was a conqueror of sorts: he had gained the throne
of England by conquest, though he was subsequently disinclined
to emphasize the fact; he had campaigned successfully against
France in Brittany in 1497; and he had put down by force at least
two serious armed uprisings at home. In addition, although he
was by no means outstandingly learned in his own right, he had
been an important patron of arts and letters, on a grander scale
than had been known in England at least since the beginning of
the fifteenth century.[23] Nevertheless, Alberici's motive for using
the topic was probably rhetorical and political rather than merely
encomiastic. The notion underlying the concluding allegory of
Alberici's *Tablet* – that a *rapprochement* of arms and letters,
accomplishment in both warfare and learning, comprised the particular variety of virtue most able to yield long-lived glory – was

not original with him. This 'arms and letters' theme was common. Alberici's use of it would have derived from Italian sources, however, possibly more specifically from sources to be associated with Urbino;[24] Alberici's evocation of the theme may have been calculated to flatter Henry VII by likening him to the dukes of Urbino. The theme had been central to ducal propaganda since the time of Federico da Montefeltro (d 1482). The best-known example is probably the symbolically weighty double portrait of Federico and his young son Guidobaldo: in it, Federico, dressed in armour and girt with a sword, sits studying a book (fig 3). The theme figures in numerous other ducal monuments as well, and its association with the duchy was propagated in literature by Cristoforo Landino, Vespasiano da Bisticci, and Baldassare Castiglione – all of them, like Odasio, the early prose translator of the *Cebes' Tablet*, in the employ of dukes of Urbino at one time or another.[25]

Duke Federico had been elected to the Order of the Garter in 1474, during the reign of Edward IV, and contacts between the English and Urbinesque courts were continuous and extensive.[26] Moreover, recent events had lent Urbino a particular importance for English affairs, just at the time of Alberici's presentation.[27] Henry VII's heir Arthur had died in 1502, leaving Catherine of Aragon a widow. Henry needed papal dispensation to marry the widow to his eldest surviving son, Prince Henry. The pope from whom the dispensation had to be obtained was Julius II, a notorious nepotist, and he had familial interests in Urbino. His brother was married to the sister of the present Duke Guidobaldo, who was childless; his brother's son was due to succeed to the duchy on Guidobaldo's death. Guidobaldo promoted the English cause with Julius II, and, like his father, he was elected to the Order of the Garter. In 1506, probably the year of Alberici's arrival, Castiglione also travelled to England, to act as Guidobaldo's proxy in the Garter installation ceremonies at Windsor.[28]

It is not possible to be precise about the relations of Alberici's work to these events.[29] Nonetheless, Alberici's concoction, of an Urbinesque 'arms and letters' theme and the *Cebes' Tablet*, should have served to evoke Urbino for its English audience and to flatter Henry VII by the association; certainly, Urbino's increased importance to England, and the increased diplomatic traffic between England and Urbino, including Castiglione's mission, would have made such allusions more striking at the time Alberici presented his work to the English king.

Alberici's version of the *Cebes' Tablet* was literary work of quality; it was also somewhat long and complex. His analysis of the 665-line poem into a series of six chapters, with a distinct prologue, where neither the Greek original nor any other Latin version then in circulation had had any; his provision of prose summaries for each of these chapters – again, an unprecedented gesture – and his addition of marginal subheadings within the chapters; all seek to ease the work's demands on a reader. A contrast with the early printed editions of the Odasio translation is instructive: the 1498 edition comprises twelve pages, solid with abbreviated prose, forty lines per page, in a small type; at the head of the text is a title and at its foot occurs a colophon, each set off with a paraph mark, but between them there is not so much as a single visual break (fig 4). Reading it hurts. In the manuscript copy of Alberici's version, on the other hand, the provision of explicits, the summaries of what is to come, differently formatted and in a different script, and the rubricated chapter-headings every few rectos would have made using the book easier: the *mise-en-page* of the materials effectively imposes an alternation of reading and repose.

This analysis of the poem, by means of the layout and decoration of the manuscript, is complemented by the manuscript's program of illustrations. Between each prose summary and rubricated chapter heading occurs a full-page painting, always facing the beginning of the chapter it illustrates; these form a sequence evidently unique to the manuscript. There may have been a particular ancient work of art with which the *Tablet* was associated; certainly, there were ancient and later renaissance attempts to translate the writing's description of a picture into visual terms, the best known of which is Holbein's woodcut omnibus title-page, used for various books printed after 1521 (fig 5). The Greek manuscripts of the work, which survived into or were made during the late fifteenth century, were unillustrated. Only with the publication of the Frankfurt edition of 1507 did the renaissance tradition of illustrating the work begin.[30] Characteristically, this renaissance tradition represented the *tabula* synthetically: the Holbein woodcut, typical in this, attempts to show the whole allegory of the writing all at once, in the sort of single picture that the Greek work purports to describe. Even as reductive as they must be, such synthetic representations of the *tabula* are nevertheless confusingly crowded; and the analytic alternative – representation of the allegory as a series of discontinuous scenes, in a series of different pictures – was eventually tried in a printed book, produced at Paris in 1543.[31]

This analytic alternative is also tried in Alberici's manuscript. It illustrates his version of the *Tablet* with six independent full-page paintings. The first sets the scene, showing a gathering of people in a temple, among whom is the narrative's *Senex*, using a pointer to direct his audience's attentions to an oval-shaped *tabula* hung high overhead (fig 6). The second illustration shows the first of the three *circi* described in the poem: babies coming along a path, over which hangs a placard inscribed 'Hac itur ad gemitus' ('This way to miseries'), and being admitted, by *Genius* and *Deceptio*, to a walled enclosure, labelled 'vita humana,' wherein are represented *Luxuria*, *Inertia*, *Instabilitas*, and *Fortuna*, around whom are grouped men labelled either 'Fortunati' or 'Infortunati,' and a group of women labelled 'Virtutes' (fig 7). The third shows the second circle: three women, labelled 'voluptas in malis,' directing a young man (who reappears also within the circle), by way of *Gula*, to a second walled enclosure, within which appear *Occisor*, *Fur*, *Periurus*, and then *Poena*, *Dolor*, *Luctus*, and *Penitentia* (fig 8). The fourth, fifth, and sixth illustrations show portions of the third and final circle: the fourth represents personifications of *Falsa Disciplina*, *Falsus Poeta*, *Sophista Nugator*, *Mendax Astrologus*, *Nox*, *Paupertas*, and *Circe*, but also a bearded man pointing to a reptile- and snake-strewn path, labelled 'Via veritatis,'[32] at the end of which sits a unicorn, and beside which stands a tree supporting a placard, inscribed 'Set forth, if your mind is pure' (fig 9);[33] the fifth shows a young man being led, by *Promissio*, *Spes*, *Voluptas*, and *Solertia*, to the feet of *Constantia*, whose banner reads 'Persevere, youth, if you have the will,'[34] and beyond whom stands a naked, smiling *Veritas* (fig 10); and the final illustration shows *Virtus* herself finally, flanked by *Aeternitas* and *Gloria* and enthroned in her garden, at the gate of which sit *Studium* and *Mars* (fig 11).

What little is lost by the analytic approach to illustration adopted here – by way of the illustrations' infidelity to the writing, which purports to describe a single picture – is compensated by the increase in clarity that the analytic approach makes possible. The illustrations in the Alberici manuscript are still reductive, but less so than their synthetic counterparts: thirty-four of the thirty-seven personifications mentioned in Alberici's writing are depicted and labelled in the program of illustrations; of those omitted – *Vanagloria* (285–9), *Tristitia* (324–7), and *Verus Poeta* (390–407) – only one, *Vanagloria*, is mentioned in the prose summaries of the work.[35] There are also a certain small number of incongruities about the illustrations – such as the unicorn at the end of the *via veritatis* in the third illustration (fig 8) – items not mentioned in the writing, but appearing in the illustrations, as if at the illustrator's irregulated initiative.[36]

Except such few deviations, the illustrations follow the writing remarkably nearly, to such a degree that the illustration program must be regarded as having been designed specifically for Alberici's work. Most of the artist's information could have come from the prose summaries or the marginal subheadings within the chapters, rather than the work itself; it could conceivably have come from a knowledge of some other version of the *Tablet* or of some other illustrative cycle, except that the program shows Alberici's peculiarities at several points. The inscribed banners quote Alberici's poem, for example.[37] The figure of *Gula*, in the third illustration (fig 8), is original with Alberici,[38] as are other personifications that appear in the illustrations: the followers of *Falsa Disciplina* shown – *Falsus Poeta, Sophista Nugator, Mendax Astrologus* (fig 9) – are Alberici's creations;[39] likewise, Alberici's personifications of the dangers along the path to *Virtus* – *Nox* and *Paupertas* – are original with him[40] yet do occur in the illustration (fig 9).

The illustrations contributed, significantly, to making Alberici's complicated piece of writing comprehensible and memorable. Complementing the prose summaries, chapter divisions, and subheadings of the work, the illustrations clarify his writing, summarizing it again, in effect, in a way which would have eased access to the writing in the first place and then would have eased memorial reconstruction and retention of it afterwards. The same can be said of the painting at the head of Alberici's poem 'De mortis effectibus' (fig 2), which likewise sums up the crucial, concluding section of that poem. At least as important, however, from Alberici's perspective, the qualities of his manuscript's pictures as pictures – the planning, the skilled labour, and the materials expended on their production – would have augmented, also significantly, the objective, material value of his gift to the king. The pictures are modestly attractive art, particularly so perhaps in the context of early sixteenth-century English illustration. Their incorporation into the book should also have suggested to the gift's recipient that Alberici meant his work and his presentation to be taken seriously.

Alberici's gift to Henry VII had these several qualities, which combine to make it an outstanding example of its literary-artistic type, the humanist presentation manuscript. Its main item is a sophisticated rendering of a fashionably little known Greek work, being imported into England probably for the first time; it had the additional virtue of being comfortably old-fashioned as well, by virtue of its participation in the familiar genre of the sapiential literature of the ancients and the prominence of personification allegory in it. Additionally, on to the piece he received from the Greek tradition, Alberici grafted an original, unprecedented ending. His conclusion flattered the work's recipient, by its representation of the English king as the embodiment of a renowned virtue, only to be approached by way of *Studium* and *Mars*. Finally, the manuscript's inclusion of other writings sets Alberici's accomplishment with the *Cebes' Tablet* in the context of a whole literary career; he had more than one poem to present; he had connections at Cambridge, if only in the person of Bretoner; and although he might have presented his work to someone else, he had singled out Henry VII, to whom he claimed he was already known and whom he claimed already to have served.

The material context in which this writing was presented should also have favoured Alberici: by its design, the manuscript does well at representing a long, complicated piece of writing clearly and attractively. Its disposition of the work into chapters, each with distinctively marked headings, and its alternation of differently formatted and differently written prose summaries with these verse chapters, combined with the manuscript's illustrations to make the work easily legible. In addition to their contribution to the work's legibility, the manuscript's full-page paintings and borders also assert the manuscript's objective value. They are eye-catching, of course, and also articulate Alberici's self-esteem. He invested heavily in the book's production, not only of his talent and skill, but also of his money, thereby asking after recompense almost explicitly.

Nevertheless, Alberici's gift failed, in the terms by which the success and failure of such gifts are to be measured. There is no evidence that Henry rewarded Alberici's efforts, by means of either a recompensatory gift outright or an appointment to office – both varieties of favour that Henry showed others. To the contrary, what can be known of Alberici's career in later years suggests that his ambitious, elegant, and eloquent gift was met with nothing or little. He wrote piously after his return to Italy, and he held positions of importance in his Servite order there. But such successes as later came to him came not immediately of the skills as a learned writer that he demonstrated to Henry VII with his presentation of 1507, nor did they come to him in England or from the English.

Alberici's failure to thrive in England is difficult to account for with any precision; intangibles, imponderables figured, no doubt, which want evidentiary confirmation. It is possible that Alberici's work with the *Cebes' Tablet* was too sophisticated; knowledge of Greek literature at the English court may have been too little advanced by 1506–7 for Alberici's distinction to be recognizable. Such an explanation probably underestimates English culture, or overestimates Alberici's achievement; more plausible may be an explanation from some shortcoming on Alberici's part. It may be that, his denial notwithstanding, Alberici had already presented his work, or was believed to have already presented his work, to some other patron. In addition, the introductions he laid claim to were not impressive. He knew Henry VII's physician, Giovanni Boerio, and through Boerio he might have gained introductions to others at the Tudor court. However, the only person whose acquaintance Alberici advertised was Joachim Bretoner, a minor figure at best; and Alberici remained so ignorant of English affairs that he later mistook Bishop Fox's Christian name, in print.[41] In addition, Alberici's writings may have seemed too abstract for England's worldly monarch. The concluding allegory of *Studium* and *Mars* as Virtue's doorwardens would have flattered Henry VII, in a precisely appealing way: Henry had political and military ambitions, some involving Julius II and the ducal families of Urbino, as well as an evident desire to be regarded as a magnificent patron of art and learning. On the other hand, there was nothing forthrightly political or politically useful for Henry in the manuscript that Alberici presented, and the writers who are known to have succeeded with Henry seem to have done so by offering works that spoke directly to his statesmanlike concerns.

Finally, by 1506–7 Henry was already supporting what he may have regarded as a sufficient number of humanists. He had employed such men to teach his children, who were by now beyond education; he currently had a humanist Latin secretary in Pietro Carmeliano; and he currently had a humanist historiographer in Bernard André.[42] To such men, Henry VII and his heir remained surprisingly loyal, even after their usefulness was past and their accomplishments had been overmatched by younger humanists; for his part, Bernard André, for example, was capable of being zealous in defence of his position, particularly when under apparent threat from the ambitions of others.[43] Be that as it may, Henry may even have resisted the ambitions of the likes of Baldassare Castiglione.[44]

The possible reasons for Alberici's apparent failure are many; and, though they were largely beyond his or any other individual writer's control, they suggest a list of factors regulating the success and failure of patronage seekers in early Tudor England, quite apart from the literary and artistic qualities of the work involved: the timeliness and specificity of appeal of a given piece of work, for a particular patron, in particular circumstances, including accidents of temperament and inclination, which loomed large in a system of economic exchange still essentially constituted of personal transactions, between persons situated inequitably in the social and economic scheme of things; the extent of the patronage seeker's connections and the quality of his personal introductions, constituting for the patronage seeker a reticula of subpatrons, in effect; and, finally, the state of the market, so to speak, particularly the ratio of patronage to patronage seekers at a given time. Still, Alberici's presentation was exceptional, both in the qualities of the work contained in the manuscript he offered the king and in the frustration with which the ambitions embodied in it were met.

Chapter 2

Politicking and Manuscript Presentation:

Pietro Carmeliano's Development of Publishing Methods 1482–1486

Filippo Alberici's *Cebes' Tablet* manuscript was a remarkable performance: an attractive verse rendering of an important, accessible Greek work, accompanied by other writings that established Alberici's credentials, packaged in an intelligently, expensively decorated book. It was first-rate in all respects, except the only one that could have mattered to Alberici: it failed to bring him profit. Some twenty years earlier, in late 1486 most likely, another itinerant Italian humanist, Pietro Carmeliano, had presented Henry VII with another manuscript, with altogether different results. Carmeliano's presentation – a slimmer, more modestly decorated volume, containing only a single poem, on the birth of Henry VII's heir, Prince Arthur – succeeded where Alberici's failed; Carmeliano was pensioned by the king soon after the manuscript's presentation, and thereafter, to the end of his life, he continually enjoyed the benefits of royal patronage.[1]

Some measure of the success of Carmeliano's 1486 presentation may have been occasional. At least two others, Bernard André and Giovanni Gigli, also wrote poems celebrating Arthur's birth and enjoyed subsequent royal patronage. The copies of their poems that they would have circulated at court or provided the king do not survive, however, and it may be that these copies were not formal presentation copies, like Carmeliano's. In fact, both André and Gigli seem to have enjoyed already some standing with Henry by the time of Arthur's birth, and so need not have been as anxious to succeed by the occasion as Carmeliano evidently was.[2]

The manuscript that Carmeliano presented to the king was a formal, deluxe presentation copy, of sufficient merit to have been preserved, probably in one of the royal collections.[3] This merit resides in a combination of features: the tastefulness of the manuscript's decoration and script, the stylish humanism of the poem in it, its political pertinence, and the timeliness of the manuscript's delivery into precisely the right hands. In each of these regards, the presentation could have served as a model of publication for other ambitious writers to emulate in later years of the Tudor dynasty. Carmeliano had no such models to follow, however. In his career, this 1486 presentation came at the end of a series of experiments with publication; in part by trial and error, only with this work did he discover a formula for success.

Carmeliano came to England in the early 1480s, finding employment, probably secretarial, in the Rolls House in London. Little is known of his life before this: he was in lesser clerkly orders, it seems, but he was never ordained a priest, nor did he belong to a religious order.[4] In 1482, deciding to pursue royal patronage, Carmeliano wrote a poem and presented a copy to Prince Edward, Edward IV's eldest son. He explains his poem's genesis in these terms, in the epistolary preface accompanying the poem, in which he also asks for cause to feel 'me diligi' by the prince and promises to write more:

> I pondered for a long time, illustrious prince, how I might make myself known to your highness; in the end, I decided that such a thing was possible were I to give you some of my verses, of a sort that might be able to please you in some measure, either by their substance or perhaps their form. Therefore, I approached new material, namely, the description of Spring, the first part of the year ... If I perceive that my writings please you, doubtless my soul and heart will exult for exceeding joy, and our talent will be challenged to write greater poems and to attempt grander matters. Of this matter, the chief theme will be that I, an unknown, and a wanderer nearly to the ends of the earth, have felt myself esteemed by a prince so great and so excellent.[5]

The poem itself ends with the same sort of plain entreaty:

> Farewell now, prince, and receive these three hundred verses; and know that I am your servant and possession. On another occasion, I will set down your praises; I will sing of you, your brother, and your father. I commend myself to you, most renowned prince; for my poverty and my exile burden me.[6]

The ultimate object of Carmeliano's articulate ambition, however, was not the boy prince – no matter how precocious he may have been – so much as the prince's father, Edward IV. Earlier, Carmeliano had given the king a copy of Cicero's *De oratore*, in which he had inscribed comments and some lines of verse;[7] and Carmeliano flattered Edward IV in the letter with which he addressed his son in 1482.[8]

The tool Carmeliano built for furthering the ambition he voices in his letter to Prince Edward was a three-hundred-line Latin poem in celebration of spring.[9] Carmeliano's *De vere* is a long list, basically; a recitation of the responses of various natural kinds – plants, animals, and elements – to the advent of spring. Carmeliano was able thereby to show off his skill as a classicist. The most remarkable feature of the poem may be an absence: it avoids allegory and Christian doctrine. Its form – elegiac distichs – and diction are ancient, and its enumeration of kinds enables Carmeliano to use an impressive supply of arcane and strictly ancient terms for flora and fauna: *aesculus, alcyon, barrus, chenalopex, coracinus, inulae, nasturitium, salvia, scolopendra, succula, verres,* and *verves* outstanding among them. Whereas medieval bestiaries, lapidaries, and the like glossed their descriptions of natural phenomena with references to the religious import of the properties of creatures and things, Carmeliano, in discussing the same phenomena, avoids Christianizing the natural world.[10] Even though the poem was presented as an Easter gift,[11] he forgoes reading the book of nature as if it were a supplement to the Bible. The only source named in the poem is Pliny, and like Pliny, Carmeliano prefers to keep to arcane (and again strictly ancient) information and literary allusion.[12] There is a long digression on the *philomena*, predictably, and an allusion to the owl that screeches from Dido's roof in the *Aeneid*, as well as more obscure references, such as to the ancient use of the woodpecker in augury, the sacredness of the dove to Venus, and the warring of cranes against the pygmies.[13]

The poem's steadfast classicism is complemented by its material setting in the extant presentation copy. It is a small book, 212 × 144 mm. Its first page – the beginning of the prose dedicatory letter – has a full border, of springlike flowers and leaves, incorporating the English royal arms at the foot of the page (fig 12); the first letter of the poem proper, on a subsequent page, is illuminated,[14] and small paraphs, in an ink of a contrasting colour, occur intermittently throughout the text. With these modest exceptions, the book is plain. No doubt Carmeliano was not in a position to spend much more at the time. On the other hand, the book's want of other foci for visual attention highlights the bookhand itself, which was worthy to be highlighted. The manuscript provides unusually generous margins[15] – quantities of a high-quality vellum left blank, not wastefully but purely decoratively – to set it off. For publication of this poem, as of his later ones, Carmeliano worked as his own copyist; and the script he used was one of the first humanist hands, a cursive of Italian derivation, to see circulation in England.[16] The difference between Carmeliano's script and others in use in England and Northern Europe at the time is akin to the difference between Carmeliano's poem and a gothic bestiary. Like the poem, the script proclaimed Carmeliano's allegiance to the new learning.

Carmeliano prospered greatly later, and he could have afforded to present more expensive books, with more extensive and more richly coloured paintings and decoration. For the duration of his career as a presenter of manuscripts to English kings, however, he kept the basic design and format that he worked out for his first royal presentation, his *De vere* manuscript of 1482.

The manuscript also provides a surprising direct attestation to its own success, by way of an epigram added to it, on its last page, entitled 'Carmeliani ad Edwardum illustrem Wallie principem pro munere collato gratiarum actio.' Carmeliano's letter at the beginning of the manuscript is unequivocal about his material ambition; the epigram on the manuscript's last page – written in the same hand as the body of the book, but in a different ink, evidently at a later date, by Carmeliano himself – thanks the prince for rewarding the manuscript's presenter:

You have given me a great gift, prince, in return for a small

one; in return for my verses, I have received a worthy reward. The days are now come again, in which hope for poets
is born, but you, prince, you bring it about all by yourself.
See how all of the muses now ready their song on your
behalf, ever to raise your praises to the stars. I am unable
to give sufficiently the thanks I owe you, but whatever I
have I will give, Edward. May the fates give you long life,
Edward, most famous of princes; may all deities favour you:
you are the very honour of your realm, most comely of
princes, and you are your people's chief glory. Youths and
boys, like with their elders, rejoice in you, and all the stars
rejoice in your face. Justly do you have the king's visage,
best of dukes, for the kingly sceptre awaits you after your
father.[17]

Apparently, Carmeliano presented his work; was rewarded for
doing so; took the book back, for as long as was needed to com-
pose and inscribe this epigram in it (not long, one supposes); and
then gave the book again to the prince.

There is this evidence for the presentation's success; though
the epigrammatic postscript may intend less *gratias agere* than
to obligate the prince to Carmeliano further, the presentation did
return to the poet something that he could bring himself to describe as 'praemia digna.' But whatever favour Carmeliano may
have gained from the success of his *De vere* – a modest success,
at best – can have been only short-lived, like Prince Edward himself. The prince's father, Edward IV, died in April 1483, a year
after the date of the *De vere*; the prince, still a minor, reigned
as Edward V for a period of two or three months before his disposition in favour of Richard III, and he lived no more than a
few months thereafter. These events would have dissipated the
gains Carmeliano had made, and there was nothing he could do
about them. Worse, Carmeliano's association with Edward IV and
Edward V might have worked against him, the favour of the previous monarchs tending to preclude the favour of the new one.
From the perspective imposed by these changed circumstances,
it may have appeared fortunate to Carmeliano that his successes
with the two Edwards had not been greater; more to the point,
Carmeliano had no scruples. Although he could not undo Richard
III's accession, he could behave as if he had had no commerce
with Richard's now useless predecessors, and so he did.

Carmeliano next put into circulation, at some indeterminable point during Richard III's brief reign, between June 1483 and August 1485, a long Latin verse life of St Katherine of Alexandria.[18] The poem embodies a clever, if indirect, argument in favour of support for humanist scholars and writers, among whom Carmeliano meant himself to be counted. It casts the saint's life in the form of Vergilian epic: passages of action are narrated tersely, with emphasis falling instead on set speeches. These are exemplary bits of classicizing oratory, ending inevitably with such Vergilian locutions as 'dixerat,' 'his dictis finierat,' and 'nec mora.' The classicizing archaisms of the poem's diction are also more substantive: for example, Carmeliano uses the term *princeps* in its most restricted ancient sense – 'centurion' or 'captain' of a royal bodyguard – a sense attested in the work of the best ancient historians, such as Livy and Caesar, but for which there would have been few if any post-Augustan examples on which to draw.

The poem's form and diction are classicizing, its substance Christian. Its set-pieces of stylish oratory include descriptions of the glories of heaven, suasions to belief in Christ, and exhortations to strengthened devotion; its epic narrative remains a religiously edifying tale of martyrdom, useful for all Christians in its provisions of examples of faith made greater by adversity, and then rewarded. Carmeliano's poem approaches the oxymoronic: a humanist hagiography. But it is in this peculiar combination of affiliations – stylistically to the ancient, pagan past and substantively to the post-antique culture of Christianity – that the virtue of the poem inheres. Carmeliano would answer back a fear of humanism, sometimes latent, sometimes overt, that saw in the veneration of antiquity an at least implicit disavowal of the achievements and promise of Christianity.[19] The fear may or may not have been well founded; Carmeliano's work wants to deny that there was any reason for it: his *Vita S. Katerinae* is a practical demonstration that the innovations of the new learning could be put to work serving traditional Christian ends. In one of the epistolary prefaces he wrote for the work, Carmeliano claims as much himself, implicitly, in describing the genesis of his poem:

> After I had come to the point where I could not furnish myself with the bread of life out of the inventions of the

muses and rhetors, nor could I see that any aid would come
to me from those who were both able to provide it and ought
to have done so, by reason of the likeness between their
studies and mine, having done with poetic trifles and putting aside the rhetors' windy orations, I determined to de-
vote myself to sacred studies; not indeed for the sake of
begging a living for myself from them, but rather that I
might have better set before me examples by means of which
I would be able to suffer with more equanimity the savagery
of the profligate behaviour of our age and, if I might not
altogether extinguish my woes, I would at least mitigate
them.[20]

What Carmeliano offers is a cake that can be eaten and kept
too: the blend of humanist classicism and Christian doctrine
manages to be daringly innovative and comfortingly traditional
at the same time, in this respect like Alberici's *Cebes' Tablet*.
Carmeliano might have treated the life of any saint in this same
way, serving up the same combination of the fashionable but
threatening with the comfortable but outdated; treating the life
of St Katherine in this manner, however, helped him make his
point the more clearly, because Katherine is the patron saint of
learned eloquence.[21] Carmeliano claims her as a saint for humanists, as if thereby to claim ecclesiastical sanction or protection for the new learning; his writing about her offers potential
patrons the prospect of investing in a literary avant-garde that
has already been domesticated, in a humanism serving Christian
devotion, hallowed already by saintly approbation.

This life of St Katherine is not itself explicitly political. As
he had done also with his *De vere*, however, Carmeliano circulated epistolary prefaces with the poem, and these demonstrate
a considerable if unsavoury sophistication about politics on his
part. The *Vita S. Katerinae* was dedicated to Richard III; and although the copy does not survive, it seems all but certain that
Carmeliano did in fact present it to the king.[22] The poem survives
instead in the form of two other manuscript presentation copies,
the one for John Russell, Richard III's lord chancellor, and the
other for Robert Brackenbury, Richard's constable of the Tower
of London.[23]

These two surviving copies are as identical as a pair of hand-

made books can be; in size, materials, page design, decoration,
script, and text, they can hardly be distinguished. Their design
closely resembles that of Carmeliano's earlier *De vere* manuscript, of which they are only somewhat more costly versions –
longer and illustrated with miniatures. Where the *De vere* had
begun with a full-page border, only the upper and inner margins
of the first page of the poem in the *Katerina* manuscripts are
decorated, with the same feather-like pen-work in both copies,
and in both copies the first letter of the poem is illuminated (figs
13 and 14). The *Katerina* manuscripts both have a small illustration, facing the beginning of the poem, of the saint and her wheel,
and they comprise greater numbers of vellum sheets, as copies
of a poem over twice as long as the *De vere*.[24]

The two *Katerina* manuscripts differ from one another
slightly in contents: the one opens with a letter addressed to
Russell, and the other opens with a different letter, to Brackenbury. In the letter to Russell, the ecclesiast, Carmeliano ex-
pounds his view of the right relations between humanism and
Christian doctrine; in his letter to Brackenbury, Carmeliano lauds
Richard's virtues, in explaining his decision to dedicate the work
to the king:

> I found no prince more worthy than him, to whom my work
> might be dedicated. But lest I should seem to extol his maj-
> esty unreasonably, you personally, wisest of men, will be
> my witness, as to whether I speak the truth or falsehood. If
> we look first to his religion, does our age have any prince
> more religious than him? If we look to his justice, whom in
> the world will we think fit to be set before him? If we con-
> sider his wisdom, in guarding peace and in waging war,
> whom will we judge ever to have been his like? With regard
> to both the wisdom and the greatness of his mind, as well
> as his modesty, second to whom will we place our King
> Richard? What Christian emperor or prince can be proven
> with certainty to be more liberal and munificent to those
> who merit it? None, simply none. By whom are robbery,
> banditry, debauchery, adultery, homicide, usury, heresy, and
> other crimes most unspeakable more detested than by him?
> No one, clearly. Therefore, not without reason did I dedicate
> and present my brief work to his highness.[25]

It is difficult to imagine precisely what Carmeliano intended by publishing his *Katerina* in multiple copies, presented to Richard III, Brackenbury, and Russell. Although the work is persistently dedicated to the same person, the king, Carmeliano probably hoped to earn three gifts outright, however small, instead of just one. He may also have hoped that one of his three recipients might offer permanent employment, and he may have hoped that his secondary marks – Brackenbury and Russell – would intercede on his behalf with his primary target, the poem's dedicatee.[26] Other humanists later dedicated the same piece of writing to different persons, by the expedient of attaching different prefaces to different copies. Carmeliano may seem to anticipate the scheme with his differently prefaced copies of the *Katerina*; but it is more likely that he was only trying a variation of the indirect approach that he had used, with some success, in addressing himself to Edward IV through Prince Edward in 1482.

There is nothing to suggest that Carmeliano's supine effusion on the virtues of Richard III, or his other work writing and publishing his life of St Katherine, earned him anything. Richard Brackenbury was a soldier, first promoted for helping to put down Buckingham's rebellion against Richard III in 1483, and finally put in command of troops loyal to Richard at Bosworth Field, in 1485, where he too died. He now looks like a person with little potential as a patron of humanists, though he was close to Richard III; the king himself looks scarcely better. Russell may have been a more likely mark, as both a political survivor and a person of some learning. He served Edward IV, a restored Henry VI, Edward IV again and his son Edward V, then Richard III and finally Henry VII; and Thomas More later described him as 'a man of remarkable virtue and practical wisdom, and undoubtedly the most learned man of his time.'[27] Even Russell, however, had to attend carefully to the 'tragicall doinges' of Richard III.

It was a bad moment to be looking for favours in England, it seems; those in power had little leisure for patronage, and the reign of Richard III appears to have been a lean time for Carmeliano. For some portion of it at least, he gave up London (along with his appointment at Rolls House, presumably) for Oxford; there, he did editorial hack-work for Theodoric Rood, Oxford's printer.[28] Later in the reign, he did similar work for William Caxton, at Westminster, editing for his press a piece of Venetian propaganda.²⁹ Only with the accession of Henry VII did royal favour light on Carmeliano again.

Carmeliano's manufacture of three presentation copies of his *Katerina* had tripled his costs. His outlay for publishing the poem may have been six times greater than for the *De vere*, inasmuch as the *Katerina* is twice as long, and the manuscripts have paintings. Moreover, Carmeliano increased his investment without increasing his return, so far as we can tell. The failure could have been instructive, however. Out of this and his earlier experience in the reign of Edward IV, he seems to have developed a sophistication about the publishing process that would bring him success early in the reign of Henry VII. By August 1485, he had been in England for three to five years, during a period of constant political upheaval; and he knew the political game and players in a way he could not have on first arriving. In addition, Carmeliano had seen the impact that political circumstances could have on his work's reception: the death and deposition of a pair of monarchs had aborted his profitable access. Yet he was learning how to adapt his work to the situation. Though neither of the poems he had yet published was directly political, the preface to his *Katerina* that he wrote for Brackenbury – with what may have seemed timely, well-placed flattery of a new monarch – demonstrates an awareness that politics affected his fortunes.

Experience honed Carmeliano's political reflexes; it also educated him in methods of self-publication. Early on, Carmeliano invented a book form suitable to both his resources and the nature of his work. The modesty of the decoration of the pages of his books highlighted his humanist script, making objective and visual the affiliations with the new learning that were the basis of his appeal to patrons. In addition, since Carmeliano acted as his own copyist, the decorative plainness of his books meant that his only expenses in producing them were writing materials – vellum, pens, and ink – perhaps some modest professional decoration, and binding; and after his experiment with the *Katerina*, Carmeliano went back to the kind of shorter composition with which he had begun: his next poem was nearer three hundred than six hundred lines long. Finally, he gave up on the indirect approach and the distribution of multiple presentation copies; they cost too much. Given the prevalent literary economy, the approach most likely to yield patronage was the direct one, to a work's dedicatee; and the best dedicatee, the prospective patron with the greatest potential, was the monarch himself.

Henry VII caused his reign to be dated from 21 August 1485.[30] He was therefore not a rebel when he did battle against Richard III at Bosworth Field on 22 August: because of the dating, Richard was the traitorous usurper, Henry already the legitimate king. The episode gives notice of what was a central concern of Henry's: not only assuring the continuity of his dynasty but also, more fundamentally, obviating the possibility of internecine fighting among the powerful families ruling England.

The next major political events of Henry's reign had also to do with assuring the succession and dissolving conflict over it. In late January 1486, Henry married Edward IV's only surviving child, Elizabeth of York. In late September 1486, with remarkable precision, a male heir was born to the combined fortunes of the houses of Lancaster and York, and he was christened Arthur. The birth was capable of anticipation, of course, unlike Henry VII's accession; and Carmeliano was ready for it, with a poem entitled 'Suasoria Laeticiae ad Angliam pro sublatis bellis civilibus et Arthuro principe nato epistola,' which he presented to the king in a fine copy probably not long after the prince's birth.[31]

As a piece of book-making, the *Suasoria Laeticiae* manuscript resembles Carmeliano's previous presentations; about the length of the *De vere*, and furnished with a miniature, like the *Katerina* manuscripts.[32] A full-page border surrounds the beginning of the poem, and on the verso facing it is a full-page painting (fig 15). The illustration features the English royal arms, supported by a pair of angels; it juxtaposes red and white roses, the badges of Lancaster and York, though not yet (typically, so early in the reign) the characteristic red and white rose of the Tudors; and it also incorporates a white greyhound and a red dragon. Henry's grandfather Owen Tudor had used the red dragon, historically the badge of Cadwalader, the last of the British kings, to assert his claim of descent from King Arthur, a claim Henry VII also asserted in a number of ways, not least of which was the name he gave his heir;[33] and the white greyhound was a badge of the house of Lancaster, with which Henry was connected. But for this comparatively lavish decoration at the beginning, Carmeliano's *Suasoria Laeticiae* manuscript replicates his earlier presentations, in size, materials, page design, and script.

Nor does the poem much differ stylistically from his earlier work; again, the *Suasoria* is decidedly humanist. It differs from his *De vere* and *Vita S. Katerinae* strikingly, however, in its greater degree of political engagement. As indicated (at least) by the heraldry the king used – the greyhound, dragon, and the Tudor rose – Henry VII was anxious to legitimate and secure his rule. The appearance of these heraldic emblems in the decorative program of Carmeliano's presentation bespeaks his awareness of Henry's political problems too; the poem contained in the manuscript is in fact permeated with current affairs. Carmeliano's *De vere* was politically evasive; his poem on St Katherine was not itself political, though his decisions about where to present it and the prefaces he attached to it were informed by political considerations; now, finally, his *Suasoria Laeticiae* was a thoroughly, explicitly political piece of writing.

As the poem's full title suggests, Carmeliano's *Suasoria Laeticiae* speaks in detail about recent events in England, focusing particularly on the *sublata bella civilia*. It relates the fortunes of Henry VI, Edward IV, Edward V and his younger brother; it narrates at some length Richmond's exile in Brittany and France, his return from France to Milford Haven, his success at Bosworth Field, his acclamation as Henry VII, and his courtship and marriage of Elizabeth of York; and it concludes with a celebration of the event that should then have seemed to cement Henry VII's other successes, the birth of Prince Arthur, a male heir to him and his Yorkist wife. It is a primary source of information, written by a contemporary witness; the poem's representation of events is slanted, however, to flatter Henry VII. Some portion of the flattery is simple praise for Henry, of the sort that could have been written about any monarch: it likens him to Apollo (217), for example, in suggesting that he is possessed of 'tanta praestantia formae' that the people say 'this is not a man's, but a god's likeness'; and it describes him at one point as 'Magnanimous, outstanding, noble, decent, pure, brave, just, patient in adversity, merciful, eloquent, liberal, and pious.'[34]

The better part of the poem is more specific to English circumstance. It denigrates Richard III thoroughly, in what represents another opportunistic reversal for Carmeliano. The person whom he had lately lauded at such length, in his letter to Brackenbury – 'By whom are robbery, banditry, debauchery, adultery, homicide, usury, heresy, and other crimes most unspeakable more detested than by him? No one, clearly,' and the rest – is characterized in the *Suasoria Laeticiae* as a criminal tyrant, habituated to evil-doing ('sceleratus et ille tyrannus,' 'promptus ad omne nefas' [205, 92]), who, by the time of Henry's advent to England, 'had committed so many crimes that his mind, conscious of his sins and guilt, was already defeated' ('crimina praeterea tot tot commiserat, ut mens / Peccati et sceleris conscia victa foret' [193–4]). The poem pronounces him guilty of murdering, by his own hand, not only the two princes in the Tower of London (88) but also Henry VI. Richard is the poem's only villain, a person doubly guilty of regicide – the crime that Henry, who might himself have been thought guilty of the same crime by some, need have been especially vigilant to see precluded, especially in the early, insecure part of his reign.

The correlative of the poem's denigration of Richard III is its praise of Henry VI – here represented as among the saints in heaven – and, more interestingly, its mild and even mildly flattering representation of Edward VI. Henry VII's blood relations with Henry VI, the last of the Lancastrian kings, comprised his sole claim to the throne by heredity. It was not a very good or clear claim, but it was politically expedient for him to make it. It was his only alternative to bald assertion of the fact that he had come to the throne by force of arms, a fact with unappetizing implications; for if Henry VII were king only by *force majeure*, his reign encouraged anyone possessed of a *force* still *majeure* to attempt to oust him. The campaign for Henry VI's canonization, carried on into the reign of Henry VIII, was in large part the Tudors' attempt to sanctify this their sole claim to hereditary legitimacy.[35] Carmeliano's poem contributed to the campaign, early indeed in its development; more immediately, the *Suasoria* also spelled out the relations between Henry VI and Henry VII, in such a way as to represent Henry VII as the only legitimate heir to Henry VI's prerogatives. The poem explains that, once Henry VI himself and his son Edward Plantagenet had been killed,

Henry VI's familial right would have been destroyed ('extinctum ius genus atque foret'), had God not taken care to save Henry VI's 'nepos,' Henry Tudor (105–12).

The poem allows that Edward IV had deposed Henry VI (86), but it avoids condemning him for it. Unobtrusively, it insists on the legitimacy of Edward's claim to the throne, calling him 'that bravest of kings' ('regum fortissimus ille' [85]). This respect for Edward IV is a gesture of deference to his daughter Elizabeth, whose marriage to Henry VII the poem also celebrates; at the same time, it also contributes to the poem's peculiar representation of the Wars of the Roses. Paradoxically, the *Suasoria* flatters Henry for his part in the wars by downplaying the fact that his accession represented a victory for the house of Lancaster.

In the view that Carmeliano propounds in the *Suasoria*, the dynastic strife of recent decades was a struggle between two equally legitimate branches of the English royal line:

> There are twin lines of descent, deriving from the blood of their kings, and each lays claim by right to the royal sceptre. The one part of the people favours the one claimant, the other favours the other, and the crowds of fighters favour their masters. The one party follows the house to which Lancaster gives its name, to which Brutus gave the realm and sway over it; the other keeps and guards the Yorkist line by force of arms, waging fierce war.[36]

Because of this attitude it must take towards Elizabeth of York – Henry VII's wife and the mother of the heir – and towards her family, the poem tends to glorify the Wars of the Roses, and this end it accomplishes in part by likening them to the epic struggles of antiquity. Henry's part is not that of a figure who decides the struggle one way or the other, however; for to make Henry a victor would be to legitimate dynastic struggle and to encourage its perpetuation. Instead, the poem represents Henry as a peacemaker, as a figure who dissolves conflict, marrying Elizabeth of York and producing an heir with her. When Edward IV and his sons had died, his daughter Elizabeth – 'titulum quae genitoris habet' (134) – was the only remaining legitimate heir to the Yorkist fortunes, as was Henry to the Lancastrian *titulum*.[37] Elizabeth's marriage to Henry conjoins the two competing but equally legitimate branches of the royal family: 'Thus of the twinned lines will one line be made, and afterwards one house shall hold sway' ('Sic solus gemino fiet de sanguine sanguis, / Una domus post haec imperiumque petet' [135–6]). The poem represents the product of this conjunction, Prince Arthur, as the physical embodiment of unity: a boy – 'than whom no other is more noble, whether you look more to the mother or to the father' ('quo non generosior alter, / Seu matrem quaeras seu magis ipse patrem') – born 'of the twinned blood of kings' ('gemino de sanguine regum'), to be 'the sure salvation of the kingdom and its perpetual ornament' ('Firma salus regni perpetuumque decus' [255–8]).

The poem's political burden, then, is not that Henry VII had emerged the victor from England's recent dynastic struggles. The *Suasoria* allows that both Lancaster and York had legitimate claims. Carmeliano's point is the more subtle one, more useful to Henry VII, that Henry's accession, his marriage to Elizabeth of York, and their production of a conjoint heir had instead done away with the causes of the dynastic struggles that England had lately known, any recurrence of which could ruin the Tudor king.

In the *Suasoria*, Carmeliano alludes to Lucan's epic of Roman civil strife repeatedly: his characterization of Richard III as 'promptus ad omne nefas' ('ready for every wickedness' [92]), for example, and his description of Henry VII's advent to England with the phrase 'gelidas cursu superaverat Alpes' ('he had hastened his course over the frozen Alps' [187] – a nonsensical statement except by light of its source, where the verb's subject is 'Caesar' – are both quotations from it.[38] These uses of the *Pharsalia* are part of Carmeliano's general rhetorical strategy in the *Suasoria*: he dresses the current English political situation in the clothes of antiquity. The poem's classicism is a matter of diction and allusion – above all to Rome's preeminent epic poet, Vergil, as well as to Lucan – but also of narrative. Sometimes the fancy dress works; sometimes the ill fit of the antique garments is striking.

The *Suasoria* opens with a convocation of the *sancti* in heaven, called by God, who has looked down on England and seen that 'the land was everywhere wet with its citizens' blood':

'Let there be an end to this great war and its madness,' he
said; 'it is enough that they have surpassed the Roman pa-
triciate. Neither the son-in-law and father-in-law (albeit that
their war was the greatest), nor Marius, nor warlike Sulla
ever consumed such a quantity of Roman blood, no matter
that their empire was the larger and their might the greater.'[39]

God would have counsel of his assembled *sancti*, as to how to
end England's *bellum civile*, and the *sancti* nominate one of their
number, England's late king Henry VI, to speak for them. After
describing the state of England's affairs at some length, Henry
VI advises his 'omnipotens genitor' (54) to deliver Henry of Richmond from his captivity: 'order him to demand, by force of arms,
the rights owed him; to take back his paternal realm, and drive
out the savage tyrant; and to restore his country.'[40] In his boundless wisdom, God of course agrees.

This uneasily Christianized *concilium deorum* section el-
evates England's Wars of the Roses to the epic level of those
ancient conflicts on which the pagan gods had taken counsel: the
Trojan war, the struggle of the Seven Against Thebes, the Roman
civil wars, and so on. Even as Carmeliano maintains this rhetorical strategy, however – he describes God as 'pater hominumque
deorum' (69), for example, and the counsels of God's *sancti* 'pla-
cuerunt ... Tonanti' (137) – his remarks also suggest a self-con-
scious, self-depreciating irony about the misguidedness of his
application of ancient decoration to contemporary events. He
was aware of the incongruity involved in depicting Christian
sancti giving counsel to the Christian God like so many pagan
deities intriguing with Jupiter. The assembled *sancti* answer God's
request for counsel by reminding the *Omnipotens* that their advice is needless to him, 'for you see all things, all by yourself;
you know everything' ('singula nam vides per te; tu singula nosti'
[54–5]); and Henry VI apologizes to God for telling him, something he already knows, 'how this bellicose furor can be lifted':
'you are God; you know everything' ('Ast igitur dicam – quamvis
Deus omnia nosti – / Qua queat hic tolli bellicus arte furor'
[79–80]). Carmeliano's irony in these passages is disarming, in the
same way as had been his earlier remarks, in his preface to the
Vita S. Katerinae, on the relations between humanism and Christian doctrine. Classicist pretensions could issue in absurdities and

offence, and Carmeliano allows his potential detractors so much, even implying that he could agree. All the while, however, his poem continues to show off its writer's humanist skills.

Carmeliano's most striking, and possibly most important, insistence on such classicism is in his representation of the birth of Prince Arthur. The choice of a name for the boy was politically motivated, one among several attempts to advertise the Tudor claim to descent from Britain's original kings, themselves ultimately of Trojan origin, according to the legend. The most famous of them was of course King Arthur, England's worthy among the Middle Ages' Nine Worthies, whose 'name has reached into all lands' ('nomen terras penetravit in omnes') [271]), as even Carmeliano knew. Henry VII's uses of this putatively Arthurian ancestry, as a prop for his otherwise somewhat insecure hereditary right to the throne, have been well documented.[41]

Carmeliano was aware of the Tudor claim to ancient British ancestry: for example, he describes the House of Lancaster, Henry VII's house, as the one 'to which Brutus gave the realm and sway over it.' As his understanding of the politics of the claim would have dictated to him, Carmeliano alludes to Arthurian legend in his celebration of Prince Arthur's birth, particularly to the Galfridian legend of King Arthur's return; the occasion seems to have been designed to elicit precisely this association.[42] Although he could scarcely have avoided Arthurian legend in a poem written to celebrate the birth of a Prince Arthur, Carmeliano prefers to substitute a classical frame of reference for the medieval one the occasion supplied. 'Nascitur ecce puer' is the refrain-like phrase that Carmeliano uses four times in his poem (254, 255, 257, 263):

Nascitur ecce puer, per quem Pax sancta resurgit;
    Civilisque cadit tempus in omne furor.
Arthurus rediit, per saecula tanta sepultus,
    Qui regum mundi prima corona fuit.
Ille licet corpus terris et membra dedisset,
    Vivebat toto semper in orbe tamen;
Arthurum quisquis predixerat esse secundo
    Venturum, vates maximus ille fuit:
Arthuri nomen terras penetravit in omnes,
    Perpetuum faciunt fortia facta virum.
Aurea iam redeunt cum principe secula tanto;

Queque diu latuit, iam dea virgo redit;
Bellica iam tandem rediit cum principe virtus,
Antiqumque decus, Anglia pulchra, tuum.   (263–76)

Behold, a boy is born, through whom holy peace rises up
again, and civil strife ends for all time. Arthur has returned,
buried for so many ages, who was the prime glory of the
kings of the world. Although he had given his limbs and his
body to the earth, nevertheless he lived forever throughout
the world; whoever had predicted that Arthur was going to
come a second time, he was the greatest of seers. The name
of Arthur has reached into all lands; his brave deeds make
the man immortal. Now the golden age returns, with so
great a prince; now the virgin goddess returns, who was long
hidden; now at last martial virtue has returned and, with
the prince, O beautiful England, your ancient glory.

The passage refers unambiguously to Geoffrey of Monmouth and
his epigones ('Whoever had predicted that Arthur was going to
come a second time, he was the greatest of seers'); it is more
fundamentally permeated, however, by the influence of Vergil's
Fourth Eclogue, echoes of which run right through the passage:

Ultima Cumaei venit iam carminis aetas;
Magnus ab integro saeculorum nascitur ordo.
Iam redit et Virgo, redeunt Saturnia regna,
Iam nova progenies caelo demittitur alto.
Tu modo nascenti puero, quo ferrea primum
Desinet ac toto surget gens aurea mundo,
Casta fave Lucina: tuus iam regnat Apollo.
Teque adeo decus hoc aevi, te consule, inibit,
Pollio, et incipient magni procedere menses;
Te duce, si qua manent sceleris vestigia nostri,
Inrita perpetua solvent formidine terras.
Ille deum vitam accipiet divisque videbit
Permixtos heroas et ipse videbitur illis,
Pacatumque reget patriis virtutibus orbem.

The last great age the Sibyl's song foretold / Rolls round:
the centuries are born anew! / The Maid returns, old Saturn's

reign returns, / Offspring of heaven, a hero's race descends. / Now as the babe is born, with whom iron men / Shall cease, and golden men spread through the world, / Bless him, chaste goddess: now your Apollo reigns. / This age's glory and the mighty months / Begin their courses, Pollio, with you / As consul, and all traces of our crimes / Annulled release earth from continual fear. / He shall assume a god's life and see gods / Mingling with heroes and be seen by them, / Ruling the world calmed by his father's hand.[43]

Carmeliano prefers to represent Arthur's birth, not in terms drawn from the medieval Arthurian legend, lying readily at hand, but in more recondite terms, drawn from farther afield. He describes Arthur's return as the return of the *aurea saecula* of antique mythology, as the fulfilment not so much of the medieval, Galfridian prophecy as of the messianic prophecy of Vergil. Again, this is Carmeliano's demonstration of humanist credentials; this is what a humanist poet can do: magnify the present by likening it to glorious antiquity. In addition, here again too, Carmeliano's humanism is disarmed and disarming, already domesticated: Vergil's Fourth Eclogue is an ancient and pagan poem, of course, but one with a long history of assimilation to Christian tradition, by virtue of medieval exegesis of it as an inspired prophecy of Christ.[44]

Carmeliano's pervasive classicism, common also to his other poems though most pronounced in the *Suasoria Laeticiae* – here taking the graphic form of his substitution of the ancient myth of the *aetas aurea* for the Middle Ages' legends of King Arthur – had broadly political implications, of which Henry VII or those around him may have been sensible. Humanism *per se* may have been politically appealing to Henry VII and his court, in a way that Carmeliano's *Suasoria Laeticiae* helps to clarify. By framing his celebration of the birth of Prince Arthur in terms discontinuous with the immediate medieval literary past of Arthurian legend, Carmeliano, who means to announce himself as an Italian-born and -trained humanist, avoids yoking his work to the Middle Ages' literary heritage. In so doing, he also avoids yoking the Tudor Prince Arthur to the medieval past, if only in literary terms. The historical equivalent of the literary past of Arthurian literature was a real-world, political past of dynastic struggle and the overthrow of established monarchs; Carmeliano's denial of the Middle Ages, in the literary terms appropriate to his sphere of work, by means of the alternative, antique images of the birth of the prince that he offers in the *Suasoria*, also, if only implicitly, proposes an analogous denial of the Middle Ages in the political sphere in which Prince Arthur would have to work. Carmeliano found little literary use for the medieval past of Arthurian legend, in a political circumstance in which the monarch to whom he was appealing similarly stood to benefit from an equivalent suppression of his medieval legacy in the sphere of politics. By substituting Vergilian messianism and Roman imperial glory for Arthurian legend, and so dissociating Prince Arthur's birth from the literary Middle Ages, Carmeliano evoked, if only by analogy, a lifting of the burden of the political legacy of the Middle Ages from the prince's shoulders. Carmeliano's break with the Middle Ages in literary terms is the literary realization – an enactment in literary terms – of the politically crucial break with the Middle Ages that Henry VII would have wanted the birth of his and his Yorkist wife's heir to be.

There is little to indicate that Henry VII was so subtle a reader – or even a reader – of the literary work that was presented to him. Likewise, there is no evidence that at any point he adopted a grand strategy for patronizing humanists, on the basis of an intuitive grasp of the deep, long-ranging political implications of a movement still only emergent in England. To the contrary, Henry was by all accounts a practical person, and it seems that his dealings with writers early in his reign were improvised.[45] In cultural terms, humanism represented a break with the medieval past; in this respect, it bore a resemblance to what Henry VII needed to do to solve the so-called Tudor Problem[46] – freeing the dynasty from the threat of the kind of independent exercise of power by the feudal nobility that had so scarred the political landscape during England's late Middle Ages – namely, enact an analogous break with the past on the political front. That Henry VII could have understood humanism in such terms seems unlikely; immediately, however, it did not matter much one way or the other.

What Carmeliano's *Suasoria Laeticiae* could have demonstrated to Henry VII that he would have appreciated was that writers – humanist writers specifically – could be useful to him, in the practical realm of political affairs, in two ways: as propagandists and as ornaments, not always readily distinguishable. As Carmeliano had not done before, in the *Suasoria Laeticiae* he demonstrated a willingness to speak directly to current political conditions and a concern to promote the king's part in them. That in so doing Carmeliano also exhibited a sophisticated grasp of the king's position – most crucially in his insistence that Henry VII had not won the dynastic struggle for the Lancastrians so much as dissolved it, preclusively, by his marriage to Elizabeth of York and by the birth of Prince Arthur – only made plain his possession of the requisite apologetic skills.

Any clever writer, similarly in need of eliciting royal patronage, might have offered Henry VII as much. What Carmeliano also demonstrated by the *Suasoria Laeticiae*, however, as well as by his other, earlier work, was his affiliation with an avant-garde cultural movement that, in 1486, had yet to become firmly rooted in England. Carmeliano's presentation of the *Suasoria Laeticiae* offered Henry VII not only an opportunity to enlist a skilled propagandist, but also a chance to acquire stock in humanism, along with such credit as might then be extended to him, locally and internationally, for so exhibiting good taste. Employing Pietro Carmeliano, or others like him, could begin to lend tone to Henry's court, a semblance of princely 'magnificence,' that would enable Henry to begin to appear to be the sort of man of wealth and taste whom other, more sophisticated continental princes would have to treat as an equal.[47]

Carmeliano came to fulfil both of these functions, for Henry VII and for his successor. As a propagandist, in 1489 Carmeliano put into circulation a poem castigating a French ambassador, for negotiating in bad faith; in 1508 he published a celebration of the betrothal of Henry VII's daughter Mary to Prince Charles of Castile, later the emperor Charles V; and in 1513 he published a celebration of the English victory at Flodden Field.[48] As decoration, Carmeliano was Latin secretary, carrying on his kings' correspondence and replacing medieval *dictamen* with his brand of Ciceronian eloquence; he accompanied Henry VII to France for his military campaigns of 1513 and for the Field of the Cloth of Gold meetings with Francis I in 1520; and, generally, he supplied the kind of presence at court that, near the end of his life, could cause Thomas More still to speak respectfully of him.[49]

Carmeliano was richly rewarded for these services. The details of the multiple churchly benefices and other benefits he was given by the crown are long to repeat; a salient detail is enough to suggest the wealth to which he attained: for the forced loan assessed in 1523, to fund the French wars, he was assessed at three hundred and thirty-three pounds, six shillings and eight pence, whereas Polydore Vergil, now much better remembered, was assessed at two hundred pounds.[50] Carmeliano's material success seems to date precisely from the presentation of the *Suasoria Laeticiae*. The object of the celebration of the poem, the birth of Prince Arthur, took place on 19 September 1486; on 27 September 1486, Carmeliano was first pensioned by the king.[51]

From a certain perspective, the fact that Carmeliano was pensioned for the *Suasoria Laeticiae*, but was given only a one-time gift of some sort for the *De vere*, and does not seem to have earned any return at all from his three presentations of the *Vita S. Katerinae*, is difficult to explain. The three poems and four surviving manuscripts have much in common. What finally distinguishes the *Suasoria Laeticiae* from its predecessors is a greater political sophistication, of two sorts: about the politics of publication, so to speak, and, more generally, about the political situation of the presentation's recipient.

The conditions for publication of humanist work in England were different under the Tudors, but in ways Carmeliano could not control and could not have anticipated. Not surprisingly, Henry VII was determined to reign long and to found a dynasty; more unexpectedly, by light of recent history, it turned out that he was successful, and his successes had palpable consequences for the fortunes of Carmeliano and others like him, particularly in continuity of benefits. Carmeliano never again had to start from a position of abjection, with a new monarch or a new royal family. Nevertheless, no late medieval or early modern English monarch's political successes could be traded on in advance, as Carmeliano's dealings with Edward IV and the short-lived Edward V would have taught him. Likewise, Henry VII found that he could use humanists,[52] and, again, the long-term consequence of this discovery was increased patronage, royal, noble, and ecclesiastic. Carmeliano's dealings with Henry VII early in his reign probably played a part in the discovery and so in improving the long-term prospects for humanists in England; otherwise, Carmeliano could do nothing about the size and wealth of the market in England. Carmeliano can hardly be expected to have foreseen the general condition's change for the better, any more than he could have been individually responsible for it, nor, even if he did foresee it, could he have felt sure that he would be the beneficiary of any such change. While material conditions for humanists in England did improve and he benefited from the improvement, Carmeliano remained as little a master in the realm of state politics under the Tudors as he had been under Edward IV, Edward V, and Richard III.

Within determinate limits, though, Carmeliano was the master of his own labours, and his experience seems to have taught him how to approach a royal patron and with what to present such a patron. There was a timeliness to Carmeliano's presentation in 1486 – a factor not only of the suitability of the birth of an heir for celebration with presents of one sort or another, but also of a new monarch's openness (itself a factor of the political insecurity of Henry's position) to the appeals of humanist propaganda and flattery. There was a preciseness of fit about the presentation – not only the fit of a humanist-style piece of writing to a humanist-style piece of book production, but also the fit of what Carmeliano offered to what Henry VII needed. And there were, finally, directness and sophistication about the poem's address to current politics. For all of these features of the work, Carmeliano was responsible; he did control them, and they would appear to be the causes of his success with the *Suasoria Laeticiae*. It too was an exemplary presentation, though not necessarily of the best that could be done in literary and artistic terms, as was Alberici's. It was a model of what worked to elicit patronage.

 Chapter 3

Authorial Self-Fashioning:

Collected Works, in Manuscript and
Print, in Bernard André's Later Career,
1509–17

Pietro Carmeliano was not the only humanist to enjoy success
at the English court during the early years of Henry VII's reign.
Numerous others came and went, among them Cornelio Vitelli
and Desiderius Erasmus, to mention only two; in the same period,
still others – including Stefano Surigone, Caio Auberino, and Lorenzo Traversagni – settled for patronage from lesser English
sources.[1] The perception evident among such persons, that Tudor
England, and especially its royal court, were potential sources of
support for humanists, was in some measure a product of the
fact that Henry VII did patronize and employ them regularly.
Most of those who came stayed only briefly, but to those who
presented him with literary gifts Henry often gave presents of
his own in return, usually money.[2] In addition, there were a few
whom Henry employed over periods of years, being provided not
only with occasional gifts but with regular annuities as well. John
Skelton was one of them; a writer whose later work has tended
to obscure his early humanist affiliations, he was at court in some
official capacity from early in the reign until about 1502. Likewise, Giovanni Gigli supplied propaganda and oratorical skills,
and was finally collated to the bishopric of Worcester, shortly
before his death in 1497, and Pietro Carmeliano's royal support
too lasted for years, beginning almost with the accession of the
Tudors.[3]

The pre-eminent figure, however, of the humanist *grex poetarum* to be associated with the court of Henry VII was Bernard André.[4] Carmeliano may have been sharper about the benefactions that came to him and so may ultimately have profited more from his royal connection. On the other hand, André was more productive than Carmeliano; consequently, over time, he was the more useful writer to the Tudor monarchy, and he always had at least a gift of money at New Years' from his kings.[5] Carmeliano did not publish major work after 1486; while others came and went, sought favour, lost it, and regained it, André stayed at court, always writing and always publishing, throughout the period running from Henry VII's accession to Thomas More's appointment to Henry VII's council. For a period of thirty-five years, from late 1485 until 1521 or 1522, when he last published,[6] André helped shape the development of court writing in England, and he was well rewarded for his labours.

Over the course of his long career, he tried various kinds and methods of publication. Early on, he used presentations like Carmeliano's. In the sixteenth century, he began to work with collections of his writings, the contents of which could be designed to show off his particular skills or services that he had rendered. Finally, at the end of his life, he was one of the earliest English humanists to turn to print, recognizing the help it could lend a writer trying to build or sustain a reputation. Professional circumstances changed for André in the sixteenth century, as they had for Carmeliano earlier; André too adapted his publishing practices to meet current situations. The competition for patronage became fiercer, and so it became increasingly important to craft an attractive face for display at court and for the general learned public.

Like Carmeliano, another wholly Tudor creature, André too is fittingly unknown before his arrival in England in late 1485 or early 1486. He was born in Toulouse, probably c 1450, *ortu claro* according to later but uncorroborated testimony,[7] and entered the Augustinian order, probably at Toulouse, probably late in the 1460s. Before coming to England, he earned the right to be styled 'utriusque iuris doctor,'[8] though the identity of the university at which he studied canon and civil laws remains unknown, as do all other details of his education. His later work confirms, however, that he acquired a good knowledge of Roman poetry at some point, as well as of patristic literature.

Though not at Bosworth Field with Henry VII, André witnessed Henry's entry into London after the battle, on 3 September 1485; the event occasioned his earliest essay in Tudor propaganda.[9] It has been conjectured, plausibly, that André's talents had been brought to Henry's attention while the future king was still abroad, in Brittany or France, by the agency of Richard Fox, subsequently bishop of Winchester, whom André named his 'Maecenas.'[10] In any case, by late 1485 and early 1486 André's pen was busy in the service of England's new king, and no later than November 1486, as 'poeta laureatus,' he was in receipt of an annuity from Henry VII.[11] Until the end of his life, André continued to receive this and other royal benefactions: ecclesiastical preferments, salaries, and irregular, occasional gifts of cash.

For his kings' patronage, André leased them his skill as a literary apologist. He did much other writing as well. From 1496 to 1500, he was responsible for the education of the heir and produced a number of scholarly and pedagogic works. After 1500, he began to produce *annales* of a sort – encomiastic recitations of his king's *gesta* in a particular year, or topical orations, touching on current affairs – which he usually presented as New Years' gifts. He also wrote works of devotion, including saints' lives and liturgical pieces.[12] But André seems to have established himself at court in the first place with the kind of work that brought Carmeliano success with Henry VII: topical, political writing, of a humanist bent, occasioned by significant public events. Its production seems to have been André's principle, possibly exclusive occupation, until about 1496. Between late 1485, when André wrote his poem celebrating Henry VII's triumphal first entry into London, and late 1518, when he put about an *epithalamium* for the betrothal of Henry VIII's two-year-old daughter Mary to the infant dauphin of France, André published eighteen still-known poems of this sort.[13]

By comparison with the sophisticated reading of policy that characterizes Carmeliano's *Suasoria Laeticiae*, André's politically occasioned poetry tends to comparatively simple flattery; still, his work in this vein differs little from Carmeliano's, in purpose or style. For example, the poem André wrote to the same occasion addressed by Carmeliano's *Suasoria*, the birth of Prince Arthur

Tudor in September 1486, similarly garbs the contemporary event in ancient dress. As in Carmeliano's poem, the point is to praise Henry VII and the English by likening them and their doings to fabled antiquity: the poem makes a Roman *imperator* of Henry VII, crowned 'triumphali lauro' and pouring out libations, while the happy *plebs* enjoys a day of pomp and circuses in honour of the heir, wreathing brows with festal garlands and shouting 'Io Paean,' while the *tibia* sounds.[14] Likewise, André's poem on England's 1513 victories, calling Henry VIII 'Caesar' and 'Augustus,' promises: 'Whoever wishes to hear the triumphs of a great king, let him read of the mighty deeds of Henry VIII.[15]

By means of his politically occasioned poetry, André fulfilled the same functions for Henry VII as did Carmeliano: André too was a propagandist for the court, and he too was an ornament to it, to the extent that his displays of humanist learning brought him an esteem that might also attach to his patron. Likewise, André probably discharged these functions in the reign of Henry VII by the same means that Carmeliano also used: publication, by presentation of the individual poems, to the king in person. André describes the process himself, with such phrases as 'versus a nobis qui sequuntur editi sunt' ('the verses that follow were made public by us'), 'versus a nobis hi extemporaliter editi sunt' ('these verses were published by us extemporaneously'), 'palam hoc carmen cecini' ('I performed this piece in public'), and 'coram regia maiestate Henrici septimi recitatus' ('it was read out in the presence of his royal majesty Henry VII');[16] however, the surviving material evidence for André's methods of initial publication, particularly in the reign of Henry VII, is not good.

Much of André's writing is lost, known only through brief references at second hand; much of what remains – particularly of his early poetry – survives only in later, second-generation copies. Few original presentation copies of writings of André's from the reign of Henry VII survive; little indeed of his politically occasioned verse survives in such forms from any part of his career. There are extant perhaps nine manuscripts that Bernard André can be believed to have presented to Henry VII or Henry VIII; only one of them is a presentation copy of a politically occasioned poem – a copy of a poem on England's victories of 1513 over the French and the Scots – and six of the nine, including this verse manuscript, post-date the accession of Henry VIII.[17]

The seemingly low survival rate of presentation copies of

André's political poetry, and the uneven distribution over the reigns of Henry VII and Henry VIII of the original presentation copies that do survive, are probably not altogether due to accidents of transmission; André's personal condition and a change of circumstances accelerated by the death of Henry VII in 1509 probably pertain. André was blind.[18] His surviving presentation manuscripts suggest that he was not as attentive to the physical appearance of his writings as his sighted contemporaries. His manuscripts are less decorated and less carefully designed than those of Alberici or Carmeliano (fig 16); consequently, they were perhaps less likely to be preserved. Moreover, throughout his career, André boasted of an ability to improvise Latin verse;[19] lost poems of his, and poems surviving only in belated copies, may have been published at court orally in the first instance, with the king's blind *vates* declaiming or reciting them *coram rege*.

There is reason to think that André's access to the king may have been less free in the reign of Henry VIII, and that Henry VIII took less and less interest in André's work, especially as new, more accomplished men came to prominence at court. If so, after 1509, André would have had to rely more on written copies for putting his work before the king. More significantly, André may have begun to publish a different kind of book to Henry VIII. To the sorts of writing that he had published in the reign of Henry VII, André added selections and collections of his work. As compilations of distinct pieces, these did not lend themselves to spontaneous invention or oral circulation; in fact, the point of such compilations was that they were not extemporaneous.

The *Vita Henrici Septimi* that André presented to Henry VII in about 1502 is in part a retrospective collection of this sort. Made comparatively early in André's career, it brings together a quantity of his previously published political verse within a new historiographic framework. The work retells the *res gesta* of Henry's reign up to late 1497, in prose that the preface says began to be written in 1500. The retrospective narrative frames quotations – re-presentations, in effect – of whole poems that André had written and published at the time. Within the *Vita*'s account of the coronation of Henry VII's queen, for example, is quoted the poem that André had written and made public on the occasion, entitled 'Reginae coronatae praenosticum'; likewise, within the

Vita's account of the birth of Prince Arthur in 1486 is quoted the poem André had written and published at the time, 'in natalem principem.' All of the poems collected in the *Vita* occur in it in this manner, framed by reference to their previous publication.[20]

André did more with collections of his work after Henry VII's death, and more of them survive from this period; the shift in the kind of publication that he worked with answered to changes in his circumstance. At the time of the death, in April 1509, the perception was that the accession of a new king would change the pattern of distribution of royal patronage among humanists. Lord Mountjoy wrote Erasmus – whose efforts to find an English place for himself in 1499 and subsequently had met with frustration – to encourage him to expect greater success under Henry VIII: of the new king, Mountjoy wrote:

> If you knew how ... warmly he is attached to men of letters, then I should go so far as to swear upon my own head that with or without wings you would fly to us here to look at the new and lucky star ... Heaven smiles, earth rejoices; all is milk and honey and nectar. Tight-fistedness is well and truly banished. Generosity scatters wealth with unstinting hand.[21]

Likewise, in the suite of poems he wrote to celebrate Henry VIII's coronation, which he presented to the new king, Thomas More emphasized precisely this possibility for change: 'He now gives to good men the honors and public offices which used to be sold to evil men. By a happy reversal of circumstances, learned men now have the prerogatives which ignoramuses carried off in the past.'[22]

These perceptions adumbrate important properties that the English situation for humanists had taken on by the end of the reign of Henry VII, which would have had repercussions for Bernard André, the senior established figure. Evidently, by 1509 at the latest, the humanist supply in England had come to exceed patronal demand. More humanist talent was seeking to share in a quantity of patronage no longer sufficient to go around. The situation was the result of several factors: the legendary tight-fistedness of Henry VII's last years; the king's loyalty to those, like André, who had begun to serve him early in his reign; the rising expectations of humanists, after a period during which patronage for humanism had become generalized and institutionalized in England to an unprecedented degree; an over-production of talent in Italy, combining with the political disruption of the peninsular wars of the 1490s to cause an exodus of learned Italians, seeking livings for themselves in the ever more widely scattered, northerly markets that were not yet saturated. The most important factor, however, may well have been the maturation of a pool of humanist talent native to England during the decade or so leading up to 1509. It had become possible by that date to become educated in humanism, even in Greek, without leaving England; in addition, a subsequently prominent group of Englishmen who had gone to Italy to study began to come home.[23]

By the time of the death of Henry VII, then, a second generation of English humanists – including William Lily, Thomas Linacre, Thomas More, Richard Pace, Thomas Lupset, and others, as well as such foreign born *sodales* of theirs as Andrea Ammonio and Erasmus – had come of age; they were ready to enjoy royal favour but found the way to it blocked. The maturation of this new group led to a kind of intergenerational warfare, a series of intermittent clashes between members of the two generations, mostly attacks by new men on the old, lasting throughout the first two decades of the sixteenth century.[24] The death of Henry VII only exacerbated the situation. Eventually, within a decade or so, the hopes that More and Mountjoy had voiced in 1509 were realized: the accession of a new king did in time result in a redistribution of royal patronage.[25] But the advent of Ammonio, Linacre, More, Pace and other new men to prominence at court was not immediate on the accession of Henry VIII. In fact, for some period after 1509, it cannot have been clear that the change of monarch would necessarily work to the benefit of the second generation.[26] In the meanwhile, for the recipients of the late king's favour, Henry VII's death increased the anxiety they would already have been feeling; for the second generation, the new king's accession incited ambition further.

The short-term consequence was an intensification of the competition for patronage already current among England's humanists, in a buyer's market. After about 1500, and certainly by

1509, the problem for the humanist patronage seeker in England appears no longer to have been attracting patronage to humanist work in contrast to other kinds of literary or cultural work. The problem had become creating repute, a matter of the comparative standing of humanists, in competitive relation to one another.

Throughout the reigns of Henry VII and Henry VIII, André continued to publish at court unique copies of single pieces of writing of his, prepared as prompted by particular occasions. After 1500, and especially after 1509, however, this kind of publication seems not to have appeared adequate to him any more. He tried two publication tactics that were new for him, often in combination with one another. He re-presented work that had been seen at court before, and he published, not single pieces, but collections of his writings. André did not invent these techniques for England: about a century earlier, John Gower and Thomas Hoccleve had published versions of their own collected writings;[27] among the early humanist visitors to England, Antonio Beccaria and Stefano Surigone would seem to have circulated collections of their poems that had been published separately before;[28] within the first year or two of Henry VII's reign, Giovanni Gigli used a collection of writings to ingratiate himself with Richard Fox and possibly with others prominent at court;[29] Giovanni Opizio, Filippo Alberici, and no doubt other itinerant humanists presented Henry VII with collections of their work;[30] and within a year or two of his accession, Henry VIII had been presented with collections of writings by Thomas More and John Skelton,[31] not to mention André. Nor were these publication techniques new for André only after the accession of Henry VIII, since he had already presented his *Vita Henrici Septimi* to Henry VII in about 1502. Nonetheless, collections of writings figure more significantly in André's sixteenth-century career than they had before.

The republication of old work, in collections of some sort, be they of exclusively old work, or of old and new work at once, served purposes different from those of single, occasional pieces. Republications and collections were more efficient tools for reputation-building – for public self-fashioning – than single-item publications. Presenting the same piece of work at court a second time, as André did with his *Vita Henrici Septimi*, for example, served to remind his royal patron of the literary service André had already done. His repeat presentations affirmed the fact of his career: that he had persisted over time in doing literary service, and had come already to hold standing and reputation at court because of it.

Collections of work served the same authorial interest, in asserting a persistence of success. In addition, collecting writings together has the effect of shifting interest, away from the particular pieces of writing themselves towards the author of the writings, from their qualities to his skills. The *Vita Henrici Septimi* has these properties. At the time of the individual poems' initial publication at court, the poems bespoke their author's talents, inevitably; but they also then spoke, more directly and immediately, to the occasions they addressed and to patronal wants and needs. By the time of their collection and representation some years later, the immediacy was out of them. The poems continued to recall their initial occasions, of course; once collected, however, their emphasis necessarily shifted to the only still immediate unifying factor, the authorial talent, as employed over time, on a variety of occasions, to meet a variety of patronal needs.

André appears to have recognized the efficacy of this sort of publication for meeting the circumstances that obtained in England after April 1509. After Henry VII's death, André could have expected to rely to a degree on what he had already achieved. Still, he was faced with a need to ingratiate himself with a new king, to whom his claim to continued standing would have to be put, and his competition had grown stronger. His publications were designed to fit this new situation. For what may have been André's first offering to Henry VIII, he presented a collection of writings rather than a single, occasional piece.[32] It is a comparatively plain, small paper book, in size and decoration much like André's other surviving presentations, only uncharacteristically long; its title page announces that it comprises three separate items:

[1] an *Exposition du Pseaulme huitiesme*, a brief invocational 'prayer' in French;
[2] a Latin verse *Vita Beate Katherine*; and

[3] an *Aristotelis ad magnum Alexandrum de vite institutione oratio*, in Latin prose.[33]

The collection seems especially well designed for display. Each piece shows off a particular talent or aptitude; together, they summarize Bernard André's qualifications and call to mind the quality of his career as a court orator and poet over the previous twenty-five years.

The *Exposition du Pseaulme huitiesme* is a series of French verses in 'aeternelle louange de Dieu et du tresfauste et magnificque roy Henry huitiesme et de la tres noble et tressaige royne Catherine dEspaigne deuxiesme de puys la conqueste,' 'aplicque en leur tresglorieuse louange par chascune lectre de leurs royaulx noms.'[34] In other words, it is an encomium of king and queen the lines of which are arranged in an acrostic, forming the phrase 'HENRI HUITIESME ET CATHERINE DEUXSIESME DESPAIGNE TRESIL-LUSTRES ROY ET ROYNE DE ANGLETERRE ET DE FRANCE ET SEIGNEURS DHIRLANDE AULX Q[uelx] D[ieu] DOINT S[ante] E[t] L[ongue] V[ie].'[35] Although this brief piece claims to be an exposition of the psalm, in fact it only flatters Henry VIII, his wife, and Tudor rule. The psalm in question appears to have been chosen for its numerological aptness more than anything else. The poem's relation to it is not close: along with its references to 'Phebe' and 'les ancians,' however, the poem does quote the psalm, in Latin, applying to Henry VIII the words with which the psalmist had addressed God. Addressing Henry, for example, André wrote that God 'ta donne vertu infinye,

> Toy exaltant et ta lignye.
> Je puys donc bien attribuer
> En ce que dict la prophetye
> Saincte: Domne, dominus noster,
> Magnificque tu doibs regner
> Esleve toult en excellence;
> Entendement ne peult penser,
> Trop nexsaucer ta reverence,
> Car huitiesmes en permanence
> A ce noble et puissant regnom.[36]

gives you boundless virtue, exalting you and your line. Well

> may I therefore apply to you herein what the holy prophecy
> says: O Lord, our Lord, in magnificence you deserve to reign,
> wholly elevated in excellence; the understanding cannot
> comprehend, nor exalt your reverence too highly, for you
> are the eighth to succeed in this noble and mighty kingdom.

The poem demonstrates some facility with antiquity, and somewhat greater facility with Scripture and scriptural typology; but
before all else, it demonstrates André's willingness, and something of his ability, to flatter his monarch, abjectly. It also establishes his qualification to do so in French, another distinction
that André enjoyed at court.[37]

The *Vita Beate Katherine* in the same collection is by no
means so abject. When Pietro Carmeliano published his version
of the same saint's life in 1483–5, it has not the advantage that
might have accrued to André's by virtue of the fact that the queen
was the saint's namesake; still, the life of St Katherine of Alexandria remains in André's version what it had been earlier for
Carmeliano: an implicit encomium of learned eloquence, as capable of serving pious ends.[38] The saint herself best exemplifies
such skill; but in writing her life as he does, André exhibits his
own ability to exemplify it, too – putting his own learned eloquence to work piously, for devotional purposes. André's version
of the life is briefer and less overtly polemical than Carmeliano's;
it is also less self-consciously classicizing, less epic-like, in its
treatment. Nevertheless, it is in hendecasyllabics, rather than the
hexameters and elegiac distichs that Carmeliano had used, and
its metre thus asserts another distinction of André's. He was
metrically adventuresome, making distinctive, early use of various lyric metres. Finally, the manuscript claims that the *Vita*
was 'extemporaliter composita.' The claim is impossible to confirm. There can be no question but that André composed and
reworked poems put in print or otherwise published as 'ex tempore' pieces.[39] On the other hand, André must have been possessed of a powerful auditory memory for Latin verse, to have
been able to retain as much as he did without sight. In view of
the frequency with which he claims ex tempore composition, and
the absence of such claims by others, it seems likely that oral
improvisation or recitation was another skill by which André

distinguished himself at court, of which he meant to remind the new king here.

These two introductory pieces are slight by comparison with the third item: a prose piece, nominally an oration addressed by Aristotle to Alexander. During the Middle Ages, there had grown up a substantial body of writing making this same pretence, to be Aristotle's work, written for the edification of his princely charge. André's 'Aristotelis ad Alexandrum de vite institutione oratio' alludes to this medieval tradition of wisdom handed down from antiquity, but without making any claim actually to be antique itself.[40] Albeit full of ancient wisdom, the piece is André's modern address to his modern prince. André uses the fiction to put a case, obliquely, for the continuation of royal favour that he needed; given the circumstances of its presentation to Henry VIII early in the reign, the piece requires to be read as an *alieniloquim*, a kind of allergory. In it, Aristotle argues two points for Alexander: his main one, that the way to virtue (and, thereby, to eternal renown) lies in pursuit of and respect for learning; and the subsidiary one, that in forming friendships and dispensing benefactions, sons do well to emulate their fathers. Allegorically, the *Oratio* exhorts Henry VIII to emulate his father in benevolence towards the treatise's author, Henry VII's proven friend Bernard André, and it is a product and an embodiment of the sort of *sapientia* that, it argues, again by its characteristic indirection, Henry VIII ought to pursue, respect, and reward.

The Aristotle-Alexander fiction enabled André to cloak his arguments in a semblance of disinterest – the treatise represents Aristotle addressing Alexander, not André pleading with Henry directly – while also serving to flatter both the king and André himself. The fictional conceit enables André to make a set of equations. André offers to play Aristotle to the young king's Alexander, and with the *Oratio* itself, he does so. The promise is that by knowledge and emulation of ancient examples – by means of the kind of knowledge that André could claim to have provided Henry VII for years, was in fact providing Henry VIII in the form of the *Oratio*, and could continue to provide – Henry VIII could expect to surpass his father by as much as Alexander had surpassed his father, Philip of Macedon. By means of the *Oratio* itself, both its substance and its form, its advice about

learning and the use to which it puts its classical material, to
offer present guidance, André makes his own contribution crucial
to fulfilment of this promise. The piece paints André as capable
of making an Alexander of Henry VIII by means of the knowledge
of antiquity with which he could instruct the king.

Aristotle's ostensible purpose with the oration is to per-
suade his noble, young charge to pursue virtue rather than transient 'dona fortunae naturaeque': 'I will try to teach you, in brief
compass,' he is made to say, 'what studies and arts will bring you
to virtue and enable you to attain glory in the eyes of all.'[41]
Learning turns out to be the treatise's answer to this question it
poses: 'alone of all things, *sapientia* is immortal.' More specifically, the *Oratio* suggests, the most useful knowledge is of matters 'que literarum monumentis sunt tradita': 'Use your leisure
for studying the canonical authors, handed down in the monuments of letters, for thereby matters that others find difficult
will be easy for you to understand.'[42] That this learning is to be
an education in the *literae* and *mores* of antiquity is emphasized
again in the words with which Aristotle concludes:

> If it is fitting for a mortal to hazard guesses about the mind
> of God, I believe that God showed in those nearest him what
> befalls the soul for its good and evil inclinations. For when
> Jupiter fathered Hercules and Tantalus, as the story goes,
> he made the one immortal, on account of his virtue, and
> the other he condemned to suffer the worst of tortures, on
> account of his vices. Whoever would profit from these ex-
> amples should be eager, not only to abide by the precepts
> we have laid down herein, but also to read and study the
> useful and good writings that poets and orators have left us.
> We see the bees light on all plants, and take from each what-
> ever they know will be useful to them; it befits you who
> are eager for learning to do likewise: to prove yourself will-
> ing to try everything, and to gather diligently what you judge
> will be useful to you; for without such diligence, scarcely
> anyone is able to overcome the wrongs of affairs and the
> inconveniences of nature.[43]

In addition to thus insinuating that the sort of teaching

André was equipped to provide was the most useful that the prince might have, the treatise also emphasizes respect for a father's example. 'You must take the greatest care not to be too quick to show true affection to those whom you receive into your friendship; it is right to persist in benevolence with them forever,' Aristotle cautions Alexander. Since such benevolent *amicitia* is to be permanent, the good friend will be one whose worth has been proven in relations with earlier benefactors: 'You should make no one your friend until you have carefully looked into how well he observed the laws of friendship with others before. For it is not to be doubted but that he will prove to be the same sort of friend to you that he was to his other friends before.'[44] By this sort of evidence, that Bernard André was qualified to receive permanent benevolence should have been clear to Henry; if not, the *Oratio* more simply asserts that the son should emulate the father:

> I have sent this oration to you as a gift, to show evidence of my benevolence towards you and my habit with your father Philip. For it is fitting that the sons should inherit their father's friendships as well as their patrimony. And indeed I see that time and fortune favour us in this matter, for you are eager to learn and I to teach.

The passage establishes that there had been friendship between Aristotle and Philip, and it asserts that Alexander should inherit his father's friendships; therefore, it argues, Alexander is bound to reciprocate Aristotle's 'erga vos benevolentia.'[45]

The oration has prescriptive passages, of sound general counsel, in the manner (and occasionally the form) of the *Disticha Catonis* – 'time Deum, amicos verere, parentes honora, legibus pare,' for example[46] – but the better part of it is given over to matters nearer Bernard André's professional heart: to advice about dispensing benefaction. One needs to be wary of flatterers, Aristotle warns.[47] On the other hand, Aristotle also advises, 'Take care not to be too hard and haughty with everyone who approaches you; be open and kind.' The purpose of wealth is virtuous benefaction, which is to be exercised considerately; although the greedy and the opportunistic should of course be shunned, there is nothing greater than benefaction. 'Do well by good men,' is the burden of Aristotle's advice on this point; 'for to honour the best is the finest of treasures.'[48]

John Skelton wrote something similar, entitled *Speculum principis*. Like André's *Oratio*, it too is a piece of pedagogy, the advice of a senior teacher to a young student; it too makes much of ancient exempla and incorporates gnomic, Cato-like precepts among its other, more developed points of counsel. The difference is that, whereas André's *Oratio* is a fictional address, of Aristotle to Alexander, the *Speculum principis* is plain Skelton. For a time, André and Skelton were situated similarly in the royal household, both of them tutors to Henry VII's sons, André to Arthur and Skelton to Henry; and they left their jobs at about the same time, around 1500–1502. Skelton wrote the *Speculum principis* for his pupil in August 1501, to mark the end of his tutorship. Later, at some point between 1509 and 1512, after Prince Henry had become Henry VIII, Skelton refurbished the piece and represented it to his former student, as part of a collection of his writings, incorporating also a pair of previously published poems and a newly written postscript.[49] That Skelton wrote a valedictory summation of his teachings when he left his tutorship raises the possibility that André wrote something similar for a similar occasion. That Skelton recopied and represented his valediction, along with other pieces of his writing, after the boy whom he had taught had become king, again raises the possibility that, in presenting a copy of his *Oratio*, André too was representing something he had published at court before.

In any case, the *Oratio* remains the most important piece in André's collection of writings. It speaks most directly to the fundamental issue: continuing André's royal patronage after the death of Henry VII. The *Oratio* establishes that André knows how to use his classical learning and humanist talents to make Henry VIII a virtuous and thereby glorious king. If it had been published before, it could also serve to remind its royal recipient of services previously rendered and to recall its presenter's career. It did not appear alone in the manuscript, however. By the collection of other writings with the *Oratio*, André's collection also showed that he could make propagandistic eulogy, Latin or French, as in his *Exposition du Pseaulme huitiesme*, and that he could entertain and instruct, with a combination of learning and piety, as

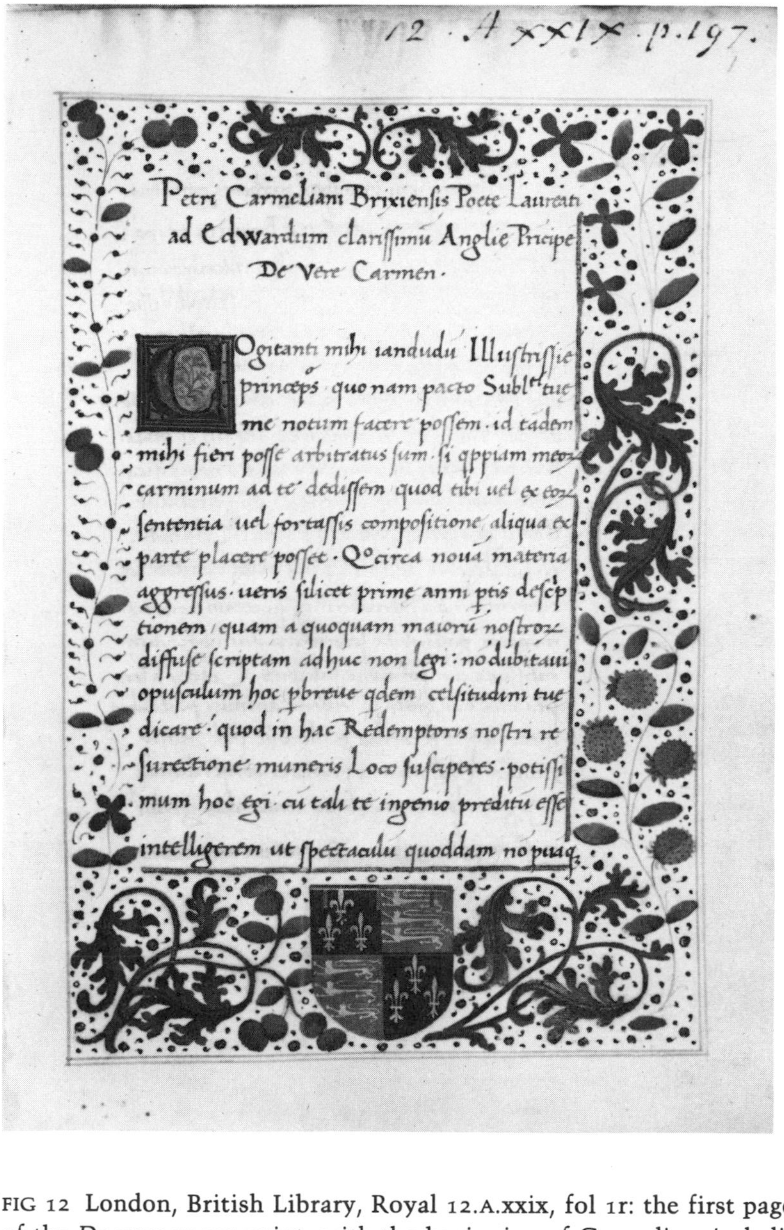
12 . A xxix . p. 197.

Petri Carmeliani Brixiensis Poete Laureati
ad Edwardum clarissimu Anglie Pricipe
De Vere Carmen ·

COgitanti mihi iandudu Illustrissie
princeps quonam pacto Sublte tue
me notum facere possem · id tadem
mihi fieri posse arbitratus sum · si qppiam meoz
carminum ad te dedissem quod tibi uel ex eoz
sententia uel fortassis compositione aliqua ex
parte placere posset · Qocirca noua materia
aggressus · ueris silicet prime anni ptis descp
tionem quam a quoquam maioru nostroz
diffuse scriptam adhuc non legi : no dubitaui
opusculum hoc pbreue qdem celsitudini tue
dicare · quod in hac Redemptoris nostri re
surrectione muneris Loco susciperes · potissi
mum hoc egi · cu tali te ingenio preditu esse
intelligerem ut spectaculu quoddam no puiq

FIG 12 London, British Library, Royal 12.A.xxix, fol 1r: the first page of the *De vere* manuscript, with the beginning of Carmeliano's dedicatory letter (dated 7 April 1482) to Prince Edward. The full text of the letter is given in appendix 3. Vellum page, 212 x 144 mm; writing, 122 x 77 mm

me tempare nequiueris atq; in legendum
sese mihi sponte sua capilli sepius insurgent.
Hanc staq; deuotissimā martirem protectri
cem meam proprio motu mihi delegi eius
q; uitam sanctissimam i heroicu carmen col
l ectis omnibus ingenij mei uiribus deduxi.
Quocirca eu pncipale opus Serenissimo regi
cofecrarim tibi quoq; q lingue Latine pnci
patu iter tuos conalies possides q libaliu3
disciplina3 oiu3 peritia3 q3 maxima tenes;
q q; doctos uiros fauore et beniuoletia pse
queris exemplu unu scribendu esse duxi;
Illud igitur Sereno tuo uultu Legito meq; tui
. cense. Vale.

Sponsa dei Katerina deū in redde benignū
Et crebras pro me te rogo funde preces;

FIG 13 Cambridge, Gonville and Caius College, ms 196/102, pp 4–5: the copy of Carmeliano's *Vita B. Katerinae* presented to John Russell, dating from 1483–5, showing the end of the prefatory letter, the miniature, and (at right) the beginning of the poem itself. Vellum page, 192 x 122 mm; writing, 100 x 85 mm

¶ In Beate Katerine Egyptie christi
Sponse uita̅ Prohemiu̅ feliciter iapit.
V̅nina si ueteres celebraru̅t falsa Poete
Et uanas illis Laudes titulos q̄ dedere
Quid nos horremus sanctox̄ gesta referre
Qui christu̅z toto sitientes pectore ueru̅z
Sunt diros passi cruciatus uerbere multo
Cu̅ q̄ suo intrepidi sparseru̅t sanguine uita̅z   Propositio
Ergo age Musa cane quo sit Katerina parete
Qua regione sata que christi Sponsa uocata est
Et uita̅z mortes q̄ sua̅z recto ordine pande
Digna qde̅z puro Katerina est carmine na̅q̄
Post matrem christi uirgo hec celebrima p̄mu̅z
Virginitatis habet titulu̅ casti q̄ pudoris.

　　　¶ Inuocatio
At tu q̄ terra̅z Pelagus Celi q̄ gubnas
Su̅me̅ Opifex mu̅di per quem p̄rit oi̅a tellus
Et mare̅ concutitur per quem polus astra reuoluit
Et quo nascitur pereu̅t q̄ animatia cuncta

FIG 14 Oxford, Bodleian Library, Laud Misc 501, fols 2v–3r: the corresponding opening of the copy of Carmeliano's *Vita B. Katerinae* presented to Robert Brackenbury, dating from 1483–5. Vellum page, 195 × 125 mm; writing, 100 × 85 mm

FIG 15 London, Addit 33736, fols 1v–2r: the first opening of the *Suasoria Laeticiae* manuscript, dating from 1486, showing the full-page painting facing the beginning of the poem. Vellum page, 190 x 128 mm; writing, 102 x 85 mm

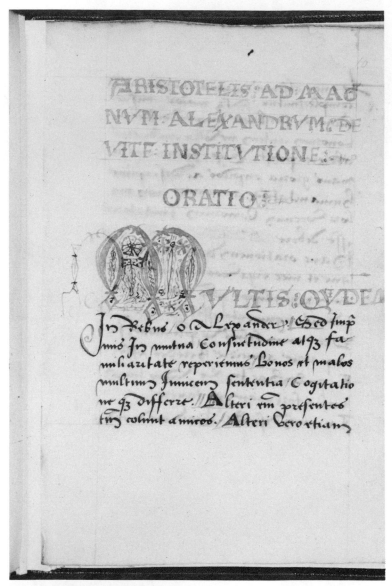

FIG 16 London, British Library, Royal 12.B.xiv, fol 10r: the beginning of André's 'Aristotelis ad Alexandrum de vite institutione oratio,' presented to Henry VIII, probably early in his reign. Paper page, 197 × 127 mm; writing, 133 × 97 mm

In Hymnos Chriſtianos p̄ Bernardū Andreã Regiū poe
tã compoſitos Ad Henricum octauum Angliȩ regem in⸗
uictiſſimum:eiuſdem Bernardi Apologeticon.

Vrelius Prudentius Cæſarauguſtenſis
poeta chriſtianus iam ſeptimū & qnqua
geſimū annum agēs:res eccleſiaſticas va
rio metrorū genere cœpit cōponere:in⸗
genioſe quidē & elegāter:ſed ſpta inter⸗
dū ſyllabarū q̄titate in peregrinis dictio
nibus & maxie grȩcis:id ipſum ego quo
q̄ vere dicere poſſum p̄terq̄ q̄ ingenioſe & elegāter.Cum
em̄ ſcriberē hȩc natalis Chriſti currebat milleſimus & qn
genteſimuſnonus annus:regni vero celſitudinis tuȩ regū
inuictiſſime ſecūdus.Quo tēpore annoꝝ tātūdē vt ille for
ſan & ampli⁹ agebã:nūc nō ſine graui dolore repetēs q̄ iu
ueniles annos viridioris ȩtatis nequiter exegerim:fret⁹ au
tē dei miſericordia q̄(vel ſero)pœnitētes nō deſpicit:iſcri
ptū opus chriſtianȩ fidei a paucis antea q̄tum meminerim
attentatū id eſt de hymnis ſanctoꝝ per totius anni circu
lū tã Rōano q̄ Anglicano vſu ſcribere ſum aggreſſus.Spe
rans eoſdē in partē ſatiſfactionis ac pœnitentiȩ flagitiorū
meoꝝ a miſericordiſſimo deo ſuſcipiendos,qd vt ſua largi
flua bonitate in extrema ſenecta mea mihi largiatur : vos
oēs qui hoc iã caſtigatū opus lecturi eſtis, illū mecum vſis
p̄cibus exorare non grauemini.

⸿Hoc aūt hymnoꝝ exile op⁹ trifariã diſtribuit.Prima em̄
pars aduſq̄ ſalutiferȩ crucis inuētionē p̄tendit:quo qdem
die cōceptū,ipſum auſpicati ſum⁹.Secūda vero ad eiuſdē
crucis exaltationē p̄durat.Porro tertia a triūphali crucis
exaltatiōe ad toti⁹ calcē opis decurrit.Atq̄ obiter aiaduer
te reuos lectores boni,velim:me primū diui Seuerini de cō
ſolatu philoſophico metra retrouerſum oĩa eſſe imitatū:
& diui Andrȩȩ vitã totidē metroꝝ gñib⁹ ſic tenuiter depĩ
xiſſe.Poſt hȩc vero ad vernãtia carminū ſuoꝝ prata Venu
ſin⁹ nos acciuit Horati⁹.Hȩc idcirco iure p̄miſeri vt ſcribē
tis ītētio vos minie lateat.Fauete icœptui lectores optimi.

A iii

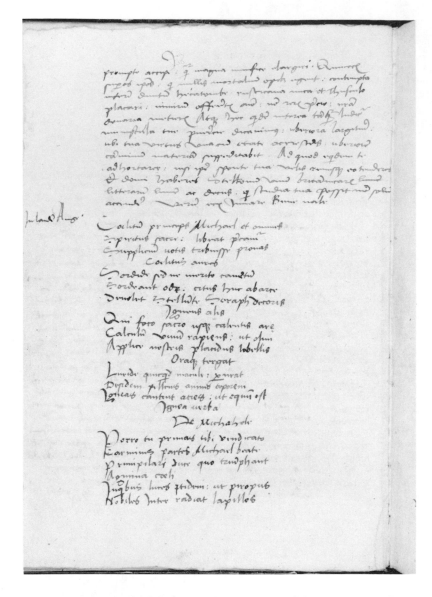

FIG 18 London, British Library, Egerton 1651, fol 1v: the end of Erasmus' Ep 104 and the beginning of his poem 'In laudem angelorum,' in an apograph dating from about 1500. Paper page, 280 x 188 mm; writing, 215 x 145 mm

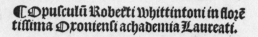

¶ Opusculū Roberti Whittintoni in floꝛē
tissima Oꝛoniensi achademia Laureati.

¶ Ad inuictissimū pꝛincipem Henricū regem Angliae ⁊ franciae. Pꝛinci
pem walliae et dñm Hiberniae:de octenario numero Epygramma.

¶ Ad honoꝛificentissimū dñm Thomam woley Cardinalem ⁊ Legatum
de latere Libellus de difficultate iusticiae seruādae in reipublicae guber-
natione.

¶ Ad eundem panegyꝛicon a laude quattuoꝛ Uirtutū cardinalium.

¶ Libellus Epygrammaton.

¶ Ad eximiū pꝛincipem Carolum Bꝛandon Suffolciae ducem.

¶ Ad illustrem virum Thomam Moꝛe:vnū ex praepotentissimi Regis
Angliae Henrici octaui cōsiliariis vtriusꝗ lingue Censoꝛem.

¶ Ad lepidissimum poetäm Sceltonem Carmen.
¶ Eiusdem inuectiua ad quendam zoilum.

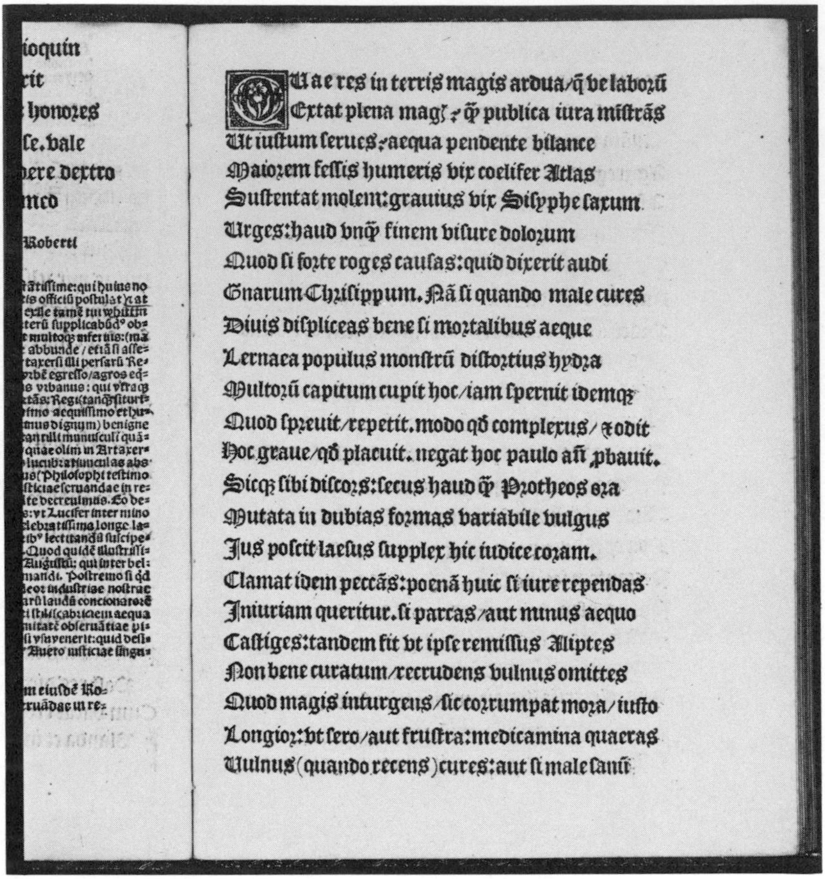

Quae res in terris magis ardua/q̄ de laborū
Extat plena mag ; ꝙ publica iura mīstrās
Ut iustum serues;aequa pendente bilance
Maiorem fessis humeris vix coelifer Atlas
Sustentat molem:grauius vix Sisyphe saxum
Urges:haud vnq̄ finem visure dolorum
Quod si forte roges causas:quid dixerit audi
Gnarum Chrisippum. Nā si quando male cures
Diuis displiceas bene si mortalibus aeque
Lernaea populus monstrū distortius hydra
Multorū capitum cupit hoc/iam spernit idemq̄
Quod spreuit/repetit.modo qđ complexus/ fodit
Hoc graue/qđ placuit. negat hoc paulo añ ꝓbauit.
Sicq̄ sibi discors:secus haud ꝙ Protheos ora
Mutata in dubias formas variabile vulgus
Jus poscit laesus supplex hic iudice coram.
Clamat idem peccās:poenā huic si iure rependas
Jniuriam queritur.si parcas/aut minus aequo
Castiges:tandem fit vt ipse remissus Aliptes
Non bene curatum/recrudens vulnus omittes
Quod magis inturgens/sic corrumpat mora/iusto
Longior:vt sero/aut frustra:medicamina quaeras
Uulnus(quando recens)cures:aut si male sanū

FIG 20 *Opusculum Roberti Whittintoni* (London: de Worde 1519 [*STC* 25540.5]) sig A4r: the beginning of Whittinton's poem 'De difficultate iusticiae servandae in republica administranda,' addressed to Wolsey in the printed collection, showing the same text as copied by hand in fig 21. Copy: San Marino, California, Huntington Library, RB 59198. Paper page, 185 x 134 mm; type, 145 x 90 mm

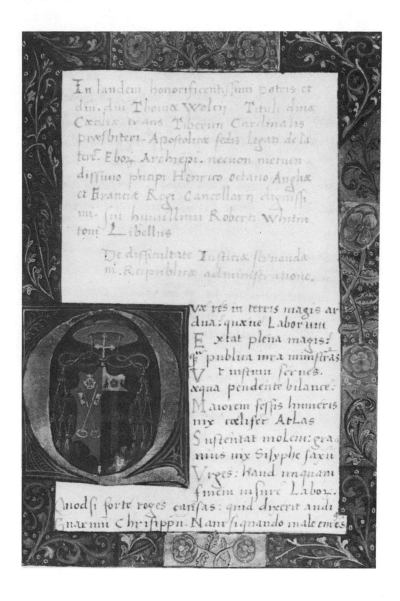

FIG 21 Oxford, Bodleian Library, Bodley ms 523, fol 4r: the beginning of Whittinton's 'De difficultate iusticiae servandae,' in the manuscript copy that he had made for Wolsey c 1519, showing the same text as printed in fig 20. Vellum page, 232 x 164 mm; writing, 134 x 94 mm

FIG 22 Oxford, Bodleian Library, Bodley ms 523, upper cover: the earliest surviving English gilt binding, covering the presentation manuscript
that Whittinton gave Wolsey c 1519

demonstrated in his life of St Katherine. In a way that no single work could have done, the collection exhibited to advantage André's several qualities, and it did so in a circumstance – the over-supply of humanist talent competing for a new monarch's attentions – which called for an assertion of potential and accomplishment.

As an effort to secure continued favour, this manuscript collection should have worked well. All the evidence indicates that it did.[50] Nevertheless, there were jobs that unique presentation manuscripts could not do, no matter how well designed. This one that André offered Henry VIII early in his reign, Skelton's similar *Speculum principis* manuscript, and other contemporary publications, though they might assert or articulate a reputation, could not broadcast or aggrandize one. Unique presentation manuscripts – be they new single works or collections of represented, old work – put work only into single pairs of hands. Patrons' hands were critical, to the extent that they were still the best source of immediate material support for writers; still, the unique presentation copy remained an instrument by which to reach, exclusively, a particular potential patron.

Unique manuscript presentation copies had worked well enough for the likes of Carmeliano and André early in the reign of Henry VII, while the local humanist population remained small; and publications of this sort retained importance. With the growth of the English humanist community in the sixteenth century, however, putting work into the hands of the many took on a new significance. It was no longer sufficient to impress the king himself, nor was it possible to succeed by impressing the king alone. A reticula of subpatrons – patrons of lesser power and wealth than the monarch, and persons who might intercede between writers and patrons, who were themselves in fact patrons of a sort – had also to be wooed; for such subpatrons, particularly other humanists, could contribute to the manufacture of a paying reputation. Reputation, more difficult to acquire in the first decades of the sixteenth century, concomitantly became more important to success, and the creation and aggrandizement of reputation was more the work of the many, acting together, than the work of the single patron, judging alone.

Humanists could and did damage one another's prospects,

and they also could and did benefit one another, both materially and immaterially. They provided one another loans, lodging, introductions, and so on; they also provided praise in one form or another, and thereby contributed to the creation of reputation, an immediately intangible thing, but something that might eventually be transvalued into material benefits. André practised both kinds of behaviour in the course of his career. When Thomas Linacre appeared before Henry VII in 1499 or 1500, to present the king with a copy of his translation of Proclus' *De sphaera*, André condemned the work, in terms that caused the king to conceive an *inexpiabile odium* for Linacre, who did not then gain royal favour until the next reign.[51] On the other hand, when Erasmus was visiting England, André both loaned him money and arranged that he might lodge at the Austin Friars' London house; he also sought, unsuccessfully as it happened, to introduce Erasmus to Richard Beere, abbot of Glastonbury, in person taking Erasmus to call at this potential patron's residence.[52] In another case from the same period, André saw printed an epigram praising the work of William Horman, a young, humanistically inclined grammarian.[53] The impact on a reputation of formal, public praise of this sort can be comparatively evident; less formal, private acts of praise – a word or two in conversation, of the sort André might have offered Beere on Erasmus' behalf – are by their nature less in evidence but must have occurred and must have been of prime importance, as the stuff of which reputation was made.

The tangible benefactions that humanist compeers did one another in early Tudor England were forms of patronage in themselves; the intangible benefactions helped their beneficiaries gain patronage in an intermediary way, by heightening standing within the humanist community. In the long run, these intangible benefactions – the contributions that humanists made to building one another's reputations – paid the greater dividends; for, all else being equal, high standing in the humanist community made a patronage seeker the more attractive to patrons, inasmuch as patronizing someone with a good reputation in turn paid to the patron greater dividends in esteem.

For purposes of impressing humanist peers, that they might be so favourably disposed as to provide praise and occasional material benefactions, unique manuscript presentation copies, of the sort that André had used with his kings, would have been exceedingly inefficient, involving great immediate outlay of money to produce copies, to be recompensed only by some slight, transient material benefit or by an intangible return in the form of praise. Wooing the many – the larger learned community, both patrons and humanist peers – necessitated publication in multiple copies, but copies of a sort that could be produced more cost-efficiently.

Publication in multiple copies was tried with manuscript technology. Carmeliano had experimented with it in the publication of his *Vita S. Katerinae*, but unsuccessfully. He may have chosen the recipients of his copies poorly, and, more to the point, because he chose to use costly formal presentation copies, it turned out to be a prohibitively expensive experiment. He did not repeat it.[54] There is also evidence for the circulation of work in multiple informal manuscripts, copies produced cheaply. In the *Vita Henrici Septimi*, for example, André tells of an operation of the *grex poetarum* attached to Henry VII's court: in 1490, the French ambassador Robert Gaguin wrote an epigram denigrating Henry VII, and Gaguin was answered with poems by Giovanni Gigli, Pietro Carmeliano, Cornelio Vitelli, and André himself, from each of which André quotes a few lines. No formal copies of any of the verse from this incident survive, and there may not have been any; the English responses against Gaguin may have been 'presented' at court orally, if at all. Nor do other kinds of contemporary copies from the incident survive; by their physical nature and the nature of the uses to which they were put, copies not meant for formal presentation are unlikely to be preserved. The poetry of the 1490 Gaguin episode is known only from André's account of it, and, in a pair of cases, from copies made later, at second or third hand, in manuscript miscellanies. The facts imply the circulation of numerous ephemeral copies of the several poems, most likely copied on single sheets, by various informal copyists, and then passed from hand to hand, among the members and patrons of the court's *grex poetarum* and others.[55]

In most cases, however, printing was the more efficient technology for this sort of job. Printing was costly to writers in several ways, among them that it depersonalized publication; by reason of this depersonalization, for example, printed copies were not regarded as suitable to be offered immediately to patrons and were not in fact presented.[56] Potential patrons, who were to pay directly, wanted something special; and so unique, purpose-built copies – therefore necessarily manuscript copies – remained in use. The writer's numerous peers, on the other hand, who offered chiefly immaterial returns, wanted a kind of copy that could be produced cheaply and in quantity. And printing – to leave aside for the moment whatever else it might have cost or accomplished for the writers who tried it – was then unrivalled as a means by which to proliferate cheap copies.

Printing, too, was something that Bernard André tried. In July 1517, he saw issue from the Parisian press of the scholar-printer Josse Bade a book of his, entitled *Hymni Christiani* (fig 17).[57] Apart from the fact that it is a printed book, the *Hymni Christiani* shares much with André's earlier publications. It is again a collection, in this case of nearly two hundred items, all in verse. Some of the poems are major compositions in their own right, of two to three hundred lines, and the whole comprises about four thousand verses – a quarter as long again as the four books of Horace's *Odes*. Stylistically, the collection is again often self-consciously classicizing. Here as elsewhere, André worked with the ancient lyric metres, using all of Horace's and Boethius', and a number of the poems are modelled closely on particular Horatian odes. In addition, the collection's basic conception involves it closely with a pair of ancient works, the *Fasti* of Ovid and the *Cathemerinon* of Prudentius, for the *Hymni Christiani* collection too has a thematic coherence. It is an annual cycle of hymns for the feasts of the Christian year. In it are poems on saints, major and minor, of the Roman and English calendars, as well as poems on various other feasts of the Church, the Circumcision, the Invention of the Cross, and so on.

As advertised in the preface,[58] André's cycle includes poems on English saints, even some seemingly obscure figures; in fact, the English saints chosen were the politically important ones. Among them are the national saints David, Chad, Patrick, and George; the royal saints Edward the Confessor and the West Saxon King Edward; and several who were of particular moment in the history of the English church, including Wulfstan, Cuthbert, Etheldred, and Winifred.[59] That the collection incorporates such poems – devotional lessons, but with political import – bespeaks

André's continuing willingness to serve the political objectives of the Tudor monarchy, to use even his religious poetry to flatter the dynasty: the whole is dedicated to Henry VIII; individual pieces within it address other members of the royal family, including an Office and Mass of the Immaculate Conception dedicated 'ad serenissimam regiam matrem' and a eulogy memorializing Prince Arthur's death; and political issues enter into the poems themselves, as when, for example, a poem on the Visitation ends with a prayer:

> Grant our prayer, holy virgin: look down favourably on our King Henry VIII, as well as on his great wife, now with child, and on our pious realm. Put the hideous sisters of Erebus to flight; let dear peace reign over the whole world; and let our good prince long wield the sceptre. Amen.[60]

André had been at work on the collection for at least eight years by the time of its publication in 1517.[61] It seems that in the meanwhile – if not in fact earlier – André had published by other means some of the pieces that appear also in the printed volume: the *Vita S. Katherine* printed in the *Hymni Christiani* in 1517 is the same one surviving also in his earlier manuscript collection, with the *Exposition du Pseaulme huitiesme* and Aristotle's *Oratio* to Alexander; the *Vita S. Andreae* printed in the volume seems to have had separate circulation before; and there is evidence to indicate that the three offices printed here had had previous circulation too, evidently in the form of copies dedicated and presented to Margaret Beaufort.[62]

The printed book thus worked to benefit André in the same ways that earlier manuscript publications of his had. By offering his royal patron flattery, in the form of his eulogies of saints dear to the Tudors and his gestures of deference to the royal family, the collection intended to insinuate its author still further into the favour of England's rulers, as his earlier, more overtly propagandistic work had done. In addition, by showcasing André's abilities to write in a variety of verse forms and on a range of subjects, as well as his persistence in his vocation over a number of years, the collection stood to benefit his reputation, focusing on it, as had his earlier manuscript collections. But because the

Hymni Christiani collection was printed, the book could also have worked to aggrandize André's reputation in ways new for him.

By virtue of the fact that printing put copies of his work into comparatively many hands, the *Hymni Christiani* brought André and his writing to the attentions of a larger audience than they had reached before. The technology solved for him the problem of producing and circulating multiple copies of the same work. And the fact that the collection was put into print set André apart from his peers. No English printer worked closely with humanists or regularly printed work of interest to humanists, after the manner of such continental printers as Bade, Manutius, or Froben, whose products attracted international attention. Consequently, up to about 1520, English born and England-based humanists seeking publication in print had to go abroad; but to going abroad in this way certain benefits accrued. From André's perspective, Bade's willingness to put out his book was a mark of distinction for him; Bade's trademarks about the book were a widely legible sign of André's insinuation into the international mainstream of humanist culture.[63]

Bernard André's 1517 *Hymni Christiani* adumbrates the varieties of benefits that might come of the publication of collected and, in some instances, reused work, in multiple printed copies; potentially, the benefits for reputation and so, indirectly, for patronage, could be great. By the qualities the book had as a collection of its author's work, the *Hymni Christiani* asserted André's several claims to standing in the learned community. Moreover, by consequence of a printer's willingness to intercede in the work's circulation, André's assertion was able to reach a comparatively wider public, in the learned community in England and on the continent, than could have been reached otherwise. By means of the 1517 printed book, Bernard André was to be widely known as the author of a sizeable collection of verse, politically useful and religiously circumspect, produced over a number of years and in part already circulated.

The *Hymni Christiani* was Bernard André's last major work, and the last innovation in publishing methods that he tried. After it, he reverted to kinds of publications that he had used before, and he published little between 1517 and his death, probably in 1522;

he presented unique copies of purpose-specific writings to Henry
VIII – an *oratio* and poem for New Year's 1518, another *oratio*
for New Year's 1520, and an apology for his own increasing
feebleness, with some appended verses, for Accession Day 1521
or New Year's 1522.[64] From this perspective, the *Hymni Christiani* concludes André's career, and the line of historical development he represents, from manuscript to print. He wrote much
and tried various kinds and means of publication: single-item
presentations, characteristically of politically occasioned work,
especially in the early part of his career; collections of his writings, including items previously published in other forms, especially after 1500; and, finally, in 1517, a similarly designed
collection put into print. His several publications adumbrate the
properties that collections of work, republication, and printing
had as tools, by means of which André and his contemporaries
could approach potential patrons and attempt to build reputations for themselves among their learned peers. André's use of
different kinds of publication demonstrates an ability to adapt
his writings and his publishing activities to changing circumstances, to fit his work to the particular professional situation at
hand; and these skills, as a writer and a self-publisher, brought
him consistent success, attracting royal patronage as long as he
continued to write and publish.

 Chapter 4

Authorial Parsimony:

The Circulation of Some Poems of Erasmus, c 1495–1518

Erasmus was more sophisticated about the business end of humanism than any of his contemporaries, in England or elsewhere in Europe. Perhaps he was bound to be: unsuited by temperament for regular religious life, disinclined to enter ecclesiastical or governmental service, and without inherited means of support, he had few options other than cultivating reputation and patronage. This may seem a mean aspect of his accomplishment; it was fundamental to it nevertheless. Erasmus occupied himself with matters greater than his own material well-being. Had he not seen to making a living, however, the causes of *bonae literae* and a pacific, reasonable Christianity that he espoused would have suffered. He made his living by writing and publishing.

Like Bernard André, Erasmus had a long career; he too was prolific, and he too worked with a range of publishing methods: presentation manuscripts, collections, and printed books among them. Erasmus was still busier, though, about writing and rewriting, and about publishing and republishing his work; Erasmus tried everything that André did and more, and he earned greater success by it, material and otherwise.

Because of the wealth of epistolary and printed evidence, along with the lucky survival of an Erasmian manuscript of a sort not often preserved, it is possible to reconstruct Erasmus' publishing activities in some detail for a period early in his career,

during the decades on either side of 1500, centred on his visit to
England in 1499–1500.[1] In general, the evidence tells that, even
in the fifteenth century, when his reputation was being made,
Erasmus paid close attention to his work's publication and was
clever about it.

The principle governing Erasmus' publishing activities was
parsimony. By managing his publications, he was able to maxi-
mize the profits accruing to him from his labours. Among his
peers, he was distinctively skilled at mining the available supply
of patronage and maintenance for returns from the authorial and
scholarly work he did, while conserving and economizing his
expenditure of effort. By no means was he indolent. Simply, Erasmus used everything twice, at least. His readers, his printers,
and his patrons complained about the practice, but he could not
afford to mind.

Erasmus himself sought to account in part for this behaviour
by reference to his perfectionism. When Johann von Botzheim
complained about being tricked into buying the same book of
his twice, Erasmus tried to exculpate himself from the charge of
dishonest dealing by saying 'as long as we live, we are devoted
to self-improvement, and we shall not cease to make our writings
more polished and more complete until we cease to breathe.' In
considerable detail, he explained that friends had hurried him to
publish, prematurely; that printers had pressured him to provide
new or revised copy; that his knowledge had grown, so obligating
him to issue corrections of work that he had issued previously;
and so on. Various factors, Erasmus claimed, largely beyond his
control, had forced him to publish, and then to republish, repeatedly.[2]

Erasmus' account of his publishing practices in his reply to
Botzheim is credible, as far as it goes. Erasmus' parsimony, however, was not a matter of his perfectionism, the pressures on him
to publish, or his habit of revising work that he had already made
public. Others felt and behaved as he did in these regards. It was
instead a matter of reusing work already finished once, to profit
by it a second time, no matter what led to the reuse, no matter
whether he revised for republication or not. Whatever his reasons, Erasmus did reuse work, over and over again, in various
ways; and he profited by the practice.

In replying to Botzheim, Erasmus evaded the issue, arguing

instead that Botzheim ought not to be angry about the sharp trading practices of Erasmus and his printers. Thereby he conceded Botzheim the point. Erasmus' printers were tricking book-buyers into paying for the same thing twice, by offering them 'new and improved' editions of the same old works, and Erasmus was conniving at it with them.[3] Josse Bade, Erasmus' principal printer until 1514, had to complain to him, repeatedly, of the losses his press suffered from Erasmus' habit of providing the same copy to more than one printer; still, the problem did not cause Bade to discontinue working with Erasmus. To the contrary, Bade's letters are conciliatory and flattering. They plead for more copy to print, and give voice to what was the crucial point, for both writer and printer. If the matter of reprinting old work, in revised form or not, was carefully managed, both could still help one another profit by it, no matter that readers might complain. Erasmus understood the printing business well;[4] he was profiting only from what profited his printers too. 'Your admirable book, the *Parabolae*, has arrived safely,' Bade wrote once;

> With your usual modesty you express the wish that I should do what I can for it; but it is your book that will do a great deal for my printing house, except that I have some misgivings about causing other men to suffer the loss many of them inflict on me. Do you take my point? What I mean is this. Such is your reputation among your fellow men, that if you announce a revised edition of any of your works, even if you have added nothing new, they will think the old edition worthless; and losses of this kind have been forced on me in respect of the *Copia*, the *Panegyricus*, the *Moria*, the *Enchiridion* (I had undertaken for 500 copies), and the *Adagia*, of which I had bought 110. It would be thus greatly to our advantage if you would assign each individual work to a single printer, and not revise it until he had sold off all the copies; a practice which you have observed in the *Parabolae* to some extent, if you have given your previous printer prior warning, and not encouraged Martens to print it. On your own encouragement I sent a fair quantity of your *Panegyricus* into Germany; but since they had already been printed there, this was owls to Athens with a vengeance.[5]

Erasmus faced similar complaints from patrons. In 1506, during his second English sojourn, Erasmus was insulted to hear it insinuated that he made a habit of presenting the same piece of work, as if anew, to different patrons. He presented William Warham, the archbishop of Canterbury, with a copy of a translation of Euripides' *Hecuba* dedicated to him. Warham paid Erasmus money for the dedicated presentation, on the spot; but Erasmus thought the amount small and later asked William Grocyn, who had introduced him to Warham, to explain. In Erasmus' account of the episode, Grocyn answered that

> the suspicion told against me that I might perhaps have dedicated the same work elsewhere to someone else. This took me aback; and when I asked him what on earth could have put that idea into his head, he laughed (and a mirthless laugh it was) and said 'It is the sort of thing you people do,' suggesting that men like myself make a habit of it. This barbed shaft remained fixed in my mind, which was not used to such two-edged remarks.

Here too, Erasmus evaded the implied accusation. He took offence at the insinuation but did not deny its substance, and there is evidence suggesting that he may have previously presented this translation elsewhere.[6] On at least one other occasion, Erasmus did give the same piece of work – rededicated and otherwise somewhat revised – to more than one potential patron: the *De conscribendis epistolis* was dedicated and presented, serially, to Robert Fisher, to Adolph of Vere, to William Blount, Lord Mountjoy, and finally to Nicolas Bérault.[7]

Embarrassed as Erasmus was by it, the belief that he dealt on the market in this way – the perception of duplicity about publishing practices that his contemporaries regarded as characteristic of him – had some basis in fact. He did pass over sometimes from sharp into dishonest dealings; most often, he did not. In either case, however, the same basic principle – twice the return for half the work – underlies much of Erasmus' publishing.

Instances of each of these distinctive practices come up in the publication histories of a group of poems Erasmus circulated in England during his first visit, in 1499 and early 1500. Thomas More, who was at the time only a recent acquaintance, presented

him to the Tudor royal children in the summer; Erasmus recounted the episode some years later, in his autobiographical
Catalogus lucubrationum, the 1523 letter to Botzheim in which
he describes the genesis of his poems:

> A long time before that, I had published some verses in a
> mixture of heroic hexameters and iambic trimeters in praise
> of King Henry VII and his children, and also of Britain itself.
> This was three days' work; but work it really was, for it was
> now some years since I had either read or written anything
> in verse. It was extracted from me partly by embarrassment,
> partly by irritation. I had been carried off by Thomas More,
> who had come to pay me a visit on an estate of Mountjoy's
> where I was then staying, to take a walk by way of diversion
> as far as the nearest town; for that was where all the royal
> children were being brought up, except only Arthur, who
> at that time was the eldest.

When the party arrived at Eltham palace, it was welcomed 'in
aulam' by the children and their adult handlers. Then More offered a literary gift of some sort to the eldest of them present:

> More and his friend Arnold greeted the boy Henry, under
> whose rule England now flourishes, and gave him something
> he had written. I was expecting nothing of the kind, and,
> having nothing to produce, I promised that some day I would
> prove my devotion to him somehow. At the time I was
> slightly indignant with More for not having warned me, all
> the more so as during dinner the boy sent me a note, calling
> on me to write something. I went home, and even in despite
> of the Muses, from whom I had lived apart so long, I finished
> a poem within three days. Thus I got the better of my an-
> noyance and cured my embarrassment.[8]

The poem mentioned here is that now known as the 'Prosopopoeia Britanniae,' Erasmus' only poem 'heroico hexametro et
iambico trimetro mixtum' that could be described as 'de laudibus
regis Henrici septimi et illius liberorum, nec non ipsius Britanniae.'[9] As his account indicates, the poem is a bit of flattery,
written hurriedly for presentation to Prince Henry in 1499; the

poem and the covering letter accompanying it were subsequently put into print, initially in late 1500 and then again repeatedly in the early sixteenth century.

In 1922, Percy Allen identified the manuscript Erasmus says he presented to Prince Henry in 1499 with a manuscript in the collections of the British Museum Library, which had come to Allen's attention only lately. It was, he wrote, 'an illuminated MS. (Egerton 1651) of ten leaves octavo, containing Ep. 104 [ie, Erasmus' 1499 letter to Prince Henry] prefixed to a number of poems, most of which are by Erasmus ... Though the MS. does not contain the *Prosopopoeia*, it is very likely a special copy of some of Erasmus' poems prepared for presentation to Prince Henry after the visit to Eltham in the autumn of 1499.[10]

The manuscript in question – a small, thin one – is unusual in that it seems to represent a type of manuscript since become rare, Allen's suggestion that it is a presentation copy notwithstanding. It looks like a contemporary collection of poetry, not made as expensively as possible, for a patron like Prince Henry, but made cheaply, most likely by a humanist scholar for personal use (fig 18). It probably owes its survival, if not to chance, to its associations with Erasmus, which appear to have been close, for the manuscript has none of the qualities as a piece of book-making – illustration, illumination, attractive script, deluxe binding – that would have caused it to be treasured, nor is there evidence to indicate that it was once in royal or noble ownership.[11]

The Egerton manuscript is on paper, not vellum. The often repeated remark that the manuscript is 'illuminated' is mistaken: it is without decoration or ornament of any kind, except for pen-work flourishes, of the simplest sort, which appear more functional (marking the beginning of new items) than decorative. The manuscript was written casually, with much abbreviation and error, only some of it corrected *currente calamo* by the copyist, in a hand of around 1500. Although Erasmus worked as his own copyist, skilfully and well as the need arose, the hand of Egerton 1651 does not appear to be his or a professional's. In spite of numerous mechanical errors, the texts in the Egerton manuscript are unusually good ones; that is, but for various slips of the copyist's pen, the texts are authorial.[12] Included in it are eleven items, all in Latin verse, with the exception of the first; the composition of none of them appears to postdate 1500:

[1] a letter to Prince Henry, in Latin prose, headed 'Generosissimo duci Henrico Herasmus,' written in 1499 in England;

[2] 'In laudem angelorum,' written before early 1496, probably in Paris, comprising subsections headed 'De Michahele,' 'Gabrielis laus,' 'Raphahelis laus,' and 'De angelis in genere';

[3] 'Hendecasillabum carmen,' addressed to Robert Gaguin probably in 1495 in Paris;

[4] 'Epigramma Gaguini,' probably contemporary with [3];

[5] 'In Gaguinum et Faustum Herasmus,' written a few months later than [3] in Paris;

[6] 'Carmen extemporale,' written in 1499 in England;

[7] 'In castigationes Vincentii contra Malleoli castigatoris depravationes,' written in 1496 in Paris;

[8] 'Ad Gaguinum de suis rebus,' written in the spring of 1496;

[9] 'Contestatio salvatoris ad hominem sua culpa pereuntem carminis futuri rudimentum,' probably written in 1499 in England;

[10] 'In dive Anne laudem Rithmi Iambici,' probably written in 1497–9, probably not in England; and

[11] 'Ad Skeltonum carmen ex tempore,' the first three lines only of [6] above, followed by the annotation 'ut habetur.'[13]

As Allen's provisional tone suggests, identifying this manuscript with Erasmus' 1499 presentation to Prince Henry is no straightforward matter. The Egerton manuscript is too humble in design and execution to seem fit for presentation to a prince, even at short notice.[14] Its errors of copying are unlikely to have been made by the writings' author, or to have seemed passable to him without correction.[15] Most to the point, the Egerton manuscript is a collection of items, comprising a representative selection of Erasmus' early verse compositions, yet both the account of the presentation in the *Catalogus lucubrationum* and the letter Erasmus wrote Prince Henry in 1499 to cover his presentation speak as if he presented Henry with a single poem.[16] Finally, the Egerton manuscript wants the singular *carmen* that Erasmus says he presented to Prince Henry in 1499. The letter with which the 'Prosopopoeia Britanniae' was printed in the sixteenth century does occur in the Egerton manuscript, as its first item; the poem itself does not.

Evidently, Erasmus presented a manuscript to Prince Henry in 1499, containing the 'Prosopopoeia Britanniae' and its covering letter. This may have been a somewhat humbler presentation than usual, by the standards of Erasmus as well as those of Henry, given the rush with which it had to be prepared. But the Egerton manuscript is not the presentation manuscript that Erasmus can be believed to have given Prince Henry in 1499; the 1499 presentation is now lost.

There is other evidence that Erasmus circulated his poetry in England in 1499, by means of another, different kind of manuscript. On 20 August 1499, exit from England without royal licence was prohibited,[17] and Erasmus chose to pass the period of obligatory delay in Oxford. While there, from about the beginning of October 1499 until January 1500 when he returned to Paris, Erasmus stayed at St Mary's College, the Oxford hall of his Augustinian order, the prior of which was then Richard Charnock. Charnock introduced members of the local learned community to his guest; in some measure by Charnock's good offices, Erasmus formed in Oxford at this time a number of friendships that were to remain important to him over the years, among them his friendship with Colet.[18]

During this stay with Charnock, about 27 October 1499, Erasmus received a letter from Joannes Sixtinus, a fellow Low-lander also resident in Oxford at the time, praising Erasmus' poetry, which Sixtinus had seen in something that Charnock had made available to him:

> Our most gracious master, Prior Richard Charnock, showed me today some poems written by you which showed uncommon grasp of metre; had they been carefully finished off they would, I think, deserve to earn some little reputation, but, considering that they are said to have been worked out and composed by you extempore, one can hardly believe that a single critic, of any talent at least, after he has finished reading your verses, will fail to award you a place upon the level of the distinguished poets of antiquity. For they are fragrant with a kind of Attic charm, and with the extraordinary sweetness of your mind.[19]

Neither Sixtinus' letter nor Erasmus' surviving response to it – a letter in which, with an at times patently false modesty, Erasmus denigrates his accomplishments[20] – is specific about the poetry in question. Sixtinus refers to a collection of poems by Erasmus ('quaedam abs te carmina,' for example), demonstrating a mastery of various metres ('non vulgari numero trivialive currentia'), at least some of which pretend to have been written 'ex tempore.'[21] The collection must have been such that by it Sixtinus considered himself adequately informed to pronounce on Erasmus' poetic skills: that is to say, again, that the subject of the exchange of letters was a collection, and it would have to have included substantial pieces of writing.

In his reply to Sixtinus, besides belittling his 'versiculos,' Erasmus suggests that the poetry must have been old stuff; his muses, he claims (falsely), have been enjoying ten years' rest:

> As for your urging me to rouse my Muses from slumber, you must understand that it would take the wand of Mercury to wake them ... Indeed I did awaken them recently, much to their indignation, from a sleep of more than ten years' length, and forced them to utter the praises of the king's children. Unwillingly, and still half asleep, they did indite a strain of a kind, a ditty so somnolent that it could lull anyone to sleep. Since the piece vastly displeased me, I had no difficulty in allowing them to slumber again.[22]

The implication of this reference to the 'Prosopopoeia Britanniae' is that it was not among the poems Sixtinus saw; Erasmus had to describe the poem for him, the point being that the poem so extremely displeased Erasmus ('mihi vehementer displiceret') that he would not want anyone to see it.[23]

Because neither Erasmus nor Sixtinus is any more specific about the collection of poems, neither quoting from nor describing or naming any of them, and there is no evidence besides their letters, it is not possible to delineate with precision the contents of the collection or the form that it took.[24] But inasmuch as it seemed sufficient to Sixtinus for identifying the materials in question to say that he had received them from Charnock, Erasmus can be believed to have passed the collection directly to his host Charnock; in other words, the collection Charnock ob-

tained and passed along to Sixtinus most likely derived immediately from Erasmian autographs. Since Erasmus was Charnock's
guest at the time, Charnock may have had access to Erasmus'
foul papers – Erasmus' drafts of the poems, perhaps written on
single, ungathered sheets of paper. These Charnock might have
passed by hand, as they were, to Sixtinus, who was also locally
resident at the time, and from them Sixtinus could have taken
copies of his own. Alternatively, Charnock may have taken copies
of the poems – all that were available to him or only selections
– in a book or on single sheets that he could then have passed by
hand to Sixtinus.

Such a process of transmission would eventually have yielded
up a text like the Egerton manuscript, with its unauthorial errors,
its apparent lacunae – above all, the failure to incorporate the
'Prosopopoeia Britanniae,' which 'vehementer displiceret' its author – and its confused treatment of the 'Carmen extemporale'
addressed to Skelton, which it begins to include twice. It is more
likely that the Egerton manuscript is a humble, defective, confused copy, or had its origin in such a copy, taken from Erasmus'
foul papers, by Charnock or Sixtinus or some other learned Ox-
onian, during Erasmus' stay with Charnock in Oxford in the fall
of 1499, than that the Egerton manuscript is an authorial presentation copy for a Tudor prince.

In any event, the letters that passed between Sixtinus and
Erasmus indicate that, while he was in Oxford in the fall of 1499,
Erasmus again published poetry of his: in some manuscript form
or other, he made a collection of his verse available among learned
peers of his there, much as, shortly before, he had made poetry
of his available at court, in the form of the no longer extant
presentation manuscript he gave Prince Henry in the summer.
This Erasmian collection published at Oxford may have shared
something with the manuscript he had published earlier at court
– if not the 'Prosopopoeia Britanniae,' perhaps the letter to the
prince that had covered it, which reappears at the head of the
Egerton manuscript – and the collection circulated in Oxford was
probably much like the extant Egerton manuscript, if it is not
identical with it. The Egerton manuscript contains the only extant poems that Erasmus could have circulated in Oxford in late
1499. He may have circulated fewer or more poems in Oxford
than are preserved in the Egerton manuscript, or some selection

otherwise variant from it; almost certainly, he would not have been in a position to circulate a collection in Oxford wholly different from that surviving in the Egerton manuscript.

In the absence of additional information, the physical and scribal properties of the Egerton manuscript, the authoritative nature of the texts it transmits, its presumptive English provenance, and, most telling, the fact that its selection of Erasmus' writings includes only pieces written before 1500, the most recent of which are products of Erasmus' first English visit, all taken in light of what the correspondence reveals about Erasmus' publishing activities in England in 1499–1500, make it reasonable to believe that the Egerton manuscript is a by-product of Erasmus' publishing activities in the country at the time. The Egerton manuscript is not what Erasmus gave to Prince Henry; it might be what Joannes Sixtinus saw. It is not an autograph, authorial papers either fair or foul, but appears to be an apograph, a copy taken, at a remove or two, from authorial papers made available by Erasmus – published, in effect – while he was in England in 1499–1500.

The Egerton manuscript is indicative of what Erasmus had to show for himself as a poet by 1500; its contents are representative of the poetry he had written up to the end of his first English visit. The cognate correspondence – the account of his English sojourn in his *Catalogus lucubrationum*, Erasmus' letter to Prince Henry, and the October 1499 exchange between Erasmus and Sixtinus – sheds additional light on his behaviour at the time. The correspondence, the design implicit in the manuscript's selection of contents, and the histories of the texts transmitted by it are guides to how Erasmus published himself: how he used his poetry to make himself known among his contemporaries in England and elsewhere, circulating his work by the variety of means available to him among potential patrons and his learned peers. This evidence makes plain the prosaic, strictly mechanical details of how Erasmus built a reputation for himself in the learned community at the turn of the sixteenth century, and, by building his reputation, attracted the patronage from which he lived.

As a collection, the Egerton manuscript seems well designed to elicit the sort of respectful, favourable response that Sixtinus' letter represents. It is exemplary of what a humanist verse collection published among learned peers should be. It demonstrates its author's range of skills with various forms and literary kinds. It comprehends work in both prose and verse, including verse in several metres, with the emphasis on the less common lyric metres, all of antique descent; the letter; the occasional, personal epigram, as well as longer, more formal verse encomia; hymnlike laudations of saints and angels; narrative verse; and the dramatic monologue. In aggregate, the work shows Erasmus to be in command of an impressive array of technical skills; moreover, the collection characterizes Erasmus as someone able to combine Christian piety and knowledge of *mores antiqui*.

At least equally impressive and important is the collection's assertion of Erasmus' standing. It characterizes him as already well connected and widely esteemed, thereby laying further claims on the respect of the collection's audience. Most suggestive in this regard is its inclusion of an item that Erasmus did not write: an epigram by Robert Gaguin, addressing Erasmus, occurs among the epigrams that Erasmus had circulated in Paris before coming to England. Such an item cannot demonstrate the collection's author's talents; what it can do, however, is establish that Erasmus was so esteemed by Gaguin, a person of considerable international repute, as to have earned his verse correspondence.[25] Other items in the collection function similarly: the Parisian poems and epigrams establish Erasmus' standing with Fausto Andrelini and Augustin Vincent Caminade,[26] and for an audience of Oxford scholars, the letter to Prince Henry and the laudation of John Skelton would demonstrate that Erasmus enjoyed standing at the Tudor court.

The Egerton manuscript makes no mention of the fact; nevertheless, with a possible exception or two, all its writings had been previously published, in some form, before they circulated in England in late 1499. In some cases, the point of pieces' inclusion in the collection would have depended on an audience's ability to recognize that they had been previously published. To be appropriately impressed by the Parisian epigrams and the English court pieces, for example, the audience would have had to take it for granted that these items – the poems for and from Gaguin, Andrelini, and Caminade, the letter to Prince Henry, and the poem addressed to Skelton – had already been published, if only by means of manuscript copies, formal or informal, passed hand to hand. Some of the contents of the Egerton manuscript had certainly been published already, in manuscripts, printed books, or both; the pieces in the collection that had not yet been demonstrably otherwise published by 1499–1500 would later be published again, in manuscripts, printed books, or both.

The Parisian poems were in origin items exchanged among Erasmus and humanists already established at Paris when he came there in the spring of 1495: the two leading lights of local humanism, Robert Gaguin and Fausto Andrelini, and a *vir* more *obscurus*, Augustin Vincent Caminade. Initially, these epigrams would have circulated hand to hand, in ephemeral, ungathered copies, among the concerned individuals and their close associates; such quasi-private circulation was fit for the initial purpose of such epigrams, which was to make introductions and cement connections among humanist peers. Joannes Sixtinus enclosed a poem of this sort with the letter by means of which he introduced himself to Erasmus in 1499.[27] Later, such poems could also be reused, to aggrandize reputation; the poems could be recirculated more widely, beyond the circle of persons immediately concerned in them, asserting for the wider audience their author's claim on the esteem of such estimable persons as Gaguin, Andrelini, and Caminade.

Erasmus' early Parisian poems were all subsequently reused, repeatedly, with the exception of the epigram that he wrote for Caminade. The exception is instructive. In 1498, both Caminade's edition of Vergil and a rival to it were printed at Paris. Erasmus' epigram voices support for Caminade at a time when Erasmus was financially dependent on him, as he was intermittently throughout the period July 1497–December 1500. By the evidence of the Egerton manuscript, Erasmus recirculated the poem, now deracinated from this original context, in England in 1499. He never so used it again, however. By the end of 1500, Caminade had ceased to be of much use or interest to Erasmus: Erasmus' financial situation improved and his reputation grew, while Caminade remained obscure and comparatively impoverished. Thereafter, there was nothing in it for Erasmus to advertise his association with Caminade, or to recirculate the epigram.[28]

Erasmus' other early Parisian poetry had a different publication history. After initial circulation hand to hand, the two poems addressed to Gaguin and to Gaguin and Andrelini were published again at Paris, in 1496, in Erasmus' first verse publication in print, a collection of his poetry known by the title of the piece it features most prominently, the *De casa natalicia Jesu.* Likewise, Erasmus' longer, later poem to Gaguin, the 'De suis fatis,' appeared as Erasmus' second verse publication, in a volume *Sylva odarum* by his friend Willem Hermans, printed at Paris in January 1497.[29] The Egerton manuscript suggests that Erasmus reused these poems again in 1499; knowledge that they had been previously printed might have made them more impressive to his English audience. The poems were later published, again and again, to wider and wider audiences: in the earliest of the versions of the 'collected poems' of Erasmus, the second volume of the 1506–7 edition of the *Adagiorum collectanea,* printed by Bade at Paris; in the 1518 *Epigrammata* printed with More's *Utopia* and *Epigrammata* by Froben at Basel; and elsewhere.[30] Erasmus did invest some editorial labour in these republications, and he also seems on occasion to have revised or polished poems of his before republishing them;[31] nevertheless, he used and reused this group of Parisian poems over a period of twenty-five years and more, to the benefit of his reputation but at minimal cost of authorial labour.

The same story, of publication and republication, with little new investment of labour, can also be told about the other poems represented in the Egerton manuscript, with similar exceptions. Erasmus' suite of poems 'In laudem angelorum' was commissioned, probably in 1495, by an unnamed 'magnus vir' for use in a chapel. The commissioner was disappointed, finding the poetry too avant-garde, and Erasmus was paid less for the work than he had hoped.[32] Still, Erasmus' labour was not wasted: he had the suite printed in his *De casa natalicia* collection in 1496; by the evidence of the Egerton manuscript, he used it again in England in 1499; and the suite was copiously reprinted, at Antwerp in 1503, at Strassbourg in 1515, 1516, and 1517, and twice at Basel in 1518, in editions the publication of which Erasmus authorized.[33]

Similarly, the 'In laudem Anne,' which Erasmus was probably writing while in England in 1499, was published in a presentation copy (with the predictable dedicatory letter) to Anna van Borssele, the Lady of Veere, in January 1501, whom Erasmus visited both before and after his first English sojourn. Again, the

presentation seems not to have earned Erasmus the kind of recompense he would have liked.[34] Still, he was able to use the
work again later to take additional profits: the poem had probably
circulated in informal copies among his English acquaintances in
any case, before it was presented to Anna; Erasmus used it again
in print, in a somewhat amplified version, in a series of books
printed beginning in March 1518; eventually, the poem gained
such esteem as to earn the honour of an edition with learned
scholia, by Jacob Spiegel, printed at Augsburg in 1519.[35]

The poetry Erasmus wrote in England in 1499 for use initially with local audiences – just as the Parisian poems, reused
in England in 1499, had been prepared initially for Parisian audiences – have similar histories of publication and republication.
The exception here is the 'Carmen extemporale,' written for John
Skelton in 1499. Erasmus seems never to have reused it. The only
surviving text is that included in the Egerton manuscript. A copy
passed to Skelton in 1499, when Skelton was in the royal household serving as a tutor to Prince Henry, would have served to
ingratiate Erasmus with him; the poem's collection with other
work and circulation in England later in 1499 would have served
to impress the audience of a collection like the Egerton manuscript with the quality of Erasmus' connections at court. After
the poem had fulfilled its immediate purpose for Erasmus, however, circumstances intervened to diminish its usefulness. Soon
after Erasmus' visit, Skelton left the royal household for a decade
or more of rustication as the parish priest of a Norfolk village.
Thereafter, there was no benefit for Erasmus in cultivating Skelton or advertising whatever connection had existed between them;
neither Skelton nor an acquaintance with Skelton could be turned
to profit anymore.[36]

In the Egerton manuscript occurs a dramatic verse monologue, in the voice of Christ, therein entitled 'Contestatio salvatoris.' The poem's occurrence here, as the 'carminis futuri
rudimentum,' suggests that Erasmus wrote and circulated it in
England in late 1499, and it has been suggested that the poem
was first drafted with John Colet in mind.[37] Nothing more is
heard of the poem until a revised, amplified version of it, entitled
'Expostulatio salvatoris,' appeared in a printed book of about
1510. In the meanwhile, Colet had become dean of St Paul's and
overseen the refoundation of the St Paul's School under the head-

mastership of William Lily, in 1510 – a school, in Erasmus' phrase, 'in which he [sc Colet] meant the children to be educated and brought up in religion as well as booklearning.'[38] At Colet's request, Erasmus – a proponent of the combination of learning and piety to which the St Paul's School was to be dedicated – provided Colet with a collection of his writings for use in the school. The collection included the prose *Concio de puero Jesu*, half a dozen shorter poems, and the 'Expostulatio salvatoris.' It did Erasmus good to have his influence acknowledged as it was by Colet in 1510 or so, when Colet asked for something to use in his school; of course, the Erasmian writings not only were used at the St Paul's School but also were put into print, as a collection, dozens of times and throughout Europe, over the next few years, as writings 'in schola Coletica pronuncianda.'[39] Some of the benefits accruing to his reputation from this episode cost Erasmus no more than the labour of refurbishing an old piece of work, which had served some use already, in 1499, but with which Erasmus had not been able to do anything else in the meanwhile.

Finally, predictably, the letter and poem that Erasmus addressed to Prince Henry in 1499 were also repeatedly reused, with little new investment of labour, to take additional profits. Like the 'In laudem Anne' and the dedicatory letter presented with it to Anna van Borssele in 1501, the 'Prosopopoeia Britanniae' and its dedicatory letter were in origin presentation pieces, contrived to capture the benevolence of their immediate, highly placed audience – Prince Henry, as well as other interested members of the Tudor royal family and household, like Skelton. It is not known what sort of immediate recompense, if any, this particular presentation earned Erasmus. No matter; again, as with the 'In laudem Anne,' Erasmus was able to reuse the work that he had put into the presentation, first, by republishing some of the writing among his learned English compeers soon afterwards. Erasmus disapproved of the 'Prosopopoeia Britanniae,' he told Sixtinus, and there is no evidence to suggest that the poem was recirculated in England during Erasmus' first visit. On the other hand, the dedicatory letter presented with the poem does occur in the Egerton manuscript, suggesting that Erasmus regarded it as useful for impressing such peers of his as would have seen something like the Egerton manuscript in England in 1499.

Unlike John Skelton, Prince Henry remained at court. The

boy who had been a cadet in 1499 became the heir in 1502 and king in 1509. From cultivating such acquaintance as he had begun earlier with the prince, in 1499, Erasmus stood to gain: by cultivating Henry afterwards, Erasmus might yet turn the benevolence he had earned at first into some tangible benefit. Moreover Henry's elevation made Erasmus' connection the more creditable, no matter how tenuous it may have been. By means of the 'Prosopopoeia Britanniae' and its prefatory letter, Erasmus was in a position to advertise that he enjoyed the correspondence – implicitly the intimacy and esteem – of a prudent and benevolent monarch, a connection that Erasmus could manage in public in such a way as to translate it into respect among his peers and the esteem of other patrons. This he did. The 'Prosopopoeia Britanniae' and its 1499 covering letter were republished in print, in half a dozen forms for which Erasmus was responsible, before the end of 1518: in collections of his work or as addenda to other work, as filler, in effect, that also managed to make these other publications more wide-ranging, more flattering representations of Erasmus than they would otherwise have been. The republications in print after 1499 continued to flatter Henry and so should have inclined him further to Erasmus' favour.[40]

The publication histories of the pieces contained in the Egerton manuscript epitomize the range of publishing practices that Erasmus used for circulating his more inconsequential writings; he treated his New Testament work differently. These early publication histories indicate that there were two audiences or markets that Erasmus meant to address: potential patrons, of course, the highly placed individuals who paid him immediately, whose material support he needed to survive; and his humanist peers, those situated more or less equally in the social scheme, who might house or feed him from time to time, who paid him more importantly with their praises, enhancing his reputation and so improving his chances of attracting patronage proper. For Erasmus in the period of the work represented in the Egerton manuscript, around 1495–1500, among the first group were the unnamed 'magnus vir' who commissioned the 'In laudem angelorum,' Anna van Borssele, and Prince Henry; among the second were such persons as Robert Gaguin, Fausto Andrelini, and Augustin Vincent Caminade in Paris, John Colet, Richard Charnock, and Joannes Sixtinus in Oxford, and John Skelton at the Tudor court, as well as others, no doubt, whose contact with Erasmus cannot now be documented.

Erasmus published his writings to these groups in two different configurations: he published single, occasional items, addressed to particular sets of circumstances, whereby he could expect to capture the favour of particular peers or patrons; and he published collections, whereby he could expect to build a general esteem for himself, in a way more focused on him and his talents. The decision to use single items rather than collections would seem to have had more to do with occasions than with audiences, for Erasmus published single items indifferently to peers and patrons. At various times, single items probably went to Gaguin, Andrelini, and Caminade, Skelton and possibly Colet, on the one hand, but also to Prince Henry, Anna van Borssele, and the 'magnus vir.'

Generally, it seems that whereas single items were published to the individuals concerned on the occasions for which they were composed, the circulation of collections was more likely to be prompted by a change of professional situation. So the 'Prosopopoeia Britanniae' and the 'In laudem Anne' were written for particular patrons and were presented singly to them; similarly, Erasmus' epigrams on Caminade's Vergillian *castigationes*, and on Gaguin's *Historia* and Andrelini's *Ecloga* were occasioned by the publication of these works and would have been published singularly to Caminade, Gaguin, and Andrelini, at the time. On the other hand, it was a collection that Erasmus saw printed in Paris soon after his arrival there – the *De casa natalitia Jesu* collection, including his 'In laudem angelorum' and other poetry – and it was a collection that Erasmus circulated when he first came to Oxford in 1499, the papers seen by Charnock and Sixtinus and at least reflected in the surviving Egerton manuscript.

More varied were the tools, the technical means that Erasmus used to put his work into the hands of his target audiences. These means included both printed materials and manuscripts, and manuscripts of discernibly different sorts, each of which had particular properties and meanings, advantages and disadvantages, of which Erasmus appears to have been sensible. Erasmus used cheap, ephemeral manuscripts. Few such copies survive, because of their fragile nature and the uses to which they were put; nevertheless, the correspondence indicates that, like Carmeliano, André, and others, Erasmus too circulated single ungathered pieces of paper, on which could be copied brief items, without decoration.[41] It is possible that Erasmus used similarly ephemeral, unornamented manuscripts, but made up of multiple sheets, for circulating collections of his work; none survives, and none is described unequivocally in the correspondence, but contemporaries of his did so.[42] In any case, Erasmus seems to have used such ephemeral manuscripts strictly for publishing work to his peers; and in this practice, he concurred with his peers.

Patrons – the rich – are different, and for them Erasmus used something else, in this as well concurring with his compeers' practice: deluxe, handmade copies, fit for formal, presentation; of vellum, typically, with pages less closely written, and decorated, with rubrication, other ornamental pen-work and occasionally illustration. It happens that none of the original manuscripts by means of which Erasmus presented his early poetry survives; nevertheless, it is probable that the 'magnus vir' who commissioned the 'In laudem angelorum,' Anna van Borssele, and Prince Henry, even under the circumstances of Erasmus' contact with him in 1499, would have merited books as materially impressive as the surviving Erasmian presentation copies, or the presentation copies of contemporaries like Carmeliano or Alberici.[43]

Erasmus also used print. Because they were mass-produced, printed books, as issued immediately from presses, were strictly for peers and inferiors in the interested community; potential patrons seem to have required manuscripts or manuscript-like printed books specially prepared for the purpose – printed on vellum, with hand-painted illustrations or decoration, and often with unique pages inserted. Like other contemporaries, Erasmus offered potential patrons manuscript copies even when printed copies were or were soon to be available.[44] The salient advantage of printing for Erasmus, however, as also for Bernard André seeing his *Hymni Christiani* published in print, and for others, was that it made possible putting copies into the hands of the many and so made possible greater returns of increased esteem.

Others in England also used these means of publication. In this respect, Erasmus distinguished himself only in that he managed to use all of the available means all of the time. He was able, industrious, and interested in matters of moment, and so he was prolific; however, he was able to publish as much as he did, by such a variety of means, over such a long period of time, also because he published everything more than once. His writings almost always went on from publication in manuscript to publication in print, or from one sort of manuscript to another, and from singular to collected republication, in manuscript or print, in a bewildering range of configurations, often also undergoing revision along the way. One consequence of this material and formal variety, and of the frequency with which Erasmus published and republished, is that Erasmian bibliography is a tangle. From Erasmus' perspective, on the other hand, skilful management of his various options for publication was a tool by which to make a living.

 Chapter 5

Printed and Manuscript Reduplication of the Same Piece of Writing:

Robert Whittinton's Printed *Opusculum* of 1519 and a Manuscript for Cardinal Wolsey

Robert Whittinton was a prominent humanist grammarian who, in about 1519, began to suffer from ambition. Attracting the rewards he wanted for the sort of literary and scholarly work he could do entailed making a name for himself, and building a reputation entailed writing and publishing, both to peers and to patrons. Evidently, he grasped these basic principles and, by adhering to them, succeeded. In 1519, when Whittinton began to seek court preferment, he took both the avenues of approach to his goal that the work of his humanist predecessors and contemporaries would have taught him to regard as likely to yield results. On the one hand, he sought to aggrandize his reputation, his relative standing among his peers, competitively; at the same time, he sought to ingratiate himself with potential patrons, directly. To heighten his standing among the learned, he picked a fight in public, which he could have expected to win, with a putatively rival group of humanist educators, publishing various polemics against them, answering back imagined and real attacks against him. To attract patronal favours immediately, he composed a series of poems flattering his well-placed marks and flattering himself, and these he published, in print and, in one instance, in a deluxe manuscript copy duplicating contents of the printed book, which he presented to Thomas Cardinal Wolsey.

    The kind of reduplicative publication that Whittinton practised – making a manuscript copy of a part of his printed book and then presenting the manuscript copy to a potential patron – was common. Writers did it, and even printers did it, basically because manuscript copies, by their nature, could be expected to make a more favourable impression on potential patrons.[1] Reduplication, as in the case of Whittinton's work, helps clarify the difference in meaning between manuscript and printed publication. In the period of transition from manuscript to print – when publication in print had become possible but before it became synonymous with 'publication' *tout court* – it seems that 'manuscript' meant one thing, and 'printed book' meant another. Whittinton and his humanist contemporaries were attuned to the difference, which they treated as of sufficient importance to merit observing and preserving. For the sake of the distinction, they did what Whittinton did in 1519: they went to the expense of creating reduplicative handmade copies of writings already available in print.

The decision to go to this added expense is all the more remarkable in Whittinton's case, because printed publication had an unusual importance for him and his ambitions. For others who printed collections of their verse at the time – André, Erasmus, Ammonio, More, and others – printing figured simply as the more effective tool for reputation-making; it made possible the circulation of their writings in larger numbers of copies than would otherwise have been possible. No doubt printing had this attraction for Whittinton, too, but it had an added appeal for him, by virtue of the nature of the poetry he put into print. Printing's ability to broadcast pieces of writing widely made it useful for spreading propaganda,[2] and the poetry that Whittinton collected and saw printed in 1519 was propagandistic, most emphatically in the case of the poems in the volume addressed to Wolsey. These advocate the cardinal's positions on particular issues, recalling, for example, the specificity of Pietro's Carmeliano's discussion of the conditions of Henry VII's accession in 1486. In other words, some part of Whittinton's appeal to his potential patron Wolsey would have been not only his ability to frame Wolsey's positions in an attractively humanist vocabulary but also this access to print, and, by means of print, access to a sizeable learned audience. Whittinton's success as a petitioner for Wolsey's favour depended on demonstrating his skill as a propagandist; demonstrating his skill as a propagandist on Wolsey's behalf in turn depended on his ability to see his propaganda into print. To the extent that printing could matter to the cardinal in this way, it had also to matter to Whittinton. Nevertheless, when it came time for Whittinton to make his work known to Wolsey, he chose, neither a copy of the printed book nor a dressed-up printed copy, but a specially fabricated, deluxe manuscript presentation copy.

Unlike Alberici, Carmeliano, André, Erasmus, and others prominent in the early history of humanism in England, Whittinton was a native, and his career appears to have been entirely English.[3] He was educated at the Magdalen College School – William Waynflete's foundation, one of two or three English schools already putting humanist educational principles into practice as early as the 1480s – where he probably knew as masters John Stanbridge, the school's most important fifteenth-century master in educational terms, and John Holt, subsequently tutor to Cardinal Morton's boys at Lambeth Palace and to Prince Henry in the royal household, who was also something of a mentor to the young Thomas More. With all that happened later, it is easy to lose sight of the fact that Wolsey, who also suffered from ambition, was also at the Magdalen College School early in his career; he was a graduate of the school and had been its master in 1498, a time when Whittinton, too, was probably affiliated with it in some capacity.[4] Whittinton went on to Oxford University, and was awarded a laureation in 1513, an advanced degree in grammar, evidently, taken by persons already experienced as masters, who typically went on from it to pursue further careers in education.[5]

In 1510, John Stanbridge died, and responsibility for reissuing and editing his numerous, widely influential grammar-books fell to Whittinton. In addition, in about 1511, textbooks under Whittinton's own name began to issue from the presses of Wynkyn de Worde, Stanbridge's former printer. These Stanbridge-Whittinton grammar books and the books credited to Whittinton's sole authorship – printed and reprinted by de Worde at a remarkable rate throughout the second decade of the sixteenth century and beyond, comprising a significant portion of a prolific printer's business – made up the preeminent series of books in use in England for teaching grammar during the early sixteenth century, not wholly dislodged from market dominance until the promulgation of the 'Lily grammar' by royal fiat in 1540.[6]

The fight Whittinton picked in 1519, when be began to seek a change, has come to be known as the 'Grammarians' War,' and his antagonists were chiefly William Horman and William Lily, masters at Eton and the St Paul's School respectively.[7] In late 1519, for instructing his schoolboys at Eton, Horman had had printed a *Vulgaria*, a book of English phrases, accompanied by exemplary Latin equivalents, to be used as a basis for translation and composition exercises. Predictably, in the preface to his book, Horman adopted the expedient of running down others' work in order to build up his own; Whittinton took umbrage, understandably perhaps, in light of the prominence of his work in established grammar curriculums.

Horman's remarks were innocuous, exemplifying a well-worn topos of humanist reputation-making; and Whittinton's response was so exaggerated as to appear over-determined. He was touchy, it seems. Soon after the publication of Horman's *Vulgaria*, someone naming himself 'Bossus' – almost certainly Whittinton – nailed to the door of the St Paul's School a poem attacking Horman and William Lily, who had contributed commendatory verses to Horman's book. From this provocative gesture ensued a lengthy exchange of apologies and counter-attacks, which took the form of Latin epigrams and verse epistles from the pens of Lily, Horman, Whittinton, John Skelton, and others.

Some of the writings may have been publicly posted, as was the epigram at St Paul's; more likely, the various polemics were circulated hand to hand, within and between the opposing camps, in ephemeral manuscript copies.[8] Belatedly, but still remarkably, the controversy also made its way into print. By the spring of 1520, Whittinton had had his own *Vulgaria* printed, as an exemplary answer to Horman, and early on, he also took to using the title pages of new editions of his old books for publishing epigrams against his opponents. Only in 1521, however, towards the end of the affair, did print figure more directly in it. Wynkyn de Worde, the publisher of Whittinton's grammars, printed in a single volume three of Whittinton's contributions, republishing together pieces written at different points over the course of the affair and no doubt previously circulated separately; Richard Pynson, the publisher of the *Vulgaria* of Horman, printed a collection of the polemical contributions of Horman's party, again pieces of writing originally put about separately, in manuscript. The printed volumes seem to have concluded the *bellum grammaticale* by summing it up; no more attacks either way are known to have been made.[9]

The consensus is that Whittinton lost. Lily is the hero of the story of the introduction of humanist pedagogy into English schools, and the tendency has been to represent the Grammarians' War as a triumph of the new learning – putatively championed by Horman and Lily – over bad old medieval pedagogy – as personified in Whittinton. In fact, both sides were in the same humanist camp; both endorsed the notion that 'true knowledge of lernyng that hath long tym be hydde in profounde derknes by dylygence of men in this tyme is nowe brought to open lyght,' as Whittinton put it.[10] At issue was status within this camp; and although, in the long run, after mid-century, Whittinton's reputation suffered by the controversy, in the short term it seems to have heightened his public stature.

The episode is instructive about humanist publication, perhaps most so as evidence of the use of public posting. Luther's theses and their consequences were so unprecedented that his mode of publishing them now tends to appear likewise unprecedented. In fact, posting pieces of writing in public places was a common, time-honoured way of making writing public, particularly controversial and topical writing, both before the advent of printing and afterwards in circumstances where access to presses was limited – even then, public posting must still have had vivid effects that printing could not match. Contemporary learned writers besides Whittinton did it; at the outset of the Grammarians' War, Whittinton, like Luther, was only using the most efficient and rhetorically effective means available to him for putting his views before the interested public.[11]

The printers' belated involvement in the controversy is likewise instructive. Evidently, by 1521, the controversy had generated sufficient interest that both de Worde and Pynson thought they could make money out of it; each imagined it worthwhile to produce a summary volume of the affair. The printers' actions suggest that, whatever its effects in the longer term, the short-term consequence of the Grammarians' War was an increase in public prominence for those who participated in it.[12] It is difficult to calculate the consequences of such augmented standing for the fortunes of Whittinton or the other participants; nevertheless, Whittinton did attract royal patronage to himself in the course of the Grammarians' War. He was appointed master of the henchmen – tutor to the royal pages, in other words – at some point in 1521.[13]

Most of the responsibility for the Grammarians' War seems to have been Whittinton's. Nailing the epigram up at Lily's schoolroom door set it off, and his subsequent sallies fuelled it; the contributions of Lily and Horman were always apologies, answering Whittinton back. On the other hand, Whittinton had required the provocation of Horman's *Vulgaria* to begin. From this perspective, starting a public fight, in order to aggrandize his reputation, in order to better his chances of attracting patronage, was not a process over which Whittinton could exercise complete control. All he could do was take advantage of the opportunity Horman offered him, and hope for a good result. There was not this degree of accident about Whittinton's other publishing activities in 1519. Before the outbreak of the Grammarians' War late in the year, Whittinton had already tried the direct approach to potential patrons and benefactors among his peers in the learned community. In April 1519, the publisher of Whittinton's grammars issued what was for him, and for English printing generally, an unusual book: a collection of contemporary English humanist poetry in Latin.

A small number of English and England-based humanists had seen their work printed – including Linacre, Ammonio, André, and two or three others – but always abroad rather than in England; and English printers had printed a few works of some humanist interest – Theodoric Rood's edition of the letters of Phalaris or Caxton's edition of contemporary Venetian correspondence, for example, both edited by Pietro Carmeliano – but always work only of pedagogic value, like the Phalaris, or of topical import, like the Venetian letters. Before April 1519, no English printer had published anything of general interest by an English humanist, for the domestic learned market. After the publication of Whittinton's collection, other such books followed shortly: the

Epigrammata of John Constable, issued from the press of Pynson in September 1520, the printed books summing up the Grammarians' War in early 1521, a selection of the poetry of William Lily in 1522, and others. The printers' behaviour in this period suggests the emergence of a collective perception among them that the home market for contemporary humanist writing had reached critical mass, the point at which the demand had grown great enough to make aiming printed products directly at it seem likely to prove profitable.[14]

De Worde's publication of Whittinton's poetry may bespeak a new willingness on the printer's part to bet on the profitability of the humanist market, though it may be that in this case the writer brought some special form of pressure to bear, monetary or otherwise. Whittinton's grammars may have yielded such an important part of de Worde's profits that Whittinton was in a position to ask de Worde to print other work of his to an anticipated loss. Or Whittinton may have paid de Worde outright to print his book of poems.

A letter Erasmus wrote to Aldus Manutius in 1507, proposing a new edition of Erasmus' translations from Euripides, adumbrates the range of relations that might obtain between writers and printers:

> I should consider that my efforts were given immortality if they were to be published in your type, especially that small font which is the most elegant of all. In this way, the book will be very small and the publication will cost but little. If you find it convenient to take the business on, I shall supply you the corrected copy that I send by the bearer's hand free of charge, and ask only that you should send me just a few copies for presentation to my friends. And I should have no hesitation in arranging for the printing at my own cost and risk, had I not to leave Italy in a few months' time; so that I should like the business to be finished as soon as possible. It would hardly take ten days. Now if you absolutely insist that I take one or two hundred copies, though Mercury, the god of profit, is not as a rule particularly favourable towards me and it will be highly inconvenient to have this parcel conveyed, still I will not boggle even at this, so long as you fix a fair price in advance.[15]

No doubt Whittinton's 1519 book of poems was printed by de Worde on the basis of one of the three kinds of relations suggested here: first, the printer paid the writer for copy to print, in cash or in kind (the implication of 'free of charge' is that on other occasions or in other circumstances, there would have been a payment for the corrected exemplar; in the present case, Erasmus asks instead for 'just a few copies' of the printed book that he could present, or sell or trade); second, the writer paid the printer for a portion of the print run, an arrangement whereby writer and printer shared immediate costs, in effect, for production and distribution, each then taking profits separately, from sales of the book ('if you absolutely insist that I take one or two hundred copies ... still I will not boggle even at this, so long as you fix a fair price in advance'); or third, the writer bore all costs of production and responsibility for sales ('I should have no hesitation in arranging for the printing at my own cost and risk, had I not to leave Italy in a few months' time').[16]

Printers had the upper hand – the power to decide, in view of each option's potential for profit in a particular case, which sort of business relations would obtain – because they had the greater economic clout. Even when writer and printer shared immediate costs – of paper, ink, and labour – the greater ongoing expenses, of acquiring and maintaining a press, were carried by printers alone. Nevertheless, all the arrangements to which Erasmus alludes provided benefits or the possibility of benefits for both printer and writer. The differences among them are matters of the apportionment of risk: in the case of the first option, the writer's benefit is looked after in advance, and the printer takes the chance; in the case of the second, the risk is shared by partners, in effect, each individually responsible for recouping investment by looking after the marketing of part of the edition; and in the case of the third, the printer takes profits in advance and the writer runs the marketing risk. For the printing of Whittinton's grammars – which de Worde did continually, for years – de Worde's interest would have been best served by persuading Whittinton to settle for some version of the first option; for the printing of Whittinton's verse *encomia* of 1519, Whittinton may have had to settle for some version of the third.

The volume that issued from de Worde's press in April 1519 was a small one, thirty-six pages in octavo, entitled *Opusculum*

Roberti Whittintoni in florentissima Oxoniensi achademia Laureati,[17] comprising the following dozen items:

[1] A comparatively brief, introductory epigram, in praise of the king, 'Ad invictissimum principem Henricum regem ... de octenario numero';

this followed by a group of pieces forming the core of the book, and its bulk, addressed to Cardinal Wolsey:

[2] a generally introductory epigram addressing the cardinal, fulsomely entitled 'Ad reverendissimum in Christo patrem et dominum Thomam miseratione divina Eboracensis Archiepiscopem, Divae Ciciliae trans Tiberim Cardinalem presbiterum, Apostolice sedis legatum de latere, metuendissimique principis Henrici octavi Angliae et Franciae regis cancellarium dignissimum, sui humillimi Roberti Whittintoni Laureati epygramma'; followed by
[3] a prose letter, introducing the topic of the matter that follows, virtue and Wolsey's embodiment of its several distinct kinds, 'Ad eundem dominum cardinalem eiusdem Roberti Whittintoni Epistola';
[4] a poem 'De difficultate iusticiae servandae in republica administranda,' in 167 hexameters, the longest piece of verse in the book, addressed 'Ad eundem dominum Cardinalem et legatum';
[5] an eighteen-line verse 'Appendix' to the 'De difficultate iusticiae servandae'; and
[6] an envoy-like epigram for the same, 'Ad eundem dominum eiusdem Whittintoni'; and finally,
[7] a prose encomium of Wolsey's virtues, the longest piece in the book, 'Ad eundem dominum legatum et cardinalem eiusdem Whittintoni panegyricon a laude quattuor virtutum Cardinalium.'

This series of pieces addressed to Wolsey is followed by verse laudations of others prominent at court:

[8] a verse encomium of the king's reluctant brother-in-law Charles Brandon, duke of Suffolk, 'Ad illustrissimum prin-

cipem Carolum Brandon Suffolciae ducem Roberti Whittintoni laureati poetae Oxoniensis panegyricon';
[9] a verse encomium of the king's lately appointed coun-
sellor Thomas More, 'Ad illustrissimum virum Thomam
Morum praepotentissimi regis Angliae Henrici octavi con-
siliarium ac utriusque linguae censorem perspicacissimum
Roberti Whittintoni incultum carmen';
[10] an envoy appended to it, 'Ad eundem eiusdem Whittintoni hexastichon';
[11] a verse encomium of John Skelton, 'Eiusdem Roberti
Whittintoni in clarissimi Scheltonis Lovaniensis poetae
laudes epygramma'; and finally
[12] an invective epigram 'in quendam Zoilum,' who is not
otherwise identifiable.[18]

In format and design, by comparison with contemporary
printed products, this book appears modest or even mean. Its
title page is decorated with a woodcut, showing the royal arms
supported by a pair of angels (fig 19), but it is a stock woodcut
that de Worde used over and over again. It is ill proportioned
for its setting here, a make-do occurrence; its width had to be
built up, with stock type-ornaments, and still the fit is wrong.
Ornamental capitals occur at the beginning of each item, but
stock capitals again. Two sizes of type were used: a smaller font
for headings and prose, and a larger font for the verse (fig 20);
both were black-letter fonts, however, rather than Roman, the
type otherwise associated with humanist work. The choice of an
octavo format and other design decisions would appear to have
been determined by the printer's wish to economize; the result,
as an example of contemporary book-making, was an undistin-
guished product, perhaps even typographically off-putting.
    For a general learned readership, the appeal of the writings
that de Worde had packaged so demeaningly would have resided
in their literary stylishness, apart from any political or other import they may have had. Whittinton's ability to turn a phrase is
now most widely known from his description of Thomas More
as 'a man for all seasons';[19] the same skill informs his Latin verse,
which also shows an engaging agility of mind. Above all, however, his verse is strikingly, ostentatiously learned. Whittinton
uses Greek terms frequently and informedly, usually preserving

their Greek morphology, rather than Latinizing the declensions: *prothoplastea, Protheos, cataplasma, athleta, sophos, stratagemate, tyche, Atropos,* and *scomma* among them. In addition, Whittinton tends to choose a more strictly classical Latin term, the more obscure the better, in preference to terms that had remained or become current in post-ancient usage: *Solymi,* for example, or *Nabathea,* or *Dindyma.* This preference for recondite antiquities extends also to references to figures of myth and history. The predictable allusions occur, to 'Cneum Pompeium,' Artaxerxes, 'rigidus Cato,' Croesus, Themistocles, Brutus, Sulla, Hyppolita, Solon, Alexander, Vespasian, Cyrus, Ulysses, Achilles, Nestor (who is also called 'Pylius'), Themis, Achates, and so on. More obscure references are also put to use, though, indeed with dismaying frequency: to Ctesiphon, the 'Peonis artes' (medicine), Cleon, Chiron, 'Pompilius' (Numa), Philoctetes, the Orchomeni, Ocnus, 'Pleiones nepos' (Mercury), a poet 'genuit quem Teia tellus' and another 'quem tuleratque Paros' (Anacreon and Archilocus), and Tyrtaeus. Likewise Whittinton predictably quotes Sophocles, Plato, Cicero (who is also called 'Arpinas orator'), Vergil, Horace, Seneca, and Homer; but he also quotes Chryssipus, Cratippus, Mark Antony, Bias, and Apollonius of Tyana. Finally, the concern to demonstrate the writer's humanist credentials that animates these verbal and topical tricks seems also to have extended to the book's editorial finishing at press. Unlike most other comparable contemporary printed books, the papers from which this one was typeset had been so carefully prepared, or the compositors who set it were so instructed, or proofs of it were corrected with such care, that it approaches orthographical perfection: ancient names appear spelled 'correctly,' and the ancient diphthong *ae* is regularly spelled out.

These features of the book flattered its author. Like other collections published in manuscript, this printed one showed what its author could do; it demonstrated an outstanding grasp of matters that counted in the learned community: knowledge of, and skill at using, ancient history, myth, literature, and languages, including Greek. It probably also flattered Whittinton that the collection imputes to him enjoyment of the intercourse of his betters – the king, the noble courtier-counsellor, and the chief officer of state – as well as prominent learned peers of his – Skelton and More. On the other hand, for putative connections of this sort to flatter Whittinton, his audience would have to be willing to credit him with genuine acquaintance with Henry, Brandon, Wolsey, Skelton, and More; they would have to believe that Whittinton had at least presented copies of his work to them and had earned some measure of their esteem by doing so. There is nothing about the printed book to suggest manuscript presentations of this sort; neither do the poems themselves foster the notion that they had already been presented at court.

From this perspective, in printed form the poems may have done more to flatter the persons whom they address than the person who wrote them. The use of print mattered in this regard, for thereby the persons addressed in Whittinton's poems stood to gain and their benefit could have been expected to return something to Whittinton. In the case of Skelton and More, Whittinton's learned peers, the benefits were indirect. Both already stood high in the esteem of the learned community and the court. Skelton's court affiliation dated back to the late 1480s, and, although he had spent about a decade away from court, approximately 1502–12, by 1519 he had been back for some years and had not yet begun his series of public attacks on Cardinal Wolsey.[20] By 1519, More had published and republished the *Utopia*, and had more recently been appointed to Henry VIII's council; Whittinton's poems use these facts to praise him.[21]

Whittinton's 1519 encomia of these two men might have ingratiated the poems' author with them, if the poems had only been presented to Skelton and More in manuscript copies. In print, however, the same poems served to broadcast the two men's praises more widely. For such advertisement, however negligible or intangible its consequences, both Skelton and More may have felt grateful to Whittinton, and in this connection, their positions in the Grammarians' War are noteworthy. More stood aloof from it altogether. He was busy with a quarrel of his own at the time, with Germain de Brie; nevertheless, whatever his reason, and even though the effective chief of the anti-Whittinton party was More's long-time intimate William Lily, More did not contribute.[22] Skelton behaved differently. Though there is nothing to suggest an affiliation between Whittinton and Skelton prior to the April 1519 publication, Skelton lent Whittinton his support in the controversy thereafter.[23]

Whittinton's poems for Henry VIII and Charles Brandon in

the collection are similar: generally flattering and so probably ingratiating, and, because of the use of print for their publication, more profitably flattering than they would otherwise have been.[24] In a few passages, however, the poem for Brandon does something that those for Henry VIII, More, and Skelton do not: it addresses issues. Brandon was undergoing rehabilitation at the time of the publication of Whittinton's book, and Whittinton may have meant his poem to further the process. Of ignoble birth, Brandon had been a favourite of the king's and had enjoyed constant support from the similarly low-born Chancellor Wolsey. Brandon had drawn Henry's displeasure down on himself by clandestinely marrying the king's sister in 1515. The couple retired from court, but by 1520, when Brandon accompanied Henry to France for the 'Field of the Cloth of Gold' meetings, the duke of Suffolk had been fully restored to the king's good graces. Wolsey had probably contributed something towards the restitution.[25] Whittinton's poem in praise of the king's re-emergently important boon-companion raises the issue of low birth, a source of complaint against Brandon (as also against Wolsey) among the counsellors and courtiers who opposed his influence with Henry;[26] it also addresses the problem of resistance to Brandon's rehabilitation. Because of Brandon's virtues, the king favours him: 'Therefore King Henry VIII embraces you with great love, enriching your merit with honour.' If the duke is so virtuous as to have earned the king's manifest esteem, and 'if outstanding virtue justly obligates us to love,' Whittinton asks, 'why should envious Fortune still be spiteful to Charles?'[27]

A similar topicality looms larger in the central section of Whittinton's 1519 book, the suite of writings addressed to Wolsey. Here again, printing made possible broadcasting the views espoused in the writings among a larger audience than could have been reached by means of manuscripts; but because the views espoused were of greater consequence for Wolsey, the potential for reaching a wider audience was in turn also of greater consequence. Letting the learned many know how highly Whittinton could praise More, Skelton, or the king, or the principles that might be invoked to justify the duke of Suffolk's return to court, could have made relatively little difference to More or Brandon or the others; persuading the learned many that specific policies of Wolsey's were good policies was another matter.

Whittinton's ultimate purpose was to attract Wolsey's patronage, as he makes clear enough: his wish for Wolsey is 'May
the benificent Fates grant you the highest honours, and may the
gods also grant that you be mindful of my welfare.' But in order
to cause Wolsey to 'remember your servant Whittinton from time
to time,'[28] Whittinton had to do something for the cardinal in
the first place. Whittinton flatters Wolsey, lauding his qualities
at length – 'in contemplating the immensity of which I seem to
measure out a journey everywhere larger and more impassable
than Ocean itself'[29] – for the most part in general terms, not much
different from those he had used to praise Henry, Brandon, More,
and Skelton.

Whittinton chose to focus, however, with some persistence,
on Wolsey's administration of English justice, an area in which
he made important, popular contributions in the early years of
his lord chancellorship. The first of the two main pieces addressed
to Wolsey is a poem 'De difficultate iusticiae servandae in republica administranda'; the other is a prose 'Panegyricon a laude
quattuor virtutum cardinalium' – either 'the cardinal virtues' or
'the cardinal's virtues' – putting justice ahead of the others, 'for
this virtue by itself (to use the words of Cicero) is mistress and
queen of all virtues.'[30] The poem is ostensibly counsel on how
iusticia is *servanda in republica administranda*: 'I warn you,'
Whittinton writes Wolsey ponderously, for example, 'hold to the
middle way, between Scylla and Charybdis.'[31] As here, the advice
tendered is too general to be of much use; in any case, the point
is not so much to counsel Wolsey as to praise him. The poem
characterizes his responsibilities as difficult and burdensome; for
discharging them, it claims, Wolsey is equipped with his own
considerable abilities and a special dispensation from God:

> What earthly matter is more arduous, or what more full of
> labours, than preserving justice in administering civil law,
> balancing the scales equitably? ... Still, if such mystical gifts
> have been given by the gods above to any mortal, in this
> age the high priest Wolsey is he whom the charitable spirit
> enriches with the gift of counsel, that the whole world might
> hymn his fame.[32]

In the prose treatise, Whittinton emphasizes Wolsey's ac-

cessibility and the even-handedness with which he dispensed justice, at a time when the saying had been 'justice is a fat fee;'[33]
and he calls attention to Wolsey's most public, most popular
contribution to contemporary English justice: his campaign against
private profiteering, especially enclosure. 'It would seem criminal,' Whittinton begins,

> to pass over in silence that most holy decree of our senate,
> on the opening of enclosed fields, which was recently ra-
> tified, with you as its author; in it, the greatness of your
> soul shines forth with a wonderful splendour. For they are
> to be held brave and magnanimous, says Cicero, not who
> do, but who defend against injury. On this account, the deeds
> of mighty Edgar, once king of the English, are worthy of
> memory; for it is said that, inspired by the same greatness
> of soul, he drove out of this realm not only all the wild
> beasts but also all the beastly men. With like soul, you strive
> to root out, not the beastly men, but the beastly customs of
> those men who, hating the gods and humankind, spurn the
> community of life and measure all in terms only of their
> own benefit ... You open enclosed fields; you uproot the
> hedges and destroy them; you order demolished buildings
> rebuilt anew; huge fields, long unaccustomed to the plough,
> you order planted and farmed. Carry on, therefore, as you
> have begun, and persevere bravely on this field of battle;
> and as long as England stands unconquered, your honour,
> your name, and your praises will always remain.[34]

Whittinton's work for Wolsey did this something specific
and definite for the lord chancellor: it made propaganda for him,[35]
singling out for praise his most prominent policies in the areas
of domestic administration with which he was at the time most
to be associated. From this perspective, the use of print was of
consequence for both Wolsey and Whittinton. Wolsey would have
needed no persuading of the rightness of his own positions; to
do something for Wolsey, and so to earn something by way of
return, Whittinton had to put his favourable representation of
Wolsey's work about more widely. He had to see the work printed,
and this he proved able to do.

A number of factors seem likely to have contributed to Whittinton's success at gaining a court appointment in 1521, while the Grammarians' War was still going on. One of them may have been the public prominence brought him by his role in the controversy; another, the quality of the verse he published just before its onset. His efforts to ingratiate himself with persons placed to further his ambitions may also have helped – his encomia of Skelton, More, Brandon, Henry VIII, and Wolsey. Most important, though, were probably his relations with and work on behalf of Wolsey. Wolsey was probably the more susceptible to Whittinton's appeals because some affiliation between them should have existed already: Whittinton would have been known to Wolsey from Wolsey's time at the Magdalen College School. From this perspective, Whittinton's decision to single out Wolsey by the shape he gave his April 1519 publication makes sense. Whittinton not only gave over the bulk of his printed collection, and its centre-piece, to praise of Wolsey, however; he also singled out Wolsey by presenting to the cardinal a manuscript copy of those portions of the printed book addressed to him.

The manuscript in question is not egregiously expensive, perhaps, when compared to other manuscripts given as gifts to persons of Wolsey's stature. In comparison to a copy of the cognate printed volume, however, it is a more lavish book. On vellum, it has larger pages and larger margins than the printed book, and varieties of decoration that the printed copies wanted: fine borders, and initial capitals in colour and gilt, including a small illumination, of Wolsey's arms, at the beginning of the volume (fig 21). Whittinton's presentation survives in a contemporary binding – a rare occurrence – and he seems to have gone to extraordinary expense for its provision as well, if he was indeed responsible for it: it is the earliest English bookbinding with gilt decoration to have survived (fig 22).[36]

There are other English presentation manuscripts of this sort – deluxe duplicates, in effect, of work already in print. Carmeliano, for example, and Linacre presented such books in England before the end of the fifteenth century.[37] In the instance of Whittinton's encomia of Wolsey, however, the book is the more remarkable because of the importance of print to Whittinton's project. Under the circumstances, Whittinton might well have chosen to present a copy of the printed book, possibly a specially prepared, decorated or augmented printed copy, in order to confirm that the work had in fact reached print. Alternatively, he might have chosen to present a manuscript done up to look practically indistinguishable from the printed book, and so have the best of both worlds, both a manuscript presentation and an intimation of his use of print.[38] That even in these circumstances Whittinton elected to present a manuscript copy, of the standard humanist presentation type, making no allusion to the existence of any printed copy, bespeaks the persistent importance of manuscripts, even after the advent of printing.

Manuscripts persisted in having special importance for two reasons. On the one hand, a manuscript copy could be produced more cheaply – and so more freely – than a printed book. Equipped with no more than paper and writing implements, any literate person could make one. Because of the technology's low cost and simplicity, it was possible for individuals to publish themselves in manuscript, unconstrained by the economic, social, and political factors that limit access to more costly and complicated publishing technologies like printing. Consequently, when freedom to put work about and a wish to do so surreptitiously or at little cost were prime requisites, manuscripts continued to be found useful.[39] The publication of epigrams and other occasional work in ephemeral manuscripts, by their circulation hand to hand among one's personal contacts, was one such use common among the humanist writers of early Tudor England.

On the other hand, it is also possible for manuscript copies to be more costly than printed books, and it would seem to have been this potential for expense that made manuscripts the preferred method of publication to patrons.[40] Manuscripts have shortcomings that printed books need not have. They are always imperfect and irregular, in ways that the mechanical reproduction of texts can reduce or eliminate altogether. In these regards, printed books might have been preferable; in fact, it would seem to have been just such irregularity – whatever evidence of manual production made it possible to distinguish a hand-made book from machined goods – that rendered manuscripts persistently desirable for patrons.

The pages of a manuscript book were more susceptible of costly decoration than those of a printed book; redprinting, woodcuts, and ornamental capitals in printed books attempted to substitute for, but could never be as expensive as, the hand-painted rubrication, illustrations, and illuminations of manuscript books, in terms of the cost of either labour or materials. Some printers, most extensively Antoine Vérard, tried the expedient of introducing hand-painted illustrations into specially prepared copies of printed books, in the places where simple woodcuts would otherwise have appeared; still, even specially decorated printed copies could not match manuscripts.[41] What printed books would always fail to do – Colard Mansion bankrupted his business, in part, by trying – was to reproduce scribal idiosyncrasy, the irregularities born inevitably of the process of copying by hand. Such irregularities need not have been (and ideally were not) matters of scribal error, deformations of the textual materials; they were matters of presentation, of the lay of the textual materials on the page. Mansion had cut for his press exceedingly costly fonts of type, comprising as many as one hundred and sixty sorts – one hundred and sixty differently designed kinds of pieces of type; nevertheless, pages printed in these fonts are palpably more regular in appearance than hand-written pages.[42]

In the final analysis, imagining all else to be equal, scribal idiosyncrasy left irreducible evidence that a quantity of manual labour had been expended on the production of the book in question, and evidence of the expenditure of labour was what made manuscripts more valuable to patrons than printed books. In material terms, manual copying and manual decoration produced books; at the same time, however, less concretely, they also served as signs, for humanist writer and patron alike, of a conspicuously lavish expenditure of human effort. For the humanist author using deluxe presentation manuscripts, this lavish expenditure of labour asserted self-respect, a belief in the worth of the literary work put into the form, work shown by the form to be intended for serious attention. At the same time, lavish expenditure in production also articulated respect for the patron for whom the book had been prepared. A conspicuously lavish book was as valuable an object to receive as it was costly to give, and in part at least because such a book could flatter its recipient in a particular way, no matter its literary contents.

Expensive books represent their recipients as the opposite of needy, to the extent that the costs incurred in such books' production were not needful costs.[43] Simply useful, utilitarian copies might have been offered instead, and the labour to have been invested in ornament would have remained available for making something else, something equally or more utilitarian. Conspicuously wasteful expenditure on book production – expenditure beyond that needed to produce plain copies – implies that the person for whose sake the costs are incurred has risen above any need for the useful, into a social and economic position where the only remaining want is for means by which to demonstrate a freedom from want. Patrons and potential patrons were persons whom writers perceived to have money to spend, more or less wastefully, on non-industrial labour, in such inessential areas as art and entertainment; to offer such persons wastefully expensive manuscript copies of literary work was to remind them of this surplus of wealth that they disposed, and to advertise their exalted social and economic standing in public.

There was more to humanist manuscript presentations than conspicuous waste and conspicuous consumption, to use Veblen's terms. The writings always attempt to do more: to instruct, to stimulate devotion, to make propaganda, to entertain, to ingratiate, and so on. But such literary ends would have been served as well by plain as by fancy copies. Evidently, there was an imperative implicitly in force, that patrons and prospective patrons were to be given, not utilitarian copies, but expensive ones. Heeding such a dictate makes sense only if the writers who used deluxe copies could expect to recover their extraordinary costs; and all that conspicuously costly copies could do to earn patronal recompense, which plain copies of the same work could not, was flatter, both their authors' literary work and, more to the point, their prospective patrons' potential for munificence. From this perspective, the practice of presentation was subtly coercive. Its point was to force on the patron an obligation to recompense the patronage seeker's labour and expenses. Lavish books not only created a greater sense of obligation in the patron to return something to the presenter in the presumptive exchange; they were also more apt to appeal to a patronal desire to demonstrate wealth by demonstrating a freedom to waste it on writers.

The basic distinction determining behaviours of this sort, the 'invidious distinction' as Veblen calls it, between cheap copies and dear, between the utilitarian and the conspicuously wasteful, shaped and so lent meaning to publishing activity in early Tudor

England. Fancy copies meant serious work written in deference to patrons. Plain copies did not speak so directly to the issue of the seriousness of the writing transmitted in them, but they did have meaning as signs of the relations between a writer and an audience. Plain copies meant equality of writer and reader, or a superiority of writer to reader, though in neither case is the authorial deference indicated by fancy copies meant. These meanings inherent in the forms of copies inhered also in the work itself: separation of form from content in these instances is impossible.

Printing lent nuance to the system. It created more, and more subtle, gradations, along a scale from the most fancy to the most plain, by making possible a greater number of contrasts among alternative forms of publication. The difference between an ephemeral manuscript copy, on paper, carelessly written and unadorned, and a deluxe manuscript copy, on parchment, carefully written, illustrated, and decorated, was stark and outspoken. The difference between a plain paper manuscript copy and a plain paper printed copy – in such a case, the printed copy bespeaks a difference between self-publication and the sanction of a printer's collaboration; it implies greater expense, since it implies the existence of an entire edition rather than of a single copy only; it may thus also imply comparative popularity, as opposed to intimacy, for the writing; but it need not otherwise differ much from the manuscript in stating a relation between writer and audience – or the difference between a special printed copy, on vellum, with hand-painted illustration and rubrication, and a similarly deluxe manuscript copy of the same work: these differences too are eloquent, albeit more subtle.

Printing lent nuance but did not change the most fundamental difference between the cheap and the dear, which continued to motivate the giving of lavish presentation copies to potential patrons. In presenting his deluxe manuscript copy to Wolsey in 1519, Robert Whittinton behaved as if he understood his business in these terms. Whatever else printing did for him, it would have given greater point to his decision to present Wolsey with a deluxe manuscript. The manuscript takes on its meaning as an expensive object, of especial conspicuousness, not only by implicit contrast with the cheap manuscript it was not, but also by contrast with the printed products it also was not. That on the occasion Whittinton might instead have given Wolsey a plain printed copy of his work, or even a printed copy decorated in imitation of a deluxe manuscript copy, made the manuscript he chose to give appear a more lavish gift.

✿ Chapter 6

Printers' Needs:

Wynkyn de Worde's Piracy
of William Lily's *Epigrammata* in 1522

In late 1522, there appeared a printed book much like Whittin-ton's *Opusculum* of 1519: the *Epigrammata Guil. Lilii*, printed by the same printer, Wynkyn de Worde. The *Epigrammata Lilii* was shorter, and it contained shorter, generically somewhat different poems. It also differed from the Whittinton volume in that it was printed throughout in Roman (fig 23). This typography – an unusual one for de Worde – was a sign, for those educated to read it, of the humanist proclivities of the book's contents, and, no matter that the earlier volume was less clearly marked as such typographically, this basic orientation is something that the *Epigrammata Lilii* shared with Whittinton's *Opusculum*, its predecessor.[1] Like the Whittinton volume, the *Epigrammata Lilii* was a collection of poems by a single author, another humanist schoolmaster and grammarian, William Lily.

For all the similarities between the products themselves, the paths by which the two collections came to be put into print appear divergent. The evidence is that de Worde issued the Whittinton volume only advisedly; there is reason to imagine that Whittinton may have had to offer de Worde something in the way of inducement to print the book. De Worde had no experience of dealing with such books; it would have appeared a risky proposition to him; the publication would not have done much for his business – probably other, external factors figured in his calculations. In any event, Whittinton appears to have been a partner in the publication, providing his printer, with whom he already had a long-standing working relationship, with an exemplar from which to set type, and supervising the process of textual manufacture, if not by correcting proof at press personally, then probably at least by instructing the compositors and correctors at the press.[2]

The *Epigrammata Lilii*, on the other hand, appears to have been a piracy, that is to say, a book brought out by de Worde on his own initiative, speculatively, without the cooperation, let alone the collaboration, of the author of the writings in it. There is no direct witness, one way or the other; nevertheless, the nature of the contents of the book, the histories of their previous circulation, and the existence of other, better verse by Lily, all argue that Lily had nothing to do with the book's production. Consequently, the *Epigrammata Lilii* raises the question of a printer's interest – what was in it for the printer, to manufacture these books? – in a purer form than something like Whittinton's *Opusculum*. In the case of the Whittinton book, it is possible that the printer's involvement was bought. In the case of the *Epigrammata Lilii* – if it is a case of piratical printerly speculation – the printer's interest must have been a belief that the book by itself could turn a profit, without authorial subvention or any other form of patronage. In addition, the development of such a belief – that there was a potentially profitable domestic market for humanist work – tells of the maturation of humanism in England by about 1520; for among de Worde and his colleagues, survival in business required an ability to estimate market potentials.

The book that de Worde issued in 1522 under Lily's name, calling it *Epigrammata Lilii*, contains the following items:

> [1] a poem entitled 'Praecepta morum,' in eighty-six lines of elegiacs;
> [2] a suite of eight related poems or epigrams, with various headings, in praise of Henry VIII and the emperor Charles V, who visited London in June 1522; and
> [3] an eighteen-line poem 'De rege Castelle Philippo naviganti in Hispaniam.'

Each of these items would appear to have been publicly available in some form, already, by the time de Worde printed the *Epigrammata Lilii*; in other words, in making up the book, de Worde was in a position to republish writing that Lily had already made public.

The final item – the 'De rege Castelle Philippo naviganti in Hispaniam' – concerns a portent that occurred in London at the time of Prince Philip's shipwreck on the English coast in January 1506. The same storm that had shipwrecked Philip had also blown a bronze eagle, surmounting a wind-vane, from the top of St Paul's, causing it to fall on a sign in the street below. Lily's epigram read out of these events an augury: 'Does not the eagle seem to have unfolded the Eagle's fate, saying that the ship too was coming into the king's protection?'; for Philip's badge was the eagle, and the sign on which it fell in the city street showed the 'insignia regis' of Henry VIII.[3] Lily's epigram is not known to have been printed at the time; on the other hand, Sydney Anglo suggests that the poem 'may have been read as part of an official greeting,' publicly, when Philip came up to London in early 1506, after his shipwreck;[4] certainly, the epigram would have been made public at the time by public posting, perhaps, or by circulation hand to hand.

The first item in de Worde's collection dates from about 1510. Also known by the title 'Ad discipulos de moribus,' this longest and most widely circulated of Lily's poems was nominally an address to the boys of the St Paul's School from their master, detailing the kind of conduct to be deemed proper at the school. Many of the *precepta* are quaintly pedestrian, making points of perennial schoolmasterly concern: stay in your scat ('Tu quoque fac sedeas, ubi te sedisse iubemus; / Inque loco, nisi sis iussus abire, mane'); don't speak out of turn ('Est etiam semper lex in sermone tenenda, / Ne nos offendat improba garrulitas'); be good, and don't hit the other children ('Clamor, rixa, ioci, mendacia, furta, cachinni, / Sint procul a vobis, Martis et arma procul'); and so on. Others reveal specifics of Lily's historically crucial pedagogy: 'If I dictate, you will write it out, correctly at every point, and let there be no blot or blunder in your writing'; 'look back often at what you have read, and think it over again'; 'every time you speak, remember to speak Latin, and keep away from barbarisms as from rocks in the sea';

If you want to learn the laws of grammar aright, if you desire to learn to speak with more sophistication, study the elegant writings of the ancients, and the authors whom the Roman crowd teaches. Now Vergil, now Terence, now Cicero want to take you by the hand; whoever does not study these writers sees nothing but nightmares, and he struggles to survive in a fog of Chimeras.[5]

The poem appears to have been written expressly for use at the St Paul's School, which was reopened in about 1510, with Lily as its master. At the same time, John Colet, the Dean of St Paul's, who was responsible for the school's refoundation, for the design of its pedagogy, and for Lily's appointment, also commissioned other verses for use at the school from another prominent humanist *sodales* of his, Erasmus. Copies of both Erasmus' and Lily's verses went on display in the school itself or otherwise circulated there. In addition, Erasmus' *carmina scholaria* were separately printed; and Lily's *precepta* were likewise printed, if only as prefatory matter in the grammar book first used at the school, Colet's *Aeditio*. Although copies from no edition of this book earlier than 1527 survive, it was probably in fact already in print by about 1510. Moreover, although the earliest still attested editions, before 1534, were printed in the Netherlands for export to England, or by Pynson or Peter Treveris in London, de Worde too is known to have printed texts of Lily's *precepta* in still extant grammar books that he produced later; it seems possible that de Worde himself had already printed Lily's preceptive poem in some no longer attested edition of a grammar for the school, before reprinting it in the *Epigrammata Lilii* in 1522.[6] In any event, by 1522 Lily's 'Precepta morum' had been publicly posted, circulated in manuscript copies, and printed, possibly printed by de Worde himself, over a period of ten years; by any of these means a text of the poem could have reached de Worde for printing in 1522 without his needing recourse to the author.

The other poetry in de Worde's *Epigrammata Lilii*, the suite of epigrams praising Henry VIII and Charles V in the middle of the book, was written in 1522, probably in May, for use in the public celebrations that greeted the emperor's entry into the City of London. The imminence of Charles's visit was made known early in the year. In anticipation of it, City authorities began to plan pageantry; and as part of the preparations, they commis-

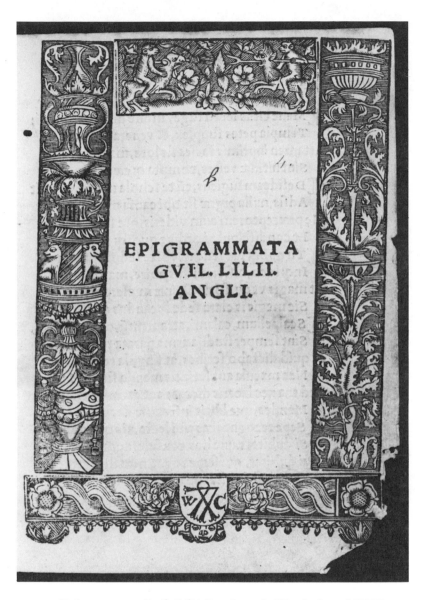

FIG 23 *Epigrammata Guil. Lilii* (London: de Worde [1522] [*STC* 15606.5]) sig A1r: the title page of the collection of Lily's epigrams that de Worde pirated in 1522. Copy: Trinity College Library, University of Dublin. Paper page, 170 × 113 mm

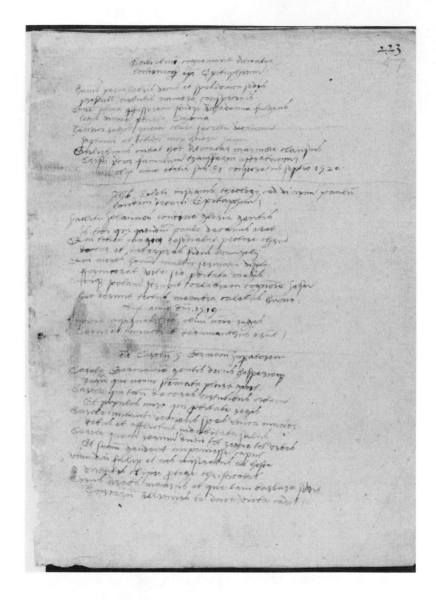

FIG 24 London, British Library, Harley 540, fol 57r: a manuscript copy of Lily's epigrams dating from the Elizabethan period, but probably derived from a manuscript collection from about the time of Lily's death, in December 1522. Paper page, 200 x 142 mm; writing, 173 x 112 mm

Hic Incipit magnus Catho.

J deus est aīmus nobis vt carmina dicūt
Hic tibi precipue sit pura mente colendus
For thy that god is in wardly the wit
Of may andz gyueth hym vndirstandingz
As dictees sayne therfore shalt þ vnshit
Thyn hert to thy souueraīn lord e kyng
Andz principally a boue al other thing
Geuyng hym laude ꝛhonnour e reuerence
Whiche hath the endowed with excellence
Plus vigila semper ne sompno deditus esto
Nam diuturna quies vicijs alimenta minīstrat
A wake my child andz loue no slogardye
In moche slepe loke thou neuer delite
Yf thou purpose to worship for to stye
Longe slepe e slouthe to vice won men excite
Jt maketh men dul Jt maketh hem vnperfite
Jt fosterith vp filthes of the flesshe
Jt palleth also e wasteth blodes fresshe
Virtutem primā puta esse compescere linguam
Proximus ille deo qui scit racione tacere
Trusteth wele also the first of vertues alle

Ys to be stille andz kepe thy tonge in mewe
Of tonge vntied moche harme may falle
Leue me wele this is as the gospel trewe
Who that can delaviance of wordes eschewe
Andz reste with reason this is strey text
To god aboue that may is alder next
Sperne repugnando tibi tu contrarius esse
Conueniet nulli qui secum dissidet ipse
Aduise the wele that thou neuer trauerse
Thyn owne sentence for therof sueth shame
Sey not oon andz efte the contrarie reherce
Suche repugnāce wol make thy worsh ip lame
Where stedfastnesse wol cause thy good fame
For he shal neuer accorde with may on lyue
That with hym self wyl ay repugne e stryue
Si vitam inspicias hoīm si denīqz mores
Cum culpas alios nemo sine crimine viuit
Yf thou aduertise andz beholde aboute
The lyves of men andz maners also
Bothe of thy self andz other the withoute
In myndelerth thou shalt finde who
That in some part nys to vertue foo
Blame no may therfore yf you do a right

¶Petri gryphi pisani iuris consulti/nuntii et protonotarii apostolici/oratio ad serenissimum et inuictissimum Anglie regem pro recessu suo. ❧

Quam fortasse/ et alieni moris videbitur tibi sacer ꝫ
inuictissime Rex/quod cuz huc primu ad te venissem/
iussu summi sanctissimiꝗpontificis/non publice/vt par
erat.Maiestate tua salutauerim non (vt pleriꝗ facere
ꝗsueuerut) in circustantiu corona oratione habuerim/
sed priuatim potius a te ꝫ suscipi/ꝫ audiri ꝫtenderim.
Nunc vero recedes iam iamꝗ ad iter accinctus propala/ꝫ in aspectu dicturus adueniam.Uerum si id inspiciatur intentius/consulto ac recte ꝫ
me factum esse iudicabitur.Quippequonia nullam omnino mea virtutem eiusmodi esse sentiebam/vt licere tunc mihi putarem quicquã coram audere/quando satis superꝗ fore mee exiltati existimabã. Primo
congressu contemplari splendore/admirari dignitate tue maiestatis.
Et in presentiarum ratio diuersa se offert.Namꝗ humanitas ꝫ indulgentia tua iam experientia et vsu mihi perspecta et cognita timore vincit admiratione/in amore/fide/obseruantiaꝗ conuertit/eatenus vt qui
prius dicere erubueram/nunc linguã continere non valeo/quin sponte
sua exiliat/extrinsecusꝗ prodat/quod pectus intrinsecus cocepit/de tua
rum pene celestium virtutu cumulo/testetur animu significet volantate
et in ipso recessu gratias agere tue amplitudini totis viribus gestiat.Et
quod a principio fuisset comendabile/si obiecta maiestatis veneratio et
stupor tui numinis nõ me deteruissent/nuc tua benignitate et comitate
securus/quasi acceptum mutuu ad die iure persoluam.
¶Indecorum naꝗ videretur pontificis oratore a catholico rege quasi
silentem recedere e regno Romanis potificib9/obsequetissimo/et de Ro
mana sede ac dignitate benemerete.Habet eni celit9 hec regio est noie
Romano/nescio quid precipue ac mutue caritatis ꝗ vicissitudine beneficiorum ac vnanimi voluntatis ꝫcursu/ꝫ hactenus inter se strictiore quo
dam nexu coniunxit hec nomina/ꝫ nuc magis ac magis tua bonitate et
gratia Rex sacratissime inuicem ea deuinciat.Nam si paulo altius repetamus eande esse origine Romanis ꝫ Inglis reperire obuium erit.
J troiano enim Enea primordia sua Roma conumerat.Inglia a Bru
to et Troiano et Enee pronepote primam cultam illustrataꝗ vestre
memorie prodiderut.Non igitur ab ratione est/si generis affinitate co
stans quoꝗ beniuoletia subsecuta est.Sed certiora proximiorag extat
necessitudinis argumenta/quod qui primus omniu Romanum peperit
imperiu.Auctor imperatorii nominis Julius cesar/bis Angliam itrauit/
bis incolaru animos ꝫcilianit Romanis/inita pace federeꝗ percusso in
auspicinm future inter Romã et Angliam perpetue amicitie.Obmitto
Claudium vespasianu seuerum/aliosꝗ multos Romanos imperatores
qui tam vigili studio tantoꝗ labore insudarut/ne Britanorum animi
a Romanis alienarentur/pretereo quot prefectos nobilesꝗ proconsu
A.ii.

FIG 26 Pietro Griffo *Oratio* [of November 1506] (London: de Worde
1506 [*STC* 12412.5]) sig A2r. Copy: Oxford, Christ Church College
Library, f.4.32. Paper page, 173 × 120 mm; type, 146 × 94 mm

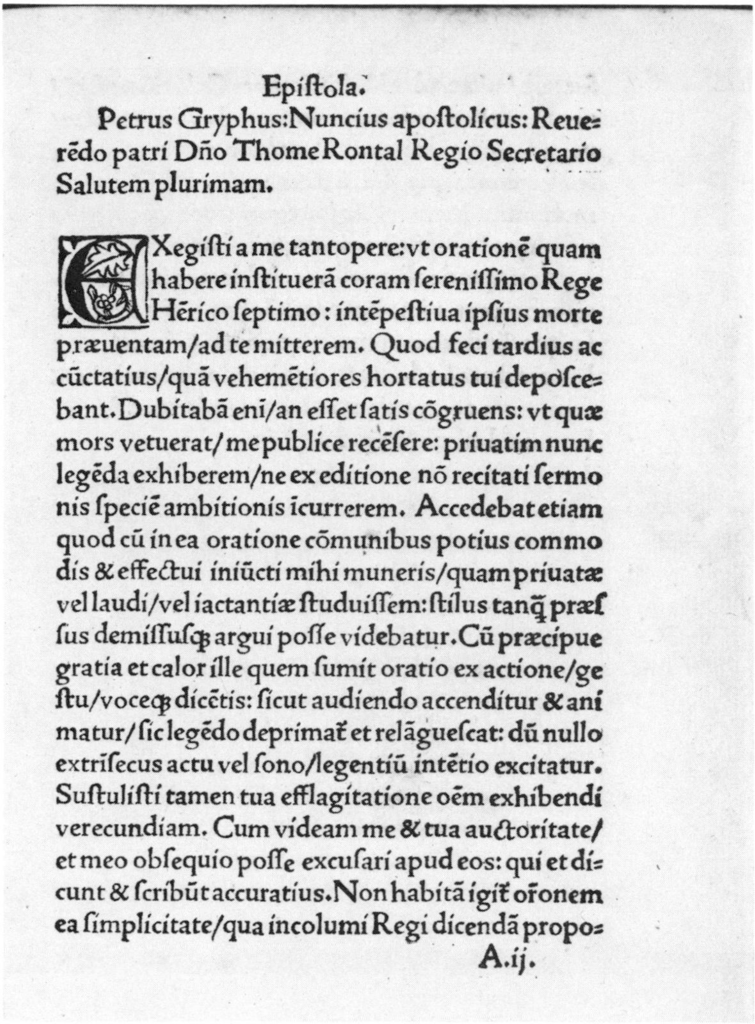

Epiſtola.
Petrus Gryphus:Nuncius apoſtolicus: Reue=
rēdo patri Dño Thome Rontal Regio Secretario
Salutem plurimam.

EXegiſti a me tantopere:vt orationē quam
habere inſtituerā coram ſereniſſimo Rege
Hērico ſeptimo : intēpeſtiua ipſius morte
præuentam/ad te mitterem. Quod feci tardius ac
cūctatius/quā vehemētiores hortatus tui depoſce=
bant. Dubitabā eni/an eſſet ſatis cōgruens: vt quæ
mors vetuerat/me publice recēſere: priuatim nunc
legēda exhiberem/ne ex editione nō recitati ſermo
nis ſpeciē ambitionis īcurrerem. Accedebat etiam
quod cū in ea oratione cōmunibus potius commo
dis & effectui iniūcti mihi muneris/quam priuatæ
vel laudi/vel iactantiæ ſtuduiſſem: ſtilus tanq̄ præſ
ſus demiſſuſq; argui poſſe videbatur. Cū præcipue
gratia et calor ille quem ſumit oratio ex actione/ge
ſtu/voceq; dicētis: ſicut audiendo accenditur & ani
matur/ſic legēdo deprimat̄ et relāgueſcat: dū nullo
extrīſecus actu vel ſono/legentiū intētio excitatur.
Suſtuliſti tamen tua efflagitatione oēm exhibendi
verecundiam. Cum videam me & tua auctoritate/
et meo obſequio poſſe excuſari apud eos: qui et di=
cunt & ſcribūt accuratius. Non habitā igit̄ oronem
ea ſimplicitate/qua incolumi Regi dicendā propo=
A.ij.

FIG 27 Pietro Griffo *Oratio* [of May 1509] (London: Pynson 1509 [*STC* 12413]) sig A2r: the first book printed in England in Roman type. Copy: London, British Library, G.1203. Paper page, 205 x 135 mm; type, 155 x 100 mm

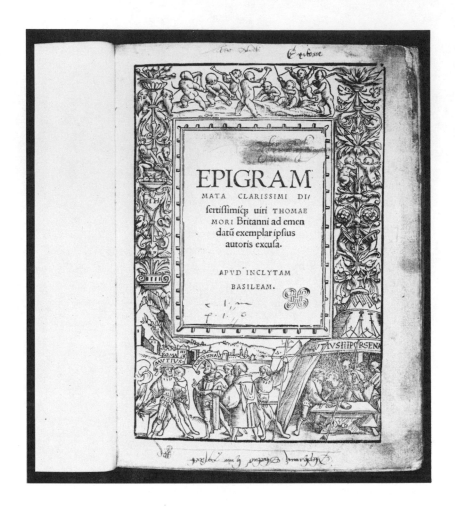

FIG 28 Thomas More *Epigrammata* (Basel: Froben 1520) sig A1r; the title page of the second edition of More's Latin poems. The border, by Hans Holbein, whose initials occur at the left, had also been used in the March 1518 first edition. Copy: San Marino, California, Huntington Library, RB 351520. Paper page, 205 x 155 mm

In suscepti Diadematis diem
Henrici Octaui Britanniæ
Galliarumq; Regis augusti[s]
sim faustissimi: Ac Cathe
rine' Reginæ eius foelicissinæ
Carmen gratulatorium Tho
mæ Mori Londinensis

S̲i qua dies unq̃: si quod fuit Anglia temp̃?
Gratia quo superis esset habenda tibi:
Hæc est illa dies, niueo signanda lapillo.
Leta dies, fastis annumeranda tuis.

FIG 29 London, British Library, Cotton Titus D.IV, fol 4r: More's 1509 presentation manuscript for the coronation of Henry VIII. Vellum page, 160 x 118 mm

olim Tiberio principi uisa est, Iliensium illa consolatio,
qua eum de morte filij, iamdiu defuncti, consolaban,
tur. quam ille faceta dicacitate delusit, respondens se eo
rum quoçz uicem dolere, quod bonum militem amisis,
sent Hectorem. uerum eorum officium, ad luctum nõ
senescentem modo, sed planè præmortuum, non po,
tuit esse non ridiculum. meum uero ab hoc uitio uendi
cat immésa illa de celebri coronatione tua lætitia. quæ
quum pectoribus omniũ tam efficacem sui uim ac præ
sentiam impresserit, ut senescere uel integra ætate non
possit, effecit nimirum, ut hoc meum officium non sero
re peracta atçz euanida, sed præsens in rem præsentem
peruenisse uideatur. Vale princeps illustrissime, &(qui
nouus, ac rarus regum titulus est) amatissime.

❧IN SVSCEPTI

DIADEMATIS DIEM HENRICI OCTAVI,
ILLVSTRISSIMI AC FAVSTISSIMI BRI
TANNIARVM REGIS, AC CATHERI
NAE REGINAE EIVS FELICIS,
SIMAE, THOMAE MORI
LONDONIENSIS CAR
MEN GRATVLATORIVM.

I qua dies unçz, si quod fuit Anglia tẽpus,
Gratia quo superis esset agenda tibi.
z Hæc est

FIG 30 Thomas More *Epigrammata* (Basel: Froben March, 1518) p 181:
the printed page corresponding to the manuscript page shown in
fig 29. Copy: Toronto, Centre for Reformation and Renaissance
Studies. Paper page, 210 x 152 mm

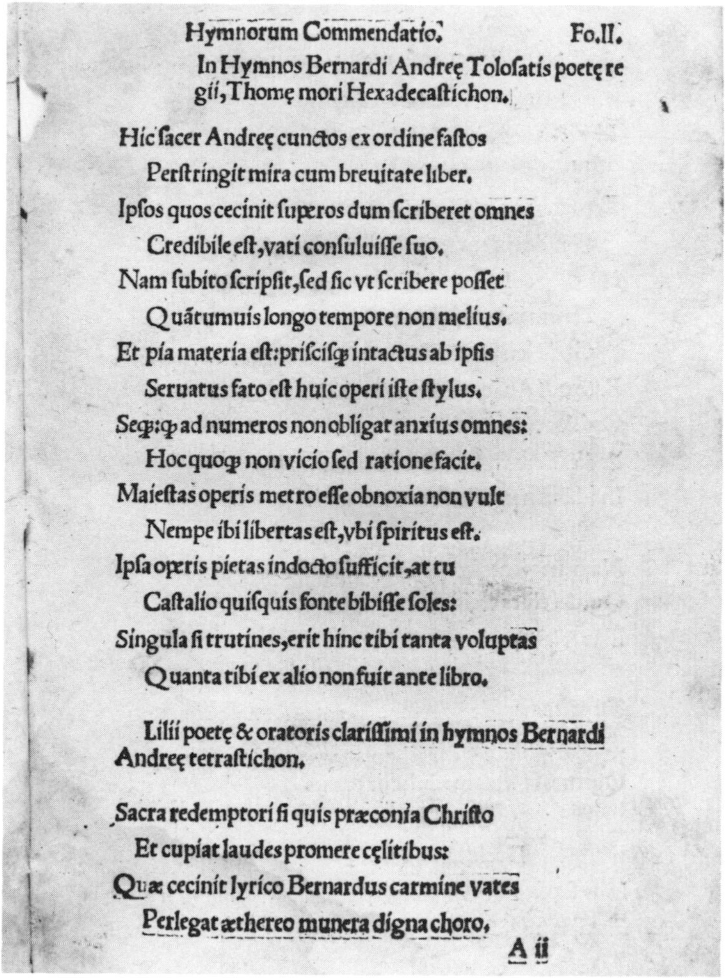

In Hymnos Bernardi Andreę Tolofatis poetę re
gii,Thomę mori Hexadecaftichon.

Hic facer Andreę cunctos ex ordine faftos
    Perftringit mira cum breuitate liber.
Ipfos quos cecinit fuperos dum fcriberet omnes
    Credibile eft,vati confuluiffe fuo.
Nam fubito fcripfit,fed fic vt fcribere poffet
    Quátumuis longo tempore non melius.
Et pia materia eft:prifcifcp intactus ab ipfis
    Seruatus fato eft huic operi ifte ftylus.
Secp:cp ad numeros non obligat anxius omnes:
    Hoc quocp non vicio fed ratione facit.
Maieftas operis metro effe obnoxia non vult
    Nempe ibi libertas eft,vbi fpiritus eft.
Ipfa operis pietas indocto fufficit,at tu
    Caftalio quifquis fonte bibiffe foles:
Singula fi trutines,erit hinc tibi tanta voluptas
    Quanta tibi ex alio non fuit ante libro.

Lilii poetę & oratoris clariffimi in hymnos Bernardi
Andreę tetraftichon.

Sacra redemptori fi quis præconia Chrifto
    Et cupiat laudes promere cęlitibus:
Quæ cecinit lyrico Bernardus carmine vates
    Perlegat æthereo munera digna choro.

A ii

FIG 31 Bernard André *Hymni Christiani* (Paris: Bade 1517) sig A2r: a
page devoted to 'Hymnorum commendatio,' with liminary epigrams,
including that of Thomas More. Copy: Oxford, All Souls College,
The Codrington Library, C.6.27. Paper page, 187 x 118 mm; type,
160 x 85 mm

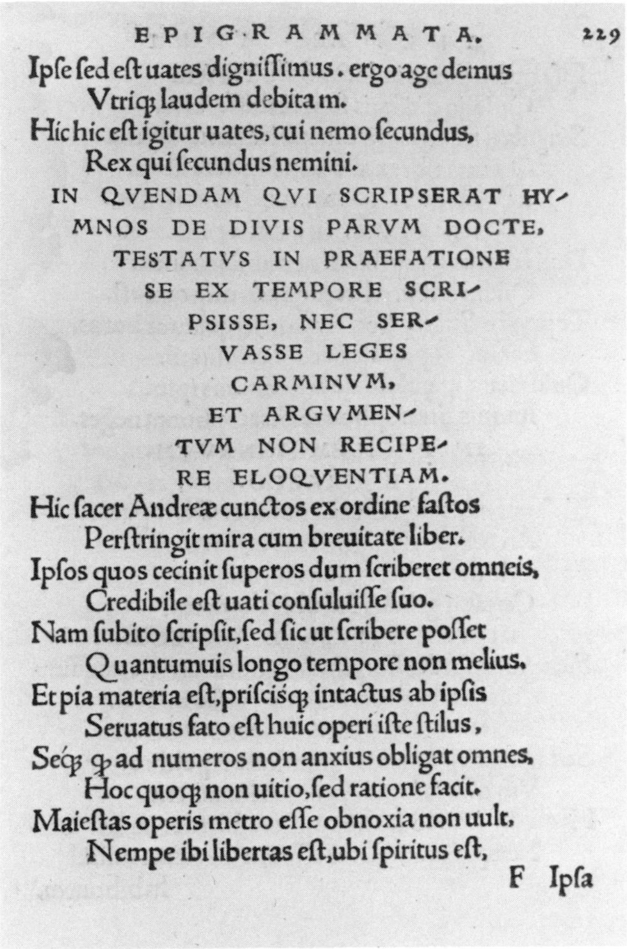

Ipſe ſed eſt uates digniſſimus. ergo age demus
    Vtriq; laudem debita m.
Hic hic eſt igitur uates, cui nemo ſecundus,
    Rex qui ſecundus nemini.

IN QVENDAM QVI SCRIPSERAT HY-
MNOS DE DIVIS PARVM DOCTE,
TESTATVS IN PRAEFATIONE
SE EX TEMPORE SCRI-
PSISSE, NEC SER-
VASSE LEGES
CARMINVM,
ET ARGVMEN-
TVM NON RECIPE-
RE ELOQVENTIAM.

Hic ſacer Andreæ cunctos ex ordine faſtos
    Perſtringit mira cum breuitate liber.
Ipſos quos cecinit ſuperos dum ſcriberet omneis,
    Credibile eſt uati conſuluiſſe ſuo.
Nam ſubito ſcripſit, ſed ſic ut ſcribere poſſet
    Quantumuis longo tempore non melius.
Et pia materia eſt, priſcisq; intactus ab ipſis
    Seruatus fato eſt huic operi iſte ſtilus,
Seq; q; ad numeros non anxius obligat omnes,
    Hoc quoq; non uitio, ſed ratione facit.
Maieſtas operis metro eſſe obnoxia non uult,
    Nempe ibi libertas eſt, ubi ſpiritus eſt,

                    F Ipſa

FIG 32 Thomas More *Epigrammata* (Basel: Froben March, 1518) p 229:
the same epigram as reprinted in More's book eight or nine months
after its publication in André's book. Copy: Toronto, Centre for Reformation and Renaissance Studies

sioned Lily to write verses for the pageants. Charles landed at Dover on 26 May; on 28 May, the court of aldermen sent to Lily, requiring that he deliver his work; when Charles entered London on 6 June 1522, he was greeted with the series of pageants that the City authorities had mounted, at the standard spots along the route from London Bridge to St Paul's Cathedral, six of the pageants decorated with placards inscribed with the Latin verses Lily had written to commission.[7] As had been recognized for some time, public interest in such celebrations was open to exploitation by printers; in this instance, it was the royal printer Richard Pynson who put a record of the pageantry in print soon after it occurred, reprinting in his book the verses that Lily had contributed along with English translations of them.[8]

Like the other materials in the *Epigrammata Lilii*, then, Lily's poems for the entry of Charles were already in the public domain by the time de Worde came to print the book. De Worde could have had access to these writings too either in manuscript form – possibly in copies circulated hand to hand, as to the City authorities and their agents and artisans, of which there must have been some number, or in copies taken from the public displays themselves, which also may have been numerous[9] – or in the form of Pynson's cheap mass-market publication. Here again, de Worde would not have needed Lily to obtain texts to print.

Lily's 1522 pageant verses are humanist in that their commonest technique for magnifying the event and its principals is to draw parallels between the present and antiquity. For example, Charles and his host Henry VIII are bidden, 'Live happily, for as many years as Nestor lived; live as long as the Cumaean Sybil':

> As much joy as Jason gave Ariadne, winning the golden fleece of Phryxus; as much joy as Pompey and Scipio brought the city of the Romans with their triumphs over their foe; so much do you bring us, Caesar, clement prince, accepting the hospitality of Prince Henry.

> Famous Rome lauds its magnanimous Catos; the Punic realm sings the praises of its Hannibal; great King David is the glory of the Jewish people; Alexander is the chief glory of his people; and the fame of Arthur glorifies the brave Britons. Likewise do you glorify your people, Caesar; and may

God favour your empire, I pray, defeating the enemy, that the amicable repose of peace may reign over the world.[10]

The allusions are the predictable ones, and none is more arcane than appropriate for the verses' original royal and imperial audience. As in this last example, Lily's verses also touch occasionally on political concerns, though only obliquely and fleetingly; predominantly, the verses keep to vague praises. Bilateral issues of the relations between Tudor England and the empire or of their alliance against France are avoided; only once does Lily refer to a specific cause, albeit a safe one: Charles's ambition to crusade against the Turk. 'Live long, happily,' Lily addresses him; 'and taking pity on Christians, protect them from the enemy with the shield of justice. With you for our leader, may Moor, Arab, Syrian, and the flood of Turks, now raging so barbarously, fall conquered.'[11]

Lily's pageant verses are *Unterhaltungskunst*, to use the term of Hans Robert Jauss, 'precisely fulfilling the expectations prescribed by a ruling standard of taste,' fit for consumption on the particular occasion for which they were composed, but otherwise disposable, negligible, unremarkable.[12] The verses for the pageants at the little conduit in Cheap or Gracechurch Street, for example, continue to sound more or less satisfactory; they have little to say, however, and in fact make little sense, once they have been deracinated from their original context of the displays on the streets of London, 1522:

The rejoicing mingled with much noise attests, O Caesar, the great love with which the people embrace you. Horns, tubas, trumpets, voices, lutes, and pipes (harmonious even though their reeds are unequal in length) all welcome you. You alone they celebrate; you alone they all thus greet: hail Caesar, ornament and glory of all things.

O Charles, ornament of Christendom, whom the chronicles tell has a lineage that descended from Charlemagne; and you too, Henry, famous in pious praise of your virtue, for learning, intelligence, devotion, and trustworthiness; Praetor, Consul, and holy Senate and people, rejoice that you have been borne hither, under a favourable star.[13]

By their nature, such verses are unsuitable for collection and republication; and the same can be said of the rest of the materials printed by de Worde in the 1522 volume. All are restrictedly occasional verses, in the sense that they yield up little of interest or use to audiences other than the original ones for which they were written: the schoolboys and masters of St Paul's and their like, the City audience of June 1522, and the City's visitors. The epigram on Philip of Castile's shipwreck is something of an exception; it works its conceit nicely, showing Lily's epigrammatic agility to advantage. The rest neither so effectively serve the interests of those whom they address, nor so flatter their author, as to call for further circulation. The *Epigrammata Lilii* is not made up of the kinds of poems that someone like William Lily would have wanted to see collected and put into print.

Furthermore, by 1522 Lily had written other verse – more flattering to him, his friends, and his betters – that he would have wanted to include, had he been involved at the time in collecting and republishing his work. The Latin verse translations from Greek that he had seen printed in 1518, next to More's renditions of the same sources, show off his linguistic skills; and his liminary poems – including one written for André's *Hymni Christiani* – show an ability on his part to promote others' interests as well.[14] In addition, a manuscript written by John Stow in the reign of Elizabeth preserves a series of other poems of his: epitaphs for Henry VII's queen Elizabeth of York, John Colet, the bishop of Lincoln William Atwater, and his own wife Agnes; two witty exchanges with Polydore Vergil; three or four Latin verse translations of epigrams from the Greek Anthology not otherwise attested; a lengthy encomium of Cardinal Wolsey; and others (fig 24).[15] All these bespeak literary talent and skills in Lily, more clearly than anything in the *Epigrammata Lilii*, and several of them speak effectively to patronal needs as well.

Stow was a considerable collector of others' writings, and it is possible that he was able to assemble this collection of Lily's poetry by himself, from diverse sources, mostly manuscript but possibly also some printed.[16] The alternative, which seems a more likely hypothesis, is that Stow's collection derives from an earlier, probably authorial collection, assembled not long before Lily's death in December 1522 or, possibly, as a memorial of sorts just afterwards. By contrast with the *Epigrammata Lilii*, the Stow

manuscript collection is made up of the sorts of poems that someone like Lily would have wanted to bring together and recirculate;
in this regard, it is noteworthy that the Stow manuscript and the
Epigrammata Lilii share only the 'De rege Castelle Philippo naviganti in Hispaniam' and the first of the poems for Charles v,
the longest of the pageant series and a poem that may have been
presented rather than incorporated into the pageantry.[17]

Here again, the evidence is not so detailed as to admit cer-
tainty. Nevertheless, there are these reasons for regarding the
Epigrammata Lilii as something printed and distributed without
Lily's involvement or authorization: by 1522 he had written other
poetry, not included in the printed book, though better than the
work that was; and, more clearly, it would have been possible
for de Worde to have done the book on his own, because all the
work in it had already been published otherwise, in forms to
which de Worde would have had access. Even were the *Epigrammata Lilii* an authorized publication, however, the question of
de Worde's interest in it would remain. De Worde had recently
had experience in printing a similar collection by another
humanist schoolmaster in Whittinton's *Opusculum*. Nevertheless, it remains true that until about 1518–22, England's printers,
de Worde prominent among them, had had little to do with humanists. De Worde's publication of the *Epigrammata Lilii*,
especially though not exclusively if it was an unauthorized, speculative venture, is one among a series of events signalling a change
in the working relations between humanists and English printers.

The salient concern of business life for printers in the early period
was marketing. The concern was imposed on them by the economics of the technology with which they worked. When William Caxton set up England's first press in the autumn of 1476
at Westminster, the book trade in England was largely a bespoke
trade, and booksellers dealt almost entirely in satisfying articulate demand.[18] A book-buyer would approach a bookseller and
commission the manufacture of a single copy of a title, settling
in advance such incidentals of the product as format and decoration; the bookseller might then subcontract production to the
appropriate scriveners, limners, and bookbinders, and would finally deliver their work to the book-buyer, who may have paid
in advance. For the book-buyer, who would almost always have

had to wait for satisfaction, the arrangement was not as conve-
nient as it must have been for the bookseller, who was enabled
by it to avoid obligating assets to stock: the early printers' contemporaries who worked the bespoke trade did not need to concern themselves as the printers did with questions of whether
copies of a particular title would move or would sit, because the
nature of their trade did not commit them to investing in advance
in large quantities of copies of particular titles.

For Caxton and the rest of England's early printers, on the
other hand, creating demand, rather than simply satisfying already articulate, readily quantifiable demand, was the pre-eminent problem, for the economics of printing – the idea of the
technology itself – mandated producing in advance of articulate
demand large quantities of copies of single titles. The larger the
quantities, the greater was the potential for profit, as unit costs
decreased; however, the early printers could never be certain
whether or not they would be able to sell enough of the books
that they had to commit themselves in advance to producing to
break even or to profit. Solutions to the early printers' other
problems, commercial and otherwise – accumulating the skills
and the capital necessary to acquire and to run a press, and continually reaccumulating the capital to sustain it, to obtain paper,
to store stock of bulky and slow-moving unbound printed sheets,
and so on – were all predicated on solving this fundamental problem, creation of demand, in the absence of which the rest of the
undertaking could not be made to work.[19]

To suggest that the manuscript book-trade was exclusively
a bespoke trade, and the printed book-trade exclusively was not,
would be to exaggerate. Early printers produced what were in
effect bespoke editions, commissioned by authors or other interested parties, the whole press runs of which (or large portions
thereof) would have been paid for in advance. Likewise, the commercial *scriptoria* that had begun to develop late in the fourteenth
century in London seem occasionally to have speculated on the
market, to have produced copies of books in advance of articulate
demand, in the expectation that buyers could be found.[20] These
behaviours were uncharacteristic, however, and uncommon, too,
except in the unusual half-century or so on either side of the date
of the invention of printing and its advent to England. In any
case, it remains true that printers were compelled to face the

problem of creating demand for their products by the nature of the technology that they sought to profit from using. Traders in manuscript books were free to try to create demand for their products, if they wished, but were not under the same obligation to do so that contemporary printers faced.

In attempting to fulfil the technologically imposed injunction to create demand, the early printers tried various mechanisms. Some proved inefficient and were abandoned. The large, intricate *bâtarde* types that Caxton used at the outset, for example, like printing on vellum, made printed products look more like manuscript books and so should have made them more attractive to buyers habituated to deluxe manuscripts; on the other hand, such types were uneconomical to use, in terms of the expense of both their manufacture and their appetite for paper, proportionately always the early printers' most costly supply (fig 25).[21] Other marketing tools tried among England's early printers have since come to seem commonplace in the trade. William Caxton, for example, printed handbills advertising his wares – the earliest extant one announcing a printed *Ordinale* to be had at his shop 'good chepe' – and, more sophisticatedly, he also used his prefaces to foster demand, like twentieth-century blurbs. Liminary verse, including liminary Latin verse by humanists, did this same job.[22] Caxton also introduced the printer's device into England, a form of advertising not known in the manuscript trade, and the next generation of English printers introduced the title page – a needless thing in a bespoke trade and by consequence virtually unknown in manuscript books before printing, but a necessary tool for advertising a book's contents to potential buyers, to whom the book's appeals might otherwise remain obscure.[23]

In general, the most important element of the marketing strategies of the early printers was editorial management of the output of their presses.[24] Decisions about which titles to produce and when were the decisions that made the most difference to the success or failure of their businesses over time. England's early printers tried different approaches. Caxton addressed a good deal of work to the more up-market segment of the potentially book-buying public, if not only the nobility then at least also those lower on the social scale who wished to emulate the patterns of noble consumption. Caxton's often remarked love for chivalric prose romance, for example, or for translations of courtly French works, seems in fact to reflect his commercial sense that the greatest potential for profit lay in the market for such literature.[25] Caxton's heir Wynkyn de Worde moved the business from Westminster into the City in 1500, the same year that his most important competitor, Richard Pynson, made the same move; the relocation reflects their changed perception of where the best markets were located. Both de Worde and Pynson published less to the courtly market that Caxton had cultivated, more to the city market: 'books on subjects known to have a popular appeal – religious and homiletic, practical and instructional,' issued 'in easily handled volumes likely to attract readers who would recoil from large and expensive volumes.'[26] The most profitable lines for England's early printers were those addressed to markets whose need for books was already well established: the market for service books, for example, or the schoolbook market which de Worde worked extensively, or the market for law-books, in which Pynson specialized.[27] Such markets need not have been created or even much expanded; they were already sufficiently sizeable simply to be farmed for profits by the printers.

Commercial exigencies of this sort probably fostered the editorial conservatism that characterizes early English printing.[28] In the field of letters, England's printers stuck with the 'classics' of the late Middle Ages: prose romances in English, the poetry of Chaucer, Gower, and Lydgate, and devotional and edifying writings like the *Legenda aurea*. In any case, the early English printers seem not to have perceived much of a market in England for books of humanist interest, and for the first forty years or so of the trade in England, they contributed little indeed to creating one.

The 'stigma of print' had this obverse face for humanists in England until about 1520. Certain contemporary writers – the amateur, aristocratic ones and their epigones – may have avoided print, in a belief that printing made vulgar. In the etymological sense, it did, and their avoidance of it tells something about their work.[29] The humanists do not appear to have felt stigmatized by print, however. Printing could broadcast their work and their names among the *vulgus*, which was still a relatively learned and well-placed crowd; vulgarization was beneficial to their professional progress, something they needed and wanted.[30] From the perspective of England's printers, on the other hand, needfully attentive as they were to problems of marketing, it was humanism that would appear to have been the perceived stigma. The English printers' reluctance to involve themselves with humanism can be explained in these terms: scepticism among the uncommitted – and there were no scholar-printers, persons like Bade or Manutius, among the English – about the size of the domestic market and the potential for profit from books of humanist interest.[31]

In a career that saw him produce eighty-nine editions of books, Caxton printed only three that might have been attractive to a humanist market. The first, a publication indicative of the nature of Caxton's interest in books of this sort, was the *Nova Rhetorica* of Lorenzo Traversagni, issued in 1479 and again in 1480, in an abbreviated form, as the *Epitome Margarita eloquentiae*. It is a treatise on Latin speech-making after the humanist manner, the work of an Italian who spent some years trying to make a living lecturing in England, while also seeking patronage there, before giving up and returning to Italy. Caxton printed the book to Traversagni's commission: Traversagni evidently supplied copy for typesetting, ordered the editions printed, and undertook to market the books himself among his students.[32]

Caxton's two other humanist publications were also either schoolbooks or commissions or a combination. In 1490, Caxton issued the *Donatus Melior*, an 'improved' version of the ancient grammar of Donatus, prepared by another Italian humanist, Antonio Mancinelli. How Caxton came to issue this book, which survives only in fragments, is not as clear as in the case of Traversagni's grammar; nonetheless, the *Donatus melior* too was a schoolbook.[33] In 1483, Caxton had issued another book that might have seen use in schools, an edition of *Sex epistole*: as the title describes it, 'Six most elegant epistles concerning the war on Ferrara, of which three were written by the supreme pontiff Sixtus IV and the holy College of Cardinals to the illustrious Doge of Venice Giovanni Mocenigo, and the same number by the Doge himself, to the aforesaid Pontiff and Cardinals.' The letters were edited for publication by Pietro Carmeliano, who acted as an agent of Venice, secret and otherwise, during the period; and in spite of the claim put forward in Carmeliano's liminary epigram, that the book's purpose was to provide elegant epistolographic models for emulation, it is in fact propaganda for the Venetian position, what George Painter called 'a Venetian White Paper.' Venetian subvention, channelled to Caxton through Carmeliano, seems probable.[34]

The rest of England's fifteenth-century printers – William de Machlinia, John Lettou, the St Alban's Schoolmaster, and Theodoric Rood, those who printed in England exclusively in the fifteenth-century – produced books of humanist interest still more rarely, with the exception of Rood. The St Alban's printer reprinted Caxton's edition of Traversagni's *Margarita eloquentiae* and printed an edition of Agostino Dati's *Libellus super Tulianis elegantiis*; the partnership of Lettou and Machlinia offered only two editions of the same *Vulgaria Terentii* which Rood also printed for use in schools.[35] Theodoric Rood, on the other hand, the first printer of Oxford, worked the university market, and nearly half of the seventeen titles he is now known to have issued would have held some appeal for humanist tastes. His catalogue included the first ancient text printed in England, Cicero's oration *Pro Milone*; Francesco Griffolini's Latin translation of the letters of pseudo-Phalaris (edited for Rood by Pietro Carmeliano); Leonardo Bruni's Latin translation of the *Nicomachean Ethics*; and, by way of more elementary textbooks, a *Vulgaria Terentii* and three Latin grammars, among them grammars of John Anwykyll prefaced by liminary epigrams from Carmeliano. Ominously, however, Rood's business failed, within about eight years, even though it enjoyed the financial backing of an established Oxford stationer.[36] Of the one hundred and forty-four editions of books printed by these exclusively fifteenth-century printers in England,[37] not more than fifteen of them, editions of only nine different titles, were of any humanist interest; with the possible exception of Carmeliano's propagandistic *Sex epistole* published by Caxton in 1483, all were schoolbooks; and nearly half of them, seven of the fifteen, were the work of Theodoric Rood alone, printed at Oxford between 1478 and 1486.

Between about 1492 and 1518, a period during which they had nearly the whole domestic trade to themselves, de Worde and Pynson followed the pattern established by Caxton and the others in the fifteenth century.[38] With the exception of humanistically oriented grammar-books – including the work of the natives Anwykyll, Stanbridge, Whittinton, Holt, Horman, and

Colet, as well as better-known contemporary Italians, Giovanni Sulpizio and Nicolò Perotti – de Worde and Pynson, not to mention their contemporaries, published little that would have had even a marginal appeal to a humanist audience. A pair of specially occasioned publications issued by Pynson, the one an account of the public celebration of the *sponsalia* of the princess Mary Tudor and Prince Charles of Castile, later Charles V, in 1508, and the other an account of the English victory at Flodden Field in 1513, incorporated new humanist poetry by Pietro Carmeliano.[39] Likewise, in 1506, de Worde printed a stylistically humanist oration of Pietro Griffo, again a piece specially occasioned by Griffo's arrival in England as a papal emissary (fig 26); and in 1509, Pynson printed another, the first book printed in England in Roman type (fig 27).[40] Also worth mention is an edition of Erasmus' Latin translation of Plutarch's *De tuenda sanitate precepta*, dedicated to John Yonge, Master of the Rolls, which Pynson printed in 1513; and in about 1510, Thomas More's translation of *The Life of Pico* was printed, by John Rastell, More's brother-in-law.[41] Except for these half-dozen books, most of them specially occasioned, out of perhaps seven hundred printed editions produced in England in the same period, neither de Worde nor Pynson, nor their five contemporaries in the English trade after 1490 and before 1522 – Julian Notary, William and Richard Faques, John Rastell and Henry Pepwell – printed contemporary work of a general or predominant humanist interest, by English or England-based humanists.[42]

A shift in the English printers' attitude towards the publication of humanist writings is discernible in 1518–22. Earlier, they printed humanist books only rarely, with humanist schoolbooks being an exception; beginning in 1518–22 and continually thereafter, they printed humanist books frequently and regularly. It appears as if only at this point, belatedly, did the English printers realize that the size of the domestic humanist market had reached the level at which publishing for it could be profitable. A characteristic publication of the years of change is the *Epigrammata* of John Constable, printed by Pynson in September 1520. Constable had been trained at the St Paul's School and at Oxford, and his career was entirely English. The epigrams in his book are humanist exercises, perhaps only modestly successful; also, they are often of domestic interest, on or addressed to such English figures as Lily and More.[43] His book does not appear to have been specially occasioned, nor would it have had much appeal as a schoolbook. It was a new kind of publication for English printers: contemporary humanist writing, broadly or generally appealing, to a domestic market of learned readers with humanist tastes.

The production of such books in the period 1518–22 exceeded their total production in the previous forty-year history of English printing. Among them were various specially occasioned, more or less official items again, such as had been issued earlier, including Richard Pace's *Oratio in pace* and Cuthbert Tunstall's *In laudem matrimonii oratio*, both printed by the royal printer Pynson in 1518; among these may also be included the volume Pynson printed to commemorate Charles v's 1522 entry into London, featuring Lily's poetry, and perhaps also the king's own *Assertio septem sacramentarum* – sufficiently stylish as to arouse suspicion that its true authors had included Erasmus – printed by Pynson in 1521. A few were certainly schoolbooks, albeit first English editions, like that of the Johannes Murmellius *Composita verborum*, printed by de Worde in 1520, or that of a Latin translation of the *Progymnasmata* of the ancient Greek *sophista* Aphthonius, printed by Pynson at about the same time, or that of Cicero's *Philippicae*, printed by Pynson in 1521. Others may also have been meant for the schools, like the two editions of Erasmus' *Colloquia* printed by de Worde 1519–20; at about the same time, de Worde also printed an edition of Erasmus' *Christiani hominis institutum*, which was reprinted by Pepwell in 1520 – this activity following the publication of only one edition of an Erasmian work in the prior history of English printing. Likewise practical in orientation are the Latin translations of Galen, including two by Linacre, printed by Pynson in about 1522, and Pynson's 1522 edition of the *De arte supputandi* of Cuthbert Tunstall. Also printed in the same five-year period were a series of general interest humanist titles, including More's *Epistola ad Brixium* (Pynson 1520), and the volumes occasioned by the other current controversy within the humanist community, the Grammarians' War: the *Antilycon* of Whittinton (de Worde 1521), the *Antibossicon* of Horman and Lily (Pynson 1521). Finally, these years also saw the publication of Whittinton's verse encomia by de Worde in April 1519, the *Epigrammata Lilii* by the same printer in 1522, and between them the publication of Constable's *Epi-grammata* by Pynson.[44]

The appearance of a sharp increase in English printers' interest in humanism in the years 1518–22 that this evidence supports may be illusory to some extent. The domestic humanist market can be supposed to have grown constantly since the last decades of the fifteenth century, when humanist pedagogy began to take hold in England's schools and universities. The work that the printers did specifically for scholastic markets would appear to corroborate this hypothesis of steady growth. De Worde produced nearly two hundred and fifty editions of humanistically oriented grammar-books over the course of his roughly seven-hundred-book career, and these editions seem to have been regularly distributed throughout it.[45] The English printers' work with schoolbooks may therefore be a better guide to the extent and development of their interest in humanism.

Likewise, special circumstances, accidentally coincident in 1518–22 – the public events that occasioned the orations of Pace and Tunstall, and Lily's pageant verses for the entry of Charles V; the controversies involving English humanists, More against Germain de Brie, Lily and Horman against Whittinton, as well as perhaps Henry VIII (and whoever else contributed to his *Assertio*) against Luther – may help to account for the apparent change. The recent success English humanism had earned abroad, by way of Thomas More's *Utopia* – first printed at Louvain in November 1516, and most recently reprinted by Froben at Basel, in March and December 1518, along with More's collected epigrams – may have contributed too. By about the same time, a second generation of English humanists was coming to enjoy an increased prominence domestically as well, by virtue of their services to Henry VIII.[46] Such a development, however, is probably less a cause of the change in the printers' behaviour than a parallel instance of the maturation of humanism in England.

The Grammarians' War too would have had something to do with the change. The printers' behaviour in it reflects their ongoing concern with marketing; more specifically, their participation involved them, successfully, in marketing humanism, and thereby may have led to de Worde's decision to publish the *Epigrammata Lilii* in 1522.[47] Each of the two grammarians at odds in the War was connected with a printer, Horman with Pynson and Whittinton with de Worde. From the perspective of these grammarians and their seconds, the controversy would have appeared to offer an opportunity to make or improve their reputations, with the prospect of improved material situations that could come of taking the chance. The printers lent the vulgarizing power of their presses to these humanists' efforts to build their names, by their willingness to put into print, not only the rival schoolbooks at issue, but also the volumes of controversial writings they issued later.

The printers themselves were interested parties, although their interests did not coincide exactly with those of the grammarians. Both Pynson and de Worde had an investment to protect: Pynson, by virtue of his contract with Horman for printing Horman's *Vulgaria*, the book that started the controversy, would have wanted to see Horman's reputation benefit; and de Worde, by virtue of his long-standing relation with Whittinton, as the publisher of the series of schoolbooks by Stanbridge and Whittinton, including the *Vulgaria* with which Whittinton answered Horman, would have wanted to see Whittinton's benefit. In support of this interest, it would seem, each of these printers produced collections of controversial writing in the course of the War, championing the party for which he had acted as publisher in the first place: Pynson, the *Antibossicon*, publicizing the position of his writer Horman and his party, and de Worde, the *Antilycon*, publicizing the position of his writer Whittinton and his party, such as it was.

The evidence suggests, however, that Pynson and de Worde cared less for seeing their respective parties vindicated by controversy than for the existence of controversy and its perpetuation. Interest in the controversy, incited initially by the controversial writings circulated in manuscript or posted in public, would have created demand for the printed books that were the subjects of dispute; the more broadly based interest, beyond the circumscribed circles of the humanist intimates immediately involved, incited by such printed books as the *Antilycon* and *Antibossicon*, would have created still greater, more general demand for the rival grammarians' schoolbooks. Controversy, even carried on outside print, was potentially profitable for the printers, then, to the extent that it fostered demand for printed products. In addition, publishing an *Antilycon* or an *Antibossicon* was potentially profitable twice: by sales of such controversial books themselves and by sales of the grammar-books, demand for which the controversial books incited further. Moreover, although each of the controversial books had as its ostensive purpose characterizing the work of the opposite side as negligible, without merit or importance, if the books stirred interest in general, Pynson would have benefited from de Worde's publication of the *Antilycon* and de Worde would have benefited from Pynson's publication of the *Antibossicon.*

Other work done by Pynson and de Worde during the course of the controversy tends to confirm that they were more concerned to take profits than to take sides. Pynson's shop, which issued Horman's *Vulgaria* and the *Antibossicon*, was also busy during the controversy printing editions of Whittinton's grammatical writings. De Worde did twenty-two such editions during 1520–1. Pynson did a further five, including, most remarkably, an October 1520 edition of the *Vulgaria* of Whittinton, first issued by de Worde in March of the same year.[48] Either Pynson undertook on his own to print this edition, having reason to believe demand for the title was such that the market could use a fourth edition within a period of six or seven months, or de Worde, finding the demand for the book greater than his shop could manage, shared the profits of Whittinton's *Vulgaria* with Pynson.[49] In either case, Pynson's edition confirms that his first interest in the controversy was business.

De Worde's publication of the *Epigrammata Lilii* in the same period took place within this pattern of printers' profit-taking from the humanists' quarrel. Lily had been the most vigorous and vocal of the detractors of de Worde's grammarian Whittinton in the course of the Grammarians' War; and, as evidenced in part by de Worde's publication of his epigrams at the end of the *bellum grammaticale*, Lily probably gained from the controversy more by way of enhanced reputation than did anyone else involved. No matter that this benefit to Lily's name had come of his repeated attacks on the author of books prominent in de Worde's catalogue, de Worde evidently believed that Lily's renown had in the course of the controversy so grown as to make publishing even a small collection of already public epigrams by him a profitable venture.[50]

   De Worde's willingness to speculate on the market in this way – to speculate on the marketability of humanism, probably without the connivance of William Lily – is a sign of humanism's maturation in England by this point, at least in the eyes of one of England's printers. If its publication was a speculative venture, the *Epigrammata Lilii* is good evidence for such a perception; nevertheless, it is only one among an unusually bunched series of humanist books, all printed at about the same time, suggesting that the perception was more widespread. At some point between about April 1519 and late 1522, it seems – between the publication of Robert Whittinton's *Opusculum* and that of the *Epigrammata Lilii* – English printing discovered that the English humanist activity was marketable, as if by this point it had arrived.

Chapter 7

Formal Translation:

Thomas More's Epigrams before and after 1518

In March 1518, a collection of *Epigrammata* by Thomas More was printed at Basel. By no means is it a spectacular book; nonetheless, it conveys an impression of printerly competence, solidity, and refined restraint. It is small – a quarto, measuring about 210 x 152 mm – and thick, of a little more than three hundred and fifty pages. Printed throughout in Roman type, with passages of Greek, the book is decorated with modestly ornate initials and title-page borders by Urs Graf, and by Ambrosius and Hans Holbein. The publisher was Johann Froben, the pre-eminent northern European printer of writings of humanist interest, whose shop employed scholars like Beatus Rhenanus, and who worked closely and extensively with Erasmus.[1]

As Froben printed More's poems in March 1518, and reprinted them in December of the same year, without deliberate change, the epigrams were a collection within a collection. The 'Epigrammata clarissimi disertissimique viri Thomae Mori' have a title page to themselves in the 1518 editions, with a full-page Holbein border (fig 28), and a separate colophon, giving Froben's name and a date; so do two other items continuously paginated with the 'Epigrammata Mori' in the 'single' volume: an edition of More's *Utopia*, preceding the collection of his epigrams, and following it, another collection of verse, 'Epigrammata Des. Erasmi Roterodami.' Correspondence suggests that the plan had been to print the two works by More in the company of various *lucubrationes* of Erasmus. The proposed volume grew so large, however, that Froben found himself unable to issue all of it at once, and to More's writings he adjoined instead only a brief farrago of Erasmian poetry.[2]

In part because of these peculiarities of the book, the 1518 publication of the *Epigrammata* was an important event in More's literary career. The *Epigrammata* was published as it was because More already had a name, by virtue of his friendship with Erasmus and the success of his *Utopia*; at the same time, however, the book also helped make More's name, by its design and manufacture. The collection summed up More's career in poetry, bringing together from disparate origins samples of his work in the current varieties of humanist verse-making. The poems in it had been published previously, by different means, in different bibliographic contexts, and so with different meanings, before they were made over again for the 1518 book. More and those with whom he worked most closely at making the collection – Erasmus and Froben – knew what they were doing: like other contemporary collections, the *Epigrammata* too, beyond turning a profit for its printer, had as its purpose fashioning an attractive public self for its author. In the course of designing and building a book to meet this end, by virtue of the new context of publication in which they came to be set, the individual epigrams were altered. The form and circumstances of publication mattered, in other words, for the ways the poems meant.

Stefano Surigone – a Milanese humanist who visited England late in the fifteenth century and spent some time teaching Greek at Cambridge – left a manuscript collection of his epigrams. In it, many of the poems are labelled according to their method of previous publication: some are said to have been affixed to doors, others to have been inscribed in books, and still others to have been written on the backs of letters.[3] There is nothing similar in the collection of More's poetry printed in 1518; nevertheless, the previous histories of the poems can in many cases be worked out. The 1518 collection comprises over two hundred and fifty poems, written at various periods over the preceding twenty years. Represented among them are the kinds of poetry, public and (more or less) private, that early Tudor humanists wrote, and underlying the 1518 publication are the kinds of publication that contemporary humanists used.

The largest number are personal epigrams: encomia and lampoons, polemics and apologies, epitaphs, *sententiae, xenia*, and so on. Like other similarly personal or private verse written by his contemporaries, More's poems in this vein would have been published first by means appropriate to them: privately (or at least semi-privately), in the form of personally made, ephemeral manuscript copies, passed hand to hand among those most immediately concerned. At the outset, the point of such personal poetry was to make an impression on a particular person, who could be addressed more or less as an equal. This is not to imply that the individual might not also be a potential benefactor; humanist peers did benefit one another, in both tangible and intangible ways. But for reasons of class – inattention to which might be costly – the intimacy of address that characterized personal epigrams like More's was appropriate only among equals, and appropriate to this intimacy of address was the intimacy of publication that characterized ephemeral manuscript copies passed among humanist peers. The poems transmitted by them were intimate utterances; the copies themselves were likewise intimate possessions, preserving and passing on something of the touch of the author's hand. And because such copies cost virtually nothing to make, their exchange did not engender a relation of reciprocal debt, of recipient to giver, such as was fostered by the giving of lavish copies, by respectful writers to potential patrons, in an expectation of earning something in return.

Because of the physical properties of ephemeral manuscript copies and the uses to which they were put, none survives.[4] Passages in More's correspondence, however, as well as other similar sources of information, confirm the existence of this mode of circulation and show how it worked. In 1517, for example, Pieter Gillis and Erasmus commissioned the painter Quinten Metsys to produce a portrait diptych of themselves to be given to More; receipt of the gift occasioned More's composition of a set of verses of appreciation. The poem begins with a brief section in which the painting speaks:

Tabella loquitur
Quanti olim fuerant Pollux et Castor amici,
　Erasmum tantos Aegidiumque fero.
Morus ab his dolet esse loco, coniunctus amore
　Tam prope quam quisquam vix queat esse sibi.
Sic desyderio est consultum absentis, ut horum
　Reddat amans animum littera, corpus ego.

The Picture Speaks: I show Erasmus and Giles, friends as
dear to each other as were Castor and Pollux of old. More
grieves to be absent from them in space, since in affection
he is united with them so closely that a man could scarcely
be closer to himself. They arranged to satisfy their absent
friend's longing for them: a loving letter represents their
minds, I their bodies.[5]

This is followed by a longer, metrically distinct section, headed
'Ipse loquor Morus,' in which, in his own voice, More says his
thanks for the gift, praising both Metsys' work and, tastefully,
Erasmus and Gillis as well. Referring to the depictions of those
who had given him the gift, More concludes:

Nam si secula quae sequentur ullum
Servabunt studium artium bonarum
Nec Mars horridus obteret Minervam,
Quanti hanc posteritas emat tabellam!

If future ages preserve any love for liberal arts, and if savage
Mars does not obliterate Minerva, then what a price pos-
terity would pay for this picture.[6]

The portraits in question are intimate ones: Erasmus is wear-
ing a ring given him by More, and holding open a manuscript
copy of his *Paraphrasis ad Romanos*, a copy that More could
have recognized for the autograph it is meant to represent; and
Gillis is reading a letter from More, whose handwriting Metsys
had imitated so well as to lead More to joke that he could have
a second career as a forger. The occasion too was intimate: an
exchange of gifts and thanks, which could have been appreciated
fully only by Gillis, Erasmus, and More and perhaps by a few

others who knew them well. Appropriately, then, More's poem of thanks was first 'published' (though the term is awkward for the circumstances) 'privately,' strictly to Pieter Gillis and Erasmus, in the form of a copy that More himself made and enclosed with a letter addressed to Gillis. With it, More also enclosed a second letter, this one for Erasmus, asking Gillis to pass the letter along to Erasmus, and the verses too 'si digna videbuntur.' Gillis evidently did find them worthy, for soon afterwards More expressed his pleasure at the pleasure Erasmus took in the poem.[7]

The episode shows how such personal verse was circulated among humanist peers: copies – plain ones, manufactured at home, inexpensively, for the nonce – were enclosed with letters, or were passed to friends in person. Friends might show them to other friends, who might take copies for themselves; authors might keep copies back for other uses later; and so on. Although the evidence is not so detailed in other instances – about either the occasions that led to the compositions or the initial paths of circulation – the contents of much of More's other poetry is such as to suggest that it too was more or less private in origin, at the outset more or less privately 'published,' by such means as were used to 'publish' the poem on the Metsys portrait.[8]

The 1518 *Epigrammata* also incorporates other poetry that More first circulated in manuscript, albeit more properly public poetry, meant for less intimate forms of circulation. Following the translations from the Greek Anthology, by More and William Lily, making up the printed book's opening section, there occurs a group of poems, with a prefatory letter, that More had written for the coronation of Henry VIII in June 1509. The poetry is the same as that written for the same occasion, or similar ones, by More's contemporaries. Henry's virtue, of both mind and body, is outstanding ('animi praestans una cum corpore virtus'), as was also said of his father; and Henry's wife 'surpasses Tanaquil in counsel ... and Penelope in marital fidelity,' as his mother was also described. Henry's accession represents the return of the golden age ('Aurea te, princeps, redierunt principe secla'), as Andrea Ammonio also claimed at the time; and it represents as well the fruition of the conjoining of the red rose (of the house of Lancaster) and the white (of York), a notion central also to John Skelton's coronation ode. As Bernard André had also enjoined on the occasion of the birth of Prince Arthur in 1486, the English people here too are to celebrate the event with an ancient-style burning of incense and with other ancient rites: 'If ever there was a day, England, if ever there was a time for you to give thanks to the gods above, this is that happy day, one to be marked with a pure white stone and put in your calendar.'[9]

It is possible that More circulated these poems too in ephemeral manuscript copies, hand to hand among his peers, before or after their presentation to the king.[10] Be that as it may, More's 1509 coronation suite was evidently written with presentation in mind; from the start, More conceived the poems in anticipation of publishing them by particular means on a particular kind of occasion: by presentation, in a formal copy to a social superior and potential patron on an occasion of political consequence.

The manuscript survives in this case, by which More published his poems to the king in 1509 (fig 29).[11] More's poetry recalls the earlier performances of other Tudor humanists; likewise, his manuscript recalls earlier humanist presentation manuscripts, none so much as the *Suasoria Laeticiae* manuscript that Pietro Carmeliano had presented to the previous King Henry more than twenty years before. More's 1509 manuscript is similar to Carmeliano's 1486 manuscript in length and size; likewise, the ratio of written area to blank is similarly generous in the two manuscripts.[12] Set off to advantage by the conspicuous wastage of vellum in both is a similarly humanist handwriting, and the decorative programs of the manuscript are similar, both given over to representations of well-known icons of Tudor dynasty building. Each has illuminated initials and rubrics in contrasting inks. In addition, the Carmeliano manuscript has a full-page painting and a full border facing it at its first opening, showing the Tudor royal arms, surmounted by a crown and supported by angels; the arms are surrounded by the red and white roses of the houses of Lancaster and York; and underneath appear a Lancastrian badge, the white greyhound, and a red dragon, an emblem adopted by Henry VII's father Owen Tudor, which alluded to the Tudors' claims of descent from Cadwalader and King Arthur (fig 15). For its part, the More manuscript has more but smaller (and more tasteful) illustrations: one of the characteristically red and white Tudor rose again, and another with this same Tudor rose, this time its vine intertwined with that of a pomegranate, the badge of the Aragonese house of Henry VIII's wife Catherine, with a Beaufort portcullis and a fleur-de-lys, of the English claim to France, above.

It is not necessary to imagine that More (or anyone else) had this specific 1486 manuscript of Carmeliano's in mind while designing his 1509 presentation. Numerous other manuscripts might have served as well for models, as would have also an ideal of the humanist presentation manuscript, so to speak, canonized by the publication of so many of them at the royal court in the previous reign. More remarkable is the persistence of the type. Embodied in More's 1509 manuscript is a belief that, three decades after their earliest appearance in England, design features already in use in humanist presentation manuscripts of the 1480s were still right for publishing humanist work to social superiors and potential patrons.

Other verse printed in the 1518 collection may likewise have been presented at court. No other formal presentation copies of More's survive, however, and there may not have been others. On the other hand, a number of pieces printed in 1518 appear not to have been meant strictly as personal compositions for private circulation. More wrote verses on other state occasions, including a series of poems on England's military victories in 1513 against France and Scotland. The siege of Thérouanne in Brittany and the Battle of Flodden Field occasioned much humanist versifying; Bernard André, Pietro Carmeliano, Erasmus, John Skelton, and Andrea Ammonio all spoke out as More did. Some of this work – Skelton's English poems, for example, though not his Latin ones, and Carmeliano's epigram – went quickly into print, and one poem, Bernard André's, appears to have been presented formally to the king.[13] The rest – probably along with these other items that were also printed or presented – would have been passed around informally at court, reaching the hands of the poets' humanist peers,[14] and presumably also those of the poets' social superiors, their potential patrons. More's poems apparently belong among this last group. Not poems published only among friends, or poems formally presented to a patron, they would still have circulated comparatively widely. Publications of this sort were not immediate solicitations of patronage; on the other hand, they could be expected to return more, and more immediately, than the private verse that circulated only among friends.[15]

The other sort of publication represented in More's 1518 collection is such liminary verse as he wrote for the books of others. Like poems written for publication in presentation manuscripts, liminary verse too was a kind of poetry informed from the start by a prospective circumstance of publication; for with the exception sometimes of propagandistic verse, like Carmeliano's 1513 poem on Flodden Field, liminary verse was the only kind of humanist poetry to be printed in England with any regularity before 1520. The genre owes its efflorescence, if not its existence, to the need of printers for tools with which to market their wares. Like printed handbills and title pages, liminary verse was a form of advertising. Caxton experimented with it as early as 1478, when he commissioned an Italian humanist to write a eulogy for Geoffrey Chaucer, and then printed it in one of his Chaucer editions. No matter that Caxton's experiment was ill conceived, he still imagined the commendation could help him market his Chaucer, making the book more attractive to potential buyers. This initial experiment did not dissuade Caxton from trying again; later, he and other early English printers used the technique more effectively, with such success from their perspective that the printing of commendatory verse at the beginning or the end of a book became standard practice.[16]

From the printers' perspective, liminary verse was a means of marketing product, of making their wares more attractive to potential buyers; from the perspective of the humanist poets who provided the verse, the custom offered a means to advertise themselves and their connections. The practice allotted them room to display their own eloquence publicly, while praising that of their friends; it linked the names of the commenders with those of the other authors represented in the book, again publicly, in such a way that they too stood to share in the prestige of the publication. The practice guaranteed wide distribution for the work and names of those who contributed commendatory verse, in a context calculated to augment the standing they had brought with them to the job.

More wrote half a dozen such poems, the only poems of his likely to have been intended for printed publication: two for John Holt's *Lac puerorum* around 1496; another for Thomas Linacre's *Progymnasmata grammatices vulgaria* around 1510–15; another for Bernard André's *Hymni Christiani* in 1517; and three more for Erasmus' *Novum Instrumentum* in 1516.[17] Of these, only a select few were reprinted in 1518.

The various Latin poems that More had written and circulated previously, by these different means, were brought together and republished in 1518 with a purpose. The point of the *Epigrammata* was to magnify the reputation of More. As Beatus Rhenanus pointed out in his epistolary preface, the idea was to foster admiration for More among the general learned public, persons not otherwise acquainted with him: 'Pick up this book, read it, and become an admirer of More,' he instructed.[18] What had been a series of disparate, essentially occasional poems, on a variety of topics, fulfilling a variety of functions, was made over into a single, weighty monument to More's public self, functioning to advertise his *ingenium*. The success or failure with which the 1518 *Epigrammata* met in attempting to do its job would have been results of the qualities that the writings displayed, in the form lent them at press. It was in the nature of the publication, however, in its conception and design, to have this magnification of the book's author as its basic task.

The 1518 *Epigrammata* is the way it is, in specifics as well as in general conception, in large measure because More wanted it to be so and acted accordingly. Although the decision to issue the collection of poetry in the company of his corrected *Utopia* and the Erasmian poetry seems to have been out of his hands, the 1518 *Epigrammata* itself was ultimately, though not entirely, More's doing. The collection captures authorial intentions well, in other words, but only within limits imposed by the institutions of contemporary publishing. Like all books, the 1518 *Epigrammata* was a group project: the product of collaborative labour. Though others were involved too, the contributions of Erasmus and Froben are the most palpable in the finished product. Each of them had idiosyncratic interests to pursue, and these are reflected in the book; nevertheless, the interests of the writer and those who mediated between him and his audience were complementary.

To the decision-making process leading up to production of the printed *Epigrammata* in March 1518, the crucial contributions were More's. Beyond writing the poems in the first place, he also assembled the materials – from copies he had saved, presumably, in some cases for years – and he delivered up the original, authorial copy of the collection; later, he entered into discussions about how the book should be edited and published. By comparison, Froben's contributions were belated: he translated writings and book ideas into finished products, choosing paper, format, typefaces, ornamental capitals and borders, supplying the necessary presses and labour, and so on. This is not to say that Froben's work was meaningless; for the most part, however, it was done after More and Erasmus had left off. Finally, although Erasmus' contributions were less concrete than either Froben's or More's, he too must be apportioned an important measure of responsibility. It was to him that More sent the original copy of the collection, entrusting to him some of the editorial decisions remaining to be taken, along with the job of dealing directly with the printer. Erasmus apparently had the collection recopied, incorporating final editorial decisions, into the form in which it was used for setting type. He consulted More about publishers, asking him to chose between Basel and Paris; but the decision to give the work to Froben, taken when Erasmus despatched final copy to Basel towards the end of May 1517, was probably Erasmus'; so too probably was the idea for the composite volume, incorporating the corrected *Utopia*, More's *Epigrammata*, and the Erasmian *lucubrationes*.[19]

In making the choices he did, Erasmus was no doubt guided by a wish to do well by More, for whom his affection and esteem appear to have been as genuine as they were constant. 'As regards More's *Utopia* and *Epigrammata*,' he wrote in a letter of December 1517, 'the business meant more to me than my own affairs.'[20] A composite volume, juxtaposing work of the reputable Dutchman with work of his lesser-known friend, could have been expected to draw favourable attention to More's writings; likewise, the involvement of Froben, whom Erasmus enlisted, would have been a professional boon to More. Froben's reputation for doing quality humanist work was at least as great as that of Bernard André's Parisian publisher Josse Bade – the probable alternative to Froben, had Erasmus and More decided to publish in Paris.

The book's publication served Erasmus' professional interests as well as More's, however. In delivering More's work to Froben, Erasmus was nurturing good relations with his publisher. He profited from his association with Froben over a long period. The manuscripts of his writings that he supplied Froben brought the printer profit, both directly, in sales, and indirectly, in prestige. At the same time, Froben paid Erasmus for manuscripts; in addition, Erasmus' reputation and all that it was worth to him came to rest in large measure on the printed products Froben manufactured and distributed on his behalf.[21] Once profits from sales of More's work began to reach Froben, Erasmus' favour could have been expected to better his relations with Froben, even if only intangibly. Finally, there was also something more definite in the projected publication for Erasmus, because the plan called for putting out something of Erasmus' next to More's work. The book could evoke the personal and professional bonds that linked Erasmus and the author of the famous *Utopia*. Not only was it an opportunity for Erasmus to see writings of his circulated in print again, in the company of More's most reputable work; he could also appear in public as co-sponsor of sorts for More's learning and literary efforts.

From the printer's angle, the volume Erasmus proposed, to incorporate a corrected *Utopia* as well as new work by both More and Erasmus, should have seemed an especially marketable product. Writings attached to Erasmus' name had proven themselves consistently profitable for Froben as for others; they were as near a sure bet as could be imagined. Even in a subsidiary role, they should have improved the publication's prospects. In addition, in the *Utopia*, Froben had a property that had also already proven its profitability for Martens in the Low Countries in its first printing in 1516 and, by the time Froben went to press with it again in March 1518, for Gourmont in Paris in its second printing in 1517. But herein also lay the risk for Froben, in the possibility that the market for the *Utopia* was worn out. Two editions had been brought on to the international market already, within about eighteen months; they had perhaps already met such demand as there was. The Erasmian project's design, however, answered fears about possible market fatigue. Froben was not to reissue the same old *Utopia*. By delivering to Froben copy that More himself had reworked, Erasmus put the printer in a position to produce an authorially corrected *Utopia*, preferable to the old editions, which Erasmus characterized as 'full of mistakes.'[22] In addition to this appeal of the improved that it would enable Froben to make, the plan also offered him the chance to add something new as well: the collected epigrams of the *Utopia*'s author, not to mention the various *lucubrationes* of More's esteemed associate Erasmus.

From More's perspective, the project offered an opportunity to trade on the initial successes of the *Utopia*. He would have a chance to polish the work again. In addition, a third republication for it, in a third city, by a third (and more reputable) publisher, within a year and a half, would confirm that by it More had earned wide respect among the international learned audience. More to the point, the sort of composite volume Froben issued in 1518 offered More a chance not so much to cement the success of the *Utopia* as to cement his own success. In the way characteristic of authorial collections, the volume transferred attention, and so some measure of esteem, from a particular piece of writing – the *Utopia* – to the author of the several separate works brought together in the book – the *Utopia* and the individual poems and groups of poems collected in the *Epigrammata*. By design, the 1518 volume would have yielded More a reputation the more secure to the extent that it was anchored no longer only at a single point, the greater to the extent that it was delimited no longer by a single demonstration of talent.

More understood the publication of his *Epigrammata* in these terms, as a tool for magnifying his repute. His remarks about the collection of poems before they were published ('deal with them as you may think will be best for me,' he wrote Erasmus)[23] bespeak a concern that their publication should flatter him as much as possible. A like worry animated the work that More put into gathering and arranging the poems for publication in the first place, as well as into correcting them for a second edition in 1520. The 1518 *Epigrammata* is in fact only a selection from among the larger corpus of Latin poetry More wrote. How much was left out is impossible to gauge; there is evidence, though, to indicate that there was a process of selection. With Erasmus, for example, More discussed the propriety of including one group of poems – those against Germain de Brie – and he may have decided against printing them, though if he did so his wishes were ignored.[24] Likewise, there are poems extant that More had written and circulated by 1518 which do not appear in the printed volume.[25]

Most instructive in this regard may be the selection from among the commendatory verse that More had written for others' books. Poems still capable of flattering More, or others from whose favour More might still hope to benefit, were reprinted in the 1518 volume; the rest were left out. Consequently omitted were the poems that More had published commending the work of the comparatively obscure English grammarian Holt, who was dead by 1518; omitted too were the verses he had published with Linacre's largely unsuccessful *Progymnasmata*. On the other hand, the poem More had published with Bernard André's *Hymni Christiani* in 1517 was reprinted, as capable of being turned to More's credit, and three poems he had written praising Erasmus' *Novum instrumentum* in 1516 – one addressed to Wolsey and another to the archbishop of Canterbury William Warham – were also selected for inclusion.

Editorial changes More made later to the book confirm this earlier evidence that the book was designed to cast the public monument to More from as flattering a mould as possible. In December 1520, the *Epigrammata* was reprinted by itself in a corrected edition advertised on the new title page as 'ad emendatum exemplar ipsius autoris excusa' ('printed from copy improved by the author himself').[26] Eleven poems were added, and two were dropped – the one a poem occasioned by the death of the king of Scots at Flodden in 1513, which had come to seem impolitic, and the other 'a weak effort to translate from a definitely inferior [Greek] source.'[27] Also, improvements were made to the verbal fabric of individual poems: more than twenty-five authorial emendations were introduced in this edition.[28]

Without altering the *Epigrammata* in substance, the changes served to make More look better; the immediate impetus for them, however, had been an attempt to make More look bad. The 1518 *Epigrammata* had raised controversy.[29] The book came under attack by Germain de Brie, a Parisian humanist who had studied in Italy and there made the acquaintance of Erasmus. Brie had published an epic poem, the *Chordigera*, on a sea-battle between the English and the French in 1513, imputing perfidy to the English in the incident, while celebrating French heroism. Understandably, when Brie's epic appeared in print, an English humanist wrote a group of epigrams in response. At the time, More's epigrams against the *Chordigera* probably circulated only hand to hand, among More's friends or at the English court; but then they too appeared in print, in the 1518 *Epigrammata*, possibly against their author's better judgment. Brie responded with the *Antimorus*, printed at Paris in late 1519 or early 1520, in which he castigated the 1518 *Epigrammata* as a whole, providing annotated lists of More's 'Inexcusable Mistakes in the Quantity of Syllables' and 'Utterly Disgraceful Solecisms and Barbarisms.'[30] Erasmus had tried to dissuade Brie from publishing the *Antimorus*, but Brie ignored him and lied about doing so. Their subsequent correspondence was less cordial. Erasmus then sought to dissuade More from publishing something answering the *Antimorus*. More's response, the *Epistola ad Brixium*, was printed nevertheless, though at some point More recalled his pamphlet, buying up the remaining copies and destroying them.

In the end, in practical terms, More behaved as did other humanist poets in response to their peers' criticisms – albeit usually expressed in private and prior to printed publication. More made the improvements that Brie had recommended, along with others of his own devising, for the second edition of the *Epigrammata* that Froben printed in December 1520.[31] No matter that the improvements had been suggested to him by Brie as unpleasantly as could be imagined, the result was that the 1520 *Epigrammata* was a more creditable collection than the 1518 book. More was in no position, of course, to agree with Brie's characterization of him as a person 'taken in by a love for fleeting and trivial glory' ('gloriolae captus amore levis').[32] Nevertheless, More behaved throughout as if he subscribed to Brie's formula: 'the good poet takes care to publish only good things' ('Non nisi quae bona sunt, bonus evulgare poeta / Curat'). More's work on the collection in 1518 and 1520 shows that the *Epigrammata* was the book of a 'good poet' in Brie's sense: one 'who has concern and regard for his reputation' ('cui famae est curaque amorque suae').[33]

Recasting the poems in a new bibliographic form in 1518 changed them. Because they were republished as they were, the epigrams ceased to be personal transactions, of various kinds – between More and his learned friends; between More and the potential patrons whom he approached; between More and a somewhat larger, less intimate circle of acquaintances, the audience at court – and became a single impersonal transaction between an author and a public, mediated no longer by handmade objects, but by the machined products of Froben's presses. Collected republication meant attenuating or severing the individual poems' links with their originary occasions; it also meant creating a new occasion for them, new situational and literary contexts. As with other author-collections, the gathering up of More's epigrams

inevitably shifted attention from them and their diverse occasions to the author; in other ways as well, the poems read differently by light of their juxtapositions with one another in the
single printed volume, occasioned by the professional needs of
a writer, his printer, and their go-between.

The effects of the contextual changes on the meanings of
particular poems vary, from the gross to the subtle to the hardly
sensible. The fact that they were put into print – and were put
into print as they were, by Johann Froben – changed them, even
if the change was diaphanous. The different kinds of manuscripts
More had used earlier differed from one another in meaning;
printed publication meant something different again; moreover,
there was within printed publication a range of options, each also
importing peculiar connotations. Typography was significant, for
example, at a time when markedly different styles were current:
bâtarde, black-letter, and Roman among them. Roman, the humanist standard, was not used at all in England until 1509.[34]
Meaningful too were other features of the book that Froben con-
trolled: for example, he was most likely responsible for the classicism of the spelling, and, though it is difficult to define the
difference, *laetitia* and *leticia* are different words, with different
meanings.[35]

What Froben contributed to the *Epigrammata* by his decisions about materials and specifics of presentation was above all
something intangible: a humanism by association. Froben cast
about More's writing an aura of humanist rectitude, presenting
it in the form of a correctly produced product. On the one hand,
a printer's participation provided a certain social, ultimately economic guarantee for the writings' quality. Someone had decided
that the collection merited the expense of manufacturing numerous printed copies of it, and this decision was legible in the
book. Any printer's participation could have vouched for More's
work in this way, but Froben was able to do more. Erasmus'
northern publisher had decided that More's work was a good risk
and had invested in it. It was Froben's job to make such judg-
ments, about what would attract learned buyers, and he had
proven his ability to judge the market well. Froben had been
persuaded to see More's writing as humanist writing, likely to
appeal to the humanist market; accordingly, when he published
it, he dressed it in the recognizable garb of a humanist printed

book, using the kinds of types and ornaments that he and others had used for similar books in the past. Consequently, the book's audience would have expected the product to be a quality humanist book and would have read it accordingly. Froben's seal of approval on More's work made it more authoritative and its readers more respectful than would otherwise have been the case.[36] The printer's labours and reputation thus lent meaning to More's poems that they could not have had in any other form.

The translation from manuscript to print also affected the sense of individual poems, though not always more specifically than this. When More's poems for the coronation of Henry VIII were republished in print, for example, they still complimented Henry VIII; in 1518, however, in a way new to them, they complimented More too, albeit vaguely (fig 30). An analogy with the publication histories of certain poems that Erasmus wrote complimenting his betters – not to mention More's own liminary epigrams – is suggestive: as long as the objects of his praises remained his betters, Erasmus published and republished his encomia of them, over and over, in manuscript and print; when they died, or when they fell from prominence, or when their fame faded, relatively, as Erasmus' rose, Erasmus dropped the poems from the body of his work that he put into circulation. Evidently, he believed that credit accrued to him out of the connections with the rich and famous that he might advertise among third parties.[37] More's poems for the coronation of Henry VIII were changed by their printed republication in 1518 in this way at least: by publicizing More's relations with Henry VIII after the fact, in a way they could not have done had they remained in a presentation manuscript only, the printed poems did him credit.

The effects of formal translation are more definite and specific in other cases. For example, there occurs in the collection an epitaph on Henry Abyngdon, formerly choirmaster of the King's Chapel, who died in 1497:

> Attrahat huc oculos, aures attraxerat olim
> Nobilis Henricus cantor Abyngdonis.
> Unus erat, nuper mira qui voce sonaret.
> Organa qui scite tangeret, unus erat.
> Vellensis primo templi decus, inde sacellum
> Rex illo voluit nobilitare suum.

Nunc illum Regi rapuit Deus, intulit astris,
  Ipsis ut nova sit gloria caelitibus.

Let the famed singer, Henry Abyngdon, draw your eyes
hither; there was a time when he drew your ears with his
music. Not long ago he sang in a voice marvellous beyond
compare and played the organ with incomparable skill. At
first he was the pride of the church at Wells; then the king
decided that he should lend his fame to the Chapel Royal.
Now God has taken him away from the king and installed
him among the stars to add glory to the very inhabitants of
heaven.[38]

Speaking as it does in a dignified way of Abyngdon's accomplishments and his loss, this epitaph must have had considerable emo-
tional weight among those who mourned him. Although the effect
can no longer be recovered, the difference between the poem's
impact on its original occasion and its impact when republished
in 1518 can be imagined. The poem would have been one thing
in 1497, among Abyngdon's mourners, and something else in
1518, for More's international learned public. Printed in the 1518
collection, the poem ceased to be about Abyngdon and came to
be about Thomas More's skill and taste, even without other contextual changes.
    There were other contextual changes, however. In the 1518
collection, the epitaph is juxtaposed to another speaking to the
same occasion, but in a different style and metre – in Leonines,
rhyming at the caesura and the end of the line:

Hic iacet Henricus, semper pietatis amicus.
Nomen Abyngdon erat, si quis sua nomina quaerat.
Vuellis hic ecclesia fuerat succentor in alma,
Regis et in bella cantor fuit ipsa capella.
Millibus in mille cantor fuit optimus ille.
Praeter et haec ista, fuit optimus orgaquenista.
Nunc igitur Christe quoniam tibi serviit iste
  Semper in orbe soli, da sibi regna poli.

Here lies Henry, the constant friend of piety. Abyngdon was
his family name, if anyone should want his full name. He

was once succentor of the kindly church at Wells; and later
he became chanter in the beautiful Chapel Royal. He was
the best singer among a million. And besides this he was
the best of organists. And so now, Christ, since he served
you always on earth, admit him into the Kingdom of
Heaven.[39]

This poem too must have had one meaning among Abyngdon's
mourners and another among its later, wider public. In 1497, by
itself, it could still have worked as a eulogy. Its juxtaposition in
print in 1518 with the first epitaph created new meanings, however, of two not necessarily exclusive kinds. Throughout the
printed collection occur pairs and larger groups of epigrams treating the same topic in different words; in More's work as in others', such exercises demonstrated a verbal fecundity valued in the
current rhetorical tradition. As with similarly paired epigrams
elsewhere in the 1518 collection, this juxtaposition too might do
no more than show off the *copia* of More's talent.[40]

Knowing how to take the second epitaph is difficult, however. A shift in taste was occurring just at the moment it was
written: in late medieval poetry, composition in Leonines was
regarded (reasonably) as a difficult trick, for virtuosos; among
humanists, the verse-form was to be redefined as barbarous, in
accord with ancient standards of versification, which looked down
on rhyme.[41] Combined with other medievalisms in the second
epitaph – the equivocation about quantities, the placement of the
enclitic -*que* in 'orga*que*nista,' 'sibi' for 'ei'[42] – the Leonines make
this poem starkly different from the modishly classicist first epitaph. It is possible, therefore, that the second epitaph could have
been understood as a parody even without additional evidence.

This possibility is confirmed by a third epigram, printed
following the two epitaphs in 1518. It explains that the second
epitaph is indeed meant to ridicule Abyngdon's heir 'Janus' ('This
Janus sees nothing before or behind'),[43] who found the first one
too humanist for his tastes – too ostentatiously stylish and self-
important, perhaps, given the occasion – and had made the mis-
take of wishing aloud for something else with which to bury
Abyngdon. Here, when More calls the second epitaph 'laughable
... verses,'[44] it ceases to be possible to take it seriously as a eulogy.
In another context of circulation, however, the same poem must

have been different: the Leonines, not the classicizing verses, were inscribed on Abyngdon's tomb.[45]

Three poems published next to one another in the 1518 collection; preceding their reappearance there, a series of previous publications, singly or in groups; even here, where there is no direct testimony to the original documentary forms used, the specific shifts in meaning that came over these poems as they were translated from one context of circulation into another can be imagined. The situations in which the poems were published changed the ways they meant.

The most striking case is that of the epigram on Bernard André, More's elder contemporary, the senior figure in Tudor court literary circles.[46] In July 1517, André had published his only work to see print, the *Hymni Christiani*, at the Parisian press of Josse Bade; along with several others – including Erasmus and William Lily – More had at the time supplied a liminary epigram. In André's book, it appeared on a page with other commendatory verse, under the title 'A Hexadecastich of Thomas More, on the *Hymns* of Bernard André of Toulouse, Poet Royal' (fig 31).[47] Although attentive reading reveals it to be a wonderfully ambiguous epigram, in its original bibliographical context it appears to be of a piece with the volume's other commendatory poems, asserting as it does, for example, 'that all the saints celebrated here took counsel for their poet when he wrote.'[48] At the end of the volume, moreover, André set a pair of epigrams of his own, addressed to More, singling him out from among the several commenders for particular thanks.[49]

The poem was reprinted among More's *Epigrammata* eight or nine months later. The body of the poem is essentially invariant, but it was printed in 1518 under a strikingly different title, no longer the innocuously descriptive 'In Hymnos Bernardi Andreae Tolosatis poetae regii, Thomae Mori hexadecastichon,' but now a title enjoining a different reading of the 'same' poem: 'In quendam qui scripserat hymnos de divis parum docte, testatus in praefatione se ex tempore scripsisse nec servasse leges carminum, et argumentum non recipere eloquentiam' – 'On a Certain Person who wrote Hymns on the Saints, Unlearnedly, Maintaining in his Preface that he Wrote them Ex Tempore and did not keep to the Metrical Regularities, and that his Matter did not admit Eloquence' (fig 32).[50] Under it, lines that had before looked laudatory came to look hurtful indeed: for example, 'he composed quickly, but even so, with all the time in the world, he could not have written better.'[51]

The new title goes a long way towards making this same epigram mean differently in More's 1518 collection. But the changed title was only one of the contextual changes worked around it by its 1518 republication, all of which contributed to altering the invariant poem's sense. In 1517, the epigram had occurred adjacent to others praising André and his work, in a place customarily reserved for such commendations; the running title at the top of the page on which it occurs is 'Hymnorum commendatio.' In 1518, on the other hand, in More's collection of poems, it occurs immediately following an epigram in which More unequivocally ridicules another well-known Tudor humanist poet of André's generation, Carmeliano, with whom André would have been associated; and it is followed by a series of invectives translated from Greek against parasites, drunks, *mulieres foedae*, and philosophic fakers.[52] Most fundamentally, the poem had appeared in 1517 in a book about Bernard André, an objectification of and tribute to his accomplishments as a poet. No matter that there may have been something odd about one of the liminary epigrams printed with it, the 1517 book remained a witness to Bernard André's qualities. Without André's book, More's poem could not have remained the same. It reappeared in 1518 in a differently oriented publication, a similar objectification of and tribute to the accomplishments of a learned poet, but now More in place of André.

Considered abstractly, as if it existed apart from a context of publication, More's epigram on André might appear to be a masterly bit of ambiguity. But the epigram did not exist abstractly. Poems always have bibliographic contexts, and bibliographies are meaningful. In 1518, in the changed context of publication, the 'same' epigram on Bernard André became functionally a new poem, doing different work than it had in its original context of publication in 1517. Among the rest of the commendatory verse set at the beginning of the *Hymni Christiani* – and in large measure by virtue of that original context – the epigram worked to commend André. In its new context, among More's collected occasional poetry, the 'same' epigram had to work to commend Thomas More – an end to be achieved, not by commending, but by ridiculing Bernard André. The poem passed for an encomium of André, well enough that it was printed among the *Hymni*'s other commendatory matter by Bade, who had a product to market, in part by the blurblike commendations he could put about with it, and well enough that André would write poems of thanks to More for inclusion in the book. Among More's other epigrams, however, in his 1518 *Epigrammata*, the poem functions as an encomium of Thomas More. The changes to the meanings of the lines on André ultimately stem from this most basic, most general change to the context of the lines' publication. The new title may provide immediate impetus for a changed reading of the poem, and it may serve to signal that the change is especially striking in the particular instance. In the final analysis, however, the new title only reflects a more general, more fundamental shift in perspective wrought by the new book's conception and design. The epigram would have changed anyway, and in the same way, new title or no.

This is the extreme case capable of documentation from surviving evidence: a transformation of the 'same' poem from one thing into its opposite, from apparent praise into disambiguated blame, wrought by the poem's republication in a redesigned context. To the extent that the words remained the same, the alteration is to be attributed to the context of publication. The case only dramatizes the general phenomenon, however. In the other cases, the change may appear to have been less radical, but still there was change. If only because of the subjugation of each to the new project – Thomas More's magnification – for which the 1518 publication was designed, all the poems in the 1518 volume were altered by their republication in it.

❦ Conclusion

The histories of More's epigrams and their transformation into the *Epigrammata* of 1518 confirm that modes of publication were themselves meaningful, in historically determined ways. A few current forms of publication were not involved: nothing of More's was ever published as a printed broadside or news pamphlet, for example, like Carmeliano's verses of 1513 against the Scots, nor is he known to have posted his writing in public, as Whittinton did.[1] More's publishing routines were conservative. He tried nothing that his peers and immediate predecessors had not already made standard practice, and all the main kinds of publication used by England's humanist writers in the early Tudor period are represented in his work: the presentation manuscript, the ephemeral copy, and the printed book, the single item and the collection.

The histories of More's poems offer striking instances of alteration of meaning as items move from one bibliographical context to another: the epitaph inscribed over a tomb changing when the 'same' epitaph came to be printed in More's collection among other poems, the commendatory epigram made discommendatory when moved from one printed book to another. In other cases as well, however, attention to the bibliographic details yields similar conclusions. The forms of publication current among early Tudor humanists were meaningful forms. Their meanings were fixed in part by convention, perhaps, but equally importantly by the material limits of current technology and social relations. Manuscript and print had different meanings; a book given the king differed in meaning from a book circulated among friends or offered the learned market by a printer. Those espousing the cause of *bonae literae* in England – from Carmeliano and André in the fifteenth century to Whittinton and More early in the sixteenth – made livings by using the available means of publication to win repute and to attract patronage.

Generally, it is the case that 'a text that goes unread is not a text without meaning.' In origin, writing itself may be a strictly graphic means of communication, as Roy Harris has argued, independent of speech and not necessarily obligated to verbal content. Certainly, writing has retained a graphic dimension.[2] The history of the evolution of written forms confirms over and over that the non-verbal element of written messages is meaningful. Roman capitals inscribed in stone monuments set up in public places articulated Roman authority, imperial or ecclesiastical, even among illiterate peoples. The wealth of evidence and detailed analysis accumulated by Stanley Morison for his unfinished *Politics and Script*, subtitled 'Aspects of authority and freedom in the development of Graeco-Latin script from the sixth century B.C. to the twentieth century A.D.,' shows that, while lettering changes, the fact that its formal properties are meaningful does not. For Morison, barely perceptible adjustments of written forms – the shift from monoline to letterforms of contrasted strokes, incorporating both thin and thick lines; the invention of serifs, their subsequent presence, absence, and shape (simple, elongated, wedge-like, bifurcated); the horizontal compression of letters; the placement of the thinnest lines of the contrasted letter o perpendicular to the line of writing or at an angle to it – can bespeak consequential shifts of authority.[3]

The fifteenth century saw the invention of Roman type and of the humanist cursive bookhand that yielded italic. Most fundamentally, it saw the invention of printing, and printing brought to the current system of forms of publication a degree of complexity it could not have had before. The formal differentiae at issue are more gross than those between monoline and contrasted letters or perpendicular and tilted os. Several strikingly different alphabets were in use; a more basic difference between type and

letters written by hand was also current, as were differences between handmade books, of one kind or another, and printed ones,
again of different kinds. By consequence of the quantity and
quality of current difference, the meanings of the various forms
and the connotations imparted by the forms to the words transmitted through them were the more palpable. The concerned
community of writers, readers, and bookmakers – humanists,
patrons, printers, and others – recognized the differences in
meaning and worked with them.

Late in the fifteenth and early in the sixteenth centuries,
while there remained several modes of publication still current
in use, competing with one another or complementing one another, with none yet so dominant as to deny the others a measure
of importance, there was an articulate variety of forms. Each form
of publication meant something different, being endowed with
distinctive value within the current system of publication, which
was particularly complicated at the time and mutable. The books
themselves – forms and contents emplaced in a context of material, social culture – are the best witnesses.

 Appendices

Appendix 1
Alberici's Summaries of His *Cebes' Tablet*,
London, British Library, Arundel 317

\<fol 2r\> **Operis argumentum:**
Cebes advena Saturni templum ingreditur. Aspicit depictam tabulam,
adeo cariosa vetustate confectam, quam nullatenus poterat dignoscere
quidnam vellet. Senex indigena novit eum una cum sociis de pictura
d\<i\>ffidentem. Hic rogatus a Cebete sensa figuris velata dissoluit, ac
suscaepta virga rem totam ordine demonstrat.

\<fol 6r\> **Primum circi Argumentum:**
Hic autem Vita Humana demonstratur. Infantes sunt qui in lucem ac-
cedunt et venturi doloris presagi variis nutibus cordis tristitiam pre se
ferunt. Genius, naturae deus, singulos quid acturi sint instruit. Verum
Decaeptio erroris poculum unicuique porrigit assumendum; alii plus,
minus alii degustant. Vitiorum catherva ingredientibus obviam sese in-
gerit a sinistris, Virtutes autem a dextris; pauci has, plerique illas com-
itantur. Sunt qui Virtutes amplecti vellent, sed Ignavia retinentur: hinc
Luxuria, inde Instabilitas. Est praeterea Fortuna, quae oculos vincta ro-
tundo lapidi insidet: hos ditat dextera; illos autem sinistra exspoliat.

<fol 10r> Argumentum secundi:
Illi quos antea Fortuna ditaverat genialem vitam exercent. Hos Vanagloria, Gula, Voluptasque amplexantur. Verum quum desint Fortunae
bona, protinus expelluntur; qui, ut priorem vitam reducant, alii homines
interficere, alii furtis ditari, plerique autem tenui premio deos falso testantur. Sed ii in obscura domo recluduntur, quos Dolor, Luctus, Paena
doloribus afficiunt. Inde ad albicantem domum deducuntur, ubi, a cri-
minibus expiati, possunt ad meliorem vitam reverti. Poenitentia hostium
virga propulsat, et continuo eorum corda excitat ad honesta.

<fol 13r> Argumentum prime partis tertii circi:
Falsa Disciplina offert se obviam querentibus veram scientiam, cuius
imagine decaepti mortales eam insequuntur. Cum ipsa sunt Falsus Poeta,
Mendax Astrologus, Nugator Sophista. Hinc bivium est, cuius pars dextera ad veram virtutem ducit, tota quidem senticosa ac venenosis affla-
tibus <in>fecta. Si quis autem ex his qui iter ad virtutem occoeperant
retrocesserunt, illum Nox Paupertasque flagris animadvertunt; eor-
umque verberibus cesum Circes in ferinam imaginem transfert, et denique Stygia palude demersum ab hominum memoria tollit.

<fol 18r> Secundae partis argumentum:
Via haec ad Virtutem tota quidem difficilis est et asper<r>ima. Ingredientibus divae se undique offerunt: hinc Promissio volentibus plura
pollicetur; Spes totum assequi posse confirmat. Est praeterea Delectatio,
quae cadentes ex itineris asperitate attollit; Solertia autem ad dimidiatum
iter hominem comitatur. Iacet in medio saxum ingens, de cuius fastigio
Constantia fessos exhortatur quod, quum quis preterierit, iter prorsus
facillimum experitur; et duce Veritate ad Virtutis atrium proficiscitur.

<fol 20r> Argumentum tertiae partis:
Sedet Regina Virtus in aureo solio, geminam potestatis suae vim de-
monstrans; nam libro quem tenet dextera scientias, ense autem in sinistra
posito arma significat. Via ad hanc amoena est. In vestibulo sedent Studium et Mars, qui adeuntibus fores aperiunt. Post Virtutem sunt laurus
et palma: hac victores, illa docti coronantur. A dextris est Aeternitas,
Irim manibus gestans, a sinistris autem perfulgens Gloria.

Appendix 2
False Education and Her Followers:
Parallel passages from the Greek original, the Odasio translation, the anonymous Copenhagen verse translation, and Alberici's version of the *Cebes' Tablet*.

The Greek is reproduced from the edition of Karl Praechter. The Latin translation of Lodovico Odasio, written at Urbino c 1490–5, is edited from the facsimile of the Paris 1498 edition (the second to appear, following only a Bologna 1497 edition) reproduced in Sandra Sider, *Cebes' Tablet*. The Copenhagen verse paraphrase is edited from a photocopy of the unique surviving manuscript copy, Copenhagen, Kongelige Bibliotek, Fabr 138, VI, in 4to, kindly supplied me by Mr Erik Petersen, of the Department of Manuscripts of the Kongelige Bibliotek; palaeographically and orthographically, this copy appears to be later than either Odasio's or Alberici's versions, probably nearer the end than the beginning of the period to which Lutz would allot it (ie, c 1500–40, in 'Ps. Cebes,' *Catalogus Translationum et Commentariorum* VI, 6–7). Alberici's version is edited from the British Library manuscript Arundel 317.

I. ΚΕΒΗΤΟΣ ΠΙΝΑΞ **12.2–13.2** (ed Praechter, pp **11–12**):

Οὐκοῦν ἔξω τοῦ περιβόλου παρὰ τὴν εἴσοδον γυνή τις
ἕστηκεν, ἣ δοκεῖ πάνυ καθάριος καὶ εὔτακτος εἶναι;
Καὶ μάλα.
Ταύτην τοίνυν οἱ πολλοὶ καὶ εἰκαῖοι τῶν ἀνδρῶν
Παιδείαν καλοῦσιν οὐκ ἔστι δέ, ἀλλὰ Ψευδοπαιδεία,
ἔφη. οἱ μέν τοι σωζόμενοι ὁπόταν βούλωνται εἰς τὴν
ἀληθινὴν Παιδείαν ἐλθεῖν, ὧδε πρῶτον παραγίνονται.
Πότερον οὖν ἄλλη ὁδὸς οὐκ ἔστιν ἐπὶ τὴν ἀληθινὴν
Παιδείαν ἄγουσα;
⟨ Οὐκ ⟩ ἔστιν, ἔφη.
Οὗτοι δὲ οἱ ἄνθρωποι οἱ ἔσω τοῦ περιβόλου
ἀνακάμπτοντες τίνες εἰσίν;
Οἱ τῆς Ψευδοπαιδείας, ἔφη, ἐρασταὶ ἠπατημένοι
καὶ οἰόμενοι μετὰ τῆς ἀληθινῆς Παιδείας συνομιλεῖν.
Τίνες οὖν καλοῦνται οὗτοι;
Οἱ μὲν ποιηταί, ἔφη, οἱ δὲ ῥήτορες, οἱ δὲ διαλεκτικοί,
οἱ δὲ μουσικοί, οἱ δὲ ἀριθμητικοί, οἱ δὲ γεωμέτραι,
οἱ δὲ ἀστρολόγοι, οἱ δὲ κριτικοί, οἱ δὲ ἡδονικοί,
οἱ δὲ περιπατητικοὶ καὶ ὅσοι ἄλλοι τούτοις εἰσὶ παρα-
πλήσιοι.

II. **Lodovico Odasio, trans** *Cebetis Thebani tabula* (Paris 1498) sig *B2v*

'Video,' inquam, 'ego atque extra ambitum in vestibulo mulier quedam assistit, que mundiciam constanciamque non mediocrem pretendit, apprime,' inquam.

'Hanc igitur,' inquit, 'plerique homines et vulgo vocant Disciplinam, cum Falsa potius Disciplina sit. Huc sane prius applicant qui salvi fiunt, ubi ad veram Disciplinam voluerint pervenire.'

'Numquid alius ad veram Disciplinam aditus non patet?'

'Patet,' inquit.

'Hi vero intra ambitum declinantes, quinam sunt homines?'

'False,' inquit, 'Discipline sunt amatores, decepti seque opinantes vere Discipline contubernio frui.'

'Et quinam vocantur hii?'

'Alii,' inquit, 'poete, alii oratores, ali<i> dialetici, alii musici, alii arithmetici, alii geometre, alii astrologi, alii voluptuarii, alii peripathetici, alii critici, et quicunque eiusmodi sunt.'

III. *Paraphrasis Tabula Cebetis Poetica* (Copenhagen, Kongelige Bibliotek, Fabr 138, VI, 4to, fols 4v–5r)

Anne vides igitur septum quoddam alterum, et illic
Intra vestibulum femellam, munditieque
Compositoque venustam ore? Hanc passim unde vulgus
Paedeiam appellat; nos Falsi nominis illam,
Et Graio Pseudo-Paedeiam more vocamus.
Ad quam, qui verae Paedeiae aliquando futuri
Cultores, vitae possessoresque beatae,
Divertunt primum, veluti veramque sequuntur,
Ad quam longe alia est via, longe aliaeque ambages.
Qui vero, in septi spatiantes margine, visi
Obsonare famem, et meditari multa profunde
Secum, mulcentes propexam in pectora barbam,
Astra alii speculari, alii describere terram
Lativiam, in tabula, pictosque ediscere mundos,
Psallereque, aut aliud moliri denique tale.
Isti omnes, Pseudo-Paedeiam depereuntes,
Verae se frui amore putant, illaque tumentes,
Decepti pariter, non ultra adscendere quaerunt.
Horum Oratores alii, aliique Poetae,
Grammaticique alii, Logicique aut Musicae amantes,

Astrologique, Geometraeque, horumque Magistri
Consimiles alii, fictae sapientiae alumni.

IV. **Filippo Alberici** *Tabula Cebetis* **357–475 (London, British Library, Arundel 317, fols 14r–17r)**

> Falsa Disciplina
> Illam, illam, O iuvenes, quae tercia limina septum
> Aextremumque tenet, fas sit contingere tantum
> Luminibus; vestrum non ultra immittite pectus,
> Nullaque, premoneo, teneat vos cura sequendi.
> Ora habitusque ferunt sub corpore numina, quicquam
> Nec mortale tegi signis monstratur apertis;
> Sed fictam hanc verae species virtutis adornat,
> Et cute, si quid habet sapiant quod sydera, monstrat.
> Huius et aversi precibus, vel cortice picta
> Decaepti, accessum verae ad fastigia laurus
> Committant miseri ventis atque atra sinistris
> Littora Cocyti querunt tristisque paludes.
> Intus – cerne – comas sertis surasque coturnis
> Vinctorum structis spaciatur turba cathervis.
> Illis Falsa viris Virtus sub limine primo
> Occurrit, captisque manu, 'quam queritis,' inquit,
> 'En adsum, gremio vobis demissa tonantis,
> Quisquis es. illa ego sum, cuius diffracta potenti
> Parca manu Stygiis nigrum caput occulit undis.'
> His iter inceptum recto declinat ab orbe
> Turba pedem; creditque sacris sua nomina iungi
> Numinibus, culta hac morti et dominarier atrae.
> Verum, heu, falluntur miseri, et vestigia ductu
> Pallados ignaro et caecis imitantur habenis.
> 　　Falsus Poeta
> Illum nosce caput Phoebea ex fronde revinctum
> Atque coturnatum suras, cui dextera plectrum,
> Leva gerit cytharam, nervis ebur atque canorum.
> Ne grege de Aonio referas Phoebique caterva,
> Quamvis Phoebeum dicant insignia vatem
> Armaque Musarum gremio fateantur obortum.
> Pectine pulsat ebur – fateor – vel carmina nectit,
> Talibus at sacre resonat non Phocidos aula,
> Talia nec veros Muse docuere poetas.

Verus Poeta

Pegaseos quicumque bibit – mihi crede – liquores,
Mellifluo canit ore deos, caelestia notis
Occultatque modis, superumque palatia pandit.
Hunc licet interdum Mavortis tela cruenti
Atque referre togam tenui vel pascua versu;
Cuncta tamen docta sic concinit arte tegentque
Verba salutiferos placido sub cortice sensus.
Ille autem ingenium natum ad suprema theatro
Dat decus, ex sacra caelestumque aede sororum
Numina deducit temnendae ludicra s<c>aenae.
Sive cupidineos inhonesto carmine lusus,
Seu Paphiae canit acta deae, lascivia semper
Turget et exornat Venus ipsum plurima carmen;
Non nunquam vel dente bonos hic mordicat atro,
Exhylaratque iecur tristi livore perustum,
Sanguineis sine pace modis et gaudet iambo.
Non ii, non vates, qui sic sua numina caeno
Inficiunt Stygiisque tegunt Heliconia sub undis.

Astronomus

Illum et Niliaco cui pectine pallia dorso
Texta cadunt, longam fundentem a vertice limbum
Falleris astronomum credens caelique peritum.
Nitetur inspectis praefari motibus axum
Quae Plaustri Arctophilax vector ferat ominata,
Graia quid aspectet Helicis maiore carina
Sydere, quasque orbi clades crinita minetur;
Quid Cynosura micat, quid vertice Scorpius atro,
Strictaque Mavortis Cytherea amplexibus usti.
Verum quis gremio residens telluris in imo
Pingue supercilium tantum ad sublimia tollit?
Lumine quis caecas potis est transcendere nubes,
Aera que medium fusca caligine densant?
Caetera ab ingenio motu volvuntur Olympi
Nos quoque, versicolor volucris, grex squameus undis,
Quadrupedum genus omne, caput frondosaque pinus,
Marmora, fulgentes gemmae, crepitantiaque aera,
Terra gravis, levis ignis, aqua humida, rarus et aer:
Omnia celestes vario discrimine motus
Suscipiunt; exinde eadem non omnia possunt.
Et mihi nil dubium est: si quis bene noverit astra,

Eoasque fores, et quae te, Phoebe, cadentem
Suscipiunt, Venerisque thoros, et robora Martis,
Humectum Phoebe, divum sydusque parentis,
Haec quid agant cursum, quod iter, quae tempora complent,
Ille etenim, fateor, veluti sublimis in arce
Nosceret eventus nullo et ventura magistro.
Nulla sed humano mens interclusa baratro
Tam latas videt orbis opes. Vix noscimus, heu, heu,
Nos fore mortales, vix nostraque tempora scimus.
Ille pater divum, cui sydere regia cuncto
Celsior, haud caeca circumspicit omnia mente,
Ignoratque nihil; nullo at discrimine soli
Quae sunt, quae fuerunt, et quae ventura, patescunt.
Hunc vero, quem nosse polos plebs nescia censet,
Omne fugit; pleno at tantum caelestibus ore
Nominibus sese vulgo super aetheris axes
Ipse refert, sicque aere gravi mendacia vendit.
      Sophista
Hunc ubi novistis, doctae sub ymagine falsa
Uranie, caelos, Titania pandere et astra,
Illum hic continuo revomentem ex ore trilingui
Verba et tricipiti revoluti sophismata nexu,
Conspicite, O iuvenes, vanum et videte laborem.
Ingenio haud fretus, sed vocis munere et aura,
Nititur hic rerum latitantes noscere causas.
Non his Pegaseo divis sub fornice libat,
Sacra caduciferi nec victima concidit aris;
Sed limosa palus huic est pro Phocidos aula.
Numina sunt Eccho crepitans simul atque Syringa.
Hic querulas imitatur aves, quae carmine mensas
Inveniunt nullosque ferunt pro munere fructus.
Hic quoque perplexo iuvenilia corda susurro
Captat; et, accoepta vani mercede laboris,
Verba iterumque sonos et vendit inanes.
Turpis arundineo fulcitur dextra bacillo
Dum graditur, fragili at Zephiris tibicine fracto
Decidit, et nulla potis est vi tollere casum.
Atque alii, structa quos prospicis ire chaterva,
Virtutis tantum simulata umbramque Minervae
Complexi dant scire Notis perque aera spargunt.
Serta etenim capiti spoliantur conscita baccis;

Seu mirtus, seu fulmineo defensa furore
Quercus, et nullo est laurus quae tempore tonsa.
His quoque se interdum conspecta in limine primo
Atra cohors scelerum adversa compagine miscet.
Impius at nihil astra tegunt, nec Tartara quisquam
Perfidiore colit noxa, quam criminis hospes
Ingenioque potens hominum mens, docta nequaquam.

Appendix 3
Pietro Carmeliano's Letter to Prince Edward, 7 April 1482
London, British Library, Royal 12.A.xxix, fols 1r–2v

Petri Carmeliani Brixiensis Poetae Laureati ad Edwardum clarissimum Angliae Principem De Vere Carmen

Cogitanti mihi iandudum, illustrissime princeps, quonam pacto sublimitati tuae me notum facere possem, id tandem mihi fieri posse arbitratus sum, si quippiam meorum carminum ad te dedissem quod tibi vel ex eorum sententia vel fortassis compositione aliqua ex parte placere posset. Quocirca novam materiam aggressus, veris s<c>ilicet, primae anni partis, descriptionem, quam a quoquam maiorum nostrorum diffuse scriptam adhuc non legi. Non dubitavi opusculum hoc perbreve quidem celsitudini tuae dicare, quod in hac Redemptoris nostri resurectione muneris loco susciperes. Potissimum hoc egi cum tali te ingenio preditum esse intelligerem ut spectaculum quoddam non parvamque tui admirationem omnibus preberes gentibus. Neminem equidem, clarissime princeps, te ipso digniorem inveni cui libellus inscriberetur, nisi serenissimo regi patri tuo splendidissimo id opus destinassem; sed cum praeclarissima ac memoranda eius gesta in praesentiarum edam quae brevi profecto volumine comprehendi non possunt, visum est mihi rationem etiam tui esse habendam. Accipies igitur opus veris iam tibi a nobis dicatum. Quod quidem si non fuerit ea ellegantia aut verborum gravitate compositum sicuti Celsitudinem tuam deceret, id tamen tu pro tua innata bonitate atque clementia non aspernabere; et sinceram scribentis mentem posthabita sententiarum aut verborum accuratissima compositione suscipies. Ceterum, si scripta mea tibi grata esse sensero, animus proculdubio meus atque praecordia exultabunt pre nimio gaudio, et ad maiora poemata conscribenda atque grandiores materias tentandas ingenium nostrum provocabitur; cuius rei maximum erit argumentum quod ego ipse incognitus et peregrinus in extremis fere orbis finibus abs tanto tanque excellenti principe senserim me diligi. Decimus nempe currit annus, inclite princeps, quod in speculandis orbis regionibus semper ellaboravi; cumque et provincias et insulas multas, urbes et oppida ac quamplurima loca maritima in orientali plaga transcurissem, visum fuit mihi ad occiduas oras transire, ut de iis aliquid me vidisse futuris temporibus affirmare possem. Superiore igitur anno ab urbe Roma solvens in Gallias, mox in Britanniam i<n>feriorem me contuli, videndi tantum gratia, annumque illum ea in expeditione consumavi. Nuperrime igitur ad patriam hanc appuli ut subito ad Cymbros, deinde ad Germanos transirem; sed tanta profecto huiusce patriae amoenitate atque dulcedine sum captus, ut ab ea nesciam quovis pacto discedendi occasionem quaerere. Quocirca, cum ab ineunte aetate arti tum poeticae tum oratoriae, hystoriis quoque et annalibus omni studio atque diligentia incubuerim, nolui in praesentia torpere aut inerti ocio tabescere; composui itaque libellum de vere quem sublimitati tuae inscripsi, conatus in pluribus de animantium tam caelestium, quam terrestrium et maritimorum natura aliquid succincte referre. Quem quidem pro re parva non modicam bonarum literarum cultoribus et studiosis utilitatem allaturum certo scio. Verum cum non ignorem detractores plurimos atque gravis potius supercilii quam doctrinae plenos mihi defuturos non esse, qui scripta mea suspenso naso subsannare nitantur, ignorantiam eorum ex aliorum detractione occultare se putantes, te unum, clementissime princeps, causae meae patronum atque defensorem instituo, qui tua singulari sapientia eorum insolentiam et temerariam censuram coarguas. Superest igitur ut libellum ipsum audiamus tuaque interim celsitudo bene valeat, cui me supplex commendo.

Ex Aedibus Rotulorum vii Idus Apriles M.cccclxxxii.

Appendix 4
Giovanni Gigli's Letter to Richard Fox (probably early 1487)
London, British Library, Harley 336, fol 1v

Domino Ricardo, regio secretario, Johannes de Giglis, apostolicus subdiaconus et collector, salutem plurimam dicit.
Carmelianus noster questiunculas quas iamdudum hortante reverend<o> in Christo patre domino episcopo Lincolniense de observatione quadragesimali scripseram a te michi remissas reddidit, tuoque nomine

retulit te cupere ut transcriptas alio volumine eas tibi restituerem. Feci igitur quod iussisti, libellumque ad te mitto, munus certe pro tuis erga me meritis exiguum, sed optimo et benevolentissimo animo tibi donatum. Quod cum tanti faciendum erit quanti pro summa doctrina et sapiencia tua iudicaveris, ut quoque censueris, animum, queso, non rem ipsam diiudices, que (ut dixi) exigua est; sed qui dat quod habet satis dedisse videtur. Ergo tu litteras, cum nichil aliud possideam, qualescumque in me sint, tantum a me expectato. Ego autem, si me (ut facis) amaveris, plurimum te michi prestitisse fatebor. Vale, et in dies dignitate atque auctoritate augeare.

Appendix 5
Pietro Carmeliano and Bernard André on the Life of St Katherine of Egypt:
Two Parallel Passages

The passages from Carmeliano's *Beatae Katerinae vita*, written and published between late summer 1483 and late summer 1485, are edited from Oxford, Bodleian Library, Laud Misc 501 (*B*), with variants from the other surviving copy, Cambridge, Gonville and Caius College Library, ms 196/102 (*C*), given beneath. The passages from André's *De sancta Katharina*, probably first published in 1509, are edited from the *Hymni Christiani* (Paris: Bade 1517) fols 61r–63v (*H*) with variants from the other surviving copy, in London, British Library, Royal 12.B.xiv, fols 6v–9v (*R*), where it is called 'Vita beate Katherine', given beneath.

I. **Katherine converts the philosophers by her eloquence.**
Ia. Carmeliano *Beatae Katerinae vita* 161–245:

> Nuncius ecce venit regis, comitatus ad urbem
> Quinquaginta viris, fuerat quibus inclyta virtus
> Et quos nulla hominum prorsus doctrina latebat.
> Rex videt hos gaudens; illis se dona daturum
> <165> Regia promittit, fuerit si victa puella.
> Interea terras linquens subit aequora Tytan,
> Et suadent tenebrae mortalia lumina somnum;
> Rex igitur mandat veniant ut luce sequenti
> Seque parent doctam dictis superare puellam.

<170>   Ianque caput croceum linquens Aurora cubile
         Extuleratque diem ducebat Lucifer almum;
         Membra thoro citius solito levat ipse tyrannus,
         Militibusque suis comitatus ad atria tendit,
         In quibus ipse dabat populo sua iura petenti.
<175>   Nec mora: conscendit turba comitante tribunal,
         Tergaque convolvens solio consedit eburno.
         Ianque aderant Tyrio vestiti murice cuncti
         Quinquaginta viri, studiis et veste superbi.
         Ianque aderat Costi castissima filia regis,
<180>   Quae vix tersenos aevi compleverat annos;
         Cuius erat facies tanto perfusa nitore
         Totque simul radios spargebat ab ore corusco,
         Ut dicas: 'vultus certe est divinus in illa.'
         Extemplo insonuit leni sic turba susurro:
<185>   'Virgo viros, iuvenisque senes, atque unica multos
         Si superare potest, miro est res digna relatu.'
         At Katerina Dei radiis sua pectora postquam
         Sensit plena satis, tali sic voce locuta est:
         'Non ego, vos docti, sapientum turba virorum,
<190>   Argumenta sequar quae sunt scholastica, quamvis
         His erudita satis certare et vincere possim;
         Nec mihi vobiscum mens est contendere in illis.
         Est pater omnipotens, mundi moderator et auctor,
         Rex hominum solusque Deus, qui tempore nullo
<195>   Imperium caeli caepit, sine fine tenebit;
         Omnia qui novit, cui vera scientia rerum est,
         In quo spes hominum, requies et gloria sistit;
         Qui mare, qui terras, caelum stellasque micantes,
         Cunctaque quac toto cernuntur in orbe creavit;
<200>   Per quem visa patent nobis, invisaque constant;
         Qui genus humanum paradisi munere cassum
         Non patiens nasci voluit de virginis alvo;
         Qui populis documenta dabat, quibus alta videre
         Sidera vel superas possent conscendere sedes;
<205>   Qui diram passus nostro pro crimine mortem
         Nos tenebris mersos Stygiis et carcere solvit;
         Qui fuerat postquam tumulo terrisque sepultus,
         Tercia cum staret lux, est revocatus in auras
         Aetheraque ingressus caeli suprema tenebat;

<210>   Signa Dei qui tanta dedit, quod nulla referre
         Lingua potest nemoque valet bene mente tenere.
         Hunc ego confiteor Christumque Deumque potentem,
         Et solum cui sit mundi concessa potestas;
         Hunc ego certa colo; precibusque et thure frequento.
<215>   Hic meus ardor adest; Deus hic meus et mea virtus;
         Hic facit ut tenero maneant in pectore vires,
         Virgo viros vincam, doctosque indocta repellam.'
         Haec et plura refert fidei fundamina virgo;
         Quae postquam tacuit finem fecitque loquendi,
<220>   Obstupuere patres, doctissima turba virorum,
         Et taciti secum volventes dicta puellae
         Mutua torserunt inter se lumina cuncti.
         Quos ubi conspexit princeps reticere, furore
         Plenus ait: 'Mentes quae tanta ignavia vestras
<225>   Degenerare facit generatque silentia tanta?
         Heccine virgo potest, quae nuper ab ubere matris
         Rapta fuit, superare viros quibus alta per orbam
         Fama volat, quibus est virtutis copia tanta
         Vincere quod valeant totum rationibus orbem?'
<230>   Dixerat. Assurgens cui de senioribus unus
         Sic ait: 'Est aliud bellum classemque parare
         Et populos armis et equo decorare phalanges,
         Maxenti, quam sit virtuti obsistere verae.
         Si saperes quae sint et quam sapientia verba
<235>   Virginis, horreres, nec nostra ignava putares
         Pectora. Si nobis brevibus sententia verbis
         Quae sit scire cupis, paucis adverte; docebo.
         Tu nisi, rex, nobis fidei fundamina nostrae
         Certa magis dederis doceasque haec numina vera,
<240>   In Christum natum de virgine credimus omnes.'
         Finierat senior. Rabiem Maxentius altam
         Colligit, et spumam demittit ab ore furenti;
         Atque ita terribiles sub pectore concipit iras,
         Ut iubeat magnis doctorum corpora flammis
<245>   Viva dari et meritas pro crimine solvere poenas.

166 Tytan B : Titan C   167 lumina somnum B : membra quietem
C   175 turba B : populo C   186 potest B : queat C   188 voca B :
ore C   223 Quos B : Hos C   224 ignavia B, C post corr.   231 Sic
ait: 'Est aliud B : 'Est aliud,' dixit C

1b André, *De sancta Katharina* 26–44:

<blockquote>

Quinquaginta igitur viri diserti
Venere, omnibus artibus periti.
Tunc rex in solio suo resedit,
Gemmato solido nitente et auro;
<30> Adsunt philosophi, stat et puella,
Fidens in domino Deoque vero.
Illos conspicit et fatetur ipsa
Se nescire aliud nisi Deum unum,
Patrem numine filiumque Christum,
<35> Amborum quoque spiritum videntes;
Illam doctiloquique disputantem
Muti protinus et stupent tacentque.
Ad quos sic ait imperans tyrannus:
'Quid vos degeneres tacetis ergo?'
<40> Cui sic unus ait: 'Scias profecto
Nos hac virgine protinus subactos,
In Christum pariterque credituros.'
Iratus, furibundus, imperator
Omnes tum iubet ignibus cremari.

</blockquote>

28 resedit *H* : recedit *R*   35 Amborum *H* : Et amborum *Rpc* : Et sanctum *Rac*   *inter* 38, 39 *ponit* Maxentius ad philosophos *R*   *inter* 39, 40   *ponit* Philosophi ad Maxencium *R*   42 In Christum *H* : Et Christo *R*   *inter* 42, 43 *ponit* Eiusdam crudele mandatum *R*

II. **Katherine's final prayer and decollation**
IIa Carmeliano *Beatae Katerinae vita* 600–19:

<blockquote>

<600> His oculos dictis in caelum sustulit ambos
Atque ait: 'O mundi rector, cui summa potestas,
Da, precor, ut postquam nostro de corpore noster
Spiritus exierit, quisquis celebraverit istam
Quam nunc sustineo patiens sine crimine mortem,
<605> Et quicunque meum moriens aut anxius ulla
Iactura imploret nomen, ferat omne quod optet.
At quia iam gladius supra caput astat acutus,
Hanc animam capias, quae sit tibi, sponse, propinqua.'
Vix bene desierat, cum vox est talis ab alto
<610> Reddita: 'Sponsa, veni; patet at tibi ianua caeli,
Sanctorumque chorus sanctam, dilecta, coronam

</blockquote>

Obvius adveniens portat tibi nomine nostro.
Ne dubita: dabimus quae munera cunque petisti.'
Plena Deo tali gaudet sermone puella
<615> Inclinatque caput, quod vindex publicus ense
Separat a collo. Morientia membra relinquens
Ecce fluit sacro de corpore lacteus humor.
Sanguine terra madet nullo; sed lacte recenti,
Balsama cuius odor superat Pancheaque thura.

11b André *De sancta Katharina* 99–111:

Tunc dixit, gladium morans, 'Iesu
<100> Tu Christe, accipe spiritum meique
Quotquot sunt memores, redemptor, oro,
Fac suffragia nostra sequantur.'
Tunc vox coelitus ecce facta venit:
'Huc, dilecta, veni; veni, puella.
<105> En, coeli tibi porta iam patescit,
Et quodcunque tui petent amici
Praestabo, modo iuxta me precentur.'
Post haec candida lacteam retexens
Cervicem Katharina laniatur,
<110> Amittitque caput; cruor nec ullus,
Sed lac defluit undequaque terram.

102 sequantur *H* : consequantur *R*   *inter* 102, 103 *ponit* Vox de celo
R   103 coelitus *H* : celitus *R*   105 coeli *H* : celi *R*   107 Praestabo
H : Prestabo *R*   *inter* 107, 108 *ponit* Katherine decollatio *R*   108
haec *H* : hec *R*   retexens *H, Rpc* : protendens *Rac*   109 Katharina
H : Katherina *R*

 Abbreviations

Allen
Allen, P.S., H.M. Allen, and H.W. Garrod, eds. *Opus Epistolarum Des. Erasmi Roterdami.* 12 vols. Oxford: Clarendon 1906–58

BRUC
Emden, Alfred Brotherston. *A Biographical Register of the University of Cambridge to 1500.* Cambridge: Cambridge University Press 1963

BRUO
Emden, Alfred Brotherston. *A Biographical Register of the University of Oxford to 1500.* 3 vols. Oxford: Clarendon 1957–9

CEBR
Bietenholz, Peter G., ed. *Contemporaries of Erasmus: A Biographical Register of the Renaissance and Reformation.* 3 vols. Toronto: University of Toronto Press 1985–7

CWE
Collected Works of Erasmus. Vols 1–. Toronto: University of Toronto Press 1974–

CWM
The Yale Edition of the Complete Works of St. Thomas More. Vols 1–. New Haven: Yale University Press 1961–

DNB
Stephen, Leslie, and Sidney Lee, eds. *The Dictionary of National Biography*. 63 vols. London: Smith, Elder and Co, 1885–1900

LP
Letters and Papers, Foreign and Domestic, of the Reign of Henry VIII. Ed J.S. Brewer et al. 21 vols and addenda. London: HMSO 1862–1932

Nelson
Nelson, William. *John Skelton Laureate*. Columbia University Studies in English and Comparative Literature 139. New York: Columbia University Press 1939

Reedijk
Reedijk, Cornelis. *The Poems of Desiderius Erasmus*. Leiden: E.J. Brill 1956

STC
Pollard, A.W., and G.R. Redgrave. *A Short-Title Catalogue of Books Printed in England, Scotland, and Ireland, and of English Books Printed Abroad, 1475–1640*. 2nd ed, revised and enlarged by W.A. Jackson, F.S. Ferguson, and Katherine F. Pantzer. 3 vols. London: Bibliographical Society 1976–91

Weiss *Humanism*
Weiss, Roberto. *Humanism in England during the Fifteenth Century*. Medium Aevum Monographs IV. 3rd ed. Oxford: Blackwell 1967

 Notes

INTRODUCTION

1 Here and throughout, my debt to the work of Jerome McGann, D.F. McKenzie, and other book historians and bibliographers will be clear. For me, the most important of these writings have been James Thorpe's 'The Aesthetics of Textual Criticism'; McGann's 'Keats and the Historical Method in Literary Criticism,' 'The Text, the Poem, and the Problem of Historical Method,' *A Critique of Modern Textual Criticism*, and the collection of the papers from a conference he organized in 1982, entitled *Textual Criticism and Literary Interpretation*; and McKenzie's 'The Sociology of a Text,' and his 1985 Panizzi Lectures, *Bibliography and the Sociology of Texts*. The most striking work of this sort remains that of Randall McLeod, for example, 'UN*Editing* Shak-speare,' or, more recently, 'from *Tranceformations* in the Text of "*Orlando Furioso.*"' I have remained regrettably ignorant of parallel developments in continental bibliography, with a few exceptions: Lucien Febvre and Henri-Jean Martin, *L'Apparition du livre*; Armando Petrucci 'Alle origini del libro moderno'; and a few more specialized studies, mostly Italian, cited in the notes below.

2 See Feltes' *Modes of Production of Victorian Novels*, for whose example I have been grateful.

3 These topics are discussed in greater detail in Carlson 'Erasmus,

Revision, and the British Library Manuscript Egerton 1651'
199–200. See also Cerquiglini *Eloge de la variante* 18–29; or Gerald
L. Bruns 'The Originality of Texts in a Manuscript Culture' *Comparative Literature* 32 (1980) 113–29.

4 Coined in Italy late in the fifteenth century, the terminology was
in use north of the Alps by the early sixteenth: see Campana 'The
Origin of the Word "Humanist"' 67–73, or Giustiniani 'Homo,
Humanus, and the Meanings of "Humanism"' esp 171–4. I have
found most immediately useful the cautionary discussion of Fox
'Facts and Fallacies' 9–33, seconding the views of Paul Oskar Kristeller, eg, in 'Studies on Renaissance Humanism during the Last
Twenty Years' *Studies in the Renaissance* 9 (1961) esp 17 and 22–3.
The yoking of present-oriented activism (of one sort or another)
with the reflective impulses of the return *ad fontes* that I emphasize here is discussed by Greene, 'Resurrecting Rome' esp 41–2.

5 Cf Carlson *The Latin Writings of John Skelton* 7–11, on which the
discussion here is based.

6 On Maecenas, see Dalzell; and on Roman literary patronage more
generally, cf Peter White '*Amicitia* and the Profession of Poetry in
Early Imperial Rome,' and Jasper Griffin 'Augustus and the Poets'
Caesar Qui Cogere Posset' in *Caesar Augustus Seven Aspects* ed F.
Millar and E. Segal (Oxford: Clarendon 1984) 189–218.

7 In an epigram of his preserved in London, British Library, Harley
336, fol 86v; printed in Carlson 'Politicizing Tudor Court Literature' 304, appendix 9. Other instances of this topic – humanists
calling potential patrons 'Maecenas,' a commonplace in England by
the early sixteenth century – are mentioned below, ch 2, n 27; and
ch 3, p 62.

8 Cf the formulations of Anderson 15–42, esp 18–24 and 39–42. Various recent studies tend to affirm the absolutist propensities of
even the early Tudor monarchy: see Mayer 'Tournai and Tyranny'
257–70, esp 269.

9 Gundersheimer 'Patronage in the Renaissance' 6–8; and cf Lucas
'The Growth and Development of English Literary Patronage in
the Later Middle Ages and Early Renaissance' 223–4. On the 'anti-
royalist' strain throughout the *Utopia*, see Emrys Jones 'Common-
ers and Kings: Book One of More's *Utopia*' in *Medieval Studies
for J.A.W. Bennett* ed P.L. Heyworth (Oxford: Clarendon 1981)
255–72.

10 Veblen *The Theory of the Leisure Class* esp 41–80; the remarks

that follow are much indebted to Veblen's work. Cf also the discussion of Lucas 'The Growth and Development of English Literary Patronage' 219–48, esp 225–33.

11 Hay 'England and the Humanities in the Fifteenth Century' 340.

12 The vividness of the issue of ancient republicanism is well illustrated in D.J. Gordon 'Giannotti, Michelangelo and the Cult of
Brutus' in *The Renaissance Imagination* ed Stephen Orgel (Berkeley: University of California Press 1975) 233–45; and ancient republicanism has been central to Hans Baron's analysis of the
renaissance: see 'Cicero and the Roman Civic Spirit in the Middle
Ages and Early Renaissance' *Bulletin of the John Rylands Library*
22 (1938) 72–97, or *The Crisis of the Early Italian Renaissance*
(Princeton: Princeton University Press 1955) esp 1: 38–49. Two recent articles of Thomas Mayer discuss its ramifications for humanists in early Tudor England: 'Faction and Ideology' and
'Tournai and Tyranny' esp 270–7. For Grafton and Jardine's argument for humanism's ultimate conservatism, see *From Humanism
to the Humanities* esp xii–xiv and 23–5; and see also Caspari *Humanism and the Social Order in Tudor England* esp 6–22, arguing
that humanists in England were 'the defenders of the aristocratic
order': 'The appeal of the humanists was so great because they
showed how the position of the aristocracy could be preserved'
(p 14).

13 Eg, *Epis* 1.18.

14 'Liber sum, natura quidem, sed non voluntate. Addixi enim me invictissimo meo regi, sapientissimo famulor Cardinali Eboracensi;
patriae enim servire omnem superat libertatem.' *De fructu qui ex
doctrina percipitur*, ed Manley and Sylvester, 12; my translation.
All translations herein are mine, with only the exceptions indicated.

15 Ep 250, trans *CWE* II, 211 (ed Allen I, 497).

16 This is not to say that humanists did not take on non-literary employment of one sort or another, and gain income by it; they did.
But in these cases, the employments were secondary, rewards for
success and distinction gained in the first instance by writing. The
best discussion of incipient literary professionalism in England is
Green *Poets and Princepleasers* esp 168–211. See also Thomas
Frederick Tout 'Literature and Learning in the English Civil Service in the Fourteenth Century' *Speculum* 4 (1929) 381–2 ('Medieval conditions made literature an impossible profession');

Holzknecht *Literary Patronage in the Middle Ages* 58–73; Bennett 'The Author and His Public in the Fourteenth and Fifteenth Centuries' 9–18; Lucas 'The Growth and Development of English Literary Patronage' esp 234–44; and Ebin *Illuminator, Makar, Vates* esp 196–200.

17 On literary presentation, see Green *Poets and Princepleasers* 63–5, 98, and 205–6. Root 'Publication before Printing' is concerned above all with presentation, which he is inclined to equate with publication and to treat as 'final and definite'; cf Holzknecht *Literary Patronage* 156–69.

18 Schirmer *Der Englische Frühhumanismus*; Nelson esp chs 1–2; Weiss *Humanism*; and Hay, esp 'England and the Humanities in the Fifteenth Century' 305–67, but also (emphasizing the historical background) 'The Early Renaissance in England.' Rossi, 'Enrico V dalla cronaca alla poesia' in *Ricerche sull'umanesimo e sul rinascimento in Inghilterra* esp 7–10, also has important observations on the early history of humanism in England; Rossi's 'Note sugli Italiani in Inghilterra nell'età del rinascimento' concerns the later sixteenth and early seventeenth centuries, except pp 59–61 on the reign of Henry VII and the early years of Henry VIII. The period has been most recently surveyed by Schoeck 'Humanism in England.' From these works most of the facts in the following paragraphs are drawn.

19 Weiss *Humanism* 183.

20 See now Anglo 'Ill of the Dead.'

21 One such figure is the subject of Trapp's study, 'Christopher Urswick and His Books.'

22 For what follows here, see, eg, McConica *English Humanists and Reformation Politics under Henry VIII and Edward VI* 76–105.

23 Hay 'England and the Humanities in the Fifteenth Century' 366; and cf Schoeck 'Humanism in England' 6–7.

24 This too is Hay's term, 'England and the Humanities in the Fifteenth Century' 333; cf Caspari, *Humanism and Social Order* 2–22, on the inculcation of humanist tastes in England's 'civil governing class' (p 7).

25 Cf Hay 'England and the Humanities in the Fifteenth Century' 312.

26 Cf Clough 'Federigo da Montefeltro's Patronage of the Arts, 1468–1482' 142; and Hay *Polydore Vergil* 4–5.

27 The most important discussions are in Starkey, ed *The English*

Court from the Wars of the Roses to the Civil War esp 71–118, Starkey's contribution 'Intimacy and Innovation: The Rise of the Privy Chamber, 1485–1547'; cf also Elton 'Tudor Government' esp 212–13.

28 Lord Mountjoy wrote Erasmus, 27 May 1509: 'Superioribus diebus, quum se eruditiorem optaret [sc. noster rex Henricus VIII], "Non hoc," inquam, "nos a te, sed ut eruditos amplectaris et foveas expetimus." "Quid ni?" inquit, "nempe sine illis vix essemus"' (Ep 215, ed Allen I, 450). The generational change following 1509 is discussed below, ch 3, pp 65–7.

CHAPTER ONE

1 The manuscript in question is now London, British Library, Arundel 317. The probability that this is the manuscript presented by Alberici to Henry VII is corroborated by the note, in a later hand, on fol 29v, indicating that the manuscript was once in an English royal collection: 'This booke was geven me, George Carew of Clopton, by the ladie Elizabeth, daughter unto the most highe and puissant monarch James, of England, Scotland, France, and Ireland the kinge, and with her owne fayre hand she superscribed her name. Mens. Octob. 1608'; above this, in a different hand, is written 'Elizabeth.' Subsequently, the manuscript came into the possession of Henry Howard, duke of Norfolk, as part of whose library it was noticed by Edward Bernard, in his 1697 *Catalogi librorum manuscriptorum Angliae et Hiberniae* II, 81, no 3204.306. It is also described in Kristeller *Iter Italicum* IV, 131.

   The evidence for the date of the manuscript and its presentation is likewise not unequivocal. The writings in it repeatedly made reference to Prince Henry as the heir (see below, pp 22 and 25), and so it must belong to the period April 1502–April 1509. One of the items in it was occasioned by a visit by Henry VII to Cambridge University, and the only such visit in the requisite period that I find took place in late April 1506 (see below, pp 22–3 and n 7). Since Alberici was resident in Paris by June 1507 (see below, n 4), the most likely occasion falling between April 1506 and June 1507 for the presentation of a manuscript containing the Cambridge poem, along with other writings, seems to me to be New Year's 1507.

2 The best source of biographical information about Alberici re-

mains the scattered remarks of Archangelo Giani, in his *Annales sacri ordinis Fratrum servorum B. Mariae virginis* 2nd ed, ed A.M. Garbi (Lucca 1719–25), I, 380–1 and II, 32, 35, 53, 62–3, 75, 88, 100–1, esp II, 101, where Giani summarizes Alberici's career (but without noticing any of his activities early in his career in England and in France) and states the nature of his authority (II, 103, n 2): 'Author singula de Albrisio [sic] collegit, tum ex ejusdem operibus, tum ex monumentis Albericiae Familiae, quae in ejus domo asservantur Mantuae.' Alberici's other biographers – principally, Giammaria Mazzuchelli *Gli Scrittori d'Italia cioè Notizie storiche e critiche, intorno alle vite e agli scritti dei letterati Italiani* (Brescia 1753), 286–7, and Leopoldo Camillo Volta *Biografia dei Mantovani Illustri nelle Scienze, Lettere ed Arti*, corrected and augmented ed, ed Antonio Mainardi, vol 1 (Mantova 1845) 11–13 – appear to have taken their information from Giani.

There is slight evidencè to suggest that Alberici may have travelled to England on papal business, at the behest of Julius II. Giani *Annales* II, 101, states that Alberici was 'vir nunquam otiosus,' and so on, 'multos assecutus honores, et quem a Julio Secundo in Galliam, et Angliam Nuncium, et Concionatorem Apostolicum, ac Sanctae Inquisitionis contra haereses Ministrum legatum ferunt.' I tend to regard Giani's 'ferunt' here as significant, particularly just following, as it does, his assertion of the quality of his sources; however, the claim is echoed or perhaps corroborated by the remarks of Mazzuchelli, p 287, and Volta, p 12, who states: 'Dal sommo Pontifice Guilio II venne spedito in Francia e in Inghilterra in qualità di Nunzio e predicatore Apostolico.' I am unable to find other corroboration, though; consequently it seems unlikely that Alberici came to England as Julius II's emissary.

Alberici came to England with an introduction to Giovanni Battista Boerio, Henry VII's court doctor, a familiar of Erasmus, Bernard André, and others involved in the development of early Tudor humanism. The acquaintance is attested by the account of a conversation between them, in a letter that Alberici published as a preface to the edition of his uncle Battista Fiera's *Coena saluberrima* (Paris: Josse Bade, 13 August 1508) that he prepared in Paris. The letter is reprinted in *The Letters of Richard Fox* ed P.S. Allen and H.M. Allen, no 27, pp 41–2; and the volume in which it first appeared is described in Dennis E. Rhodes 'The Early Editions of Baptista Fiera' in *Book Production and Letters in the Western Eu-*

ropean Renaissance ed A.L. Lepschy, John Took, and Rhodes (London: Modern Humanities Research Association, 1986) 237–8. On Boerio, who also contributed commendatory verse to another volume printed at Paris by Bade, Bernard André's *Hymni Christiani* (1517), see *CEBR* I, 158–9; and for Boerio's acquaintance with Alberici's uncle Fiera, see Dionisotti 'Battista Fiera' 414–15.

3 Alberici's two letters to Fox are printed in *The Letters of Richard Fox* ed Allen and Allen, nos 27–8, pp 41–3. In the first – the letter printed as a preface to the *Coena saluberrima* – Alberci wrote: 'Non enim oblitus sum quanti me haud merentem facias, quantaque abs te susceperim, qui Regis servitio tot iam pollicitationibus me addicere nitebaris. Verum non mea hec causa acta sunt, sed tue virtutis magnanimitatisque: tu enim ille es (ut brevi cuncta perstringam) in cuius animo non ab re regii pectoris archana collocantur. Vale.' And in the second – evidently the epistolary preface to a work of Alberici's, entitled *De casu animi*, of which no copy now survives, reported by Anthony à Wood, *Historia et antiquitates universitatis Oxoniensis* (Oxford 1674) II, 229 – Alberici wrote: 'Et hac spe semper operatus sum, ut tibi patrono meo studiorum meorum labores quantuloscunque offerrem. Videbor enim mihi ingrate egisse nisi meam in te venerationem literario munere ostenderim, qui elapsis temporibus potentissimum Regem, cuius consilia in te uno conquiescunt, cuius arcanorum solus es conscius, tam propitium habes.'

4 For the details of Alberici's Italian career, after May 1509, I have relied on Giani. The evidence that Alberici spent some time in Paris, after his visit to England in 1506–7 and before returning to Italy, by May 1509, when he took part in the *publicae disputationes* of the Servite General Chapter at Piacenza (Giani *Annales* II, 32), is as follows. In the prefatory letter to his *Problemata exponibilium* (Paris: Barbier and Petit, 12 June 1507), sigs x6r–x8r, a letter addressed to Alberici by the author, Jérôme de Hangest, a Sorbonne *magister*, describes a conversation among himself and the 'venerabiles religiosos, fratrem Hieronimum Castro de Placentia et fratrem Philippum Albericum de Mantua Ordinis Sancti Augustini, Servorum Beate Marie' that must have taken place in Paris not long before the book's publication. On 1 July 1507, Bade printed occasional verses by Alberici in the second volume of an edition of the *Opera* of Mantuan, (Paris: Bade, 1 July 1507); and on 8 August 1508, Bade printed the edition of Fiera's *Coena saluber-*

rima, mentioned above n 2, that Alberici prepared and for which he wrote a preface. Alberici's two letters to Richard Fox, mentioned above, n 3, were both signed at Paris, dated 8 August 1508 and 1 January 1509. Probably while in Paris, Alberici wrote the lost work *De casu animi* that Anthony à Wood saw (see above, n 3); in addition, Volta *Biografia* 12–13 says that Alberici wrote 'un Poema latino sulla Passione di Gesù Cristo, di cui si conserva un imperfetto esemplare in pergamena fra i Codici della R. Biblioteca di Parigi,' but I have been unable to locate such a poem.

5 Giani *Annales* II, 53 quotes from this work and claims that it was printed in 1515; but again, I have been unable to locate a copy. In the passage Giani quotes, Alberici describes his election as vicar-general of the Servites, at Mantua in 1515, concluding 'Ordinis nostri initium Congregationis institutionem, et B. Philippi vitam hoc anno [sc 1515] composui'; Giani continues: 'Haec Albrisius [sic] ad calcem suae historiae de Congreg. quam hoc anno [sc 1515] complevit et typis mandavit.' Cf also Giani *Annales* I, 380, and II, 101; and Giani's *Della historia del B. Filippo Benizii* (Florence 1604) 22, 75, and 91, where Alberici's work is also cited. In his *Annales* I, 380, Giani says that the work was dedicated to Antonio del Monte, a Curia cardinal who had an interest in English affairs (see Chambers *Cardinal Bainbridge in the Court of Rome 1509–1514* 109–10; and Wilkie *The Cardinal Protectors of England* 208, 212–14); however, Alberici's dedication more probably was due to the fact that del Monte was also cardinal protector of the Servites.

6 The reference to the gift to the poet from Italy occurs in London, Public Record Office, E 101/414/6, fol 30r, one of the several surviving books of accounts of payments kept by Henry's treasurer of the Chamber, John Heron, throughout the reign. On the reference, see Wormald 'An Italian Poet at the Court of Henry VII,' who thinks it may refer to Johannes Michael Nagonius; Nagonius certainly visited England c 1494. A similar later reference – in London, Public Record Office, E 36/214, fol 89v, to a 3 August 1507 gift of ten shillings 'to a monke of Italy that gave the kinges grace a boke' – could conceivably refer to a present given to Alberici, though he was probably in France at that date. The manuscript addressed by Opizio to Henry VII survives as London, British Library, Cotton Vespasian B.iv; it is described in Watson *Catalogue*

of Dated and Datable Manuscripts in the British Library I, 108, no 566, with a photograph, II, pl 889, and in Kristeller *Iter Italicum* IV, 139; see also Nelson, pp 27–8.

7 The poem survives in Arundel 317, fols 24r–24v. For Henry's 1506 visit to Cambridge, see J. Saltmarsh, in *The Victoria History of the Counties of England: A History of the County of Cambridge and the Isle of Ely* ed J.P.C. Roach, vol 3 (London 1959) 389. A number of payments, dated 1 May 1506, occasioned by the visit are recorded in the Heron account book for the period, Public Record Office E 36/214, fol 28r.

8 Cf Arundel 317, fol 24v: 'Cantabria est testis, quae dum de more coronat / Docta viros, tanto te duce [sc Henrice VII] culta nitet.'

9 For Bretoner's career, see *BRUC*, p 92. The letter, including Alberici's warrant about the poem, 'nulli adhuc nisi regi vestro eam concesserim,' occupies Arundel 317, fol. 24v. On the practice of representation, see below, ch 4, pp 83–5 and n 7, and Lucas 'The Growth and Development of English Literary Patronage' esp 239.

10 Arundel 317, fols 25v–28v.

11 'De mortis effectibus,' lines 82–4 and 87–8: 'nec mox vertere terga licet'; 'Hic (ut fama) trahunt tetricae sua pensa Sorores, / Et stabili observant relligione locum'; 'Est opus extremam tandem pertingere metam, / Et trahit aeternas exitus ad tenebras' (Arundel 317, fol 28r).

12 'De mortis effectibus,' lines 93–104 (Arundel 317, fols 28r–28v).

13 Arundel 317, fol 3r.

14 Arundel 317, fols 1r–2r.

15 In *Of Education*, Milton lists *Cebes' Tablet* as an 'easy and delightful book of education,' to be read to the young 'to season them and win them early to the love of virtue and true labor, ere any flattering seducement or vain principle seize them wandering' (*John Milton: Complete Poems and Major Prose*, ed Merrit Y. Hughes [Indianapolis: Bobbs-Merrill 1957], 633).

16 See Fitzgerald and White *The Tabula of Cebes* 1–4.

17 For these details of the *fortuna* of the *Cebes' Tablet* in the late fifteenth and early sixteenth centuries, see the survey of Lutz, 'Ps. Cebes,' esp 2–3 (overlooking Alberici's version, however), as well as her 'Aesticampianus' Edition of the *Tabula* Attributed to Cebes'; and Sider, *Cebes' Tablet* 1–4.

18 For the Latin originals of these summaries, see appendix 1.

19 Specifically, to the end of section sixteen of the Greek (ed Karl Praechter [Leipzig: Teubner 1893], 15) and to line 490 (Arundel 317, fol 17v) of Alberici's version.

20 Appendix 2 gives some extracts for comparison, of the sort that lead to this conclusion.

21 See appendix 1 for the Latin original of this summary as well.

22 Arundel 317, fols 24r–24v: 'Ingenio fortis, fortis quoque Caesar in armis'; 'Sat tibi laudis erat, nullo et peritura sub aevo, / Inclite rex, forti gloria parta manu; / Quid – nimium est – quid adhuc sacra de fronde Minervae / Temporibus statuis condere serta tuis?'; 'Iure, igitur, duplici dentur tibi signa triumpho: / Et galea et lauro te decorare decet.'

23 On Henry's patronage in general, see Kipling, 'Henry VII and the Origins of Tudor Patronage,' though the piece systematically slights Italian contributions and influence.

24 Much of what follows is indebted to Francesco Tateo's 'Le armi e le lettere: Per la storia di un topos umanistico,' which he kindly made available to me before its publication. Cf also Raffaele Puddu, 'Lettere ed arme'; and for the theme's context in larger philosophical issues, see Fritz Schalk, 'Il tema della "vita activa" e della "vita contemplativa" nell' umanesimo italiano' in *Umanesimo e scienza politica* ed Enrico Castelli (Milan 1951) 559–66. Kipling 'Henry VII,' esp 124–5 and 133–4, seeks to show that the same ideal also animated contemporary Burgundian culture and English culture under Burgundian influence.

25 On the double portrait, see esp Rosenberg 'The Double Portrait of Federico and Guidobaldo da Montefeltro.' For other examples of the theme in Urbinesque court art, see Dennistoun *Memoirs of the Dukes of Urbino* III, 459; Westfall 'Chivalric Declaration' 37; Clough 'Federigo da Montefeltro' 347–8; and Cheles *The Studiolo of Urbino* esp 18 and 56, and figs 49–51, 60, and 105, on the decoration of the east wall of the room, juxtaposing an inlay depicting pieces of armour with another depicting books and a lectern; the room also contained an intarsia portrait of Federico, in which he carries a spear and has the collar of the Order of the Ermine about his neck, but wears a humanist's robe rather than armour or more statesmanly garments. Castiglione's biographical eulogy of Guidobaldo, the 'Ad Britanniae regem Henricum de Guido-Ubaldo Monfeltrio Urbini duce' (1508), in *Le lettere*, ed Guido la Rocca, vol 1 (Rome 1978), no 191, pp 162–98, is organized in part by the

'arms and letters' theme: Castiglione describes first Guidobaldo's aptitude for military feats (ed Rocca, pp 166 ff) and then his learning and patronage of learning (ed Rocca, pp 174 ff); the transition from the one section to the other is: 'Magni in primis consilii, magnaeque prudentiae vir fuit, solus ex omnibus quos unquam viderim ad omnia quibuscumque animum intendisset natus. Nam, ut omittam belli peritiam, magnanimitatem, sollertiam in rebus omnibus dexteritatemque, liberalia studia ab aetate prima cupide semper ac diligenter exercuit.' The piece was addressed to Henry VII and the presentation copy survives: see Clough 'Baldassare Castiglione's Presentation Manuscript to King Henry VII.' On Odasio's career at Urbino, see above, p 25 and n 17, and Clough 'Federigo da Montefeltro's Patronage' 133.

26 See esp Clough 'The Relations between the English and Urbino Courts, 1474–1508.' Cornelio Vitelli had some contact with the court of Urbino before he came to England in late 1489 (possibly earlier); see Weiss 'Cornelio Vitelli in France and England' 220; and Clough 'Thomas Linacre, Cornelio Vitelli, and Humanistic Studies at Oxford' 10–21. Polydore Vergil was a native of Urbino, maintaining familial and other ties with it throughout his life, and he had dedicated an early work to Odasio; see Hay *Polydore Vergil*, esp 3–5. Likewise, it seems possible that Pietro Torregiano, who worked in England during the first decade of the reign of Henry VIII, most notably on the monuments of the Henry VII Chapel at Westminster, also had had some experience of Urbino earlier in his career; see G.F. Hill *Medals of the Renaissance* (Oxford: Clarendon 1920) 41.

27 For what follows, see esp Clough 'Relations' 206–8 and 211–14, and 'Federigo Veterani, Polydore Vergil's "Anglica Historia" and Baldassare Castiglione's "Epistola ... ad Henricum Angliae Regem"' 780–3; see also Wilkie *Cardinal Protectors* 30–1 and 35–6.

28 On Castiglione's embassy, see esp Clough 'Baldassare Castiglione's *Ad Henricum Angliae regem epistola de vita et gestis Guidubaldi Urbini ducis*' 227.

29 As noted above, n 2, it is just possible that Alberici was in England as an emissary of the della Rovere Pope Julius II. It is also conceivable that Alberici travelled to England with Castiglione, with whom he may have been acquainted, except that there is no evidence whatsoever. Before entering the service of the dukes of Urbino in 1504, Castiglione had served the Sforza dukes of Mantua,

Alberici's native city. Moreover, Alberici's uncle Battista Fiera, who also provided Alberici an introduction to Giovanni Battista Boerio, was a correspondent of Castiglione; see above, n 2, and Dionisotti 'Battista Fiera' 401. Were there anything linking Alberici to the ducal court of Urbino, or to some member of the ducal family, it might be tempting to imagine that his version of the *Cebes' Tablet* was conceived or first drafted for a duke of Urbino or some relative of one, for whom the concluding allegory of *Studium* and *Mars* would have had a particular propriety; but again, there is no evidence.

30 On the *Cebes' Tablet* in art, particularly book-illustration, see Müller 'Relieffragment mit Darstellungen aus dem ΠΙΝΑΞ des Kebes'; Boas 'De Illustratie der Tabula Cebetis'; and Schleier *Tabula Cebetis*. Holbein was responsible for as many as four versions of the *tabula*, only the latest of which, that of 1522, is reproduced here; see Schleier *Tabula Cebetis* 34–6 and 76–89, and figs 5–8. For the illustration of the Aesticampianus edition, see Lutz 'Aesticampianus' 115 and ill, and Schleier *Tabula Cebetis* 32 and fig 1.

31 See Schleier *Tabula Cebetis* 28–39 and 77, and figs 18–28.

32 A contemporary analogue for this snake-strewn path occurs in Pinturicchio's pavement mosaic for the Duomo of Siena, called the *Colle della Virtù*, designed 1504–6; cf Enzo Carli *Il Duomo di Siena* (Genoa 1979) 143–53, esp 143 and 151–2, and pl 251.

33 'Incipe, si mens est tibi candida.' The words occur as part of line 486 of Alberici's poem (Arundel 317, fol 17v).

34 'Pergite, si mens est, iuvenes.' The words occur as part of line 524 of Alberici's poem (Arundel 317, fol 19v).

35 These unillustrated figures are described at lines 285–9 (*Vanagloria*), 324–7 (*Tristitia*), 390–407 (*Verus Poeta*; a passage edited below, appendix 2) of Alberici's poem (Arundel 317, fols 11r, 12r, and 15r–15v).

36 A similar anomaly of the illustrations is the fleur-de-lys-like tree around which a banner inscribed 'fortunati' is draped in the second illustration (fig 7); both of these may make some heraldic point or other, of which I am ignorant.

37 See above, p 32 and nn 33 and 34.

38 On *Gula*, see lines 293–5 of Alberici's poem (Arundel 317, fols 11r–11v): 'Aspice, quantum illi mento palearia pendent, / Sordida cui vestis, cui brachia nuda manusque / Turgescunt: illi est cupidus pro munere venter.'

39 The passages describing these figures are edited below, appendix 2.

40 For these figures, see lines 499–506 of Alberici's poem (Arundel
317, fols 17v–18r): 'Si quis forte pedem cepto dimoverit orbe, /
Territus anguineo afflatu tristive labore, / Huic tellure datur
scaevo pro vindice nata / Nox, secumque potens flagris crudelis
Egestas.'

41 On Alberici's acquaintance with Boerio, see above, n 2. Alberici's
prefatory letter to Fiera's *Coena saluberrima* (see above, nn 2–3),
dated 8 August 1508, is addressed 'Domino Roberto episcopo Win-
toniensi, regii apud Anglos sigilli custodi' (in *The Letters of Richard Fox*, ed Allen and Allen, p 41).

42 On the tutors Henry employed, see Carlson, 'Royal Tutors in the
Reign of Henry VII'; the careers of Carmeliano and André are discussed below, in chs 2 and 3.

43 For an example, see below, ch 3, p 76 and n 51.

44 In 'Baldassare Castiglione's Presentation Manuscript' 272, Clough
suggests that Castiglione was soliciting Henry VII's favours in
1508, when he addressed his eulogy of Guidobaldo to the English
king.

CHAPTER TWO

1 See below, pp 47–58 and n 51. For Carmeliano's biography, see
James Gairdner's article on him in the *DNB*, III, 1036–7; Guerrini,
Pietro Carmeliano da Brescia, segretario reale d'Inghilterra; Weiss
Humanism 170–2, and 'Cornelio Vitelli' 223–4; C.A.J. Armstrong
Dominic Mancini 19 and n 1; Massimo Firpo's article on him in
the *Dizionario biografico degli italiani* xx (Rome: Istituto della En-
ciclopedia Italiana 1977) 410–13; Gilbert Tournoy, in *CEBR* I, 270;
and Carlson 'The Occasional Poetry of Pietro Carmeliano' and
'Politicizing Tudor Court Literature' 285–6 and 290–3. The aspect
of Carmeliano's biography that remains least well understood in
his work as a Venetian agent in England, secret or otherwise, at
least in 1504 and again in 1508–9; in 1496, Carmeliano seems to
have offered similar services to Lodovico Sforza, duke of Milan.
For the pertinent documents, see the *Calendar of State Papers and
Manuscripts relating to English Affairs Existing in the Archives
and Collections of Venice and in Other Libraries of Northern Italy*
I, 332–5 (nos 915, 918–20), 338 (no 922), 341 (no 929), 345 (no 941);
II, 9 (no 25), 12 (no 30), 28 (no 61), 30 (no 64), 32 (no 67), 105 (no

251), 419 (no 963), 578 (no 1331), 636–7 (nos 1481 and 1484), and 643 (no 1489).

2 For these poems of André and Gigli, see Carlson 'King Arthur and Court Poems for the Birth of Arthur Tudor in 1486' 167–73, where they are edited. André's poem survives only as it was later incorporated into his *Vita Henrici Septimi*, now London, British Library, Cotton Domitian XVIII; Gigli's poem survives only as it was incorporated into a larger collection of writings of his, now London, British Library, Harley 336, that he made for Bishop Fox, probably some time after the prince's birth (on it, see below, ch 3, n 29). By late 1486, André seems already to have been well established at court, as a propagandist and historiographer; for his biography, see below, ch 3 and the references given at ch 3 n 4. Gigli had been papal collector for England since 1476 and had helped Henry VII in the early months of his reign to obtain the canonical dispensation that he needed to marry Elizabeth of York; for Gigli's biography, see Mandell Creighton's article on him, in the *DNB* VII, 1190; Weiss, 'Lineamenti di una biografia di Giovanni Gigli, collettore papale in Inghilterra e vescovo di Worcester (1434–1498)'; Wilkie *Cardinal Protectors* 14, 17–24, and 55–7; and Tournoy-Thoen 'Het vroegste Latijnse humanstische epithalamium in Engeland.'

3 This suggestion that the manuscript – now London, British Library, Addit 33736 – was once part of the royal library is pure presumption, only inferred from the manuscript's decoration (discussed below, p 47) and contents, and from what is known of Carmeliano's other publishing activities. It should have belonged to Henry VII and should have gone into his collection; however, I have been unable to discover anything definite about the manuscript's early whereabouts.

4 The most important source of information about Carmeliano's career before his arrival in England may be an autobiographical passage in a letter of his, surviving in London, British Library, Royal 12.A.xxix, fols 1r–2v, given in full in appendix 3 below. In it, Carmeliano tells something about his early education in humane letters, and he says that he had left Rome about ten years earlier (ie, c 1472), travelling through France and Brittany before reaching England. The letter is signed at its conclusion (fol 2v): 'Ex Aedibus Rotulorum vii Idus Apriles M. cccclxxxii'; and, from this, Carmeliano's employment at the Rolls House has been inferred.

5 The manuscript in question is now Royal 12.A.xxix; and it is described in Watson *Catalogue of Dated and Datable Manuscripts in the British Library*, I, 154, no 888, with a photograph, II, pl 831, and in Kristeller *Iter Italicum* IV, 201. The epistolary preface translated here (the Latin is in appendix 3 below) occupies fols 1r–2v. The discussion of the work's dedication here is based on that in Carlson 'Politicizing Tudor Court Literature' 291.

6 'Ianque vale, et centum, princeps, ter carmina sume; / Meque scias servum mancipiumque tuum. / Nanque tuas alio describam tempore laudes, / Teque tuum fratrem cum genitore canam. / Me tibi commendo, princeps celeberrime; nanque / Me mea paupertas exiliumque premit.' *De vere* 295–300 (Royal 12.A.xxix, fol 10r).

7 Thomas Tanner saw this book at some point before 1748 and described it in his *Bibliotheca Britannico-Hibernica* (London 1748), 155; but it has since dropped from view. See further Carlson 'Occasional Poetry' 496–7.

8 'Neminem equidem, clarissime princeps, te ipso digniorem inveni cui libellus inscriberetur, nisi serenissimo regi patri tuo splendidissimo id opus destinassem; sed cum praeclarissima ac memoranda eius gesta in praesentiarum edam quae brevi profecto volumine comprehendi non possunt, visum est mihi rationem etiam tui esse habendam.' Cf appendix 3 below.

9 Surviving uniquely in Royal 12.A.xxix, fols 3r–10r.

10 Cf Curtius *European Literature and the Latin Middle Ages* 319–26, esp 319–21; on medieval bestiaries, see Florence McCulloch *Mediaeval Latin and French Bestiaries* 2nd ed (Chapel Hill: University of North Carolina Press 1962).

11 According to the letter prefacing it: 'non dubitavi opusculum hoc perbreve quidem celsitudini tuae dicare, quod in hac Redemptoris nostri resurectione muneris loco susciperes'; the date given at the end of the letter, 'vii Idus Apriles M. cccclxxxii,' was Easter Sunday in the year mentioned. See appendix 3 below.

12 Eg, 'Indica Testudo sequitur, quae tecta domorum / Integra sola tegit tegmine celsa suo, / Ac cymbas pariter remeantes Aequore Rubro / Efficit, ut memorat Plinius historicus.' *De vere* 97–100 (Royal 12.A.xxix, fol 5r).

13 The digression on the *philomena* occupies *De vere* 213–34; the allusion to the owl, *De vere* 167–8, with reference to *Aen* 4.462–3. For use of the woodpecker in augury (*De vere* 173), cf Pliny *Hist nat* 10.20.40–1, or Plautus *Asinaria* 2.1.10–15; for the sacredness of

the dove to Venus (*De vere* 237), cf Ovid, *Met* 15.386; and for the war between the cranes and the pygmies (*De vere* 185), cf Pliny, *Hist nat* 4.11.44, or Pomponius Mela *De chorographia* 3.8.81.

14 Royal 12.A.xxix, fol 3r.

15 The pages of Royal 12.A.xxix now measure 212 x 144 mm; the area covered by the writing – a single column of twenty lines per page, verse or prose – measures only 122 x 77 mm.

16 On Carmeliano's hand, see Fairbank and Wolpe *Renaissance Handwriting* 29–30 and plates 6 and 14; and *Duke Humfrey and English Humanism in the Fifteenth Century* 63, nos 108–9. Cf the remark on Colet's hand after his return from Italy, in Trapp 'An English Late Medieval Cleric and Italian Thought' 235.

17 'Munere pro tenui, princeps, mihi magna dedisti / Munera; pro numeris, praemia digna tuli. / Tempora iam redeunt quibus est spes parta poetis, / Sed solus, princeps, tu tamen illa facis. / Ecce parant omnes pro te sua carmina Musae / Ut tollant laudes semper ad astra tuas; / Non ego ast possum meritas tibi solvere grates / Sed mihi quicquid erit, hoc, Eduarde, dabo. / Dent, Eduarde, tibi longos, celeberrime princeps, / Fata dies; faveant numina cuncta tibi: / Es decus ipse tui, princeps pulcherrime, regni, / Maxima tuque tuae gloria gentis ades; / Te gaudent iuvenes, pueri, pariterque senesque / Et gaudent vultu sydera cuncta tuo. / Tu merito faciem regis, dux optime, gestas, / Nam te post patrem regia sceptra manent.' Royal 12.A.xxix, fol 10v; cf Carlson 'Occasional Poetry' 497, and 'Politicizing Tudor Court Literature' 291 and 301–2.

18 This 630-line poem survives in two copies, now Cambridge, Gonville and Caius College, ms 196/102, and Oxford, Bodleian Library, Laud Misc 501, discussed below.

19 As is suggested by Tertullian's often imitated questions – 'Quid ergo Athenis et Hierosolymis? quid academiae et ecclesiae?' (*De praescriptione haereticorum* 7.9) – the fundamental issue is virtually as old as Christianity; cf E. Harris Harbison *The Christian Scholar in the Age of Reformation* (New York: Scribner 1956), esp 1–67.

20 'Posteaquam ad ea tempora ventum esset, ut neque musarum neque oratorum inventis vite alimenta mihi suppeditare possem, nec opem mihi ullam ab his praestari intelligerem, qui et possent et ratione paritatis studiorum deberent, ad haec sacra studia, poeticis nugis omissis atque oratorum ambagibus posthabitis, me conferre decrevi; non ea quidem gratia, ut ex his mihi victum mendicarem,

sed ut potius proposita ante oculos haberem exempla, quibus per-
ditissimorum aetatis nostrae morum saevitiam equiore animo ferre
possem atque, si non dolorem prorsus meum extinguerem, saltem
lenirem.' Cambridge, Gonville and Caius College, ms 196/102, p 3.

21 The association was born of the sections of the standard *Vita* in
which Katherine refutes the arguments of the learned philosophers
whom the emperor had assembled against her and then persuades
them all to convert to Christianity.

22 The epistolary prefaces Carmeliano wrote for other copies of the
poem indicate that he did make a copy for Richard III and presented it to him: 'Quocirca cum principale opus serenissimo regi
consecrarim, tibi quoque, qui linguae Latinae principatum inter
tuos concives possides, qui liberalium disciplinarum omnium peritiam quam maxime tenes, quique doctos viros favore et benevolentia prosequeris, exemplum unum scribendum esse duxi' (Caius
College ms 196/102, p 4). 'Solent omnes ... qui opus aliquod nuperrime ediderint alicui principi et doctrinas et doctos viros excolenti
illud dedicare. Quocirca et ego, illorum vestigia imitatus, cum
paulo antea libellum de Beatae Katerinae Aegyptiae Christi spons-
sae vita composuissem, serenissimo regi nostro Ricardo tercio illum consecravi'; after explaining why he found Richard III worthy
the dedication, Carmeliano concluded, 'opusculum igitur meum
non ab ratione suae sublimitati ascripsi atque presentavi' (Laud
Misc 501, fols 1v–2r).

23 Caius College ms 196/102 is the copy presented to Russell; Laud
Misc 501 is the copy presented to Brackenbury.

24 Both the Caius and the Laud manuscripts of the *Katerina* are of
eighteens folios, each manuscript collating I^2 II^{10} III^6, and each
measures 192 x 122 mm; the Royal manuscript of the *De vere* is of
twelve folios (apparently, a single gathering of ten leaves with
cover sheets front and back, of uniform vellum), measuring 212 x
144 mm. The miniature in the Laud manuscript of the *Katerina*,
fol 2v, is reproduced in Pächt and Alexander *Illuminated Manuscripts in the Bodleian Library Oxford* III plate 15 no 1120.

25 'Neminem enim eo digniorem principem inveni cui libellus meus
dedicaretur; sed, ne videamur absque ratione maiestatem suam ex-
tollere, tu ipse, vir sapientissime, mihi ipsi testis eris, en vera vel
vana feram. Si religionem in primis spectamus, quemnam aetas
nostra principem magis religiosum habet? Si iusticiam, quem sibi
in toto terrarum orbe praeponendum putabimus? Si et pacis ser-

vandae et gerendorum bellorum prudentiam intueamur, quem sibi unquam parem adiudicabimus? Si vero animi tum sapientiam, tum magnitudinem, simul et modestiam inspexerimus, cui regem nostrum Ricardum postponemus? Quis sane Christianus imperator aut princeps in benemeritos magis liberalis munificusque comprobari potest? Nemo, sane nemo. Cui magis furta, latrocinia, stupra, adulteria, homicidia, fenus, heresisque et alia nephandissima scelera exosa sunt quam sibi? Nemini, plane. Opusculum igitur meum non ab ratione suae sublimitati ascripsi atque presentavi.' Laud Misc 501, fols 1v–2r. The discussion of this letter here is based on Carlson 'Politicizing Tudor Court Literature' 291–3.

26 Carmeliano asks Brackenbury directly for both kinds of help in his letter to him, both that Brackenbury should be his 'Maecenas' and that Brackenbury should speak well of him to the king: 'Visum fuit mihi, ut eiusdem opusculi nostri exemplum tibi unum hoc Christi natali transmitterem; te quoque rogatum facerem, ut serenissimo regi me notum ac commendatum faceres. Scripsi itaque manu propria hoc exemplum, quod in diuturnam mei tibi deditissimi memoriam servares. Quod si in posterum quicquam operis fabricavero, te profecto studiorum meorum et laborum participem faciam. Reliquum est, vir egregie, ut me inopiamque meam commendatam habere digneris; velis quoque meus esse Maecenas, hoc est protector. Nisi equidem tales viri sicuti es mihi opem ferant, ab omni prorsus spe destitutum me esse perspicio. Quod si aliquando maiestati regiae me cognitum feceris, spero illud fore, ut perpetuo gaudeas te mihi opitulatum esse.' Laud Misc 501, fols 2r–2v.

27 In the *Historia Ricardi Tertii*, ed and trans *CWM* xv, 360–1: 'vir et usu rerum et vitae probitate singulari, tum in litteris haud dubie sua tempestate primarius.' Cf Elizabeth Armstrong 'English Purchases of Printed Books from the Continent 1465–1526' 268–9 and 279, who calls Russell 'a keen supporter of learning and of printing'; and Martin Lowry 'Diplomacy and the Spread of Printing' in *Bibliography and the Study of Fifteenth-Century Civilisation* ed Hellinga and Goldfinch, 132–3. Russell's book-buying and reading habits are discussed in greater detail in Lowry's 'The Arrival and Use of Continental Printed Books in Yorkist England.'

28 On Carmeliano's association with Rood, see Modigliani 'Un nuovo manoscritto di Pietro Carmeliano' 90 and 101; and Carlson 'Occasional Poetry' 497–9 and nn 9–10. On the books he produced

with Rood, see Madan *Oxford Books* II, 5–6 nos 11 and 18; cf also
below, ch 6, p 135 and n 36; and Carter *A History of the Oxford
University Press* I, 4–11.

29 See below, ch 6, pp 134–5 and n 34.

30 Cf Chrimes *Henry VII* 50 and 63.

31 The poem survives only in Addit 33736; cf also n 3 above. The
poem is edited, with some annotation, in Carlson 'King Arthur'
174–83; it is also reprinted in Henry Ansgar Kelly *Divine Provi-
dence in the England of Shakespeare's Histories* (Cambridge, Mass:
Harvard University Press 1970) 317–24. The discussion of it that
follows here is based on Carlson 'King Arthur' esp 159–62 and 166.

32 The *Suasoria* manuscript (Addit 33736) collates I² II¹⁰; its pages
measure 190 x 128 mm, with single columns of writing on them,
sixteen lines of verse per page, measuring 102 mm x 88 mm at the
most. It is described in Watson *Catalogue of Dated and Datable
Manuscripts in the British Library* I, 76, no 361, with a photograph, II, pl 846, and in Kristeller *Iter Italicum* IV, 120.

33 For Henry VII's own use of such heraldry, see Carlson 'King Arthur' 150–1 and the references there given.

34 '"Non hominis," dicunt, "est, sed imago dei"' (211–12); 'Magnani-
mus, praestans, nobilis atque decens, / Integer ac fortis, iustus pa-
tiensque laborum, / Clemens, facundus munificusque, pius'
(124–6). Quotations from this poem are from my edition of it, in
'King Arthur' 174–83, with parenthetical references to the line
numbers of this edition following the quotations.

35 On this campaign and its literary context, see esp Green *Poets and
Princepleasers* 179–95; see also King *Tudor Royal Iconography*
23–31; and Anglo *Spectacle, Pageantry and Early Tudor Policy*
37–43.

36 'Sunt gemine suboles regum de sanguine ducte / Regiaque ex titu-
lis utraque sceptra petit: / Hanc populi pars una fovet; pars altera
at illam; / Atque favet dominis bellica turba suis. / Una domum
sequitur cui dat Lancastria nomen, / Cui regnum Brutus principi-
umque dedit; / Altera progeniem fovet et tutatur in armis / Ebora-
censem, fortia bella movens' (33–40).

37 'Nulla ex Eduardo superest iam mascula proles / Que populis possit imperitare suis; / Filia prima manet natu, pulcherrima virgo, /
Nubilis Elisabet, bis duo lustra tenens, / Que docta et sapiens plus
quam sua tempora poscunt: / Fratribus extinctis, ius genitoris habet' (95–100).

38 The quotations are *Phars* 6.147 and 1.183, respectively.

39 'Undique civili cum sanguine terra maderet' (7); '"Sit modus his,"
dixit, "bellis tantoque furori; / Romanos satis est exuperasse
duces: / Non gener atque socer (quamvis ea bella fuerunt / Maxima), non Marius, non quoque Sylla ferox / Hauserunt tantum Ro-
mani sanguinis unquam, / Imperium licet his, vis quoque maior
erat"' (19–24).

40 'Et iube ut armatus debita iura petat / Ac patrium repetat regnum,
sevumque tyrannum / Expellat, patriam restituatque suam' (130–2).

41 See esp Millican *Spenser and the Table Round* 7–36; Kendrick *British Antiquity* 34–44; and Anglo 'The Foundation of the Tudor Dynasty' and 'The *British History* in Early Tudor Propaganda.'

42 Cf Carlson 'King Arthur' 152–3 and, on the Galfridian prophecies
at issue, 148–50.

43 *Ecl* 4.4–17, trans Paul Alpers *The Singer of the Eclogues* (Berkeley:
University of California Press 1979) 27–9.

44 See esp. Courcelle 'Les Exégèses chrétiennes de la quatrième ég-
logue.'

45 Cf Carlson 'Politicizing Tudor Court Literature' 279–304.

46 Elton *England under the Tudors* 1–17.

47 On the history of the relations between magnificence and patronage, see Jenkins 'Cosimo de' Medici's Patronage of Architecture
and the Theory of Magnificence.'

48 One supposes that Carmeliano did more such work than has survived; on the writings mentioned here, see Carlson 'Occasional Poetry' 499–502.

49 In 1516, More wrote Erasmus, of Carmeliano, 'totus deditus est
sacris litteris, perfunctus lectione eorum pene omnium qui scri-
bunt quaestiunculas, quibus tribuit tantum ut ne Dorpius quidem
tribuit amplius. Ambitiose congressi sumus, accuratis orationibus
ac longis laudibus nos invicem scabentes. Sed ut vere dicam, plane
delectat me; videtur enim honestissimus et rerum humanarum per-
itissimus ac iam divinarum cognitioni deditissimus' (Ep 461, ed
Allen, II, 339).

50 For these assessments, see *LP*, III, pt 2, pp 1047–50, no 2483; and cf
Nelson, p 13. For Carmeliano's many benefices, see the list in
Carlson 'Occasional Poetry' 495. The impact of Carmeliano's work
for Venetian interests (see above, n 1) on his financial status is impossible to gauge. It may be that he was paid in favours rather
than money: on 1 November 1516, Carmeliano wrote the Doge

asking that favour be shown a nephew of his; on 10 September
1517, the Council of Ten acted as Carmeliano had hoped; see the
Calendar of State Papers, Venetian II, 419 (no 693) and 643 (no
1489).

51 Cf Gairdner, *DNB* III, 1036. No doubt Carmeliano's first royal pension was 'occasioned' by his presentation of this poem in much
the same sense that the poem itself was 'occasioned' by the birth
of Prince Arthur: just as there was more to the poem than the
birth itself, so there was undoubtedly more to this pension than
the presentation alone.

52 Cf Carlson 'Politicizing Tudor Court Literature' esp 295–96.

CHAPTER THREE

1 On Vitelli's contact with the English court, see Weiss 'Cornelio
Vitelli' 223–6; and cf Tournoy 'New Evidence on the Italian Humanist Cornelius Vitellius (c. 1440–c.1500).' On Erasmus' early
contact with the court, see below, ch 4. For such others as Giovanni Opizio and Jean Michel Nagonius, who also passed briefly
into and out of the ambit of the Tudor court in the fifteenth century, see above, ch 1, n 6. For the careers of Surigone, Auberino,
and Traversagni, see Weiss *Humanism* 138–40, 162–3, 197, and 199;
and on Traversagni, see also Ruysschaert 'Lorenzo Guglielmo
Traversagni de Savone (1425–1503),' and below, ch 6 and n 32.

2 A number of these are recorded in the Privy Purse account books
kept for Henry VII by John Heron; for example (from among numerous references to matters of literary interest): on 10 May 1496,
twenty pounds 'to an Italian a poete' (PRO E 101/414/6, fol 30r); on
20 September 1496, 56/8, 'to the blynde poete [ie, Bernard André]
in rewarde' (PRO E 101/414/6, fol 47r); on 28 February 1499, the
same amount 'to my lorde princes poete in rewarde' (PRO E 101/
414/16, fol 57r); on 10 January 1506, ten shillings 'to Stephen
Hawse for a balett that he gave to the Kinges grace in rewarde'
(PRO E 36/214, fol 13v); and so on. On these account books, see
Plomer 'Bibliographical Notes from the Privy Purse Expenses of
King Henry the Seventh'; and Chrimes *Henry VII* 332.

3 On Skelton's career as a court poet and his humanism, cf the discussion in Carlson *Latin Writings of John Skelton* esp 1–3 and
7–12. On Gigli's career, see the references given above, ch 2, n 2,
and cf below, p 67 and n 29; on Carmeliano's, see above, ch 2.

4 The phrase *grex poetarum* is André's own, in his *Vita Henrici Septimi*, ed Gairdner, in *Memorials of King Henry the Seventh* 57. The most recent biography of him is by Tournoy, in *CEBR* I, 52–3, which lists previously published studies. To the bibilography there given may now be added: Blackwell 'Niccolò Perotti in England – Part I' 17–19, and 'Humanism and Politics in English Royal Biography' esp pp 435–8; Gutierrez 'John Skelton' 59; and Carlson 'King Arthur and Court Poems for the Birth of Arthur Tudor' esp 153–4, 156–7, and 167–8, and 'Royal Tutors in the Reign of Henry VII' 255–9.

5 These gifts, among numerous other rewards and payments to André, are recorded in the Heron account books mentioned above, n 2. André continued to receive a New Year's gift of one hundred shillings as late as 1519 at least, and possibly later; see *LP* III, pt 2, p 1533.

6 Surviving as London, British Library, Royal 12.A.x, in which André complains of his frailty; he likely died soon after publishing this collection. See additionally below, p 81 and nn 17 and 64.

7 On André's date of birth, see esp Tournoy 'Two Poems written by Erasmus for Bernard André' 49–50. The claim that André was of illustrious birth is made by Giovanni Opizio, in his poem 'De Henrici Septimi in Galliam progressu,' line 42 (London, British Library, Cotton Vespasian B.IV, fol 4r); cf Roth 'A History of the English Austin Friars' *Augustiniana* 15 (1965) 622 n 1073.

8 Roth 'A History of the English Austin Friars,' *Augustiniana* 15 (1965) 624 and nn; cf *BRUO* I, 33, and II, ix.

9 Preserved in his *Vita Henrici Septimi*, ed Gairdner *Memorials* 35–6.

10 This is the hypothesis of Gairdner *Memorials* ix.

11 Gairdner *Memorials* ix; the grant itself is printed in A.F. Pollard *The Reign of Henry VII from Contemporary Sources* II, 233–4.

12 On André's pedagogic duties and work, see Carlson 'Royal Tutors' 255–9. A number of now lost pedagogic works of his were included in the list of his own writings that he made, in the manuscript, Paris, Bibliothèque de l'Arsenal, ms 360, printed in Nelson, pp 239–41, and, with corrections, in Roth 'A History of the English Austin Friars' *Augustiniana* 16 (1966) 457–60. Four of André's *annales* or annual orations survive, from what was probably once a much larger body of such work: those for 1505 (now London, British Library, Cotton Julius A.IV), for 1508 (now London, British

Library, Cotton Julius A.III), for 1515 (now Oxford, New College, ms 287), and for 1520 (now Hatfield House, Cecil Papers 277/2); those for 1505 and 1508 have been printed by Gairdner *Memorials*, 79–94 and 97–130. The greatest surviving quantity of André's devotional writings is in his printed collection *Hymni Christiani* (Paris: Bade 1517), some of the pieces of which certainly circulated earlier; for examples, see below, p 79 and n 62.

13 Poems for Henry VII's entry into London, for the coronation of his queen, for the birth of his heir, for his victory at the Battle of Stoke, for Arthur's creation as Prince of Wales, and for Henry VII's return from France in 1492, all survive only as later incorporated into André's *Vita Henrici Septimi*, of c 1502, ed Gairdner *Memorials* 35–6, 40–2, 52–4, 44–6, and 61–4. An epitaph for Arthur's death and an epigram on Philip of Castille's shipwreck, now lost, are listed in the Arsenal manuscript, as 'Item Arthuri principis epytaphium' and 'Philippi regis Castelle in Angliam adventus' (nos 31 and 29, ed Nelson, p 240). A French *ballade* for the Princess Mary's marriage by proxy survives in London, British Library, Cotton Julius A.III, fols 2v–3r (ed Gairdner *Memorials* 95–6); and a Flodden Field poem (which touches on much else besides), entitled 'Invocatio de inclita invictissimi regis nostri Henrici octavi in Gallos et Scotos victoria,' survives in the manuscript, Hatfield House, Cecil Papers 277/1. The *epithalamium* for Mary is now lost too, apparently; it was seen and described by Thomas Tanner, however, in his *Bibliotheca Britannico-Hibernica*, p 41: '*Ad regem Henricum viii pro hujus anni novi sc. decimi prosperrimo exordio una cum Epithalamiis in sponsalia Francisci Delphini Franciae et … filiae regis.* Princ. "*Quum superiori anno triumphum.*" Ms. penes Tho. Martin de Palgrave.'

14 This poem, surviving in the *Vita Henrici Septimi*, is edited and discussed in Carlson 'King Arthur and Court Poems for the Birth of Arthur Tudor' 156–7 and 167–8.

15 'Magnanimi regis qui vult audire triumphos, / Octavi Henrici fortia gesta legat'; 'Invocatio de inclita invictissimi regis nostri Henrici octavi in Gallos et Scotos victoria' lines 5–6 (Hatfield House, Cecil Papers 277/1, fol 1r).

16 The first three of these phrases occur in the *Vita Henrici Septimi*, ed Gairdner *Memorials* 47, 54, and 35, respectively, where they introduce quotations from André's poetry; the last phrase comes from the Arsenal manuscript list, ed Nelson, p 239, nos 5, 6, and 7.

17 The surviving presentation manuscripts, with their probable dates
of presentation, are as follows. From the reign of Henry VII: [1]
London, British Library, Cotton Domitian A.XVIII, fols 126r–228r
(originally a separate manuscript of 102 folios, the unique copy of
the *Vita Henrici*, probably presented c 1502 [see further below, n
20]); [2] London, British Library, Cotton Julius A.IV (André's annal
for Henry VII's twentieth year, probably presented at New Year's
1506); and [3] London, British Library, Cotton Julius A.III (André's
annal for Henry VII's twenty-third year, probably presented at
New Year's 1509). And from the reign of Henry VIII: [4] London,
British Library, Royal 12.B.xiv (the collection of items discussed
below, pp 68–75, probably presented in 1509); [5] London, British
Library, Royal 16.E.xi (a French poem entitled 'Le temps de lanne
moralize sur laige et vie de lhomme,' probably presented at New
Year's 1510); [6] Hatfield House, Cecil Papers 277/1 (André's Flodden Field poem, mentioned above, n 13, probably dating from late
1513 and presented at about the same time), this being the only
surviving presentation copy of a politically occasioned poem; [7]
Oxford, New College, ms 287 (a Latin prose oration, presented at
New Year's 1515); [8] Hatfield House, Cecil Papers 277/2 (a Latin
prose oration, presented at New Year's 1520); and [9] London, British Library, Royal 12.A.x (two brief poems and a prose apology,
probably presented mid-year 1521 or at New Year's 1522). Two additional items might belong in this list. The manuscript London,
British Library, Royal 16.E.xvii, containing a French poem known
as 'Les douze triomphes de Henry VII,' which dates from late 1496
(ed Gairdner *Memorials* 133–53), was certainly presented to Henry
VII; but the case for André's authorship of the poem has yet to be
made. André's Arsenal manuscript (see above, n 12), which I have
not been able to examine – its main content apparently being a
commentary on Augustine's *Civitas Dei* – may also be a presentation copy.

18 André mentions this himself intermittently (eg, in the *Vita Henrici Septimi*, ed Gairdner *Memorials* 32, 35), as do others as well:
in 1492, for example, Robert Gaguin addressed a letter to him 'Andreae Caeco' (ed Thuasne *Roberti Gaguini Epistole et Orationes* I,
347).

19 See below, p 70 and n 39.

20 The *Vita* was edited from the unique manuscript, Cotton Domitian A.XVIII (see above, n 17), by Gairdner *Memorials* 3–75. The

date of its presentation to the king is not clear. The last event narrated in it is the capture of Perkin Warbeck in late 1497; in one of its prefaces (pp 6–7), André says that he did not begin composing it until 1500; the latest event mentioned in it is the death of Prince Arthur, of April 1502 (p 42). Presumably, it was presented at some point between this event and the death of Queen Elizabeth, which is not mentioned, less than a year later, in February 1503. The poems preserved in the *Vita* occur on pp 35–6, 40–2, 44–6, 48–9, 52–5, and 61–4 of Gairdner's edition.

21 'Verum si scias ... quod studium in literatos prae se ferat, ausim meo periculo iurare te vel sine alis, ut hoc novum et salutare sydus aspicias, huc ad nos propere advolaturum ... Ridet aether, exultat terra; omnia lactis, omnia mellis, omnia nectaris sunt plena. Exulat longe gentium avaritia, larga manu spargit opes liberalitas.' Ep 215, trans *CWE* II, 147–8; ed Allen I, 450.

22 'Ille [sc Henricus] magistratus et munera publica, vendi / Quae suevere malis, donat habenda bonis. / Et versis rerum vicibus feliciter, ante / Quae tulit indoctus praemia, doctus habet.' Ed and trans *CWM* III.2, no 19.104–7 (pp 106–7).

23 The best discussion of this activity remains Parks *The English Traveller to Italy* 455–94. The case of Colet is discussed in greater detail in Trapp 'An English Late Medieval Cleric' 233–50.

24 As, for example, the attacks of Erasmus and Ammonio on Pietro Carmeliano in late 1513 (on which see Carlson 'The Occasional Poetry of Pietro Carmeliano' 502 n 13); or Thomas More's humiliation of Bernard André in 1518 (on which see below, ch 7). I discuss this generational clash in a different context in Carlson 'The "Grammarians' War" 1519–1521, Humanist Careerism in Early Tudor England, and Printing' 167–9. See also Nelson, pp 31–9; Hay *Polydore Vergil* 13–14; Caspari *Humanism and the Social Order* 24; McConica *English Humanists* 44–75, esp 74–5; and Hay 'The Early Renaissance in England' 104.

25 Witness the July 1519 letter of Erasmus (Ep 999; ed Allen IV, 22 [*CWE* VII, 24–5]), in which he boasts of the quality of the persons whom Henry VIII, 'cordatissimus Rex,' 'in familiam suam atque adeo in cubiculum non solum admittit verumetiam invitat, nec invitat verumetiam pertrahit,' listing among those whom Henry 'habet arbitros ac testes perpetuos vitae suae' Linacre, William Latimer, Tunstall, More, Pace, and others, none of whom had benefited by Henry VII's patronage.

26 André continued at court after Henry VIII's accession, of course;
likewise, Pietro Carmeliano had been appointed a king's tutor by
1513, was provided with the archdeaconship of Gloucester in 1511
and the prebend of Ealdland in St Paul's in 1517, and was finally
licensed to import annually two hundred tonnes of Gascon wine
and Toulouse woad (cf Carlson 'The Occasional Poetry of Pietro
Carmeliano' 495); and John Skelton seems to have been awarded a
patent in April or May 1512 nominating him an *orator regius* as
well (see Carlson *Latin Writings of John Skelton* 80–1). Linacre did
not become a royal tutor in Latin until 1523, but he was appointed
king's physician in 1510, early in the reign; others had to wait
somewhat longer, however: Ammonio, after six years of neglect,
replaced Carmeliano as Latin secretary to the king only in July
1511, two years after the coronation, and was appointed papal collector only in 1515; Richard Pace became a royal secretary only in
1515, subsequently replacing John Colet as dean of St Paul's when
Colet died in 1519; and although More, like others, celebrated the
accession of Henry VIII with a gift of poetry unequivocally calculated to attract the favour of the new king, it was not until 1518
or so that he was 'dragged' into the royal service. Other evidence
for More's ambition is discussed in Guy *The Public Career of Sir
Thomas More* esp 6–11; and cf Marc'hadour 'Fuitne Thomas Morum in Aulam Pertractus?' Rossi 'Profilo dell'umanesimo Enrici-
ano' in *Ricerche sull'umanesimo e sul rinascimento in Inghilterra*
26–63 details additional examples.

27 The Trentham manuscript evidently is or is derived from an authorially designed and published collection; see John H. Fisher
John Gower (New York: New York University Press 1964) 71–3,
and, for other examples in Gower's work, 116ff. On Hoccleve's
publishing activities, see esp Bowers 'Hoccleve's Huntington Holographs' esp 45–6, and 'Hoccleve's Two Copies of *Lerne to Dye*' esp
462–8.

28 A collection of epigrams by Beccaria – who was in England in the
period 1438–46 working as a secretary to Duke Humphrey of
Gloucester – survives as Durham, North Carolina, Duke University Library, ms lat 37. This particular collection appears to have
been made and circulated only after Beccaria's return to Italy;
nevertheless, that he was an epigrammatist and that a collection of
his poems circulated in Italy raises the possibility that he put
something similar about during his English sojourn. On the manu-

script, see van Kluyve 'The Duke Manuscript of Antonio Beccaria'; for information about the manuscript, I am grateful to J.
Samuel Hammond, of the library's Department of Rare Books.
The surviving collection of Surigone's occasional poems – an originally separate booklet now incorporated into London, British Library, Arundel 249, fols 94r–117v – probably circulated in England
during Surigone's residence in the country, at some point between
1454 and 1478; cf Weiss *Humanism* esp 138–40, and Rossi 'Enrico
v dalla cronaca alla poesia' in *Ricerche sull' umanesimo e sul rinascimento in Inghilterra* 9–10, n 13. The manuscript is described
in Kristeller *Iter Italicum* IV, 129–30.

29 The manuscript is now London, British Library, Harley 336, and it
comprises copies of Gigli's prose *De observantia quadragesimali*, a
verse epithalamium for the marriage of Henry VII and Elizabeth of
York, and a verse *genethliacon* and two epigrams on the birth of
Prince Arthur. The epigrams that conclude it indicate that the collection was intended to curry favour at court; the letter with
which it begins suggests that Gigli may have given or shown
something similar to others. On this manuscript, see Tournoy-
Thoen 'Het vroegste Latijnse humanistische epithalamium' esp
174; and Carlson 'Politicizing Tudor Court Literature' 293–4. (The
statement there, that Harley 336 was a presentation copy for
Henry VII, is mistaken. It was made for Richard Fox; the presentation copy or copies of the epithalamium and the *genethliacon* that
Gigli can be presumed to have given Henry VII have not survived.)
It is also described in Kristeller *Iter Italicum* IV, 154–5. The poems
for Arthur's birth in it are edited in Carlson 'King Arthur and
Court Poems for the Birth of Arthur Tudor' 169–73; the two epi-
grams with which it concludes are edited in Carlson 'Politicizing
Tudor Court Literature' 303–4; and the letter with which it begins
is given in appendix 4 below. The other surviving copy of Gigli's
De observantia quadragesimali, New Haven, Yale University,
Beinecke Library, ms 25 (*olim* Z109.041), does not appear to have
been a presentation copy; see Barbara Shailor *Catalogue of Medieval and Renaissance Manuscripts in the Beinecke Rare Book and
Manuscript Library Yale University* I (Binghamton: MRTS 1984)
40–1. On Gigli's career, see above, ch 2 n 2.

30 For the Opizio collection, see above, ch 1 n 6. The Alberici collection is discussed above, ch 1, passim.

31 On the collection that Skelton presented, see below p 74, and n 49.

More's collection of poetry occasioned by Henry VIII's coronation was presented to the new king in the form of London, British Library, Cotton Titus D.iv; on it, see below, ch 7, pp 146–8 and nn 11–12.

32 The manuscript is now London, British Library, Royal 12.B.xiv. A presentation for New Year's 1510 survives (the copy of 'Le temps de lanne' listed above, n 17 – at the end of the dedicatory letter to which the poem is said to have been written 'au premier an de vostre faustissime regne'); so I favour regarding Royal 12.B.xiv as presented at the time of Henry VIII's coronation, in June 1509, at the same time that Thomas More presented his collection of verse. There is no unequivocal evidence, however, for dating this presentation of André's. The nature of the contents of the collection tends to suggest the early years of Henry VIII's reign; cf the similar judgement of Nelson, pp 241–2. In any event, that this manuscript was part of the Royal Collection from early Tudor times is confirmed by the presence in it, on fol 1r, of an inventory number (no 1177) indicating that it entered the royal library at Westminster palace at some point before 1542; on the import of these inventory numbers, see Carley 'John Leland and the Foundations of the Royal Library' esp 17–19.

33 Royal 12.B.xiv, fols 2r–6r, 6v–9v, and 10r–28r, respectively. The titles used here are taken from the individual headings in the manuscript; the manuscript's title page (fol 1r) reads: 'En ce petit livre sont contenu<s> troys beaux petitz traictez. Lun est a la louange dez tres illustrez et mes tressouverains le roy et la royne dAngleterre. Lautre est la vie de Saincte Katherine en metre. La tiers est une moult belle oraison dAristote envoye au grant roy Alexandre.'

34 Royal 12.B.xiv, fol 2r.

35 For the acrostic, see Nelson, p 241 n 2; making sense of it, as Nelson does, requires using the whole first word of some lines rather than only the first letter.

36 Royal 12.B.xiv, fol 2v.

37 André's surviving French writings are few: a pair of poems transmitted with the annal for Henry VII's twenty-third year (ed Gairdner Memorials 95–6); the Exposition du Pseaulme huitiesme in Royal 12.B.xiv, discussed here; 'Le temps de lanne' (see above, n 17); and possibly the Douze triomphes that has been imputed to him (see above, n 17). The French prose treatise Grace entière that has sometimes been said to be a pedagogic work of André's cannot

have been written by him, since it was already in circulation in the fourteenth century; see Carlson 'Royal Tutors' 258 n 12. There were other francophones associated with the court, in literary or cultural capacities: Henry VII's librarian Quentin Poulet, for example, and his successor Giles Duwes, who was also a tutor in French to Henry VII's children. Neither of them has been shown to have circulated French poetry at court during the reign of Henry VII as André did.

38 Appendix 5 offers parallel passages from Carmeliano's and André's lives of Katherine. For the suggestion that Queen Katherine 'played a key part in the establishment of the new learning in England,' see Dowling 'Humanist Support for Katherine of Aragon' 46.

39 André's willingness to try a variety of metres – not always successfully – is best displayed in his *Hymni Christiani*, printed in 1517, discussed below, pp 78–80. The claim of extempore composition for the life of Katherine occurs at Royal 12.B.xiv, fol 6v; the same claim is made for the lines André addressed to Giovanni Gigli in early 1487, for example (*Vita Henrici Septimi*, ed Gairdner *Memorials* 54) and for items included in the *Hymni Christiani* (eg, fol 52r). In his conclusion to the *Hymni Christiani*, André wrote 'Hi sunt, rex invictissime, ... hymni quos in honorem caelestis regni per anni circulum sub nominis tui celebritate fere ex tempore concinnavimus' (fol 81v). However, some of the differences between its text of André's life of St Katherine and the 1509 manuscript text of the same 'ex tempore' composition are certainly the results of recomposition and polishing; cf the variants listed below, appendix 5.

40 This tradition is surveyed in the bibliography of Schmitt and Knox, *Pseudo-Aristoteles Latinus*, which lists André's *Oratio*, p 82, no 96; Green *Poets and Princepleasers* 140–2 discusses the tradition's development at the English royal court in the fifteenth century.

41 Royal 12.B.xiv, fols 11r–11v and 14r: 'Conabor breviter tibi precipere, quibus studiis ac artibus multum mihi et ad virtutem proficere et apud reliquos omnes splendorem assequi posse iudicare ... Quamobrem nullam tibi excogitamus oratoriam excercitationem; sed, ut tibi consuleremus quas res appetere quasve fugere, et quibus cum hominibus versari, et quomodo vi tam agere adolescentis opporteat, precepta quedam monitaque perscripsimus.'

42 Royal 12.B.xiv, fols 15v–16r: 'Sapientia enim sola omnium rerum

immortalis est.' As this claim suggests, Aristotle credits those 'qui aliquid utile docere profitentur' with considerable importance: 'Sic maxime vituperandus est qui nichil eorum didiscerit que utilia esse cognoverit. Ocium vite tue in eorum audiendorum studio consumito que literarum monumentis sunt tradita; sic enim et alii que difficillima invenerint facillima cognitu tibi contingerint.'

43 Royal 12.B.xiv, fols 27v–28r: 'Equidem si mortalem de mente Dei coniecturam facere decet, puto Deum in eius familiarissimis ostendisse quid sit animo in bonos et malos affectus. Iupiter enim, cum Herculem et Tantalum genuisset, ut est in fabulis, alterum propter virtutem fecit immortalem, alterum vero propter vitia maximis cruciatibus puniendum tradidit; quibus exemplis qui uti volent, opportebit esse avidos neque solum in his premanere que a nobis dicta sunt, sed ea etiam legere atque perdiscere que poete atque orhatores utilia et optima scripta eliquerunt. Quemadmodum enim apes videmus super omnia virgulta insidere et singulis capere que sibi utilia esse cognoscant, sic vos facere opportet qui doctrine sunt cupidi, ut nullius res expertes se probeant, sed illa diligenter colligant que sibi utilia iudicaverint; nam hoc sine diligentia qua rerum vitia incommodaque nature vix superare quis potest.'

44 Royal 12.B.xiv, fol 18r: 'Neminem tibi prius facias amicum quam diligenter quesieris quonam ipse modo et superioribus amicitie iura coluerit. Neque enim dubitandum talem ipsum erga te fore qualem antea se in superiores prebuit amicos. Valde tibi curandum est ne sis subitus ad amandum verum quos in amiciciam receperis; cum his erit perpetuo in benevolentia permanendum.'

45 Royal 12.B.xiv, fols 10v–11r: 'Hanc orationem dono ad te misi, que et mee erga vos benevolentie et cum Philippo patre tuo consuetudinis argumento esset. Decet enim filios, ut patrimonii, sic et patrie amicicie heredes esse. Equidem hac in re video tempus nobis fortunamque favere: tu enim discendi, ego vero docendi sum cupidus.'

46 Royal 12.B.xiv, fol 15r, for example: 'Noli tibi suadere, si turpe quicquam commiseris, id ceteris clam fore; nam etsi reliqui omnes ignorabunt, eris tamen ipse tibi scelerum tuorum conscius. Time Deum. Amicos verere. Parentes honora. Legibus pare. Eas venerare voluptates que sint cum honesto coniuncte; oblectatio enim honesto adiuncta res quidem optima est.'

47 Royal 12.B.xiv, fol 20v: 'assentatores non minore sunt odio quam seductores prosequendi; ambo enim eos decipiunt qui fidem sibi prestiterunt.'

48 Royal 12.B.xiv, fols 19v–20v: 'Presentium bonorum possessio non ad luxuriam sed ad honestum vivendi fructum dirigenda est. Eos maxime contemnendos esse puta qui ad parandas divitias omne adhibent studium ... Res fortunasque tuas duabus de causis non parvifacere debes, ut et possis tributum ac mulctam penamque persolvere et bonis amicis in calamitate subvenire ... Benefacito bonis; pulcherrimus enim thezaurus est de viris optimis benemereri.'

49 The surviving manuscript of the refurbished *Speculum principis*, incorporating also the other writings mentioned here, is now London, British Library, Addit 26787. On it, see Carlson *Latin Writings of John Skelton* 68 and fig 2; and on relations between the *Speculum* and ancient compendia of sapience like the *Disticha Catonis*, see Carlson 'John Skelton and Ancient Authors' 104–9. On Skelton's work as a tutor in the royal household alongside André, see Carlson 'Royal Tutors' esp 264–70.

50 For example, André continued to be given a hundred shillings as a New Year's gift, in 1510, 1511, 1512, and so on (see *LP* II, pt 2, pp 1444, 1449, 1454), just as he had before Henry VII's death.

51 On this episode, see Erasmus' account in Ep 2422, ed Allen IX, 108: 'Thomae Linacro pessime cessit quod Proclum a se denuo versum Regi huius patri dicarat. Andreas quidam Tolasates, praeceptor Arcturi Principis, et in regnum paternum successuri nisi mors antevertisset, caecus adulator, nec adulator tantum sed et delator pessimus, Regem admonuit hoc libelli iam olim fuisse versum a nescio quo; et erat, sed misere. Hanc ob causam Rex et munus aspernatus, et in Linacrum velut in impostorem inexpiabile concepit odium.' Cambridge, Trinity College, R.15.19 is possibly, if not probably, the manuscript that Linacre presented on this occasion, which André then saw.

52 For evidence of these instances, see Ep 243, 248, 254, and 1490, ed Allen I, 487–8, 495, 500 (*CWE* II, 199, 208, 215), and Allen V, 539.

53 The epigram, entitled 'Bernardi Andree poeta laureati, in grammaticum epitoma W.H. Carmen,' occurs in the *Introductorium lingue latine* (London: de Worde, c 1495 [*STC* 13809]), sig A2r: 'Grammaticem brevibus qui vis contingere normis, / Hec lege, W<ilielme>, dogmata clara tui. / Prima rudimenta et latine primordia lingue / Lucidius, brevius tradere nemo potest. / Hec igitur iuvenes teneri clarissima discant; / Hec preceptores dogmata pauca legant.'

54 See above, ch 2, pp 43–7.

55 The episode is discussed in detail in Carlson 'Politicizing Tudor Court Literature.' London, British Library, Addit 33534, fol 3r, has copies of Gaguin's epigram and Carmeliano's response; Cambridge, Trinity College, 0.2.53, fols 65r–65v, has copies of Gaguin's, Carmeliano's, and Gigli's contributions.

56 See below, ch 5.

57 For a description of the book (which is foliated), see Renouard *Imprimeurs et libraires Parisiens du XVIe siéle* II, 154 (to the two copies of the book there listed may be added another in the library of All Souls College, Oxford); and cf Carlson 'Reputation and Duplicity' 261–4.

58 *Hymni Christiani* fol 3r.

59 André's poems on these saints appear in the *Hymni Christiani* as follows: David, fol 10r; Chad, fol 10r; Patrick, fol 11r; George, fol 14v; Edward the Confessor, fols 4r and 52r–52v; the West Saxon King Edward, fol 11r; Wulfstan, fol 5v; Cuthbert, fol 11v; Etheldred, fols 24v and 53v; and Winifred, fols 55v–56r. On this last, see esp Lowry 'Caxton, St. Winifred and the Lady Margaret Beaufort' esp 110–17.

60 'Da quod optamus, pia virgo: nostro / Octavo Henrico pariterque tantae / Coniugi iam nunc gravidae pioque / Prospice regno. // Diffuga tetras Erebi sorores; / Alma pax toti dominetur orbi; / Et diu princeps regat iste sceptrum / Optimus. Amen.' *Hymni Christiani* fols 30r–30v. The dedication occurs on fol 3r; the mass in question occupies fols 72r–79v; and the eulogy for Arthur occurs on fols 47v–48r.

61 He suggests as much in the preface, *Hymni Christiani* fol 3r: 'cum enim scriberem haec, natalis Christi currebat millesimus et quingentesimus nonus annus, regni vero celsitudinis tui, regum invictissime, secundus' (2 Henry VIII did not begin until 22 April 1510, ns).

62 The life of St Katherine, intermittently improved but not fundamentally changed from the form given it in Royal 12.B.xiv, fols 6v–9v, recurs in the *Hymni Christiani* at fols 61r–63v. Both John Bale *Scriptorum Illustrium Maioris Brytanniae Catalogus*, posterior pars (Basel 1559) 139, and Tanner *Bibliotheca Britannico-Hibernica* 41, mention a separate 'Vita S. Andreae apostoli,' though the work would appear to survive now only in the form of the text of it printed in the *Hymni Christiani* fols 64r–70v. The evidence for previous circulation of the two Offices printed in the

Hymni Christiani, for the Immaculate Conception (fols 72r–79v),
for the feast of S Maria ad Nives (fols 38r–39r), and for the Presentation (fols 58v–60r), is the appearance of references to them, as
dedicated to Margaret Beaufort, in the Arsenal list of André's
writings (ed Roth 'A History of the English Austin Friars' *Augustiniana* 16 (1966) 459, correcting Nelson, pp 239–41, nos 33 and 34):
'Officium immaculate conceptionis Marie Christi parentis nobilis,
ad varias horas, missam, et processionem recitandum ad serenissimam regiam matrem' and 'Item ad eandem de festo nivali et pre-
sentatione beate Marie officium.'

63   On the relations between printers and humanists in England, see
below, ch 6. Examples of publication abroad by English and England-based humanists before the appearance of André's *Hymni
Christiani* include Thomas Linacre's translation of Proclus' *De
Sphaera*, printed by Manutius in 1499 (see Barber 'Thomas Linacre'
291–2); a selection of Latin poems by Andrea Ammonio, printed,
probably at Paris, probably c 1511–13 (see Pizzi *Un Amico di Erasmo* 42–7); and More's *Utopia*, first printed by Martens in Louvain in 1516. The best guide to such publications is M.A. Shaaber
*Check-list of Works of British Authors Printed Abroad, in Lan-
guages Other than English, to 1641*, in which the category 'British
Authors' is held to include such anomalous figures as Bernard
André and Andrea Ammonio. On Bade, see Renouard *Imprimeurs
et libraires Parisiens* II, esp 6–14; and also David J. Shaw 'Badius's
Octavo Editions of the Classics.'

64   The 1518 presentation does not survive, though it was described
by Tanner, quoted above, n 13; the presentations for 1520 and
1521–2, which do survive, are listed above, n 17.

CHAPTER FOUR

1   Erasmus' life and works have been comparatively thoroughly
studied, and there are a number of good biographies in English,
most recently McConica's *Erasmus*, which lists others important
studies. On Erasmus' English sojourns, see esp Porter, in Porter
and Thomson *Erasmus and Cambridge* 8–10; McConica *English
Humanists and Reformation Politics* esp 13–43; Thompson 'Erasmus and Tudor England,' emphasizing Erasmus' influence; and
Schoeck 'Erasmus in England, 1499–1517.'

2   Ep 1341a (= *Catalogus lucubrationum*), ed Allen I, 1–46 (where it

is not treated as part of the sequence of numbered letters) and trans *CWE* IX, 291–364. The sentence quoted here is trans *CWE* IX, 352 (Allen I, 37).

3 P.S. Allen 'Erasmus' Relations with His Printers' commented: 'So it was indeed with almost every one of Erasmus' works. Froben's issues followed Martens' almost as soon as they could be carried to Basle and set up; Schurer's followed Froben's: so, too, the printers of Cologne and Paris and Antwerp. Erasmus connived at this, for many of the new issues bear evidences of his revision, as Badius complained. The inference seems to be that though the printers deprecated imitation of their own works, and fully realized that it was unfriendly to imitate the works of others, still the situation as regards the enforcement of any protection of copyright was hopeless. They knew that they were doing one another wrong. But business was business, and in the pursuit of present gain, they were not ashamed to go on still in their wickedness. Seemingly all that they could do to protect themselves was not to print too large an edition' (p 137). Erasmus argued for Botzheim: 'Now, when you complain that your purse is empty because you have to buy the same book so often, I should like you to look at it like this. Suppose that my *Proverbs* had just appeared for the first time, and that the moment the book was published I died: would you have regretted your expenditure? I doubt it. Now suppose something else, that after several years I came to life again and that at the same time the book revived with me, better and fuller, would you regret what you had spent, or would you be delighted to see again both your friend and his immortal work? Now I know what you will say: "I should be delighted to see you alive again; but none of this has really happened." Which then do you suppose to be the more blessed state, to rise again from the dead, or not to die? If you would be pleased to see me risen, you must be much more pleased to see me alive ... Do not hope therefore that I of all people shall relieve you of this inconvenience, until I leave the stage and once and for all utter my "So farewell and clap your hands" to the whole lot of you ... so you must make up your mind whether you would rather wish for that moment, or from time to time buy a book that has been enlarged and revised. In fact, if you recall what a lot of money you had to spend on trash in the old days, you will not, I think, regret this expense quite so much' (Ep 1341a, trans *CWE* IX, 351–2 [Allen I, 37–8]).

4 On Erasmus' relations with his printers, see Allen 'Erasmus' Rela-

tions with His Printers' 109–37; Wiriath 'Les Rapports de Josse
Bade Ascensius avec Erasme et Lefèbvre d'Etaples'; Bloch 'Erasmus
and the Froben Press'; and S. Diane Shaw 'A Study of the Collaboration between Erasmus of Rotterdam and His Printer Johann Froben at Basel during the Years 1514 to 1527' esp 39–41. For most of
1508, Erasmus lived in Venice at the Aldine Press, which has been
described as a 'mixture of the sweatshop, the boardinghouse, and
the research institute'; see ibid 37–9. Erasmus' correspondence
with his several printers shows considerable sophistication on his
part about the business.

5 Ep 472, trans CWE IV, 88 (Allen II, 351). Other letters in which
Bade voiced similar complaints include Ep 263 (Allen I, 514–16;
CWE II, 231–4), Ep 346 (Allen II, 125–6; CWE III, 154), and 434 (Allen II, 271–2; CWE III, 327–8). Cf Grendler 'Printing and Censorship' 33–4.

6 The quotation is from Ep 1341a, trans CWE IX, 298 (Allen I, 5); for
the suggestion that the Euripides translations had been presented
elsewhere, see Garrod 'Erasmus and His English Patrons' 1–2.

7 See Ep 71 (Allen I, 198–9; CWE, I, 146–7), Ep 95 (Allen I, 234; CWE,
I, 187–8), Ep 117 (Allen I, 271–3; CWE, I, 233–4), and Ep 1284 (Allen
V, 63–5; CWE IX, 90–3). Cf Garrod 'Erasmus and His English Patrons' 2–4; Thompson 'Erasmus and Tudor England' 34 and n 27;
and also above, ch 1, p 23 and n 9.

8 Ep 1341a, trans CWE, IX, 299–300 (Allen I, 6).

9 Ep 1341a, ed Allen I, 6 (CWE IX, 299). The poem in question is edited in Reedijk, no 45, pp 248–53.

10 Allen IV, xxi. Ferguson Erasmi Opuscula 25–6, Garrod 'Erasmus
and His English Patrons' 4–5, and Reedijk, p 202, all concur with
Allen's view of the manuscript's origin. The description of Egerton
1651 that follows and the discussion of its provenance (pp 87–92)
are reproduced here, with some alteration, from a section of Carlson 'Erasmus, Revision, and the British Library Manuscript Egerton 1651' 201–2. The article includes a more detailed and technical
description of the manuscript, esp 227 n 8. The manuscript is also
described in Kristeller Iter Italicum IV, 143.

11 Evidence concerning ownership of the manuscript is detailed in
Carlson 'Erasmus, Revision, and the British Library Manuscript
Egerton 1651' 202 and n 11. Its whereabouts before c 1810–25,
when it apparently formed part of a modest private collection in
England, remain obscure.

12 The qualities of the texts in the manuscript, including issues of

the errors in it, are discussed in detail in Vredeveld 'Towards a
Definitive Edition of Erasmus' Poetry' 143–4 and 150–61, and in
Carlson 'Erasmus, Revision, and the British Library Manuscript
Egerton 1651' 209–25.

13 [1] = Ep 104, ed Allen I, 239–41 (CWE I, 195–7); [2] = Reedijk, nos
34–7; [3] = Reedijk, no 38 ('Ad Gaguinum nondum visum carmen
hendecasyllabum alloquitur musas suas'); [4] is reprinted in Smith
Erasmus 456–7, no 15; [5] = Reedijk, no 39 ('In annales Gaguini et
Eglogas Faustinas carmen ruri scriptum et autumno'); [6] = Reedijk, no 46; [7] = Reedijk, no 44; [8] = Reedijk, no 40 ('Ad Robertum
Gaguinum carmen de suis fatis'); [9] = Reedijk, no 47; [10] = Reedijk, no 22; [11] = Reedijk, no 46.1–3 only (cf [6] above).

For dating the composition of these items, I rely on the discussions of Allen, for the date of [1], the letter, and on Reedijk's
discussions in his headnotes to the several poems, except as indicated otherwise. The possible exceptions to the claim that all the
manuscript's contents antedate 1500 are items [9] and [10]. [9], the
'Contestatio salvatoris,' was not printed or otherwise published
until c 1511, when it appeared, as the 'Expostulatio salvatoris,' in a
form that differs greatly from the Egerton manuscript 'Contestatio.' Reasons for thinking that the 'Contestatio' was written by
1500 are: first, that the 'Expostulatio' appears to be an amplifica-
tion of the 'Contestatio,' rather than the 'Contestatio' appearing to
be an abbreviation of the 'Expostulatio,' so that the 'Contestatio'
antedates the c 1511 publication of the 'Expostulatio'; and second,
less certainly informative, that the 'Contestatio' occurs in the
Egerton manuscript. The claim that the composition of the manuscript's item [10], the 'In laudem Anne,' antedates 1500 is similarly
somewhat ill founded. Reedijk's reason for believing the poem to
have been composed 'c 1489' – a passage in the letter Erasmus
wrote to cover the poem's presentation to Anna van Borssele (Ep
145), in which Erasmus describes it as 'carmen vel rhithmos potius
a me puero lusos' and claims 'a tenellis unguiculis eius Divae pietate flagravi' – may be insufficient. The poem may in fact be
nearly as late in composition as its date of presentation to Anna
van Borssele, with Ep 145, in late January 1501; the best evidence
here – but again, it is not good evidence – for a date of composition somewhat earlier than that of the poem's presentation to the
Lady of Veere is the fact that the poem occurs in the Egerton manuscript, again in what appears to be draft form.

14 The standard for presentation copies is established by the deluxe manuscripts of Alberici and Carmeliano, among others, described above, chs 1 and 2. In the same period, however, Skelton seems to have presented his paean on the accession of Henry VIII to the king in the form of a rather plain copy indeed, now London, PRO, E 36/228, fols 7r–8v: a pair of ungathered sheets of paper, altogether undecorated, that were folded up and endorsed like a letter. The copy is reproduced in P.J. Croft *Autograph Poetry in the English Language* (New York: McGraw-Hill 1973) I, 6–8. Likewise, there is an altogether plain copy, again on paper, of a group of poems by Robert Whittinton, now Hatfield House, Cecil Papers 233/8, probably presented to Henry VIII in 1532; it is described in Kristeller *Iter Italicum* IV, 36.

15 Most telling of these perhaps is that, having copied out the poem in full once already [6], the copyist of the Egerton manuscript began to copy again at the end of the book Erasmus' poem in praise of Skelton [11], stopping here after only three lines, evidently having realized by then that a copy of the piece had already been taken, and subjoining the phrase 'ut habetur.'

16 In the *Catalogus*, Erasmus claims '*carmen* intra triduum absolvi' (Ep 1341a, ed Allen I, 6 [*CWE* IX, 299–300]). Likewise, in the prefatory letter that he wrote for the presentation, Erasmus again refers to his versified gift in the singular: he describes himself as a person 'qui *carmen* suo ingenio, suis vigiliis elucubratum nomini tuo dicat,' and says that he 'non veritus sum *hunc qualemcunque panegyricon* nomini tuo nuncupare' (Ep 104, ed Allen I, 239, 240 [*CWE* I, 195, 197]).

17 See Paul L. Hughes and James F. Larkin *Tudor Royal Proclamations* I (New Haven: Yale University Press 1964) 52–4, nos 46–7.

18 For a balanced view of the importance of this first Oxford residence for Erasmus, see Rummel *Erasmus' Annotations on the New Testament* 10–12. On Charnock, see *CEBR* I, 300–1 and the references given there.

19 Ep 112, trans *CWE* I, 219–20; Allen I, 260: 'Ostendit hodie mihi humanissimus dominus noster, Prior Richardus Charnocus, quaedam abs te carmina, non vulgari numero trivialive currentia; quae si multo labore confecta essent, meo tamen iudicio non in infima laude forent reponenda. Quum vero elaborata exque tempore a te conscripta dicantur, quem credis futurum, modo sit ullius ingenii, qui non te cum summis illis priscisque vatibus, perlectis tuis versi-

bus, sit collocaturus? Redolent enim Atticam quandam venerem mirificamque ingenii tui suavitatem.'

20 Ep 113, ed Allen I, 261–5 (*CWE* I, 220–6). On Erasmus' answer, see Vredeveld 'Some "Lost" Poems of Erasmus from the Year 1499' esp 331.

21 Ep 112, ed Allen I, 260 (*CWE* I, 219–20).

22 Ep 113, trans *CWE*, I, 225–6; Allen I, 264–5: 'Quod hortaris ut Musas meas excitem, Mercuriali virga opus esse scito, ut expergefiant ... Excitavimus nuper, et quidem iratas, a somno plusquam decenni, compulimusque liberorum regiorum laudes dicere. Dixerunt et invitae et semisomnes cantilenam nescio quam, adeo somnolentam ut cuivis somnum conciliare possit. Quae cum mihi vehementer displiceret, facile illas redormiscere sum passus.'

23 Ep 113, ed Allen I, 265 (*CWE* I, 226). Vredeveld (in correspondence) would characterize these remarks about the 'Prosopopoeia Britanniae' as 'obligatory modesty' on Erasmus' part; as he points out, Erasmus had the poem printed frequently in the sixteenth century and mentioned it among other acknowledged writings in the *Catalogus lucubrationum*.

24 On the basis of this exchange of letters between Erasmus and Sixtinus, Vredeveld 'Some "Lost" Poems' 330–1 makes the same few inferences about the nature of what Sixtinus saw; he goes on to argue, pp 331–7, that the collection seen by Sixtinus may have included also Reedijk, nos 19–21, which do not occur in the Egerton manuscript, in addition to the 'In laudem Anne' (Reedijk, no 22) and the 'Contestatio salvatoris' (Reedijk, no 47), which do. Reedijk, pp 398–9, discusses the same correspondence more pessimistically, as regards what conclusions can be drawn from the evidence.

25 Cf Reedijk, p 202; and on Gaguin's relations with the circle of humanists associated with the court of Henry VII – good relations, in fact, in spite of exaggerated public squabbling – see Carlson 'Politicizing Tudor Court Literature' 289–90.

26 On Andrelini, *poeta regius* to the king of France, who, in 1517, contributed commendatory verses for Bernard André's *Hymni Christiani*, see Tournoy-Thoen, in *CEBR* I, 53–6. On Caminade, see below, p 94 and n 28.

27 Ep 112, trans *CWE* I, 220 (Allen I, 260).

28 For the circumstances of the epigram's initial publication, see Reedijk, pp 246–7; on Caminade and his relations with Erasmus,

see Bierlaire 'Erasme et Augustin Vincent Caminade,' and *CEBR* I, 280–1.

29 For a description of the *De casa natalicia Jesu* volume, see the *Gesamtkatalog der Wiegendrucke* VIII, nos 9275–6; and for a description of the Hermans *Silva odarum*, see the *Catalogue of Books Printed in the XVth Century Now in the British Museum* part VIII, 62–3. In both instances, the printer was Guy Marchant. Erasmus' only publication in print before these poems had been a Latin prose letter, Ep 45 (Allen I, 148–52; *CWE* I, 87–91), printed with Robert Gaguin's *De origine et gestis Francorum*, first in September 1495.

30 For a description of the 1506–7 *Adagiorum collectanea*, see Vander Haeghen, Vanden Berghe, and Arnold *Bibliotheca Erasmiana: Adagia* 10–14. The 1518 *Epigrammata* – printed with More's *Utopia* and *Epigrammata* – is listed in Bezzel *Erasmusdrucke des 16. Jahrhunderts in Bayerischen Bibliotheken* no 912; see also below, ch 7. For other occurrences of these poems, see Reedijk's 'Survey of Editions and Ms Sources Containing Poetry by Erasmus' 360–80, which, although it occasionally errs, remains fundamental to attempts to trace the publication histories of Erasmus' poems.

31 For example, see Carlson 'Erasmus, Revision, and the British Library Manuscript Egerton 1651.'

32 Cf Reedijk, pp 227–8.

33 The 1503 Antwerp volume, printed by Dirk Maartens, is listed in Bezzel *Erasmusdrucke* no 968. The 1515–17 Strassbourg volumes, the work of Matthias Schurer, are in Bezzel *Erasmusdrucke* nos 846, 848–9, and 850–1; the second of these editions, dating from June 1516, adds to its title page the claim 'Ex recognitione authoris.' The two 1518 Basel reprintings of the 'In laudem angelorum' were both issued by Froben: the first in March, in the Erasmian *Epigrammata* mentioned above, n 30; the second in July, in the first Froben edition of the *Enchiridion militis christiani*, listed in Bezzel *Erasmusdrucke* no 851.

34 The dedicatory letter than accompanied the presentation is Ep 145 (*CWE* II, 12–18, Allen I, 342–6). For Erasmus' frustration with her patronage, see Ep 146 (*CWE* II, 20; Allen I, 347–8) and Ep 172 (*CWE* II, 59; Allen I, 381).

35 The poem was first printed by Froben in the March 1518 *Epigrammata* mentioned above, n 30, and again in the July 1518 *Enchiri-*

dion, mentioned above, n 33. A copy of the Spiegel edition with *scholia* – *In hymnum aviae Christi Annae dictum ab Erasmo Roteradamo scholia Jacobi Spiegel Selestadiensis* (Augsburg: Grimm and Vuyrsung 1519) – is in the British Library, shelf-mark 11405.e.14.

36 For Skelton's prominence at court in 1499 and reputation for learning, see Carlson 'Royal Tutors' 265–9; on the circumstances of his departure c 1502, most likely in disfavour, see Walker *John Skelton and the Politics of the 1520s* 42–3. The claim of Fox *Politics and Literature in the Reigns of Henry VII and Henry VIII* 26–7, that Skelton left court willingly, rests in part on misapprehension of the documentary evidence. The accounts for the 1503 funeral of Elizabeth of York (London, PRO, LC 2/1, esp fol 73r), which Fox cites second-hand, do not in fact mention Skelton.

37 See Reedijk, p 255; and Carlson 'Erasmus, Revision and the British Library Manuscript Egerton 1651' 222–3.

38 Ep 1341a, trans *CWE* IX, 300; Allen I, 6: 'in quo non minus in pietate quam in doctrina volebat [sc Coletus] institui formarique puericiam.'

39 For a description of the earliest surviving form of the printed book, see Kronenberg *Nederlandsche Bibliographie van 1500 tot 1540* II, 330 no 2887; see also the discussion of Reedijk, pp 291–3,
' and his list of reprintings of the poem, in his 'Survey of Editions.'

40 The 'Prosopopoeia' and the letter to Prince Henry were printed together in the 1500 and 1505 Paris editions of the *Adagiorum collectanea* (see Vander Haeghen et al *Bibliotheca Erasmiana: Adagia* 5 and 9); among Erasmus' collected poetry in the second volume of the 1506–7 Bade edition of the *Adagiorum collectanea* (see Vander Haeghen et al *Bibliotheca Erasmiana: Adagia* 11); and in Froben's two 1518 printings of Erasmus' *Epigrammata* (listed in Bezzel *Erasmusdrucke* nos 912–13). The 'Prosopopoeia' alone, without the letter, was printed in the 1506 Bade edition and the 1507 Manutius edition of Erasmus' translations of the *Hecuba* and the *Iphigenia*; on which see Jan Henrik Waszink, in *Opera Omnia Desiderii Erasmi Roterodami* i–1 (Amsterdam: North-Holland 1969) 195–202 and 212.

41 I believe that the two manuscripts mentioned above, n 14 – a copy of John Skelton's coronation ode to Henry VIII (now London, PRO, E 36/228, fols 7r–8v) and Robert Whittinton's 1532 collection of poems (now Hatfield House, Cecil Papers 233/8) – are physically

similar to the ephemeral manuscripts that the humanists characteristically circulated among friends and professional associates but
owe their survival to having been presented, uncharacteristically,
to members of the patronal class, probably the king. For the evidence for an early instance of the circulation of multiple ephemeral copies of single humanist poems, among the *grex poetarum*
associated with the Tudor court in early 1490, see above, ch 3,
p 77 and n 55. The existence of other such ephemeral copies
passed hand to hand among humanist compeers can be inferred,
for example, from Ep 280 (Allen I, 540; *CWE* II, 263) and Ep 282
(Allen I, 542; *CWE* II, 266), letters that passed between Erasmus
and Ammonio – the one in Cambridge, the other at Westminster –
in which they discuss a poem by Pietro Carmeliano, to which both
must have had access in manuscript form; cf Carlson 'The Occasional Poetry of Pietro Carmeliano' 502 n 13. Among letters in the
Erasmian correspondence enclosing copies of single poems are: Ep
112 (Allen I, 260; *CWE* I, 220), with a poem of Johannes Sixtinus;
Ep 234 (Allen I, 473–4; *CWE* II, 177–8) and Ep 236 (Allen I, 476–7;
CWE II, 182), an exchange of epigrams between Erasmus and Ammonio; Ep 283 (Allen I, 544–7; *CWE* II, 269–72), with which, having
criticized a poem of Ammonio at some length, Erasmus promises
to enclose a brief poem of his own; and Ep 684 (Allen III, 105–7;
CWE V, 149–51), enclosing poems by Thomas More, on which see
below, ch 7, pp 144–6.

42 The Whittinton manuscript described above, nn 14 and 41, appears
physically to be an ephemeral collection of this sort, as does also
the copy of a collection of epigrams of Stefano Surigone mentioned above, ch 3, n 28. The existence of other such ephemeral
copies of collections, circulated privately among humanist compeers – additional parallels for the collection that Sixtinus saw in
circulation in Oxford in 1499 – is to be inferred from Ep 218 (Allen I, 455; *CWE* II, 156), discussing a copy of a collection of Ammonio's poems; and from the correspondence of More and
Erasmus discussed below, ch 7.

43 Surviving manuscripts that Erasmus presented conform to this
model: Cambridge, Trinity College, R.9.26 (the Libanius translations, presented in 1503 to Nicholas Ruistre) and Cambridge,
Cambridge University Library, Add 6858 (a translation from Plutarch presented to Henry VIII in 1513, for which Henry later paid
Erasmus sixty angels: see Ep 1341a [*CWE* IX, 360; Allen I, 44]). On

these manuscripts, see Garrod 'Erasmus and His English Patrons' 8–10; and Clough 'A Presentation Volume for Henry VIII' 199. Erasmus' father had worked as a professional copyist – see now esp Avarucci 'Due codici scritti da "Gerardus Helye" padre di Erasmo' – and Erasmus was capable of making fine copies himself; cf the remarks of Garrod 'Erasmus and His English Patrons' 9–10, and Nichols *The Epistles of Erasmus* I, xvii–xviii.

44 Examples of at least two manuscript presentations of writings soon to be printed are mentioned in Garrod 'Erasmus and His English Patrons' 2–3 and 6. On the circumstances of Erasmus' (unusual) presentation of specially prepared printed copies, in place of manuscripts, see Clough 'Erasmus and the Pursuit of English Royal Patronage in 1517 and 1518,' and 'A Presentation Volume for Henry VIII' 199–202.

CHAPTER FIVE

1 In English printing, the most notorious example is perhaps the deluxe presentation manuscript of Caxton's translation of the *Métamorphoses moralisées* (Cambridge, Magdalene College, Pepys Library, ms 2124), probably copied from a lost printed edition. In general, see now Blake 'Manuscript to Print' 403–32, esp 412 and the references there given, 431 n 33.

2 This aspect of printing is discussed in Pantzer 'Printing the English Statutes, 1484–1640.' Pantzer suggests that the first printed volume of English statutes, from the reign of Richard III, was printed in some measure for 'the propaganda value of its contents' (pp 73–4), and she discusses the shift from oral to printed propagation of laws, by means of broadsides, early in the reign of Henry VIII (esp pp 87–9).

3 For Whittinton's biography, see *BRUO* III, 2039–40, and the studies of Stanier, White, and Nelson cited below. His work is also discussed by Mayer, in *Thomas Starkey and the Commonweal* 17–26, with particular attention to Whittinton's English translation of Cicero's *De officiis*, probably dating from the 1530s.

4 On the early history of the Magdalen College School, see Stanier *Magdalen School* esp 19–20, 25–41, and 56–65; and on its importance for the dissemination of humanism in England, see also Davis 'William Waynflete and the Educational Revolution of the Fifteenth Century.' On Holt's career, see Carlson 'Royal Tutors'

270–2. The connection between Wolsey's background as a grammar master and his later support for humanism and humanists is made by Hay 'The Early Renaissance in England' 105.

5 On this degree – held also, it seems, by John Skelton – see Nelson, pp 40–7. Trapp 'The Owl's Ivy and the Poet's Bays,' esp 241 and 247, also points out that, after Petrarch, the laureation became 'more and more a University affair'; see also Trapp's discussion of the development of the continental laureation in 'The Poet Laureate.'

6 A further indication of the success of Whittinton's grammars is the number of editions of them pirated by Peter Treveris (*STC* 25455.5, 25456.3, 25457, 25471.5, 25474, 25475, etc), or shared by de Worde with other printers, including Richard Pynson (eg, *STC* 25443.8, 25446.5, 25450, 25451, 25461.5, 25465, 25468.5, 25471, 25479.15, 25529, 25547.3, 25570); evidently, the demand for the Whittinton and Stanbridge-Whittinton grammars was greater than de Worde's presses alone could satisfy. On Whittinton's textbooks, see Bennett 'A Check-List of Robert Whittinton's Grammars' (the list and chronology of which are now superseded by those of the *STC* II, 454–60), and Pafort 'A Group of Early Tudor School-Books' esp 228–55; Blake 'Wynkyn de Worde' 135–6 shows reason to believe that de Worde and Whittinton worked together on the production of these books. For their importance in educational history, see Orme *English Schools in the Middle Ages* 107.

7 On this episode, see Carlson 'The "Grammarians' War" 1519–21, Humanist Careerism in Early Tudor England, and Printing,' and the accounts of Nelson, pp 148–57, and Beatrice White *The Vulgaria of John Stanbridge and the Vulgaria of Robert Whittinton* xxi–xxxii.

8 The initial epigram that 'Bossus' nailed up survives only as quoted in Lily's portion of the *Antibossicon* (London: Pynson 1521 [*STC* 15606], sig A4v; the bibliography of the quarrel is surveyed in Carlson 'The "Grammarians' War."'

9 The printed collection of Whittinton's polemics, entitled *Antilycon* (London: de Worde 1521), is *STC* 25443.2; the printed collection of the polemics of Lily and Horman, the *Antibossicon* (London: Pynson 1521), is *STC* 15606 + 13807.

10 The quotation is from Whittinton's *Vulgaria*, ed Beatrice White, p 62; cf the remarks of Orme *English Schools* esp 112, or McConica *English Humanists and Reformation Politics* 50 and 64.

11 On public posting as a means of publication, see Scattergood *Politics and Poetry in the Fifteenth Century* 25–6. A number of the epigrams of Stefano Surigone, who was in England c 1454–78 (see above, ch 3, nn 1 and 28), collected in London, British Library, Arundel 249, are therein labelled 'valvis affixi,' suggesting that the practice was common even among the learned.

12 On the role of the printers in the Grammarians' War, see below, ch 6, and Carlson 'The "Grammarians' War"' 170–2.

13 On Whittinton's court appointment, see Carlson 'The "Grammarians' War"' 163 and n 32; and Beatrice White *Vulgaria* xxx and xxxii–xxxiii.

14 Relations between English printers and humanists are discussed in greater detail below, ch 6; on English humanists printed on the continent, see above, ch 3, n 63.

15 Ep 207, my trans, following *CWE* II, 132–3; Allen I, 439: 'Existimarim lucubrationes meas immortalitate donatas, si tuis excusae formulis in lucem exierint, maxime minutioribus illis omnium nitidissimis. Ita fiet ut volumen sit perpusillum, et exiguo sumptu res conficiatur. Quod si tibi videbitur commodum negocium suscipere, ego exemplar emendatum quod mitto per hunc iuvenem gratis suppeditabo, nisi quod paucula volumina mittere volueris amicis donanda. Neque ego vererer rem meo sumptu meoque periculo moliri, nisi mihi esset intra paucos menses Italia relinquenda. Quare pervelim rem quamprimum absolvi. Est autem vix decem dierum negocium. Quod si modis omnibus postules ut centum aut ducenta volumina ad me recipiam, tametsi non solet mihi admodum propicius esse Mercurius ille κερδῷος et incommodissimum erit sarcinam transportari, tamen ne id quidem gravabor, modo tu equum praescribas precium.'

16 Ep 129, 135, 138, 172, and 181 give evidence of Erasmus' taking the risk of marketing printed books containing his writing (the 1500 *Adagiorum collectanea* printed at Paris by Philippi); Ep 263 (from Bade; cf also Ep 472) discusses payments of cash to be made to Erasmus in exchange for copy to print. On Erasmus' relations with his printers, see above, ch 4, pp 83–4, and the references given at ch 4, n 4. See also the discussions of early printer-writer relations in Grendler 'Printing and Censorship' 31–3, or Febvre and Martin *L'Apparition du livre* 234–7.

17 *Opusculum* is *STC* 22540.5; it is dated 22 April 1519. It is described by Sylvester, in 'The "Man for All Seasons" Again' esp

148–9; Sylvester also edits and translates the volume's poem on
More, pp 150–2. The better part of the volume's poem on Skelton
is edited and translated in A.S.G. Edwards *Skelton: The Critical
Heritage* (London: Routledge 1981) 49–53; see also Carlson 'Skelton's *Garland of Laurel* and Robert Whittinton's "Lauri apud Palladem Expostulatio"' 418 and n 5.

18 Zoilus of Amphipolis (fl 359–336 BC) was an ancient Homeromas-
tix whose name came to be associated proverbially with un-
founded, malicious criticism (cf Ovid *Rem Am* 336). Whittinton
was using the name as early as 1512, before the Grammarians'
War, to refer to some imagined detractor of his *Syntaxis* (London:
de Worde 1512 [*STC* 25541]), sig D4v; to the title page of a new
edition of the same book he also added new verses 'In Zoilum
suum' after the Grammarians' War began (London: de Worde 1521
[*STC* 25548]).

19 The phrase occurs in Whittinton's *Vulgaria*; see Sylvester 'The
"Man for All Seasons" Again' 147.

20 For Skelton's career at the Tudor court, see the references given
above, ch 4, n 36, and esp Walker *John Skelton and the Politics of
the 1520s* 35–52.

21 See Sylvester 'The "Man for All Seasons" Again' 150–1.

22 For an account of More's quarrel with Brie, see below, ch 7, pp
154–5 and n 29.

23 See Carlson 'Skelton's *Garland of Laurel* and Robert Whittinton's
"Lauri apud Palladem Expostulatio"' 418–19.

24 The poem for Henry VIII (*Opusculum* sigs A2r–A2v), opening the
collection, works a numerological conceit to do with the number
eight. Whittinton's manipulations of it issue in predictable topics
of general praise: 'Aurea Saturni redcunt nunc saecula fausta, /
Henrici octavi tempore pacifici'; 'Absecat omne nephas nunc virgo
Astrea, severo / Henrici octavi cum Iove regna tenens'; and so on.

25 On this stage of Brandon's career, see now Gunn *Charles Brandon,
Duke of Suffolk, c 1484–1545* 32–74, esp 66–74.

26 Whittinton distinguishes between those whose only honour is that
which they derive from their ancestors and those, like Brandon,
who do not take honour from but bestow it on their ancestors,
and he makes the Boethian, ultimately Stoic point, that nobility is
the result, not the cause of virtue: 'Laudem adimunt abavis ignavo
pectore plures; / At Carolus tritavos auget honore suos. / Unde
hec clara ducum regum quoque stemmata ducta / Ni virtute, vi-

rens qua, Carole, ipse fluis?' *Opusculum* sig C2r; cf *Philosophiae consolatio* 3.pr.6 and 3.m.6.

27 'Rex ergo Henricus te tanto octavus amore / Complectens meritum ditat honore tuum'; 'inclyta si alliciat virtus nos iure ad amandum,' 'Invida cur Carolo sors inimica foret?' *Opusculum* sigs C2r–C2v.

28 'Fata secunda tibi donent summos et honores, / Numina dentque mei sis memor'; 'tui Whittintoni aliquando memineris.' *Opusculum* sig A3v.

29 'Quarum immensitatem animo perlustranti mihi iter vel ipso Oceano spaciosius et insuperabilius longe lateque commensurare videor'; *Opusculum* sig B4r.

30 'Quae virtus una omnium est domina, ut Marci Tulii verbis utar, et regina virtutum'; *Opusculum* sig B4v.

31 'Moneo te inter Scyllam atque Carybdim / Ut medium teneas tractum'; *Opusculum* sig A4v.

32 'Quae res in terris magis ardua, quaeve laborum / Extat plena magis, quam publica iura ministrans / Ut iustum serves, aequa pendente bilance? / ... / Si tamen a superis cuiquam tam mystica dona / Sunt data mortali, hoc antistes Wolcius evo / Est is, consilii dono quem spiritus almus / Ditat, ut illius famam totus canat orbis. / ... / Iusticia hic Curius canit unus; personat alter / Hic sapiensque Solon; Theodosius ille modestus, / Eloquio Pylius senex; affabilis idem / Pompeius, (sit opus si quando) Catoque severus / Unus agit, tantos multis e millibus unus, / Tantos unus agit.' *Opusculum* sigs A4r and B3v–B4r. Like the prose piece that follows, the poem represents Wolsey's responsibility for matters of justice, as indeed for the welfare of the entire *respublica*, as all but absolute: Wolsey is 'dignus, sub principe celso / Henrico octavo, qui publica iura gubernet' (*Opusculum* sig B4r); it is Wolsey, Whittinton claims, 'cuius uni humeris sub invictissimo principe nostro Henrico octavo sustentatur toti reipublicae onus' – 'fidem facit experientia' (*Opusculum* sig B5v).

33 'Tu omnium causas audis,' Whittinton maintains; 'Quis non admiretur tuam affabilitatem, qui, non obstante tua auctoritate et dignitate, tam faciles aditus cuivis, vel infimo, admittis gemibundas viduas, meticulosos et tremebundos inopes, mitissimo vultu et commiseranti animo suscipis, aurem benignam inclinas, trepidantia corda mellifluis verbis confirmas' (*Opusculum* sig B6v). In addition, 'aurem benignam, ut alter Alexander, non minus reo quam

accusatori praebes; ... nullum denique a tuo sermone tristem, id quod in Vespasiano laudatur, discedere permittis' (*Opusculum* sig B4v).

34 'Sanctissimum illud de inclusis agris aperiendis Senatus decretum, quod, te auctore, nuper sancitum est, silentio preterire nephas videatur, in quo miro splendore praefulget tui animi magnitudo. Fortes enim et magnanimi sunt habendi, inquit Cicero, non qui faciunt sed qui propulsant iniuriam. Memorabile igitur est illud strenuissimi Edgari Angliae olim regis, qui ea animi magnitudine accensus ut omnes non modo feras sed etiam feroces homines ab hoc regno expulisse legitur. Tu vero pari animo, non feroces homines sed ferinos hominum mores extirpare contendis, qui diis et hominibus exosi, vitae communitatem aspernantes, omnia suis metiuntur commodis ... Clausos enim agros aperis; septa evellis et dissipas; aedificia diruta denuo extrui cogis; vastos campos, aratro diu dissuetas, coli et plantari iubes. Perge, igitur, quo cepisti, et in eo certaminis campo fortius persiste; et dum Anglia incolumis stabit, semper honos nomenque tuum laudesque manebunt' (*Opusculum* sigs B5v–B6r). To dismiss such a passage as mercenary and exaggerated would be the more tempting, had not a twentieth-century historian recently chosen remarkably similar terms, apparently without knowledge of Whittinton's remarks, to describe the same events: Guy *Tudor England* 92: 'Enclosing, engrossing, and conversion of arable land to pasture were attacked by statute in 1489 and 1514–15. The acts forbade new enclosures and ordered demolished buildings to be reconstructed and land restored to tillage. Wolsey, who approached enclosures from the perspective of equity rather than economics, launched a national inquiry in 1517–18 to discover how many farmhouses had been destroyed, how much land had been enclosed, by whom, when, and where. The commissioners reported to Wolsey's chancery and it was eventually decided to proceed against 264 landlords or corporations.' On Wolsey's administration of justice in this period in general, see Guy *Tudor England* 89–94.

35 There is evidence to suggest that, at a later date, Wolsey may have had a hand in employing John Skelton and Thomas More to make and publish propaganda against religious dissent; see Scattergood, 'Skelton and Heresy' 161 and 169–70.

36 The manuscript (232 × 164 mm, with writing 134 × 94 mm) is now Oxford, Bodleian Library, Bodley ms 523 (*Summary Catalogue* no

2199). On it, see Pächt and Alexander *Illuminated Manuscripts in the Bodleian Library* III, 101 (no 1174) and pl CVIII; and on the binding, see Nixon 'The Gilt Binding of the Whittinton *Epigrams*, Ms Bodley 523,' and W. Salt Brassington *Historic Bindings in the Bodleian Library* (Oxford 1891) pl VII, where it is reproduced.

37 In about 1485, Carmeliano made a manuscript copy (now Dublin, Trinity College, ms 429) of a translation of the letters of Phalaris that he edited for publication by Theodoric Rood (*STC* 19827); see Modigliani 'Un nuovo manoscritto di Pietro Carmeliano' 86–102. In about 1499, Linacre made or had made a manuscript copy (now Cambridge, Trinity College, R.15.19) of his translation of Proclus' *De sphaera*, which Manutius printed in Venice in 1499; see Barber 'Thomas Linacre' 290–1, or Carlson 'Royal Tutors' 262–3.

38 A good (if relatively late) example of a manuscript done up to look like a printed book is described by Gutierrez and Erler 'Print into Manuscript'; cf Carlson 'The Occasional Poetry of Pietro Carmeliano' 502 n 13.

39 The best discussion of the persistent uses of manuscripts after the advent of printing is Nebbiai 'Per una valutazione della produzione manoscritta cinque-seicentesca.' See also D'Amico 'Manuscripts' esp 20–4; and the example mentioned in Loades 'The Press under the Early Tudors' 39.

40 The following remarks derive from Veblen *The Theory of the Leisure Class* esp 114–18: 'The point of material difference between machine-made goods and the hand-wrought goods which serve the same purposes is, ordinarily, that the former serve their primary purpose more adequately. They are a more perfect product – show a more perfect adaptation of means to end. This does not save them from disesteem and deprecation, for they fall short under the test of honorific waste. Hand labor is a more wasteful method of production; hence the goods turned out by this method are more servicable for the purpose of pecuniary reputability; hence the marks of hand labor come to be honorific, and the goods which exhibit these marks take rank as of higher grade than the corresponding machine product. Commonly, if not invariably, the honorific marks of hand labor are certain imperfections and irregularities in the lines of the hand-wrought article, showing where the workman has fallen short in the execution of the design. The ground of the superiority of hand-wrought goods, therefore, is a certain margin of crudeness. This margin must never be so wide as

to show bungling workmanship, since that would be evidence of low cost, nor so narrow as to suggest the ideal precision attained only by the machine, for that would be evidence of low cost' (114). Nebbiai 'Per una valutazione' 239 also singles out conspicuously costly manuscripts.

41 An example is the *La vie des peres en francoys* prepared by Vérard for sale or presentation to Henry VII in about 1495, now in the British Library (C.22.c.15 [=IC.41173]), having about 120 small paintings in it, placed over woodcuts but never simply colouring the woodcuts. On Vérard's work, see esp John MacFarlane *Antoine Vérard*.

42 Painter *William Caxton* 62 and 72–81; cf also Saenger 'Colard Mansion and the Evolution of the Printed Book.'

43 Again, these remarks derive from Veblen *Theory of the Leisure Class* esp chs 3–4, pp 41–80: 'From the foregoing survey of the growth of conspicuous leisure and consumption, it appears that the utility of both alike for the purposes of reputability lies in the element of waste that is common to both. In the one case it is a waste of time and effort, in the other it is a waste of goods. Both are methods of demonstrating the possession of wealth, and the two are conventionally accepted as equivalents. The choice between them is a question of advertising expediency simply' (p 71).

CHAPTER SIX

1 Roman type was of course in origin a humanist design, as shown, eg, by Morison 'Early Humanistic Script and the First Roman Type,' and it was used in early printing characteristically for humanist writings: cf Hirsch *Printing, Selling and Reading 1450–1550* 114–17; or Goldschmidt *The Printed Book of the Renaissance* 1–26; or the more general discussion in Febvre and Martin *L'Apparition du livre* 113–22. The most interesting discussions are those of Feld, esp 'Constructed Letters and Illuminated Texts'; see also his 'The Early Evolution of the Authoritative Text'; 'Sweynheym and Pannartz, Cardinal Bessarion, Neoplatonism'; 'A Theory of the Early Italian Printing Firm,' Parts I and II.

The *Epigrammata Lilii* printed by de Worde is listed as *STC* 15606.5, and its date is there given as '1521.' For reasons discussed below, it seems clear that the book cannot have been printed before the beginning of June, 1522, when some of the poems in it were written, and it seems unlikely to have been printed after Lily's death in December, 1522, assuming that the book would have made something of his death, as a matter of interest to its potential market (see further, below, n 50).

2 See above, ch 5, pp 107–12.

3 'Nonne Aquilae visa est aquila eventus voluisse, / Dicere et in tuto regis adesse rates?' *Epigrammata Lilii* sig A4v. On the occurrence and its diplomatic context, see Chrimes *Henry* VII 288–91.

4 Anglo *Spectacle, Pageantry* 187 n 3.

5 'Si quid dictabo scribes, at singula recte, / Nec macula aut scriptis menda sit ulla tuis'; 'Saepe recognoscas tibi lecta, animoque revolvas'; 'quoties loqueris, memor esto loquare latine, / Et scopulos veluti barbara verba fuge'; 'Grammaticas recte si vis cognoscere leges, / Discere si cupias cultius ore loqui, / Addiscas veterum clarissima dicta virorum / Et quos authores turba latina docet. / Nunc te Virgilius, nunc ipse Terentius optat / Nunc simul amplecti te Ciceronis opus; / Quos qui non didicit nil praeter somnia vidit, / Certat et in tenebris vivere Cymeriis.' The poem occupies *Epigrammata Lilii* sigs A1v–A3r.

6 On Colet and his school, see Lupton *A Life of Dean Colet* esp 154–77, and Gleason *John Colet* esp 217–34. On the poems of Erasmus commissioned by Colet, their display at the school, and their publication, see above, ch 4, pp 96–7 and nn 37–9; and Reedijk, pp 291–3 and 297. The earliest surviving edition of Colet's *Aedito*, printed at Antwerp in 1527, which incorporates a text of Lily's 'Ad discipulos,' sigs E5v–E7r, is listed as *STC* 5542; for the likelihood that the work was first published c 1510, see Flynn, 'The Grammatical Writings of William Lily, ?1468–1523' 86–7 or C.J. Allen 'The Sources of "Lily's Latin Grammar"': A Review of the Facts and Some Further Suggestions' *Library* 5th ser, 9 (1954) 86–7. The pre-1534 editions of the *Aeditio* incorporating Lily's poem are listed as *STC* 5542.1–5542.8; the earliest surviving text of it printed by de Worde is in a 1534 edition of the *Aeditio, STC* 5543.

7 The verses occupy *Epigrammata Lilii* sigs A3r–A4r. For details of the entry, see Withington, *English Pageantry* I, 174–9; Baskervill 'William Lily's Verse for the Entry of Charles V into London' esp 1–3; and Anglo *Spectacle*, esp 186–202.

8 Pynson's account of the entry – *STC* 15606.7 (*olim STC* 5017) – is reprinted from the unique surviving copy in Baskervill 'Lily's Verse' 8–14. Pynson had previously published a similar volume for the 1508 *spousells* of Henry VII's daughter Mary and this same

Charles, then prince of Castile, with contributions from Carmeliano; see Carlson 'The Occasional Poetry of Pietro Carmeliano' 500–1 and n 12. On the origins of such publications, including discussion of the 1508 *Spousells*, see Green *Poets and Princepleasers* 170–2; for other examples, see Baskervill 'Lily's Verse' 6–7; Kipling *The Triumph of Honour* 72 and 173; and cf Parkinson 'Scottish Prints and Entertainments, 1508' 306.

9 Hall's quotations from and arrangement of Lily's poems for the entry seem to derive from something copied out on the spot; see Baskervill 'Lily's Verse' 4.

10 'Vivite felices, quot vixit secula Nestor, / Vivite Cumanae tempora fatidicae.' 'Letitiae quantum Minyis praebebat Iason, / Aurea Phryxae vellera nactus Ovis; / Letitiae quantum tulerat Pompeius et urbi / Hoste triumphato Scipio Romulidum; / Tantum tu nobis, Caesar, mitissime princeps, / Intrans Henrici principis hospitium.' 'Laudat magnanimos urbs inclyta Roma Catones; / Cantant Annibalem Punica regna suum; / Gentis erat Solymae rex ingens gloria David; / Gentis Alexander gloria prima suae; / Illustrat fortes Arcturi fama Britannos. / Illustras gentem, Caesar, et ipse tuam, / Cui Deus imperium, victo, precor, hoste, secundet, / Regnet ut in terris pacis amica quies.' These passages are quoted from Baskervill 'Lily's Verse' 12, 11, and 28, respectively.

11 'Vive diu felix; gentem et miseratus ab hoste /Iustitiae clypeo protege Christigenam. / Maurus, Arabs, Syrus, et que nunc tam barbara sevit, / Turcarum illuvies, te duce, victa cadat.' Quoted from Baskervill 'Lily's Verse' 10. On the diplomatic issues that occasioned Charles's visit to England in 1522, see Anglo *Spectacle, Pageantry* 170–80.

12 Hans Robert Jauss 'Literary History as Challenge to Literary Theory' in *Toward an Aesthetic of Reception* trans Timothy Bahti (Minneapolis: University of Minnesota Press 1982) 25.

13 'Quanto amplexetur populus te, Caesar, amore / Testantur variis gaudia mixta sonis. / Aera, tube, litui, cantus, citharae calamisque / Consona te resonant organa disparibus. / Unum te celebrant, te unum sic cuncta salutant: / O decus, o rerum gloria, Caesar, ave.' 'Carole, Christigenum decus et quem scripta loquuntur / A magno ductum Carolo habere genus; / Tuque, Henrice, pia virtutis laude refulgens, / Doctrina, ingenio, relligione, fide; / Vos Praetor, Consul, sanctus cum plebe Senatus / Vectos huc fausto sidere gestit ovans.' Quoted from Baskervill 'Lily's Verse' 13 and 11.

14 Lily's verse translations from Greek were first printed by Froben

in the March 1518 edition of Thomas More's *Epigrammata*, on which see below, ch 7. The liminary verses that Lily saw printed were: an epigram for Colet's *Aeditio* (printed, eg, on the title page of the 1527 edition mentioned above, n 6, probably dating from c 1510); another for Thomas Linacre's *Progymnasmata grammatices vulgaria* (London: Rastell c 1515 [STC 15635]), sig A1v; another for André's *Hymni Christiani*, sig A2r; another for William Horman's *Vulgaria* (London: Pynson 1519 [STC 13811]), sig +1v; and another praising Linacre to Princess Mary, printed with Linacre's *Rudimenta grammatices* (London: Pynson c 1525? [STC 15636]), sig G1v.

15 The manuscript is now London, British Library, Harley 540; the poems of Lily that Stow copied into it occupy fols 57r–59r. On it, see Tournoy 'La Poésie de William Lily pour le diptyque de Quentin Metsijs' 63–4 and n 12.

16 On Stow's activities as a collector of poetry, see Ringler 'John Stow's Editions of Skelton's *Workes* and of *Certaine Worthye Manuscript Poems*' esp 215; and Carlson *Latin Writings of John Skelton* 65, 93, and 119–20.

17 For the suggestion that the 'Divo Carolo imperatori semper augusto Guil. Lilii acclamatio' from the series was presented rather than put on display publicly, see Baskervill 'Lily's Verse' 4–6.

18 Cf Graham Pollard 'The Company of Stationers before 1557' esp 15–17, or 'The English Market for Printed Books' 10–11.

19 Cf de Roover 'New Facets on the Financing and Marketing of Early Printed Books' 222; or Moran 'Caxton and the City of London' 81–8, esp 83, where Moran calls Caxton 'the father of market research in the field of books'; or Rutter 'William Caxton and Literary Patronage' 470, who argues that 'Caxton should be recognized as a pioneer in the mass-marketing of books.' Febvre and Martin *L'Apparition du livre* 307–47 discuss a series of marketing problems faced by early printers; see also Coq and Ornato 'La Production et le marché des incunables' esp 305–6.

20 The earl of Arundel promised in advance 'to take a reasonable quantity' of printed copies of Caxton's *Golden Legend*, thereby enabling Caxton to produce the edition; for this and other examples of effectively bespoke editions in Caxton's production, see Painter *William Caxton* 88–91, 108, 143–4, 164–8. On the role that such patronage for printed editions played in early English printing, see Lathrop 'The First English Printers and Their Patrons,' and

Bennett *English Books and Readers 1475 to 1557* 41–7; cf also the
cautionary remarks of Rutter 'William Caxton and Literary Patronage' 440–70. A well-known manuscript thought to be the result
of speculation is the Corpus Christi College, Cambridge copy of
Chaucer's *Troilus*: see M.B. Parkes, in *Troilus and Criseyde, Geoffrey Chaucer: A Facsimile of Corpus Christi College Cambridge
Ms 61* (Cambridge: D.S. Brewer 1978) 11. Another example was discussed by Bühler 'Sir John Paston's *Grete Booke*, a Fifteenth-Century 'Best Seller.'' The so-called *pecia* system of manuscript book
production anticipated many features of printing: textual uniform-
ity, mass production, and production in advance of demand; on it,
see Graham Pollard 'The *Pecia* System in the Medieval Universities.'

21 For Caxton's *bâtardes* and their expense, see Painter *William Caxton* 62; and cf above, ch 5, p 119 and n 42. For paper's costliness
relative to printer's overhead and other supplies see de Roover
'New Facets' 227, or Febvre and Martin *L'Apparition du livre*
169–72.

22 Cf the discussion of Blake 'William Caxton' esp 69–78. On liminary verse, see below, ch 7, pp 148–9 and n 16.

23 Cf Bennett *English Books* 211–15; likewise, there is no analogue
for printers' devices in manuscript books, as Hirsch *Printing, Selling and Reading* 25 points out. See also the discussion in Febvre
and Martin *L'Apparition du livre* 122–8.

24 On this issue in general, see Bennett *English Books* 198 and
178–97, where he surveys the development of editorial policy in
English printing up to 1557.

25 Cf Blake 'William Caxton: His Choice of Texts' esp 307; and also
Belyea 'Caxton's Reading Public.'

26 Bennett *English Books* 186.

27 On the work of de Worde and Pynson, see Bennett *English Books*
esp 182–93, and Plomer *Wynkyn de Worde and His Contemporaries* esp 43–153; also, the important conclusions about de Worde's
early editorial strategy in A.S.G. Edwards 'ISTC, the Literary Historian and the Editor' in *Bibliography and the Study of Fifteenth-
Century Civilisation* ed Hellinga and Goldfinch, 229.

28 On their concomitant political conservatism, see Winger 'Regulations Relating to the Book Trade in London from 1357 to 1586'
esp 165–8; cf also Loades 'The Press under the Early Tudors' 29–50.

29 The standard discussion remains that of Saunders 'The Stigma of

Print'; see also the important cautionary remarks of May 'Tudor Aristocrats and the Mythical 'Stigma of Print.'''

30 See above ch 3, pp 77–8.

31 There is evidence to suggest that what market there was for printed books of humanist interest could have been supplied by import – all the more reason for England's printers to stay away from a trade of which they were ignorant; cf Bennett *English Books* 193. On the import trade, see esp Elizabeth Armstrong 'English Purchases of Printed Books from the Continent 1465–1526,' and Hellinga 'Importation of Books Printed on the Continent into England and Scotland before c. 1520'; also Lowry 'The Arrival and Use of Continental Printed Books in Yorkist England,' Kerling 'Caxton and the Trade in Printed Books,' and Plomer 'The Importation of Books into England in the Fifteenth and Sixteenth Centuries,' and 'The Importation of Low Country and French Books into England, 1480 and 1502–3.'

32 On Caxton's editions of Traversagni's grammars, see esp Ruysschaert 'Les Manuscrits autographes de deux oeuvres de Lorenzo Guglielmo Traversagni imprimées chez Caxton'; Blake 'The Spread of Printing in English during the Fifteenth Century' 33; and Painter *William Caxton* 96–7 and 104, who also lists all of Caxton's books, pp 211–15. On Traversagni, see above, ch 3 n 1.

33 On this edition, see Painter *William Caxton* 157.

34 The Latin of the title is 'Sex perelegantissime epistole quarum tris a summo pontifice Sixto quarto et sacro cardinalium collegio ad illustrissimum Venetiarum ducem Joannem Mocenigum totidemque ab ipso duce ad eundem pontificem et cardinales ob Ferrariense bellum susceptum conscripte sunt.' On the book, see Painter *William Caxton* 135–6, and cf Modigliani 'Un nuovo manoscritto di Pietro Carmeliano' 89; for Carmeliano's Venetian connections, see above, ch 2, n 1. For the epigram – 'Eloquii cultor, sex has mercare tabellas / Que possunt Marco cum Cicerone loqui. / Ingeniis debent cultis ea scripta placere, / In quibus ingenii copia magna viget' – see Carlson 'The Occasional Poetry of Pietro Carmeliano' 498 n 9 (where it is implied, mistakenly, I now believe, that the verses were written by Caxton).

35 These editions are described in Duff *Fifteenth Century English Books* nos 369, 111, 393, and 394. I have relied on Duff as a source of information about English incunabula except as indicated otherwise. On the editions of Terence mentioned here, including one

by Pynson, see Dennis E. Rhodes, 'Le Publication des comedies de Terence au xve siècle' in *Le Livre dans l'Europe de la renaissance* ed Aquilon and Martin, esp 289 and 295.

36 On Rood, see Carter *History of the Oxford University Press I*, 4–12; and for his work with Pietro Carmeliano, see above, ch 2, p 45 and n 28. Rood's books mentioned here are Duff *Fifteenth Century English Books* nos 104, 348, 32, 392, 28 and 29, and 239; his others are nos 3, 21, 22, 38, 234, 238, 277, 278, 300, and 363.

37 These are only editions of which at least traces survive; no doubt there were more. For the derivation of this figure, see Carlson 'Formats in English Printing to 1557.'

38 Bennett *English Books* 188 suggests that in the decades 1500–19, de Worde and Pynson had something more than 70 per cent of the domestic trade. I used the list of de Worde's publications in Bennett *English Books* 239–76, and I used Morrison *Index of Printers, Publishers and Booksellers in Pollard and Redgrave, A Short-Title Catalogue* for reconstructing the lists of Pynson and other printers discussed herein. These lists have since been superseded by those in the third volume of the revised *STC*, which was published in 1991: I regret having prepared this chapter before it appeared, with its chronological and other pertinent indices.

39 The first of these is *STC* 4659; the other is attested only by a surviving manuscript copy, London, British Library, Addit 29506. See Carlson 'The Occasional Poetry of Pietro Carmeliano' 500–2 and nn 12–13, and Gutierrez and Erler, 'Print into Manuscript' 187–230.

40 John Colet's *Oratio ad clerum in convocatione* (London: Pynson 1512 [*STC* 5545]) might be regarded as similar to Griffo's orations, which are *STC* 12412.1 and 12413. On him, see Hay 'Pietro Griffo, an Italian in England, 1506–1512'; and for Pynson's introduction of Roman type into England with the second of these, see Issac *English Printers' Types of the Sixteenth Century* 5.

41 The Erasmus volume is *STC* 20060; Pynson also printed an Erasmian grammar, *De constructione octo partium orationis*, in 1513 (*STC* 10497). The More volume is *STC* 19897.9. At this same time (c 1512–13), Rastell printed a few other titles that may have been of some humanist interest, most notably Linacre's *Progymnasmata grammatices* (*STC* 15635); Devereux 'Thomas More and His Printers' suggests that Rastell 'may well have seen himself as an English Aldus' (p 42), albeit briefly, before turning to other projects. De-

vereux also stresses the slowness of English printers to take up humanist printing, in part because of the import trade (pp 41–2 and 46), and he too shows cause to see a change c 1520 (pp 42 and 47–9).

42 For this rough figure and the contribution of these other printers, see Carlson 'Formats in English Printing.'

43 On Constable and his *Epigrammata* (*STC* 5639), see Bradner *Musae Anglicanae* 18, or Hudson *The Epigram in the English Renaissance* 86–7; and Sylvester 'John Constable's Poems to Thomas More.'

44 Pace's *Oratio in pace* = *STC* 19081a; Tunstall's *In laudem matrimonii oratio* = *STC* 24320; the volume Pynson printed to commemorate Charles v's 1522 entry into London = *STC* 15606.7 (see above, n 8); the *Assertio septem sacramentarum* = *STC* 13078 et seqq; Johannes Murmellius' *Composita verborum* = *STC* 18292.1; Aphthonius = *STC* 699; Cicero's *Philippicae* = *STC* 5311; Erasmus' *Colloquia* = *STC* 10450.6 and 10450.7; de Worde's *Christiani hominis institutum* = *STC* 10450.2 and Pepwell's reprint = *STC* 10450.3; the Latin translations of Galen = *STC* 11531.5, 11532 and 11534; Tunstall's *De arte supputandi* = *STC* 24319; More's *Epistola ad Brixium* = *STC* 18088; the Grammarians' War volumes = *STC* 25443.1, 13807, and 15606. On Whittinton's encomia, see above, ch 5; on the publication of the *Epigrammata Lilii*, see above, n 1; on Constable's *Epigrammata*, see above, n 43.

45 Bennett *English Books* 188, and cf 86–7.

46 On the advent of this second generation, see above, ch 3, pp 65–6.

47 The following remarks are based on the conclusion of Carlson 'The "Grammarians' War" 1519–1521.'

48 Pynson's October 1520 edition of Whittinton's *Vulgaria* is *STC* 25570; the other editions of Whittinton's grammatical writings that Pynson produced during 1520–1 are *STC* 25446.5, 25479.15: 25529, and 25547.3.

49 The latter of these hypotheses seems more likely. Although on at least one occasion Pynson is known to have speculatively and provocatively cut in on business de Worde was doing – Pynson published Barclay's verse translation of the *Ship of Fools* 14 December 1509 (*STC* 3545) at his own 'coste and charge,' soon after de Worde had issued a prose translation of the same work, 6 July 1509 (*STC* 3547) – Pynson and de Worde, like other early printers in England, seem more often to have cooperated, in effectively joint publishing ventures, particularly in the production of titles

much in demand, such as grammar books. Cf Bennett *English
Books* 192 and 234–6.

50 Lily's death in December 1522 would have made the potential for
profit of such a collection seem only greater, inasmuch as it would
have attracted additional buyers to the book, as a commemoration
of Lily. No doubt it did, once Lily was dead – a windfall for de
Worde. That the volume omits to exploit Lily's death argues
strongly that it was published before his death.

CHAPTER SEVEN

1 For description of the book and its later reprintings, see Gibson
and Patrick *St. Thomas More* nos 3–4 and 57, pp 7–12 and 76–7,
which reproduces all the title pages and subtitle pages mentioned
herein. On Froben, see Hilgert 'Johann Froben and the Basel University Scholars, 1513–1523'; and S. Diane Shaw 'A Study of the
Collaboration between Erasmus of Rotterdam and His Printer Johann Froben at Basel during the Years 1514 to 1527' esp 41–51. The
discussion of the book repeats some points made in a different
context in Carlson 'Reputation and Duplicity.'

2 See, eg, Ep 584, ed Allen II, 576 (*CWE* IV, 368–9).

3 Eg, 'valvis affixi,' 'a tergo littere,' etc. The Surigone manuscript is
now part of London, British Library, Arundel 249; see above, ch 3,
n 28, and ch 4, n 42.

4 But see above, ch 4, nn 4, 41, and 42.

5 Ed and trans *CWM* III.2, no 276.6–12.

6 Ed *CWM* III.2, no 276.36–9; my translation.

7 On this episode, see Lorne Campbell, Margaret Mann Phillips,
Hubertus Schulte Herbruggen, and J.B. Trapp 'Quentin Matsys,
Desiderius Erasmus, Pieter Gillis and Thomas More' *Burlington
Magazine* 120 (1978) 716–25, and 121 (1979) 436–7; Trapp 'Thomas
More and the Visual Arts' 39–42; Tournoy 'La Poésie de William
Lily pour le diptyque de Quentin Metsijs' 63–6; and Lorne Campbell *Renaissance Portraits* (New Haven: Yale University Press
1990) 165. The poem quoted is no 276 in *CWM* III.2. More's covering letter to Gillis is Ep 684, ed Allen III, 105–7 (*CWE* V, 149–51);
the covering letter to Erasmus is Ep 683, ed Allen III, 103–5 (*CWE*
V 147–9); and More's letter of acknowledgment to Erasmus is Ep
706, where More wrote: 'Gaudeo versiculos meos in tabellam tibi
placuisse' (ed Allen III, 133; *CWE* V, 190).

8 For example, the several gibes against a false astrologer, possibly

the court astrologer William Parron (eg, *CWM* III.2, nos 60–5, 67, 101, 118, 169; see also the note, pp 348–9); the lampoons of the niggardly bishop (no 71), the fraudulent doctor (no 90), and the foolish poet (no 147); the lines addressing his friends 'Tyndalus' (no 163) and Busleyden (nos 250–2); and so on.

9 'Si qua dies unquam, si quod fuit, Anglia, tempus, / Gratia quo superis esset agenda tibi, / Haec est illa dies niveo signanda lapillo, / Laeta dies fastis annumeranda tuis'; ed and trans *CWM* III.2, no 19.8–11. The other lines in More's coronation poems quoted or referred to are *CWM* III.2, nos 19.70; 19.169 and 19.173 ('prompto superet consilio Tanaquil ... Inque maritali Penelopeia fide'); 21.10; 23.3–14; and 19.192. To them, cf the poem, attributable to Skelton, 'Septimus Henricus tumulo requiescit in isto,' lines 3–4 (ed Carlson *Latin Writings of John Skelton* 59–60), and Andrea Ammonio's 'Elegia de obitu regis Henrici VII et felici successione Henrici Octavi' (ed Pizzi *Andreae Ammonii Carmina Omnia* no 3.79); Skelton's elegy on Margaret Beaufort (XX.7–8 in *Latin Writings of John Skelton*); Ammonio's 'Elegia de obitu' (ed Pizzi *Carmina* no 3.91–100); Skelton's 'Lawde and Praise' (ed Scattergood *John Skelton* 110–12) and Ammonio's 'Elegia de obitu' (ed Pizzi *Carmina* no 3.103–4); and André's 'Carmina in natalem principis' (ed Carlson 'King Arthur and Court Poems for the Birth of Arthur Tudor' 167–8). Cf Fox *Politics and Literature* 20–3.

10 Contemporaries of his are known to have passed around informally other writings similarly intended for eventual presentation to superiors: the case of Erasmus' poem on St Anne, for example, is discussed above, ch 4, pp 95–6. Ep 218, 219, and 221, in which Erasmus and Ammonio discuss a poem or poems that Ammonio intended to dedicate or present to Mountjoy, may imply a similar circulation before presentation.

11 It is now London, British Library, Cotton Titus D.IV. Two pages of it (fols 8v and 12v, the second of these being the folio illustrated with the pomegranate and rose) are reproduced in *CWM* III.2, between pp 107 and 108. The illustrations, on fols 11v and 12v, are the work of a professional *pictor*; in his prefatory letter to Henry VIII, More describes giving the poems to one for decorative finishing: 'conscriptos eos pictori exornandos dedissem' (*CWM* III.2, 96).

12 The Carmeliano manuscript (now London, British Library, Addit 33736; on it, see above, ch 2) comprises fourteen leaves, each 190 x 128 mm, each containing sixteen lines of writing, covering an area

approximately 102 x 88 mm; the More manuscript comprises sixteen leaves, each 160 x 118 mm, each containing thirteen lines of
writing, covering an area of approximately 90 x 75 mm.

13 More's poems are nos 183–4, 244, and 271 in *CWM* III.2. Bernard
André's poem survives in Hatfield, Hatfield House, Cecil Papers
277/1 (the professional illumination of which suggests that it was
a presentation copy for the king, though there is no more definite
evidence). Pietro Carmeliano's is edited in Carlson 'The Occasional Poetry of Pietro Carmeliano' 501–2 and n 13, where its publication in print is discussed; cf above, ch 6, n 39. Erasmus' is
Reedjik, no 93. Skelton's English poems, 'A Ballade of the Scot-
tysshe Kynge' and 'Agaynst the Scottes,' are edited in Scattergood
John Skelton 113–21, and the publication of the first of these is
discussed p 421; his Latin poems are nos XVII and XVIII, in Carlson
Latin Writings of John Skelton 48–50. Andrea Ammonio's is lost,
but is quoted by Erasmus in Ep 283, ed Allen I, 546 (*CWE* II,
270–2). On the poetic response to these events, see Marc'hadour
'Croisade triumphale de l'Angleterre: 1513'; Gutierrez 'John Skelton' 59–76; and Gutierrez and Erler 'Print into Manuscript' 206
n 4.

14 As the evidence of their correspondence suggests: in Ep 283 (ed Allen I, 547; *CWE* II, 272), to Andrea Ammonio, Erasmus promised
to enclose a copy of his poem on the Battle of Spurs (no 93, ed
Reedijk).

15 The important local precedent for publication of this sort is probably the humanist response against Robert Gaguin in 1490. The epigrams involved must have had a fairly wide circulation, and would
probably not have been written had it not been likely that they
would reach courtiers and king. See above, ch 3, p 77 and n 55.

16 The Italian was Stefano Surigone; his eulogy of Chaucer, printed
in Caxton's 1478 edition of Chaucer's Boece (*STC* 3199), fols
94r–94v, is reprinted in Caroline Spurgeon *Five Hundred Years of
Chaucer Criticism and Allusion 1357–1900* (1925; rpt New York:
Russell 1960) I, 59–60; cf above, ch 6, p 132 and n 22. Not only was
Surigone's English too poor for him to have read much Chaucer
(allowing, for the moment, that someone of Surigone's proclivities
would have had any interest in reading Chaucer); also, those likely
to want an English Boethius probably could not have appreciated
Surigone's humanist Latin, and those who could appreciate Surigone's eulogy probably would not have wanted Chaucer's in-

elegantly Englished *Consolation*. On the topic generally, see Williams 'Commendatory Verses' esp 1–2.

17 These poems are nos 273–4, 275, 148, and 155–7 in *CWM* III.2.

18 'Hoc libelli in manum cape, lege, et Moro ... fave'; ed and trans *CWM* III.2, 76–7.

19 On the edition's genesis, see Craig R. Thompson, in *CWM* III.1, pp lxi–lxiii; Leicester Bradner, Charles A. Lynch, and Revilo P. Oliver, in *CWM* III.2, 3–4 and 6–7; and Edward Surtz, in *CWM* IV, pp clxxxvii–cxc. The important documentary evidence is the correspondence among More, Erasmus, Froben, Beatus Rhenanus, and others, in which the book and plans for it are mentioned: Ep 424, 461, 543, 584, 597, 628, 634–5, 726, 732–3 (= *CWE* 704a), and 785. More's *Epistola ad Brixium*, written after the fact in 1520, incorporates an important account of the fashioning of the *Epigrammata* and More's role in it (ed and trans Daniel Kinney, in *CWM* III.2, 622–31). The account needs to be used with caution, however, because it was in More's immediate polemical interest to distance himself from the publication as much as possible: Brie castigated various *menda* in the *Epigrammata*; More sought to exculpate himself in some measure by claiming that the faults had crept into the book after it had passed out of his own hands, into those of Froben and his crew. Devereux 'Thomas More and His Printers,' concentrating on More's English printers, especially John and William Rastell, does not discuss the publication of the *Epigrammata*; however, he does give examples of More's carelessness about proof-correction in other cases, pp 41, 43, and 51–2. Incidental editorial carelessness is also imputed to More in Daniel Kinney 'More's Epigram on Brixius' Plagiarism: One Poem or Two?' *Moreana* 70 (1981) 37–44, esp 40. S. Diane Shaw 'A Study of the Collaboration between Erasmus and Froben' 73–7 discusses other instances in which Erasmus acted as an agent of sorts, mediating between his friends and Froben.

20 'De Mori Utopia et Epigrammatis res mihi magis erat cordi quam mea ipsius negocia'; Ep 732, ed Allen, III, 160; trans *CWE* V, 229.

21 On relations between Erasmus and Froben, see Bloch 'Erasmus and the Froben Press' 109–20; and esp S. Diane Shaw 'A Study of the Collaboration between Erasmus and Froben' 31–124. Also cf above, ch 4, n 4.

22 'Vidi tandem Utopiam Parisiis excusam, sed mendose'; Ep 785, ed Allen III, 240; trans *CWE* V, 329.

23 'Ea sic dispone omnia ut ex usu meo censebis fore'; Ep 461, ed Allen II, 340; trans *CWE* IV, 68. After the book was published and had come under attack by Germain de Brie, More's ambivalent remarks still evoke the pride he took in it. On the one hand, he maintained to Erasmus – disingenuously, it seems, by light of the work he had put into the poems' initial publication and the corrections he made for the second edition – that the book had not meant much to him. 'My own *Epigrammata* never gave me much satisfaction,' he wrote, 'as you yourself, Erasmus, can testify; and unless that book had had an appeal for you and certain other people greater than the charm it had for me, perhaps it would not exist anywhere today.' At the same time, however, More also allowed that Brie had hurt him by attacking the work, and sought to justify defending his work on the grounds of *amour-propre.* Here too, More effectively allowed that he had an interest in his reputation after all. Justifying his *Epistola ad Brixium*, More wrote Erasmus: 'The fact remains that while I still converse with mortal men and am not yet entirely deified, if I may be flippant on this not wholly serious subject, I am not afraid, I repeat, that my human and humane reader will not make allowances in me too for those human feelings which no human being has entirely thrown off.' Ep 1096; trans *CWE* VII, 275 and 277 (ed Allen IV, 254 and 255).

24 In September 1516, More wrote Erasmus: 'If later on you publish my epigrams, please consider whether you think it best to suppress those in which I attacked de Brie, for there are some rather bitter things in them; though I might be thought to have been provoked by the abuse he levelled at my country. All the same, as I say, please give them some thought'; Ep 461, trans *CWE* IV, 67–8 (ed Allen II, 340) See also Ep 1093, ed Allen IV, 241 (*CWE* VII, 264).

25 The surviving poems written but not included in the 1518 edition of the *Epigrammata* are nos 272, 273–5 and 279, and possibly also nos 276–7 (written in October and November 1517), in *CWM* III.2.

26 *CWM* III.2, 7.

27 The new poems are nos 259–69 in *CWM* III.2. The two that were dropped are nos 270–1. The quoted phrase is from *CWM* III.2, 8.

28 *CWM* III.2, 7 and 24–32. There is some evidence to indicate that the poems underwent a similar verbal polishing before their initial publication in print in 1518, chiefly the non-erroneous differences between the manuscript and printed versions of More's coronation

poems. For example, the printed edition eliminates an alliteration of the manuscript text at 19.24; cf also the variants at 19.68, 19.166, 22.14, 22.16, 23.7, and 23.9.

29 On this controversy, see Lavoie 'La Fin de la querelle entre Germain de Brie et Thomas More'; Daniel Kinney, in *CWM* III.2, 472–9 and 557–72; and Marius *Thomas More* 245–50. The main polemic documents, Brie's *Antimorus* and More's *Epistola ad Brixium*, are edited and translated by Daniel Kinney, in *CWM* III.2, 482–547 and 594–659; the cognate correspondence is Ep 620, 1045, 1087, 1093, 1096, 1117, 1131, 1133, 1184, and 1817.

30 'Lapsus inexcusabiles in syllabarum quantitate' and 'Soloecismi ac barbarismi foedissimi'; ed and trans *CWM* III.2, 514–15 and 526–7.

31 *Cf CWM* III.2, 7–8 and 25–32.

32 *Antimorus* 305, ed and trans *CWM* III.2, 498–9.

33 *Antimorus* 316–17, ed *CWM* III.2, 498–9; my translation.

34 See above, ch 6, p 123 and n 1.

35 I count fifty-five instances in which the spelling of the manuscript version of More's coronation poems and their cover letter has been classicized in the printed edition of 1518; most of these (forty-five) are substitutions of the Classical Latin diphthong *ae* for Medieval Latin *e*, but others include correcting the pseudo-classicizing *aegregius* of the manuscript to *egregius* in print. Of course it is not certain either that More was wholly responsible for the manuscript's spelling or that Froben was wholly responsible for the printed book's.

36 Erasmus, hardly a disinterested witness of course, wrote Froben: 'ea est tuae officine autoritas ut liber vel hoc nomine placeat eruditis, si cognitum sit e Frobenianis edibus prodisse' ('your press stands so high that a book can earn a welcome among the learned for no better reason than that it is known to issue from the house of Froben'): Ep 635, ed Allen III, 57; trans *CWE* V, 83. Cf the remarks of S. Diane Shaw 'A Study of the Collaboration between Erasmus and Froben' esp 77–82 and 107–9.

37 Examples are discussed above, ch 4, pp 93–8.

38 Ed and trans *CWM* III.2, no 159.

39 Ed and trans *CWM* III.2, no 160.

40 The standard work on skill of this kind was Erasmus' *De copia*, on which see esp Rix 'The Editions of Erasmus' *De Copia*.'

41 Cf the remarks of Bradner *Musae Anglicanae* 10–12, or, more generally, Derek Attridge, *Well-Weighed Syllables: Elizabethan Verse*

in Classical Metres (Cambridge: Cambridge University Press 1974)
92–100. Erasmus too wrote a poem using Leonines parodically; see
Reedijk, p 387.

42 'Hic' is long in the first line but short in the third; for the poem's
other false quantities ('mille' in the fifth line and 'ista' in the
sixth) and medievalisms, see the notes in *CWM* III.2, 381.

43 'videt hic Janus utrinque nihil,' *CWM* III.2, no 161.13.

44 'Ridendos ... versus,' *CWM* III.2, no 161.8.

45 This information is from More's epigram (no 161.10): referring to
the 'ridendos ... versus,' More writes that 'Janus' 'hos tumulos in-
scalpsit.'

46 The epigram in question is no 148 in *CWM* III.2. The discussion
that follows is based on the more detailed one in Carlson 'Reputation and Duplicity'' 261–81.

47 In André *Hymni Christiani* (Paris: Bade 1517) sig A2r.

48 'Ipsos quos cecinit superos, dum scriberet omneis, / Credibile est
vati consuluisse suo,' ed and trans *CWM* III.2, no 148.9–10.

49 *Hymni Christiani* sig L3r; reprinted and discussed in *CWM* III.2,
p 377.

50 *CWM* III.2, p 196; my translation.

51 'Nam subito scripsit, sed sic ut scribere posset / Quantumvis
longo tempore non melius,' ed *CWM* III.2, no 148.11–12; my translation.

52 *CWM* III.2, nos 147 ('In stultum poetam') and 149–57. The evidence on the question of who wrote the title for the André epigram – most likely More himself – is set out in Carlson
'Reputation and Duplicity' 278–9 and n 33.

CONCLUSION

1 For these examples, see above, ch 2, p 57, ch 6, p 127, and ch 7,
p 148; and ch 5, p 105.

2 Harris *The Origin of Writing* esp 25–6, 29–30, and 155–7; on pp
107–8, Harris develops the example of capital letters and small letters having different meanings, corresponding to nothing in speech
and not simply standing for a verbal content. The words quoted at
the beginning of the paragraph are W.W. Barker's.

3 The examples mentioned here are all from Morison's *Politics and
Script*, edited and completed by Nicolas Barker.

❧ Select Bibliography

This bibliography includes everything cited more than once in the notes to the chapters, where citations are in shortened forms, and a few other items of special interest.

Allen. *See also* Abbreviations

Allen, P.S. 'Erasmus' Relations with His Printers.' In Allen *Erasmus: Lectures and Wayfaring Sketches*. Oxford: Clarendon 1934. 109–37

Allen, P.S., and H.M. Allen, eds. *The Letters of Richard Fox 1486–1527*. Oxford: Clarendon 1929

Anderson, Perry. *Lineages of the Absolutist State*. London: NLB 1974

Anglo, Sydney. 'The foundation of the Tudor Dynasty: The Coronation and Marriage of Henry VII.' *Guildhall Miscellany* 2 (1960) 3–11

– 'The *British History* in Early Tudor Propaganda.' *Bulletin of the John Rylands Library* 44 (1961) 17–48

– *Spectacle, Pageantry and Early Tudor Policy*. Oxford: Clarendon 1969

– 'Ill of the Dead: The Posthumous Reputation of Henry VII.' *Renaissance Studies* 1 (1987) 27–47

Aquilon, Pierre, and Henri-Jean Martin, eds. *Le Livre dans l'Europe de la renaissance: Actes du XXVIIIe colloque international d'Etudes humanistes de Tours*. Paris: Promodis 1988

Armstrong, C.A.J. *Dominic Mancini: The Usurpation of Richard III*. 2nd ed. Oxford: Clarendon 1969

Armstrong, Elizabeth. 'English Purchases of Printed Books from the Continent 1465–1526.' *English Historical Review* 94 (1979) 268–90

Avarucci, Giuseppe. 'Due codici scritti da "Gerardus Helye," padre di Erasmo.' *Italia medioevale e umanistica* 26 (1983) 215–55

Baiardi, Giorgio Cerboni, Giorgio Chittolini, and Piero Floriani, eds. *Federico di Montefeltro: Lo stato, le arti, la cultura.* 3 vols. Rome: Bulzoni Editore 1986

Bale, John. *Scriptorum Illustrium Maioris Brytanniae Catalogus.* 2 vols. Basel 1557–9.

Barber, Giles. 'Thomas Linacre: A Bibliographical Survey of His Works.' In *Linacre Studies.* Ed Maddison et al. 290–336

Baskervill, C.R. 'William Lily's Verse for the Entry of Charles V into London.' *Huntington Library Quarterly* 9 (1936) 1–14

Belyea, Barbara. 'Caxton's Reading Public.' *English Language Notes* 19 (1981) 14–19

Bennett, H.S. 'The Author and His Public in the Fourteenth and Fifteenth Centuries.' *Essays and Studies* 23 (1938) 7–24

– 'A Check-List of Robert Whittinton's Grammars.' *Library* 5th ser, 7 (1952) 1–14

– *English Books and Readers 1475 to 1557.* Cambridge: Cambridge University Press 1952

Bernard, Edward. *Catalogi librorum manuscriptorum Angliae et Hiberniae.* 2 vols. Oxford 1697

Bezzel, Irmgard. *Erasmusdrucke des 16. Jahrhunderts in Bayerischen Bibliotheken: Ein Bibliographisches Verzeichnis.* Stuttgart: Hiersemann 1979

Bierlaire, Franz. 'Erasme et Augustin Vincent Caminade.' *Bibliothèque d'humanisme et renaissance* 30 (1968) 357–62

Blackwell, C.W.T. 'Niccolò Perotti in England – Part I: John Anwykyll, Bernard André, John Colet and Luis Vives.' *Res Publica Litterarum* 5 (1982) 13–28

– 'Humanism and Politics in English Royal Biography: The Uses of Cicero, Plutarch and Sallust in the *Vita Henrici Quinti* (1438) by Titus Livius de Frulovisi and the *Vita Henrici Septimi* (1500–1503) by Bernard André.' In *Acta Conventus Neo-Latini Sanctandreani.* Ed I.D. McFarlane. 431–40

Blake, N.F. 'William Caxton: His Choice of Texts.' *Anglia* 83 (1965) 289–307

– 'Wynkyn de Worde: The Later Years.' *Gutenberg Jahrbuch* (1972) 128–38

- William Caxton: The Man and His Work.' *Journal of the Printing Historical Society* 11 (1976) 64–80
- 'The Spread of Printing in English during the Fifteenth Century.' *Gutenberg Jahrbuch* (1987) 26–36
- 'Manuscript to Print.' In *Book Production and Publishing in Britain 1375–1475*. Ed Griffiths and Pearsall. 403–32

Bloch, Eileen. 'Erasmus and the Froben Press.' *Library Quarterly* 35 (1965) 109–20

Boas, M. 'De Illustratie der Tabula Cebetis.' *Het Boek* 9 (1920) 1–16 and 106–14

Bowers, John M. 'Hoccleve's Huntington Holographs: The First "Collected Poems" in English.' *Fifteenth-Century Studies* 15 (1989) 27–51
- 'Hoccleve's Two Copies of *Lerne to Dye*: Implications for Textual Critics.' *Papers of the Bibliographical Society of America* 83 (1989) 437–72

Bradner, Leicester. *Musae Anglicanae: A History of Anglo-Latin Poetry 1500–1925*. New York: Modern Language Association 1940

Bühler, Curt F. 'Sir John Paston's *Grete Booke*, a Fifteenth-Century "Best Seller."' *Modern Language Notes* 56 (1941) 345–51

Campana, Augusto. 'The Origin of the Word "Humanist."' *Journal of the Warburg and Courtauld Institutes* 9 (1946) 60–73

Carley, James P. 'John Leland and the Foundations of the Royal Library: The Westminster Inventory of 1542.' *Bulletin of the Society for Renaissance Studies* 7 (1989) 13–22

Carlson, David R. 'King Arthur and Court Poems for the Birth of Arthur Tudor in 1486.' *Humanistica Lovaniensia* 36 (1987) 147–83
- 'The Occasional Poetry of Pietro Carmeliano.' *Aevum* 61 (1987) 495–502
- 'Politicizing Tudor Court Literature: Gaguin's Embassy and Henry VII's Humanists' Response.' *Studies in Philology* 85 (1988) 279–304
- 'Formats in English Printing to 1557.' *Analytical and Enumerative Bibliography* ns 2 (1988) 50–7
- 'John Skelton and Ancient Authors: Two Notes.' *Humanistica Lovaniensia* 38 (1989) 100–9
- 'Erasmus, Revision, and the British Library Manuscript Egerton 1651.' *Renaissance and Reformation* ns 15 (1991) 199–232
- ed. *The Latin Writings of John Skelton. Studies in Philology* Texts and Studies Series, LXXXVIII.4. Chapel Hill: University of North Carolina Press 1991

- 'Reputation and Duplicity: The Texts and Contexts of Thomas More's Epigram on Bernard André.' *ELH* 58 (1991) 261–81
- 'Royal Tutors in the Reign of Henry VII.' *Sixteenth Century Journal* 22 (1991) 253–79
- 'Skelton's *Garland of Laurel* and Robert Whittinton's "Lauri apud Palladem Expostulatio."' *Review of English Studies* ns 42 (1991) 417–24
- 'The "Grammarians' War" 1519–1521, Humanist Careerism in Early Tudor England, and Printing.' *Medievalia et Humanistica* ns 18 (1992) 157–81
- Carter, Harry. *A History of the Oxford University Press.* Vols 1–. Oxford: Clarendon 1975–
- Caspari, Fritz. *Humanism and the Social Order in Tudor England.* 1954; rpt. New York: Teachers College Press 1968
- *Catalogue of Books Printed in the XVth Century Now in the British Museum.* Parts I–. London: British Museum 1908–
- Cerquiglini, Bernard. *Eloge de la variante: Histoire critique de la philologie.* Paris: Seuil 1989
- Chambers, D.S. *Cardinal Bainbridge in the Court of Rome 1509–1514.* Oxford: Oxford University Press 1965
- Cheles, Luciano. *The Studiolo of Urbino: An Iconographic Investigation.* Wiesbaden: Reichert 1986
- Chrimes, S.B. *Henry VII.* London: Methuen 1972
- Clough, Cecil. 'Federigo Veterani, Polydore Vergil's "Anglica Historia" and Baldassare Castiglione's "Epistola ... ad Henricum Angliae Regem.' *English Historical Review* 82 (1967) 772–83
- 'The Relations between the English and Urbino Courts, 1474–1508.' *Studies in the Renaissance* 14 (1967) 202–18
- 'Baldassare Castiglione's *Ad Henricum Angliae regem epistola de vita et gestis Guidubaldi Urbini ducis.'* *Studi Urbinati* 47, ns BN. 2 (1973) 227–52
- 'Federigo da Montefeltro's Patronage of the Arts, 1468–1482.' *Journal of the Warburg and Courtauld Institutes* 36 (1973) 129–44
- 'Thomas Linacre, Cornelio Vitelli, and Humanistic Studies at Oxford.' In *Linacre Studies.* Ed Francis Maddison et al. 1–23
- 'Baldassare Castiglione's Presentation Manuscript to King Henry VII.' *Liverpool Classical Monthly* 3 (1978) 269–272
- 'Erasmus and the Pursuit of English Royal Patronage in 1517 and 1518.' *Erasmus of Rotterdam Society Yearbook* 1 (1981) 126–40
- 'A Presentation Volume for Henry VIII: The Charlecote Park Copy

of Erasmus's *Institutio Principis Christiani.' Journal of the Warburg and Courtauld Institutes* 44 (1981) 199–202
– 'Federigo da Montefeltro: The Good Christian Prince.' *Bulletin of the John Rylands Library* 67 (1984) 293–348
Coq, Dominique, and Ezio Ornato. 'La Production et la marché des incunables: le cas des livres juridiques.' In *Le Livre dans l'Europe de la renaissance*. Ed Pierre Aquilon and Henri-Jean Martin. 305–22
Courcelle, Pierre. 'Les exégèses chrétiennes de la quatrième égolgue.' *Revue des études anciennes* 59 (1957) 294–319
Curtius, Ernst Robert. *European Literature and the Latin Middle Ages*. Trans Willard R. Trask. Princeton: Princeton University Press 1953
Dalzell, A. 'Maecenas and the Poets.' *Phoenix* 10 (1956) 151–62.
D'Amico, John F. 'Manuscripts.' In *The Cambridge History of Renaissance Philosophy*. Ed Charles B. Schmitt. 11–24
Davis, Virginia. 'William Waynflete and the Educational Revolution of the Fifteenth Century.' In *People, Politics, and Community in the Later Middle Ages*. Ed Joel Rosenthal and Colin Richmond. Gloucester: Sutton 1987. 40–59
Dennistoun, James. *Memoirs of the Dukes of Urbino*. Ed Edward Hutton. 3 vols. London: Longman 1909
de Roover, Florence Edler, 'New Facets on the Financing and Marketing of Early Printed Books,' *Bulletin of the Business Historical Society* 27 (1953) 222–30.
Devereux, E.J. 'Thomas More and his Printers.' In *A Festschrift for Edgar Ronald Seary*. Ed A.A. Macdonald, P.A. O'Flaherty, and G.M. Story. St John's: Memorial University of Newfoundland 1975. 40–57
Dionisotti, Carlo. 'Battista Fiera.' *Italia medioevale e umanistica* 1 (1958) 401–18
Dowling, Maria. 'Humanist Support for Katherine of Aragon.' *Bulletin of the Institute of Historical Research* 57 (1984) 46–55
Duff, E. Gordon. *Fifteenth Century English Books: A Bibliography of Books and Documents Printed in England and of Books for the English Market Printed Abroad*. London: Bibliographical Society 1917
Duke Humfrey and English Humanism in the Fifteenth Century: Catalogue of an Exhibition Held in the Bodleian Library. Oxford: Bodleian Library 1970
Ebin, Lois A. *Illuminator, Makar, Vates: Visions of Poetry in the Fifteenth Century*. Lincoln: University of Nebraska Press 1988

Elton, G.R. *England under the Tudors.* 2nd ed. London: Methuen 1974
- 'Tudor Government: Points of Contact III. The Court.' *Transactions of the Royal Historical Society* 5th ser, 26 (1976) 211–28
Fairbank, Alfred, and Berthold Wolpe. *Renaissance Handwriting: An Anthology of Italic Scripts.* London: Faber 1960
Febvre, Lucien, and Henri-Jean Martin. *L'Apparition du livre.* 1958; rpt Paris: Albin Michel 1971
Feld, M.D. 'The Early Evolution of the Authoritative Text.' *Harvard Library Bulletin* 26 (1978) 81–111
- 'Constructed Letters and Illuminated Texts: Regiomontanus, Leon Battista Alberti, and the Origins of Roman Type.' *Harvard Library Bulletin* 28 (1980) 357–79
- 'Sweynheym and Pannartz, Cardinal Bessarion, Neoplatonism: Renaissance Humanism and Two Early Printers' Choice of Texts.' *Harvard Library Bulletin* 30 (1982) 282–335
- 'A Theory of the Early Italian Printing Firm Part I: Variants of Humanism.' *Harvard Library Bulletin* 33 (1985) 341–77
- 'A Theory of the Early Italian Printing Firm Part II: The Political Economy of Patronage.' *Harvard Library Bulletin* 34 (1986) 294–332
Feltes, Norman N. *Modes of Production of Victorian Novels.* Chicago: University of Chicago Press 1986
Ferguson, Wallace K. *Erasmi Opuscula: A Supplement to the Opera Omnia.* The Hague: Martinus Nijhoff 1933
Fitzgerald, John T., and L. Michael White, ed and trans. *The Tabula of Cebes.* Society of Biblical Literature Texts and Translations no 24, Graeco-Roman Series no 7. Chico, California: Scholars Press 1983
Flynn, Vincent Joseph. 'The Grammatical Writings of William Lily, ?1468–?1523.' *Papers of the Bibliographical Society of America* 37 (1943) 85–113
Fox, Alistair. 'Facts and Fallacies: Interpreting English Humanism.' In Fox and Guy *Reassessing the Henrician Age.* 9–33
- and John Guy. *Reassessing the Henrician Age: Humanism, Politics and Reform 1500–1550.* Oxford: Blackwell 1986
- *Politics and Literature in the Reigns of Henry VII and Henry VIII.* Oxford: Blackwell 1989
Gairdner, James. *Memorials of King Henry the Seventh.* Rerum Britannicarum Medii Aevi Scriptores (Rolls Series) 10. London: Longman 1858

Garrod, H.W. 'Erasmus and His English Patrons.' *Library* 5th ser, 4 (1949) 1–13

Gesamtkatalog der Wiegendrucke. 2nd ed. Vols 1–. Stuttgart: Hiersmann 1968–

Giani, Archangelo. *Della historia del B. Filippo Benizii.* Florence 1604

– *Annalium sacri ordinis Fratrum servorum B. Mariae Virginis a suae institutionis exordio, auctore F. Archangelo Gianio Florentino ... Editio secunda, cum notis, additionibus, et variis castigationibus, opera ac studio F. Aloysij Mariae Garbij de Florentina.* 3 vols Lucca 1719–25

Gibson, R.W., and J. Max Patrick. *St. Thomas More: A Preliminary Bibliography of His Works and of Moreana to the Year 1750.* New Haven: Yale University Press 1961

Giustiniani, Vito R. 'Homo, Humanus, and the Meanings of "Humanism."' *Journal of the History of Ideas* 46 (1985) 167–95

Gleason, John B. *John Colet.* Berkeley: University of California Press 1989

Goldschmidt, E.P. *The Printed Book of the Renaissance: Three Lectures on Type, Illustration, Ornament.* 2nd ed. Amsterdam: Heusden 1966

Grafton, Anthony, and Lisa Jardine. *From Humanism to the Humanities: Education and the Liberal Arts in Fifteenth- and Sixteenth-Century Europe.* Cambridge, Massachusetts: Harvard University Press 1986

Green, Richard Firth. *Poets and Princepleasers: Literature and the English Court in the Late Middle Ages.* Toronto: University of Toronto Press 1980

Greene, Thomas M. 'Resurrecting Rome: The Double Task of the Humanist Imagination.' In *Rome in the Renaissance: The City and the Myth.* Ed P.A. Ramsey. Binghamton: MRTS 1982. 41–54

Grendler, Paul F. 'Printing and Censorship.' In *The Cambridge History of Renaissance Philosophy.* Ed Schmitt. 25–53

Griffiths, Jeremy, and Derek Pearsall, eds. *Book Production and Publishing in Britain 1375–1475.* Cambridge: Cambridge University Press 1989

Guerrini, Paolo. *Pietro Carmeliano da Brescia, segretario reale d'Inghilterra.* Brescia: Editrice Brixia Sacra 1918

Gundersheimer, Werner L. 'Patronage in the Renaissance.' In *Patronage in the Renaissance.* Ed. Lytle and Orgel. 3–23

Gunn, S.J. *Charles Brandon, Duke of Suffolk, c. 1484–1545*. Oxford: Blackwell 1988

Gutierrez, Nancy A. 'John Skelton: Courtly Maker/Popular Poet.' *Journal of the Rocky Mountain Medieval and Renaissance Association* 4 (1983) 59–76

– and Mary Erler. 'Print into Manuscript: A Flodden Field News Pamphlet.' *Studies in Medieval and Renaissance History* ns 8 (1986) 187–230

Guy, John A. *The Public Career of Sir Thomas More*. Brighton: Harvester 1980

– *Tudor England*. Oxford: Oxford University Press 1988

Harris, Roy. *The Origin of Writing*. London: Duckworth 1986

Hay, Denys. 'Pietro Griffo, an Italian in England, 1506–1512.' *Italian Studies* 2 (1939) 118–28

– *Polydore Vergil: Renaissance Historian and Man of Letters*. Oxford: Clarendon 1952

– 'The Early Renaissance in England.' In *From the Renaissance to the Counter-Reformation: Essays in Honor of Garrett Mattingly*. Ed Charles H. Carter. New York: Random House 1965. 95–112

– 'England and the Humanities in the Fifteenth Century.' In *Itinerarium Italicum: The Profile of the Italian Renaissance in the Mirror of Its European Transformations*. Ed Heiko A. Oberman and Thomas A. Brady, Jr. Leiden: Brill 1975. 305–67

Hellinga, Lotte. 'Importation of Books Printed on the Continent into England and Scotland before c. 1520' in *Printing the Written Word: The Social History of Books, circa 1450–1520*. Ed Sandra Hindman. Ithaca: Cornell University Press 1991. 205–24

– and John Goldfinch, ed. *Bibliography and the Study of Fifteenth-Century Civilisation*. British Library Occasional Papers 5. London: British Library 1987

Hilgert, Earle. 'Johann Froben and the Basel University Scholars, 1513–1523.' *Library Quarterly* 41 (1971) 141–69

Hirsch, Rudolf. *Printing, Selling and Reading 1450–1550*. 2nd ed. Wiesbaden: Otto Harrassowitz 1974

Holzknecht, Karl Julius. *Literary Patronage in the Middle Ages*. 1923; rpt New York: Octagon 1966

Hudson, Hoyt Hopewell. *The Epigram in the English Renaissance*. Princeton: Princeton University Press 1947

Issac, Frank. *English Printers' Types of the Sixteenth Century*. Oxford: Oxford University Press 1936

Jenkins, A.D. Fraser. 'Cosimo de' Medici's Patronage of Architecture
and the Theory of Magnificence.' *Journal of the Warburg and Courtauld Institutes* 33 (1970) 162–70.

Kendrick, T.D. *British Antiquity.* London: Methuen 1950

Kerling, Nelly J.M. 'Caxton and the Trade in Printed Books.' *Book
Collector* 4 (1955) 190–9

King, John N. *Tudor Royal Iconography: Literature and Art in an Age
of Religious Crisis.* Princeton: Princeton University Press 1989

Kipling, Gordon. *The Triumph of Honour: Burgundian Origins of the
Elizabethan Renaissance.* Publications of the Sir Thomas Browne Institute 6. Leiden: E.J. Brill 1977

– 'Henry VII and the Origins of Tudor Patronage.' *Patronage in the
Renaissance.* Ed Lytle and Orgel. 117–64

Kristeller, Paul Oskar. *Iter Italicum: A Finding List of Uncatalogued
or Incompletely Catalogued Humanistic Manuscripts of the Renaissance in Italian and Other Libraries.* 6 vols. London: Warburg Institute and Leiden: E.J. Brill 1965–92

Kronenberg, Maria Elizabeth, and Wouter Nijhoff. *Nederlandsche
Bibliographie van 1500 tot 1540.* 3 vols. The Hague: Martinus
Nijhoff 1923–61

Lathrop, H.B. 'The First English Printers and Their Patrons.' *Library*
4th ser, 3 (1922) 69–96

Lavoie, Guy. 'La Fin de la querelle entre Germain de Brie et Thomas
More.' *Moreana* 50 (1976) 39–44

Loades, D.M. 'The Press under the Early Tudors: A Study in Censorship and Sedition.' *Transactions of the Cambridge Bibliographical
Society* 4 (1964) 29–50

Lowry, Martin J.C. 'Caxton, St Winifred and the Lady Margaret Beaufort.' *Library* 6th ser, 5 (1983) 101–17

– 'The Arrival and Use of Continental Printed Books in Yorkist England.' In *Le Livre dans l'Europe de la renaissance.* Ed Aquilon and
Martin. 449–59

Lucas, Peter J. 'The Growth and Development of English Literary
Patronage in the Later Middle Ages and Early Renaissance.' *Library*
6th ser, 4 (1982) 219–48

Lupton, J.H. *A Life of Dean Colet, D.D., Dean of St. Paul's and Foun-
der of St. Paul's School.* 2nd ed. 1909; rpt Hamden, Connecticut:
Shoe String Press 1961

Lutz, Cora E. 'Aesticampianus' Edition of the *Tabula* Attributed to
Cebes.' *Yale University Library Gazette* 45 (1971) 110–17

– 'Ps. Cebes.' In *Catalogus Translationum et Commentariorum.* Vol. VI. Washington, DC: Catholic University of America Press 1986. 1–14

Lytle, Guy Fitch, and Stephen Orgel, eds. *Patronage in the Renaissance.* Princeton: Princeton University Press 1981

MacFarlane, John. *Antoine Vérard.* London: Bibliographical Society 1900

Madan, Falconer. *Oxford Books: A Bibliography of Printed Works Relating to the University and City of Oxford or Printed or Published There.* 3 vols. Oxford: Clarendon 1895–1931

Maddison, Francis, Margaret Pelling, and Charles Webster, eds. *Linacre Studies: Essays on the Life and Work of Thomas Linacre c. 1460–1524.* Oxford: Clarendon 1977

Manley, Frank, and Richard S. Sylvester, ed and trans. *Richard Pace: De fructu qui ex doctrina percipitur.* New York: Renaissance Society of America 1967

Marc'hadour, Germain. 'Croisade triumphale de l'Angleterre: 1513: Réflexions en marge de John Skelton: "A ballad of the Scottyshe Kynge."' *Moreana* 35 (1972) 63–8

– 'Fuitne Thomas Morum in Aulam Pertractus?' In *Acta Conventus Neo-Latini Sanctandreani.* Ed I.D. McFarlane. 441–8

Marius, Richard. *Thomas More: A Biography.* New York: Knopf 1984

May, Steven W. 'Tudor Aristocrats and the Mythical "Stigma of Print."' In *Renaissance Papers 1980.* Ed A. Leigh Deneef and M. Thomas Hester. Durham, NC: Southeastern Renaissance Conference 1981. 11–18

Mayer, Thomas F. 'Faction and Ideology: Thomas Starkey's *Dialogue.*' *Historical Journal* 28.1 (1985) 1–25

– *Thomas Starkey and the Commonwealth: Humanist Politics and Religion in the Reign of Henry VIII.* Cambridge: Cambridge University Press 1989

– 'Tournai and Tyranny: Imperial Kingship and Critical Humanism.' *Historical Journal* 34.2 (1991) 257–77

Mazzuchelli, Giammaria. *Gli Scrittori d'Italia cioè Notizie storiche e critiche, intorno alle vite e agli scritti dei letterati Italiani.* Brescia 1753

McConica, James Kelsey. *English Humanists and Reformation Politics under Henry VIII and Edward VI.* Oxford: Clarendon 1965

– *Erasmus.* Oxford: Oxford University Press 1991

McFarlane, I.D., ed. *Acta Conventus Neo-Latini Sanctandreani: Pro-*

ceedings of the Fifth International Congress of Neo-Latin Studies. Medieval and Renaissance Texts and Studies 38. Binghamton, NY: MRTS 1986

McGann, Jerome. 'Keats and the Historical Method in Literary Criticism.' Modern Language Notes 94 (1979) 988–1032

– 'The Text, the Poem, and the Problem of Historical Method.' New Literary History 12 (1981) 269–88

– A Critique of Modern Textual Criticism. Chicago: University of Chicago Press 1983

– ed. Textual Criticism and Literary Interpretation. Chicago: University of Chicago Press 1985

McKenzie, D.F. 'The Sociology of a Text: Orality, Literacy and Print in Early New Zealand.' Library 6th ser, 6 (1984) 333–65

– Bibliography and the Sociology of Texts. Panizzi Lectures 1985. London: British Library 1986

McLeod, Randall. 'UNEditing Shak-speare.' Sub-stance 33/4 (1982) 26–55

– 'from Tranceformations in the Text of "Orlando Furioso."' Library Chronicle of the University of Texas at Austin 20 (1990) 60–85

Millican, Charles Bowie. Spenser and the Table Round. Harvard Studies in Comparative Literature 8. Cambridge, Massachusetts: Harvard University Press 1932

Modigliani, Anna. 'Un nuovo manoscritto di Pietro Carmeliano: Le "Epistole" dello pseudo-Falaride nella Trinity College Library di Dublino.' Humanistica Lovaniensia 33 (1984) 86–102

Moran, James. 'Caxton and the City of London.' Journal of the Printing Historical Society 11 (1976) 81–91

Morison, Stanley. 'Early Humanistic Script and the First Roman Type.' Library 4th ser, 24 (1943) 1–29

– Politics and Script: Aspects of Authority and Freedom in the Development of Graeco-Latin Script from the Sixth Century B.C. to the Twentieth Century A.D. Ed and completed by Nicolas Barker. Oxford: Clarendon 1972

Morrison, Paul G. Index of Printers, Publishers and Booksellers in Pollard and Redgrave, A Short-Title Catalogue. 2nd ed. Charlottesville: Bibliographical Society of the University of Virginia 1961

Müller, Karl Konrad. 'Relieffragment mit Darstellungen aus dem ΠΙΝΑΞ des Kebes.' Archäologische Zeitung 42 (1884) 115–30

Nebbiai, Donatella. 'Per una valutazione della produzione manoscritta cinque-seicentesca.' In Alfabetismo e cultura scritta nella storia *della società italicana.* Ed Attilio Bartoli Langeli and Armando Petrucci. Perugia: Università degli studi 1978. 235–67

Nelson. *See* Abbreviations

Nichols, Francis Morgan. *The Epistles of Erasmus.* 3 vols. 1901–18; rpt New York: Russell 1962

Nixon, H.M. 'The Gilt Binding of the Whittinton *Epigrams,* Ms Bodley 523.' *Library* 5th ser, 7 (1952) 120–1

Orme, Nicholas. *English Schools in the Middle Ages.* London: Methuen 1973

Pächt, Otto, and J.J.G. Alexander. *Illuminated Manuscripts in the Bodleian Library Oxford.* 3 vols. Oxford: Clarendon 1966–73

Pafort, Eloise. 'A Group of Early Tudor School-Books.' *Library* 4th ser, 26 (1946) 228–55

Painter, George D. *William Caxton: A Quincentenary Biography of England's First Printer.* London: Chatto and Windus 1976

Pantzer, Katherine F. 'Printing the English Statutes, 1484–1640: Some Historical Implications.' In *Books and Society in History.* Ed Kenneth E. Carpenter. New York: Bowker 1983. 69–114

Parkinson, David. 'Scottish Prints and Entertainments, 1508.' *Neophilologus* 75 (1991) 304–10

Parks, George B. *The English Traveller to Italy.* Rome: Edizioni di storia e letteratura 1954

Petrucci, Armando. 'Alle origini del libro moderno: libri da banco, libri da bisaccia, libretti da mano.' *Italia medioevale e umanistica* 12 (1969) 295–313

Pizzi, Clemente. *Un Amico di Erasmo: L'umanista Andrea Ammonio.* Florence: Felice le Monnier 1956

– ed. *Andreae Ammonii Carmina Omnia.* Florence: Olschki 1958

Plomer, Henry R. 'Bibliographical Notes from the Privy Purse Expenses of King Henry the Seventh.' *Library* 3rd ser, 4 (1913) 291–305

– 'The Importation of Books into England in the Fifteenth and Sixteenth Centuries.' *Library* 4th ser, 4 (1923) 146–50

– *Wynkyn de Worde and His Contemporaries from the Death of Caxton to 1535.* London: Grafton 1925

– 'The Importation of Low Country and French Books into England, 1480 and 1502–3.' *Library* 4th ser, 9 (1928) 164–8

Pollard, Albert Frederick. *The Reign of Henry VII from Contemporary Sources.* 3 vols. 1913–14; rpt New York: AMS 1967

Pollard, Graham. 'The Company of Stationers before 1557.' *Library* 4th ser, 18 (1937) 1–38

- 'The English Market for Printed Books (The Sandars Lectures, 1959).' *Publishing History* 4 (1978) 7–48
- 'The *Pecia* System in the Medieval Universities.' In *Medieval Scribes, Manuscripts, and Libraries: Essays Presented to N.R. Ker.* Ed M.B. Parkes and Andrew G. Watson. London: Scolar 1978. 145–61

Porter, H.C., and D.F.S. Thomson. *Erasmus and Cambridge.* Toronto: University of Toronto Press 1963

Praechter, Karl, ed. *Cebetis Tabula.* Leipzig: Teubner 1893

Puddu, Raffaele. 'Lettere ed arme: il ritratto del guerriero tra Quattro e Cinquecento.' In *Federico di Montefeltro.* Ed Baiardi et al. I, 487–512

Reedijk. *See* Abbreviations

Renouard, Philippe. *Imprimeurs et libraires Parisiens du XVIe siècle.* Vols 1–. Paris: La ville de Paris 1964–

Ringler, William. 'John Stow's Editions of Skelton's *Workes* and of *Certaine Worthye Manuscript Poems.*' *Studies in Bibliography* 8 (1956) 215–17

Rix, Herbert David. 'The Editions of Erasmus' *De Copia.*' *Studies in Philology* 43 (1946) 595–618

Root, Robert K. 'Publication before Printing.' *PMLA* 28 (1913) 417–31

Rosenberg, Charles M. 'The Double Portrait of Federico and Guidobaldo da Montefeltro: Power, Wisdom, Dynasty.' In *Federico di Montefeltro.* Ed Baiardi et al. II, 213–22

Rossi, Sergio. *Ricerche sull'umanesimo e sul rinascimento in Inghilterra.* Publicazioni dell'Università Cattolica del Sacro Cuore. Milan: Società editrice vita e pensiero 1969

- 'Note sugli Italiani in Inghilterra nell'età del rinascimento.' In *Saggi sul rinascimento.* Ed Rossi. Milan: Unicopli 1984. 55–115

Roth, Francis, OSA. 'A History of the English Austin Friars.' *Augustiniana* 8 (1958) 22–47 and 465–96; 11 (1961) 533–63; 12 (1962) 93–122 and 391–442; 13 (1963) 515–51; 14 (1964), 163–215 and 670–710; 15 (1965) 175–233 and 567–628; 16 (1966); and 17 (1967)

Rummel, Erika. *Erasmus' Annotations on the New Testament: From Philologist to Theologian.* Erasmus Studies 8. Toronto: University of Toronto Press 1986

Rutter, Russell. 'William Caxton and Literary Patronage.' *Studies in Philology* 84 (1987) 440–70

Ruysschaert, José. 'Lorenzo Guglielmo Traversagni de Savone

(1425–1503): Un humaniste Franciscain oublié.' *Archivum Franciscanum Historicum* 46 (1953) 195–210

- 'Les Manuscrits autographes de deux oeuvres de Lorenzo Guglielmo Traversagni imprimées chez Caxton.' *Bulletin of the John Rylands Library* 36 (1953) 191–7

Saenger, Paul. 'Colard Mansion and the Evolution of the Printed Book.' *Library Quarterly* 45 (1975) 405–18

Saunders, J.W. 'The Stigma of Print: A Note on the Social Bases of Tudor Poetry.' *Essays in Criticism* 1 (1951) 139–64

Scattergood, John. *Politics and Poetry in the Fifteenth Century*. London: Blandford 1971

- *John Skelton: The Complete English Poems*. New Haven: Yale University Press 1983

- 'Skelton and Heresy.' In *Early Tudor England: Proceedings of the 1987 Harlaxton Symposium*. Ed Daniel Williams. Woodbridge: Boydell 1989. 157–70

Schirmer, Walter F. *Der Englische Frühhumanismus: Ein Beitrag zur Englischen Literaturgeschichte des 15. Jahrhunderts*. 2nd ed. Tübingen: Niemeyer 1963

Schleier, Reinhart. *Tabula Cebetis, oder 'Spiegel des Menschlichen Lebens, darin Tugent und untugent abgemalet ist': Studien zur Rezeption einer antiken Bildbeschreibung im 16. und 17. Jahrhundert*. Berlin: Gebr Mann Verlag 1973

Schmitt, Charles B., and Dilwyn Knox. *Pseudo-Aristoteles Latinus: A Guide to Latin Works Falsely Attributed to Aristotle before 1500*. Warburg Institute Surveys and Texts 12. London: Warburg Institute 1985

- and others, ed. *The Cambridge History of Renaissance Philosophy*. Cambridge: Cambridge University Press 1988

Schoeck, R.J. 'Erasmus in England, 1499–1517: *Translatio Studii* and the *Studia Humanitatis*.' In Schoeck, *Erasmus Grandescens: The Growth of a Humanist's Mind and Spirituality*. Bibliotheca Humanistica et Reformatorica 43. Nieuwkoop: De Graaf 1988. 111–25

- 'Humanism in England.' In *Renaissance Humanism: Foundations, Forms, and Legacy*. Ed Albert Rabil, Jr. 3 vols. Philadelphia: University of Pennsylvania Press 1988. II, 5–38

Shaaber, M.A. *Check-list of Works of British Authors Printed Abroad, in Languages Other than English, to 1641*. New York: Bibliographical Society of America 1975

Shaw, David J. 'Badius's Octavo Editions of the Classics.' *Gutenberg-Jahrbuch* (1973) 276–81

Shaw, S. Diane. 'A Study of the Collaboration between Erasmus of Rotterdam and His Printer Johann Froben at Basel during the Years 1514 to 1527.' *Erasmus of Rotterdam Society Yearbook* 6 (1986) 31–124

Sider, Sandra. *Cebes' Tablet: Facsimiles of the Greek Text, and of Selected Latin, French, English, Spanish, Italian, German, Dutch, and Polish Translations.* New York: Renaissance Society of America 1979

Smith, Preserved. *Erasmus: A Study of His Life, Ideals and Place in History.* 1923; rpt New York: Ungar 1962

Stanier, R.S. *Magdalen School.* Oxford: Blackwell 1958

Starkey, David, ed. *The English Court from the Wars of the Roses to the Civil War.* London: Longman 1987

Sylvester, Richard S. 'The "Man for All Seasons" Again: Robert Whittinton's Verses to Sir Thomas More.' *Huntington Library Quarterly* 26 (1963) 147–54

– 'John Constable's Poems to Thomas More.' *Philological Quarterly* 42 (1963) 525–31

Tanner, Thomas. *Bibliotheca Britannico-Hibernica.* London 1748

Tateo, Franceso. 'Le armi e le lettere: per la storia di un topos umanistico.' In *Acta conventus Neo-Latini Torontonensis.* Ed Alexander Dalzell, Charles Fantazzi, and R.J. Schoeck. Binghamton, NY: MRTS 1991. 63–81

Thompson, Craig R. 'Erasmus and Tudor England.' In *Actes du congrès Erasme.* Ed Cornelis Reedijk. Amsterdam: North-Holland 1971. 29–68

Thorpe, James. 'The Aesthetics of Textual Criticism.' *PMLA* 80 (1965) 465–82

Thuasne, Louis. *Roberti Gaguini Epistole et Orationes.* 2 vols. Paris: E. Bouillon 1903

Tournoy, Gilbert. 'Two Poems Written by Erasmus for Bernard André.' *Humanistica Lovaniensia* 27 (1978) 45–51

– 'New Evidence on the Italian Humanist Cornelius Vitellius (c. 1440–c. 1500).' *Lias* 5 (1978) 13–18

– 'La Poésie de William Lily pour le diptyque de Quentin Metsijs.' *Moreana* 97 (1988) 63–6

Tournoy-Thoen, Godelieve. 'Het vroegste Latijnse humanistische epithalamium in Engeland.' *Koninklijke Zuidnederlandse Maatschappij voor Taal- en Letterkunde en Geschiedenis* 32 (1978) 169–80

Trapp, J.B. 'The Owl's Ivy and the Poet's Bays: An Enquiry into Poetic Garlands.' *Journal of the Warburg and Courtauld Institutes* 21 (1958) 227–55

– 'The Poet Laureate: Rome, *Renovatio* and *Translatio Imperii*.' In *Rome in the Renaissance*. Ed P.A. Ramsay. Binghamton: MRTS 1982. 93–130

– 'Thomas More and the Visual Arts.' In *Saggi sul rinascimento*. Ed Sergio Rossi. Milan: Unicopli 1984. 27–54

– 'An English Late Medieval Cleric and Italian Thought: The Case of John Colet, Dean of St. Paul's (1467–1519).' In *Medieval English Religious and Ethical Literature: Essays in Honour of G.H. Russell*. Ed Gregory Kratzmann and James Simpson. Cambridge: Brewer 1986. 233–50

– 'Christopher Urswick and His Books: The Reading of Henry VII's Almoner.' *Renaissance Studies* 1 (1987) 48–70

Vander Haeghen, F., R. Vanden Berghe, and Th.-J.-I. Arnold. *Bibliotheca Erasmiana: Adagia*. Gand: C. Vyt 1897

Van Kluyve, Robert A. 'The Duke Manuscript of Antonio Beccaria.' *Library Notes: A Bulletin Issued for the Friends of Duke University Library* 41 (1969) 3–6

Veblen, Thorstein. *The Theory of the Leisure Class*. 1899; rpt New York: NAL Penguin 1953

Volta, Leopoldo Camillo. *Biografia dei Mantovani Illustri nelle Scienze, Lettere ed Arti*. Corrected and augmented ed, ed Antonio Mainardi. Vol 1 only. Mantua 1845

Vredeveld, Harry. 'Towards a Definitive Edition of Erasmus' Poetry.' *Humanistica Lovaniensia* 37 (1988) 115–74

– 'Some "Lost" Poems of Erasmus from the Year 1499.' In *Fide et Amore: A Festschrift for Hugo Bekker*. Ed W.C. McDonald and Winder McConnell. Göppingen: Kummerle 1990. 329–39

Walker, Greg. *John Skelton and the Politics of the 1520s*. Cambridge: Cambridge University Press 1988

Watson, Andrew G. *Catalogue of Dated and Datable Manuscripts c.700–1600 in the Department of Manuscripts, the British Library*. 2 vols. London: British Library 1979

Weiss, Roberto. 'Cornelio Vitelli in France and England.' *Journal of the Warburg and Courtauld Institutes* 2 (1939) 219–26

– 'Lineamenti di una biografia di Giovanni Gigli, collettore papale in

Inghilterra e vescovo di Worcester (1434–1498).' *Rivista di storia della chiesa in Italia* 1 (1947) 379–89

- *Humanism. See* Abbreviations

Westfall, C.W. 'Chivalric Declaration: The Palazzo Ducale in Urbino as a Political Statement.' In *Art and Architecture in the Service of Politics.* Ed Henry A. Millon and Linda Nochlin. Cambridge, Massachusetts: MIT Press 1978. 20–45

White, Beatrice. *The Vulgaria of John Stanbridge and the Vulgaria of Robert Whittinton.* EETS OS 187. London: Early English Text Society 1932

White, Peter. '*Amicitia* and the Profession of Poetry in Early Imperial Rome.' *Journal of Roman Studies* 68 (1978) 74–92

Wilkie, William E. *The Cardinal Protectors of England: Rome and the Tudors before the Reformation.* Cambridge: Cambridge University Press 1974

Williams, Franklin B., Jr. 'Commendatory Verses: The Rise of the Art of Puffing.' *Studies in Bibliography* 19 (1966) 1–14

Winger, Howard W. 'Regulations Relating to the Book Trade in London from 1357 to 1586.' *Library Quarterly* 26 (1956) 157–95

Wiriath, R. 'Les Rapports de Josse Bade Ascensius avec Erasme et Lefèbvre d'Etaples.' *Bibliothèque d'humanisme et renaissance* 11 (1949) 66–71

Withington, Robert. *English Pageantry: An Historical Outline.* 2 vols. Cambridge, Massachusetts: Harvard University Press 1918

Wood, Anthony à. *Historia et antiquitates universitatis Oxoniensis duobus voluminibus comprehensae.* Oxford 1674

Wormald, Francis. 'An Italian Poet at the Court of Henry VII.' *Journal of the Warburg and Courtauld Institutes* 14 (1951) 118–19

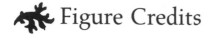 Figure Credits

The figures that appear in this book are reproduced by kind permission of the following:

The British Library, London: figures 1, 2, 6, 7, 8, 9, 10, 11, 12, 15, 16, 24, 27, 29
Alinari/Art Resource, New York: figure 3 (photo)
The Houghton Library, Harvard University: figure 4
The Huntington Library, San Marino, California: figures 5, 19, 20, 25, 28
The Master and Fellows of Gonville and Caius College, Cambridge: figure 13
The Bodleian Library, University of Oxford: figures 14, 21, 22
The Warden and Fellows of All Souls College, Oxford: figures 17, 31
Trinity College Library, University of Dublin: figure 23
The Governing Body of Christ Church Oxford: figure 26
The Centre for Reformation and Renaissance Studies, Victoria University, University of Toronto: figures 30, 32

❦ Index of Manuscripts

🐾 General Index

KING A   OLLEGE
LIBRARY